Number One Bestseller

Brian Morley

Savant Books and Publications
Honolulu, HI, USA
2010

Published in the USA by Savant Books and Publications
2630 Kapiolani Blvd #1601
Honolulu, HI 96826
http://www.savantbooksandpublications.com

Printed in the USA

Edited by Daniel S. Janik
Cover photos: by Brian Morley
Cover image design by Matt Licari Studios
Cover Models: Tara Cannistraci and multiple Purple Heart recipient
James McShane
Front and back cover layup by Daniel S. Janik

13-digit ISBN: 978-0-9829987-3-1
10-digit ISBN: 0-9829987-3-2

Dedication

To my loving and always supportive wife Linda, who of all things, means everything to me. To Mom and Dad whose love is missed but will never be forgotten.

Acknowledgements

Thanks to:

Dr. Dan Janik, a prince of a man who went out on a limb for me, and, as my editor and publisher, made this dream come true.

My sister Andrea and niece Tara who became my personal cheerleaders and whose encouragement kept me going.

Jimmy, Astrid, Raff, Uncle Joe, Aunt Caroline, sister-in-law Susan, and cousin Ray, Cathy, Heather and Patty for taking the time to read my unfinished manuscript and letting me know I was on the right track.

Number One Bestseller

CHAPTER 1

"Irish? I wouldn't know Ireland if I tripped over it, Babe," mumbled James "Mack" McConville. A homicide detective, first grade, with the New York Police Department, or NYPD as any typical New Yorker would call it, he was so dedicated to the force, his fellow officers said that when his day came, he'd bleed blue.

In his mid-fifties and built like a moose, Mack sported a shock of curly silver-grey hair that highlighted his piercing grayish-blue eyes which drew every woman's attention the minute he walked into a room. Those same captivating eyes, however, sent chills down the spine of any criminal he approached. Irish-American, with a growing beer belly that he couldn't get rid of no matter how many diets he tried or miles he ran, he was proud of his ancestry no matter how much he denied it. Babe, longtime friend and bartender, laughed in the background while cleaning the glasses.

Farrell's was one of a long list of bars Mack frequented these days. He ordered another Guinness and stared out the window, envious of the commuters hurrying home for dinner with their families. With over twenty years in the force, Mack could have retired long ago, but a drawn-out divorce in which his wife, in an effort to get him to stay, took him for everything they had, left him a permanent office resident. *I'll never forget the last thing my ex-wife said as I left her: 'Not so fast, Mack! What about that loose change in your pocket?'"*

It was a crisp, September Sunday, and twenty minutes later Mack was driving his son, Nick, to the New Jersey Meadowlands Sports Complex to watch the New York Jets play the New England Patriots. For Mack, the beginning of football season always carried sweet memories of childhood. The Indian-summer day and the free tickets he'd received from the son of an elderly neighbor he helped regularly made the occasion even sweeter. Mack provided what the eighty-four year-old man couldn't get from his high-ranking, executive son: time and attention. Mack visited the man daily, raptly listening to the man's stories, even though he'd heard them a thousand times.

"Shit!" Mack grunted aloud. "We're going to miss kick off! Why couldn't they have fixed up Shea Stadium and kept the Jets there? It may be Queens, but it's still New York. We could be drinking beers in the parking lot instead of sitting in this fuckin' traffic waiting to get to Jersey!"

Nick pointed at a cracked, dimestore clock that had been sliding loosely back and forth on the dashboard. It was hopeless to point out again that the malfeasant clock was, like always, wrong.

"You're right, as always—you and your mother," Mack grumbled, glowering at the clock. "Hell, I attached it to the dashboard with duct tape, and..."

"Good tape's the key," father and son finished together, then laughed. Laughing was something Mack could still do with his son.

Nick appreciated spending time with his father these days, because his father was more like a big brother than the overbearing dad Mack had been up to Nick's late twenties. A public school teacher with a knack for making math interesting for sixth graders, Nick was fast approaching his mid-thirties, and was still single. He'd recently given up all hope of finding the 'right girl,' secretly wanting the kind of love he had so often glimpsed between his mother and father before the marriage had ultimately failed, and now Nick craved the contentment that his memories couldn't conjure. Nick leaned over, tore the clock from its precarious perch, and began adjusting the time.

"Yeah, Dad," Nick answered with inauthentic sarcasm as he leaned back into the seat. "Tough. Real tough."

Mack laughed. "Keep giving me that fake, shit-eating grin and you'll be walking to the game. It reminds me of your mother when she was getting ready to make me look like a fool."

Nick turned serious. "Come on, Dad! You know you love playing the fool, and the laughs that come with it. Don't blame Mom for your growing apart."

Mack, noting his ex-wife's voice in Nick's attempt at playing parent, reluctantly nodded his head. "You're right. You, your mother and I had a lot of good years together. I know I was blessed, and I think she would say so, too. It was a damn good journey, but all journeys have to end. Hell, I don't want the pain of the ending to ruin my memories of our times together, that's all."

Nick knew hurt when he heard it, and, that, like other times, he'd get no more from his dad. Even so, he asked anyway, "So, Dad, what really happened between you and Mom? I mean you both seem like you still love each other, yet you haven't spoken in almost four years. When I asked Mom what happened, she says she came home one day and you were gone. She said you wouldn't answer her calls, then had your lawyer tell her it was over. All I know is, you left her without explanation. She says she's finally given up waiting, but I don't believe her."

Mack felt the dark vortex of the past suck at his mind and reflexively re-concentrated his focus on driving. Even so, the moment was enough to loosen the hundreds of nagging questions that haunted him since that fateful day. Why *had* he left, and what could he possibly say after all these years? If only for his son's peace of mind, he would never allow either of them to pry it out of him. He turned to Nick and snarled, "Why do you always have to break my balls like that when I don't want to talk. It's history. Done. Time for everyone to let it go!"

Nick, sensing the familiar barrier back between them, changed tactics. "You're right, Dad. You're just a parent," he snapped. "What fucking business is it of mine, anyway?"

Mack hesitated. "Your business right now is to please not mess up our day together…alright?"

Over the years, Nick had learned the hard way when to stop. "Alright! But one day soon I'm going to catch you drunk enough that you'll tell me."

Mack looked hard at his son. "One day, maybe, but not today." Mack's fists tightened as he looked at the bumper-to-bumper traffic."And they have the nerve to call this the Cross-Bronx expressway! I could walk faster!"

Nick sighed. "So, what's the big deal? Turn on the radio."

Mack sent his son a look of profound disappointment. "That's the problem with you, Nick: *Nothing* anymore is a big deal. Nothing, that is, except prying into your mother's and my life together. Nowadays, you don't even seem to care what time you show up for things. That's from your mother's side…" Mack added, pointing a crooked finger at his son.

Nick watched Mack and mindlessly taunted him on: "At least Mom can keep a clock working. Is the flashing twelve o'clock on the VCR at your place still covered with duct tape?"

"I should have shot you into the sink, but your mom so wanted a baby."

Nick laughed nervously, "You say the nicest things, Dad. Hey, get off the next exit. I got to take a leak."

"You're kidding, right?" Mack snorted resentfully.

"Don't worry, Dad, we have time, and it's easy to get back on from here. Trust me!" Nick looked anxiously over at his father.

Mack reached with his right hand behind the back of Nick's seat and pulled out an empty beer bottle. "Here, use this!" he said, tossing it into Nick's lap.

"What am I, fucking five or something?"

"Hey, don't cry. little boy, I'm exiting. There. Those buildings over there," Mack pointed. "They're going to be demolished. No one's in them. Go piss in one of them."

3

Nick stared at the buildings. "They're not going to fall down on me, are they?"

Mack laughed, "What are you, a moron? They're so sturdy they'll have to rip them right out of the ground, like a dentist an aching tooth."

Nick shook his head. "Moron! Ha! Had I known *you* were going to be my father, I would have begged you to shoot me in the sink!"

Mack smiled. "Just hurry and do what you have to. Football doesn't wait."

Nick got out of the stopped car, walked across a tableau of crunching debris and entered the closest abandoned building, looking around to make sure it was safe. Confident it was, and that he was alone, Nick unzipped his pants and started to urinate into a pile of rubble, constantly looking left and right, like a man who's car just stalled on a railroad crossing, Hearing a voice from behind, he jumped.

"Hey! You there! What are you doin'?"

Nick turned to see a massively built man wearing a blue police uniform standing behind him tapping the tip of a billy-club in a ham-like palm.

"I...I'm sorry, officer. I had to take a leak. I was on my way to the Jets game with my father, and with all this traffic..."

"This place is condemned. Off limits, savvy? So zip up and get your ass out of here," the patrolman demanded. "Now!"

Nick, thoroughly embarrassed, apologized profusely as he zipped up. Walking around the patrolman, his toe struck the officer's suddenly extended boot, felling him backwards like a boulder into the pool of his own, still-warm urine. "Wh... what the fuck was that for?" he yelled, trying to better view his assailant.

The patrolman swung his baton, hitting Nick on the side of the knee. "Don't fuckin' ever question my authority, you son-of-a-bitch! I know why you're really here!"

Nick grabbed for his knee as the patrolman swung, this time for his head. As Nick rolled to the side, the club made short contact with his shoulder. Grabbing a two-by-four lying on the ground next to him, Nick shoved the end towards the patrolman's shin. The boot took the brunt of the thrust, but the policeman grunted and backed off, dropping his night-stick as he reached for his own leg.

"You're a dead man," he howled, pulling out his service gun and pointing it at Nick, who immediately dropped the two-by-four and curled up in a ball, thinking, *This is it.*

The black silhouette towering above him announced with sadistic delight, "Time to die, asshole."

Nick, helpless, closed his eyes and held his breath.

In the distance, a voice yelled, "Curtis! Stop! The guy's unarmed, for Christ's sake!"

Patrolman Curtis reluctantly took his finger off the trigger and slowly pointed the gun away, all the while rubbing his aching shin. "This junkie here," he said, pointing back at Nick, rolled tightly into an unmoving ball, "attacked me. I should have wasted him right away when I had the chance."

"Shut up, Curtis," the second patrolman ordered. "You can't kill people just because you don't happen to like them. Holster your weapon. Now! He's not resisting. Take him in."

Curtis snorted and slid the gun back into its holster. The second patrolman called on his walkie-talkie for backup, afraid more of what Curtis might do next than of the young man lying on the ground, now shivering and shaking in his own urine.

"Hey! Why you callin' for backup? I caught this piece of shit right where he shouldn't be!" Curtis walked closer and kicked Nick in the ribs. Nick, fearing again for his life, grunted and didn't move.

Curtis snapped out a pair of metal handcuffs, and, prying Nick's hands away from his face, flipped the young man over, wrenched his arms behind and snapped the cuffs on. Then for good measure, he kicked Nick in the head, knocking him out.

The second patrolman yelled at Curtis, "Enough! He's cuffed and he's not resisting, you sick bastard!"

"What? You suddenly startin' to feel sorry for these druggie scumbags, Mitchell?" The two men stared at each other as sirens outside sounded the approach.

Mack, irritated at how long Nick was taking to do something as simple as urinate, turned down the volume of the radio and transferred his attention from the sounds of the pre-game show to the three squad cars screeching to a stop around him.

One of his best friends, Andre Brown, a full captain in the force, climbed out of the first car. A tall, good-looking 'man of color,' as Andre liked people to refer to him, he and Mack had been friends since they were teenagers. Andre recognized his old friend instantly and nodded; Mack laughed, thinking to himself about how big Andre's smile had been when he first told Andre the difference between a good friend and a best friend: A good friend is someone who helps you move. A best friend is someone who helps you move a body. Andre and he were best friends many times over.

Mack rolled down his window and stared at the cacophony of sound and lights. "What's going on?" he asked, as more armed officers piled out.

Andre looked confused. "What are you doing here, Mack? I thought you were taking Nick to the game."

Mack put on a face of disgust. "Yeah, if traffic breaks and Nick stops having to take a leak every twenty feet. He's in there, now." Mack pointed to the ramshackle building directly in front of the cars. "Hey, what's going on?"

Andre checked the snaps on his duty rig, explaining, "Some junkie made a move on a rookie patrol cop, and his partner called it in. I'm here to check it out. Just routine, as you've probably already guessed."

Mack opened his car door and got out. "I might as well go with you and see if I can find out what's taking Nick so long," said Mack, his disgust turning to concern.

Mack and Andre walked into the dilapidated building to find Officer Curtis dragging the suspect by a pant leg, the man's unconscious face bobbing loosely behind in the dirt.

The five officers who had entered just ahead of their Captain shook their heads. Andre, however, didn't. Instead, he locked his gaze on the rookie, frowned and demanded, "Stop! Why are you dragging an unconscious, cuffed man who's in your custody through the dirt like that?" Andre turned to the other officers. "You, men! Don't just stand around gaping! Pick the man up! Now!"

Andre immediately returned his attention back to the shocked rookie. "Curtis! Where's your partner?"

Two of the five accompanying officers positioned themselves on either side of Nick, hands on weapons. Two others knelt down and picked Nick up off of the ground, while the fifth inspected the arrestee's head for damage. It was only when the five righted the dazed and incoherent man, that Andre and Mack simultaneously realized it was Nick.

Hoping to nip Mack's reaction in the bud, Andre screamed, "Who the fuck is responsible for this?!"

Curtis arrogantly replied, "I am, sir."

That was all Mack needed. By the time the rage hit, Mack was hovering over Officer Curtis, a gun to Curtis's temple, bellowing, "Hands over your head, you motherfucker!"

The two point cops pulled their guns and swung them towards Mack while the three officers protected Nick with their bodies. Curtis had barely time to unsheathe his semi-automatic and point it at Mack's chest. Mitchell, rejoining his rookie partner after finishing his search of the building where they had caught the 'drug-dealer,' froze, rolled his eyes and stared.

"Everyone! Put down your guns!" Andre yelled, adding, "For God's sake, Mack, this guy's a cop!" Everyone except Curtis and Mack reluctantly put their guns away.

Andre tore his eyes from the rookie and locked onto Mack. "Mack! Don't! Killing this despicable excuse for an officer isn't worth throwing it all away. Hell,

Nick's been knocked around some, but he's okay, aren't you, Nick?"

Nick, now awake and aghast at being at the center of what appeared to be an armed conflict, nodded affirmatively and began shaking off the officers on either side of him. Andre signaled for everyone except Curtis and Mitchell to leave, while he continued to plead with Mack to re-holster.

Nick stretched his neck, side, leg, and groaned. "Look, Mack," Andre nervously chimed, "he's going to be fine. Curtis, you imbecile, help the man stand!"

Mack kept his gun pointed at Curtis's temple, while Curtis's eyes darted from Mack to Andre to Nick and back to Mack as Andre calmly asked Nick to explain what happened.

Nick held onto the hurt side of his chest, and tried to catch a breath. Blood was seeping from one corner of his mouth, and the side of his face was beginning to swell and discolor.

"I was taking a leak when this clown," Nick pointed at Curtis, "came up from behind me and started beating me with his club."

Andre turned to Curtis' partner. "Mitchell, is this true? Don't even think about covering for Curtis. He's not worth your career."

Officer Mitchell looked down, took a deep breath, and replied calmly, "Sir, I came up after the altercation had already begun. Everyone knows Officer Curtis here is a loose cannon. I should have been watching him closer. I assure you I have no desire to protect him. To be honest, sir, if I ever have to work with this asshole again, you can respectfully take this job and shove…"

Andre's eyes widened, taken aback by the venom in the officer's voice.

Turning back to Nick, Andre asked if Mitchell had anything to do with it. Nick nodded, explaining, "If it weren't for Officer Mitchell, I think Officer Curtis would have killed me."

Andre turned to Curtis. "Well, Curtis, you've messed up for the last time. That man with his gun at your head is a decorated NYPD detective and the guy you slapped around is his…"

Curtis interrupted, "But how was I to know?"

Mack lowered his weapon, then suddenly struck Curtis in the mouth with his other hand. Curtis dropped his weapon, gasped and choked as his mouth filled with blood. "It's not polite to talk with your mouth full, Curtis," Mack proffered.

Andre frowned, but continued, "Like I was saying, Curtis, this kind of macho act has already blinded one guy. I backed you then, as the evidence was inconclusive, but I've been watching you ever since, and this time you're going down. Hell, you're in such deep shit…"

Mack suddenly punched Curtis again, this time full fist, in the face. "So you're

7

what the force is turning out these days, eh?" Mack asked as Curtis hit the floor with a thud. From the ground, Curtis looked up to see Mack tucking into a spinal holster the revolver that, moments ago, had been pointed menacingly at his head.

Mack snorted and then looked concernedly at Nick. Reaching out, he asked, "You alright, son?"

CHAPTER 2

Nick, extending his cuffed hands out from behind him, mumbled, "I've had better days, Dad, but I'll survive."

Andre stared disgustedly at his officer on the ground, and asked Nick if he wanted to press charges.

Nick looked questioningly at his father, then made up his own mind: "Forget it, ridding the force of this *animal* will be satisfaction enough."

"You're damn lucky my son takes after his mother," Mack added, glaring down at Curtis. "I know a piece of shit when I see one, and you're really stinking up this joint."

Curtis stood up shakily, shook himself off and wiped the rivulet of blood from his jaw. "Fuck you, you old..." but before Curtis could finish, Andre and Mack had their revolvers back out and pointed at Curtis.

"Drop your rig, Curtis!" Andre commanded. "Now!"

Curtis turned pale. He looked from one to the other, and reluctantly began fumbling with the buckle of his gun belt. The moment it hit the floor, Andre snatched it up and Mack re-holstered.

Curtis, eyes wild, reached into his pocket and dangled his cuff keys at Mack. "Hey, old man, how would you like me to teach you a lesson like I did your pansy-ass kid there?"

Mack removed his revolver and gave it to Andre, replying calmly, "I'd love nothing better."

As the two raised fists and squared off, Andre whispered, "Don't do this, Mack. He may be a piece of shit, but he's twenty years younger than you and just finished Academy."

Mack ignored Andre. "Okay, tough guy. Let's see if you can beat up a decrepit old man."

Curtis enveloped the cuff-keys in his fist and lunged, full body, at Mack, attempting to tackle him. Mack, an instructor in martial arts for much of his police

9

life, stepped aside and grabbed Curtis by the arm and back of the collar as the man passed him. The rest was classic. Curtis ended up plastered against the nearest brick wall.

Shaking with rage and spitting out a fractured tooth, Curtis turned and began swinging at Mack. Mack once again stepped to the side, then kicked Curtis viciously on the side of the man's minimally injured knee. Mack's lips formed into a thin, taunting, half-smile at the resulting crunch as Curtis fell to the floor with a scream. Mack maneuvered behind the writhing man and in one fluid motion, had Curtis in a head lock ready to snap Curtis's neck.

Andre, Mitchell and Nick simultaneously yelled, "No!"

"Just seeing if you're all paying attention," Mack said, loosening his grip.

Mitchell turned disgustedly to Andre. "Captain, would it be alright if I left? I've seen enough, Sir."

Andre looked at Curtis sideways. "That, Officer Mitchell, depends on what you saw."

"I didn't see shit, Captain."

"Good. Then you can go, and while you're at it, call a 'bus' for your *ex*-partner here."

"Yes, sir," Mitchell responded, placing the call on his radiophone for the ambulance as he exited.

Mack pried open Curtis's free hand and snatched the cuff keys. Tossing the moaning cop aside in a heap, Mack strode over to Nick and unlocked Nick's cuffs. "You want me to take you to a hospital?"

Nick tested his body again. "I hurt all over, but I think I'm okay. Really, Dad, I just want out of here."

Mack slid a supportive arm around his son.

"You sure you're alright?" Andre asked, wincing as he watched Nick take an exploratory step on the damaged knee.

"I'll be fine. I've got the best of NYPD looking after me, don't I?" Nick offered, hobbling forward, enjoying the feeling of being supported by his father.

Mack took his gun back from Andre as they shuffled by. "I'll meet you at the bar when you're off duty."

"Yeah, okay, see you there." Then Andre turned his attention to the obstinate rookie, curled on the ground holding a disarticulated knee and groaning.

Mack looked momentarily back and down at Curtis, thinking of kicking him once more just for good measure, but, at the last moment, to everyone's relief, continued helping his son instead. Enough was enough. They'd all been rookies at one time, though hopefully not as rankly stupid as this one. "Fine, I'll see you then," Mack replied, his full attention directed on helping Nick back into the car.

One of the squad cars had left. Two officers sat inside another writing reports. The officer in the captain's car sat staring at the doorway Mack and Nick had just exited, waiting the captain's return. The lights on the Captain's car were still flashing, giving the area a surreal strobe-like appearance, as if they were all part of a 1940's black-and-white Hollywood movie. Mack assisted Nick into the car, but before Mack could close the car door, his son asked, "Dad, did you have to break the guy's knee like that?"

Mack slammed the car door closed as if the answer was something too sickening to say aloud. "One day you'll have a son or daughter, and, if someone, God forbid, hurts your child, you'll be surprised at how close you can come to killing him." Mack walked around to the drivers side, climbed in and fastened his seat belt, then paused, key in the ignition, as if waiting for a response from Nick.

Nick glanced sideways at his father, a man whose dark side he had always known, but rarely saw, and sighed. "Just take me home. I want to soak in a tub of hot water."

Mack feinted surprise: "You mean we're not going to the game?" Moving his right hand from the ignition switch back to the door, Mack began pushing down the door handle as if getting out, saying, "That's it. I'm going back to break his other fucking leg!"

Nick laughed, despite his pain, hoping his father was joking. "Come on, it hurts when I laugh. Take me home!"

Mack returned his hand to the keys, and the car rumbled to life. His friend, Andre, the Captain, was still inside the building, apparently reading Curtis the riot act. Mack had planned to wait for Andre but, looking back at his battered son, changed his mind and, in a cloud of dust and gravel, Mack headed the car back towards the highway and Nick's apartment.

Mack gripped the top of the steering wheel with both hands and without turning, said, "Nick, I got to give you credit. You kept a cool head back there. You did good. Reminds me of when Andre, Botch and I were growing up, and we..."

Nick looked out the side windowpane thinking, *Oh, no, not another 'Andre, Botch and Dad' story,* when he heard Mack bellow, "Aw, shit!" Looking back, Nick could see his father shaking a fist at the stalled traffic. Then to Nick's dismay, Mack quieted and continued where, a moment ago, he'd left off.

Nick knew the story: Andre and Mack had met in high school. Andre was the only black kid in the predominantly white school. He admired Mack because Mack treated him not good, not bad, but never different from anyone else. Mack was bigger than most of the other kids and tougher than all of them combined. He always stood up to anyone who crossed him or his friends and, with his quick hands and strength, he could drop an adversary so fast that those who wanted to topple him didn't try anymore.

One day, Mack invited Andre to join him in a neighborhood basketball game. Andre agreed, with hesitation, knowing he damn-well might end up getting his black ass kicked in the tight, white, Irish-Italian neighborhood. Mack went on to say that he figured Andre, being black, should know how to play basketball. Andre had initially responded with venom, only later realizing that Mack's cultural slurs were not meant to insult, so much as to get a rise.

"So which bar are we going to first?" Andre replied in retaliation. When Mack didn't get it, Andre explained: "You know; you're Irish! You'll need to get drunk first if *you're* going to play well."

Mack laughed heartily. "Good one! I love a person who can give and take a joke. I feel it's better to beat a person with a joke…"

Andre looked askance at Mack, unsure how to take what he was hearing. Here was a guy who could mop the floor with all the bad asses in the neighborhood, and was suddenly talking philosophically to Andre about his seventeen-year-old take on life. Andre understood Mack's explanation at a gut level, but he wasn't at all sure if he liked it, agreed with it or believed it.

The 'Andre, Botch and Dad' story would go on and on, filled with Mack-style homilies. "Your grandfather told me stereotypes are based on the losers in each culture, not the culture as a whole," Mack continued. "He also said that losers use this to degrade others and establish themselves as better or tougher than the rest. I guess in my father's eyes I'd be a loser. I just think people are too sensitive these days—I find teasing each other back and forth about our differences removes the obstacles. It's the best way to get to the heart of who a person really is. You know, get past *what* we are, and on to *who* we are."

Mack and Andre had hiked together over to the IS 192 schoolyard to play the proffered game of basketball. There, Mack introduced Andre to Botch, who found it harder warming up to Andre. Botch couldn't shut people up with his fists like Mack, and being friends with a black back then meant, at the least, a definite beating from whichever gang noticed and was in power at the moment. Botch also felt an impossible-to-verbalize jealousy that Mack might like Andre better than him. Botch, however, shook hands with Andre and the three stood around waiting for a pick-up game.

After a few minutes, one of several girls hanging out there came over to Mack, pointed a slender finger at Andre and asked, "Who's your friend?"

"This is my buddy, Andre. He's black and I apologize, but there's nothing I can do about his color!"

Andre, enjoying the girl's attentions, didn't know what to make of what Mack had just said, when Mack piped up, "Relax, Andre. I'm just kidding around so they'll get to know you."

Mack walked away with a couple of other friends, looking over his shoulder occasionally as if keeping an eye on Andre. Andre was smiling and had turned his attentions towards the red-haired beauty, saying, "I'm Andre and, yes, I'm black."

The girl giggled. They shook hands and talked. Andre was beginning to feel like he might fit in until he heard, "Get your dirty hands off my sister!" Andre glanced towards where Mack had been a moment ago, but Mack was nowhere to be seen. In his place was the 'kid' who had issued the challenge, a kid twice Andre's size, surrounded by three equally daunting friends.

The kid's nickname, he was later told, was 'Tiny' and Tiny was several years older than everyone else, which made him feel important enough to take the bully's lead in Mack's absence. Tiny had just finished doing a year at Riker's Island and liked to brag about it, saying he took a bullet—meaning a year in jail—for stabbing a guy nearly to death. It was Tiny's sister who had approached Andre and started to flirt, so realizing the awkwardness of her position, she volunteered that Andre *was* indeed bothering her. Andre listened, mouth agape. When Andre tried to explain, that was all the excuse Tiny needed. Tiny stabbed a prizefighter's finger into Andre's chest and threw the gauntlet: "You calling my sister a liar?"

Andre knew when to shut up, put on a game face and show no fear, so instead of answering, he simply stared back, while Tiny's friends, cracking their necks and knuckles menacingly, surrounded him. Botch, not knowing what to do, let out a whistle to which Mack came running.

"Did you bring this nigger here?" Tiny asked Mack rhetorically, ready to beat the additional intruder to a pulp—until he suddenly realized it was Mack.

In the background, Tiny's sister threw fuel on the fire: "It was the nigger who started it all. He's the one. Kick his ass, Tiny!"

Mack looked at Tiny's sister. "That's no nigger, that's your sister."

Tiny stared at Mack. "Funny, Mack. So funny, I think after I kick in the nigger's ass, I'll do yours, too!" It was a loser's feint meant to allow Tiny time to beat up Andre while thinking about how to later escape from Mack.

Tiny stripped off his shirt and began flexing his muscles ostentatiously. There was blood in his eyes; the growing crowd could smell it.

Mack unbuttoned and took off his shirt. "Tell you what, Tiny. Here's how it's going to go: I'm going to beat the balls off you, then, if necessary, I'm going to do in your three friends here, and then maybe my friend, Andre, can finish his conversation with your slut of a sister, if he cares to at that point." Mack recited the words emotionlessly, cocking his head towards Tiny's sister.

Tiny looked dumbfounded, as if suddenly reconsidering, but the crowd was already yelling, "Nig-ger! Nig-ger! Nig-ger!" and Tiny's sister, realizing the crowd's call for blood could just as easily be turned on her, added, "Kick the nigger-lover's ass, Tiny! You can do it!"

Tiny turned red in the face, forgot about Andre, and charged at Mack in a pre-emptive strike. Mack was much faster, however, and booted Tiny, sending him skidding onto the blacktop, belly-down, face-first.

Tiny pulled himself up, embarrassed at how poorly the fight was going, and drew a switchblade from his pocket. Flicking his wrist, the six-inch steel stiletto blade clicked open, glinting evilly. Tiny lunged at Mack's chest, but Mack parried the thrust and each subsequent one as if he knew ahead of time exactly what Tiny was planning to do. Tiny, huffing and puffing, made several more ineffective stabs, always aiming at Mack's torso, which Mack, at the last moment, carefully placed just out of the blade's reach. Sensing Tiny's frustration and exhaustion, Mack suddenly rammed Tiny with a left jab to the ribs. Tiny's chest caved in, drawing his head to the side. Mack followed with a quick right and left to the face. Pop! Tiny's nose surrendered to the second blow and the knife clacked to the pavement, while blood poured from Tiny's nose. Tiny, stunned and humiliated, yelled, "Grab him!"

The three thugs immediately grabbed Mack for Tiny to finish. Tiny, however, just stood there, swaying, unable to see his target through the pain, tears and blood. Andre, in the meantime, hoping to regain some lost prowess, punched one of the attackers, knocking him to the ground. Mack yelled, "Stay out of it," and threw a merciless side-kick at the second. The one on the pavement got up holding a displaced jaw and ran; the second bent over, gasping, clung onto his crotch and hobbled off behind the first. Botch in the meantime had the third in a choke hold. A moment later, the boy dropped to the ground, unconscious.

Tiny, meanwhile, had snuck up behind Mack and wrapped his arms around Mack in a bear hug. Mack struggled, at last freeing a hand, and seized Tiny's ear, twisting it with all his might. The pain from his ear and his throbbing nose together proved too much for Tiny, who decided to switch to saving what he could of the rest of his face by crying, "Uncle!"

"Uncle. Agreed." Mack responded flatly.

Tiny let go of Mack, and, cradling his bleeding nose and twisted ear, ran out of the school yard. Tiny's sister clenched her fists and looked daggers at Mack. Then she looked past Mack and Andre, threw her nose up in the air, and walked briskly towards her rapidly receding brother. As she passed Mack, her fingernails shot out as if to rake his face, but a girl from the crowd came to Mack's rescue, grabbing Tiny's sister by the hair from behind and jerking her away. Tiny's sister, eyes welling with tears, raked her taloned fingernails through the air, screaming in anger. A moment later, she broke free, leaving Mack's savior with a clump of red hair in her hand. Mack looked at the girl who had just saved him a facial razoring, and said awkwardly, "Thanks."

The girl moved close to Mack and replied, "No problem," blowing Tiny's sister's hair into his face and walking off. Mack, stunned, couldn't muster the courage to ask her name and, instead, watched her in silence as she walked away.

"Great job, Casanova. Her name is Annie," Botch shot off.

Mack smiled, entranced, and echoed the name, "Annie," as he watched his future wife fade into the distance

Andre brushed himself off, and with it any remaining feelings he had had for the red-haired girl. "Let's get out of here, the cops will be coming soon!"

The audience, hearing Andre's comment, immediately began to disperse, dissolving through numerous unseen holes in the wire fence surrounding the court. Mack, Andre and Botch joined the crowd, laughing and bragging along the way about the beating they'd given Tiny and his friends, until Mack abruptly stopped and cut the conversation with a brusque, "Who has money?"

Andre reached into his pockets. "I got a buck and a half."

Botch held up a small fold of paper. "Two bucks. Why?"

"I need some beer," Mack replied, smiling broadly.

Mack marched his two friends to Hansen's Deli, opening the squeaking screen door and encouraging everyone in like a mother hen. "We deserve it. We'll buy cheap. You know, quantity not quality." He bought a case of beer for just under their collective $3.50. From there, they climbed onto the roof of a nearby apartment building, laid down next to each other and began relishing the release of tension the golden liquid was providing. The more they drank, the more they talked; the more they talked, the more they laughed and reminisced. Andre, with a smirk, slurred, "When I drank my firs' beer, I din't like th' taste. I couldn't understan' how people could drink. Now I thi'...thin...think I finally got it. I gotta queschun for you, Mack: Whad comes firs', drunken depression or Irish music?"

"Good question," Mack laughed, downing a long swig without further comment.

Botch shook his head to clear his swirling thoughts. "If I go home like this, my father will kick my ass." Looking ridiculously serious and laughing at the same time, he added, "My father always told me to stay away from the Irish. 'They'll only get you in trouble,' he said. Can you believe that, Mack? I mean, if he really believed that, why the fuck did he move me and my mom into this mostly Irish neighborhood? An' then, why tell me to stay away from them?"

Andre worked hard to focus his eyes on Mack, "So waz your ol' man one ah' those stereotypical Irishmen, Mack? You know: a drinkin' man's drinker?" He waved his beer can in the air as if batting away an irritating fly.

"Not in his later years," Mack answered, with a hint of quiet remorse. "It was worse than that. He took the cure, and then was on my ass for everything." Mack looked over at Botch. "One day I was talking to a priest at church. Father O'Conner..."

Botch laughed, "I think I know this story..."

Mack frowned and continued. "Anyway, I went up to Father O'Conner and asked him, with a straight face, what he likes in alter boys. Well, the old priest hemmed and hawed, as if trying to answer seriously. Then he saw the smirk on my face and slapped me."

Andre, through his drunken daze, asked, "So then wha' happint'?"

"He knew then that I knew about him," continued Mack, "the fucking pervert. Anyway, I knocked him on his ass and told him that that was for every nun that beat me in Catholic grammar school and every altar boy he'd fondled. I have to admit that was the biggest release of pent-up hate in my entire life. It felt so uplifting to say what everyone knew. Of course, the hate was back later that day when my father beat me for several hours for what I'd done. I never forgave Father O'Conner or my father for the beating." Mack paused thoughtfully, then continued. "Then my father up and died before I could reconcile with him." Mack, suddenly melancholy, turned to Andre. "So what's your sad story?"

Andre, who made it his lifelong goal to avoid talking about his life, had completely succumbed to the tongue-wagging effect of the beer. In the past, whenever pressed, he replied that he grew up in South Carolina.

Actually, he explained, his father was a mechanic and his mother did everything else...literally. At thirteen, his mother died of 'pneumonia,' but all he remembered was how frantic his father had been, trying unsuccessfully to get his mother proper medical attention, which, back then, was near impossible for a black family in the South. When his mother, the only person that ever made Andre feel like he was special, died, life changed for him from rotten to unbearable.

Andre was the youngest of three siblings. His older brother moved to Canada. His sister became a nightclub singer, married her manager, and the two ran off together to L.A. That left Andre alone with his father, who hit the bottle hard, and hit Andre harder for constantly reminding his father of his deceased wife.

One day, Andre fought back. When it was over, Andre found himself standing over his father's pulverized body, ax in hand, ready to bury it into the body if it so much as twitched. Andre, regaining his composure just in time, threw the ax across the room, shattering his mother's wooden china cabinet, sending pieces of her beloved cabinet and dishes all around the room. Andre ran from the house thinking he'd axed both his father, and now his mother, too.

Eventually, he made it to a train trestle, where he decided to sit, smoke a few cigarettes, and end it all. What had begun in thought ended in his putting each cigarette butt out on his forearm to distract him from the pain in his heart. He eventually passed out between the tracks, a hand and leg extended limply over the rails.

The next day he awoke, to his surprise, intact. Perhaps, he thought, this was a sign that his father had survived. Andre had promised his mother on her deathbed that he would make something out of his life. Andre walked back to the house, relieved to find neither hearse nor sheriff's car out front. Inside, the house was cleaned up and deadly quiet, causing him fear that his father might suddenly jump out with the same ax from the shadows and finish him the way he had been considering doing to his father.

There was a pile of cash on the table with a note, saying, "I called your aunt in N.Y. This is money for the bus. Don't be here when I get back."

Andre's aunt was his mother's younger sister, and the few times he'd met her, she'd acted caringly towards him. The situation was, he decided, providential—a second chance at life.

Andre gave a drunken laugh. "And, here I yam," he chuckled, watching as Botch struggled to squeeze a pack of cigarettes out of a jean's pocket. "So, what's your story, Botch?"

Botch tried to stand up and light his cigarette, but was too wobbly to slide the match across the striker pad. Instead, he tossed the unlit cigarette and slumped down onto the floor of the roof. "My mother was Jewish, my father Italian. I met Mack in Catholic school, where the nuns tried their best to beat the Jew out of me. No one laid a hand on me at home. Of course, tonight that might prove different, but I'll just blame any drunkenness on having hung out a bit too long with the Irish."

In the car, misty-eyed, Mack smiled, reflecting further on what later proved to be the first of innumerable drunken excursions the three had together. Mack looked over at his son, Nick, as they continued to sit, stuck in traffic. He knew Nick had heard these stories a million times, each time told in a slightly different way, so Mack ignored that Nick was ignoring him, and, on a whim, added, "And that's when I realized I was gay." Nick kept up the fake nods, then suddenly froze.

Turning to Mack, he asked, "That's when *what*?"

Mack laughed. "Just checking to see if you were listening."

It was Nick's turn to laugh while instructing his father to get off at the next exit. He wanted to take the back roads in order to extend his time with his father as much as he dared.

At Nick's apartment, Nick started to get out of the car, holding his chest and knee and grunting with pain.

"You sure you don't want me to take you to an emergency room? You're looking more beat up with every passing minute."

Nick gripped the sides of the car and pulled himself out. "I'm fine. I'll see you at Farrell's later to watch the second half."

Mack nodded, pulled the passenger door closed, and drove away. As he did, he called on his cell phone to tell Botch that his plans for the day had changed. Still, he avoided telling Botch about Nick getting beat up.

"So you're not going to the game at all?" Botch asked.

"That's why I'm calling. I'm heading over to Farrell's. Andre and Nick will meet me there later. Why don't you join us?"

"Sounds good to me," Botch offered. "I have to stop at the office a moment, then I'll meet you..."

Mack disconnected before his friend finished. The only thing he hated more than long phone conversations were long goodbyes.

CHAPTER 3

Benjamin "Botch" Bartolata flipped his cell phone closed and entered FBI headquarters in Manhattan. The clack of his footsteps echoed loudly as he traversed the massive FBI insignia inlaid into the marble floor. At the far end, behind a windowpane of bulletproof glass, the night security guard watched as Botch approached the nearest turnstile.

"Mr. Bartolata, what brings you down here on a Sunday afternoon?" the speaker in the wall crackled.

Botch lied, "Forgot my glasses. Can't read the dossier's for tomorrow's briefing without them." He smiled and shrugged complacently.

The security guard laughed. "I know the feeling. Getting old sucks." The turnstile in front of him clicked and Botch walked nonchalantly through. Thank God the guard knew him, because what he'd really forgotten was his FBI identification card and walking around the streets of New York with a loaded gun and no ID was pretty stupid for a senior FBI agent. He waved as he passed the window and entered one of a row of elevators situated along the back wall, thinking how, despite his years with the service, he had never gotten used to being called "Mr. Bartolata." The elevator door slid silently shut. He pushed the floor button, and as the elevator ascended, reflected back to when and how he got the nickname "Botch."

Mack had been telling one of his typical ethnic jokes, this time comparing Ben to an Italian character in a TV show who agonized over decisions which, once made, always ended up being wrong. The character's name was Botchagaloop. Paco, a local Puerto Rican, shortened it to 'Botch' and the name suddenly stuck. At first, Botch was angry about the nickname's implication, but it ended up a blessing in disguise, as it forced him to get over his awkward, boyish shyness by requiring him to explain the nickname to everyone new he met. After a while, he realized the catchy name was actually making him popular, eventually casting him from under

Mack's shadow—everyone who heard the nickname remembered who Botch was. How the name eventually spread to the office, he couldn't remember, but the moment his boss, Walter, met Mack and Andre, that cemented it. Although deep down, he still thought "Botch" a stupid-ass name, it beat something worse like "Stinky." Or "Asswipe."

The elevator lurched to a stop, and Botch exited quietly onto the sixth floor where his office was located, looking and listening for Debbie. Botch had recently broken the primary office rule, "don't shit where you eat," by maintaining a relationship with one of the building cleaning ladies. Their friendship flamed hot for awhile then ebbed. Actually, he hadn't seen her for over a month, after she switched her work schedule to late nights and weekends to avoid him. Debbie didn't appear to be on the floor tonight. Odd, how he had inadvertently walked out without his ID, and here he was having to return to the office when she might be there.

Botch decided to take the shortcut to his office so he would be less likely to encounter the roving floor guard walking the weekend rounds who, as a formality, might just ask to see his ID. The shortcut was a door from the main hallway into a supply room that led through a second door directly into his office. Initially scheduled for removal, the supply room ended up remaining after funds ran low during the last round of building renovations. People ignored, then eventually forgot about the passageway, so Botch had the door between the small supply room and his office rigged so that he was the only one who could open it. He liked the idea of having a hidden escape route, and delighted in telling his secretary he was busy on a new case and not to disturb him, then slipping through the door to the supply room, and from there into the hallway, to the stairway and out of the building.

Standing in the hallway with the supply room doorknob in hand, he heard someone coming and hurriedly stepped in, closing the door behind him. He was about to turn on the supply room light when the voices shifted from the hallway and resumed in his office. *Damn*, he thought. It must be the floor guard conversing with Debbie while she cleaned his office. Botch couldn't hear what the voices were saying, so he reached in his pocket, pulled out his cell phone and flipped it open to minimally illuminate the room. Winding his way deftly around several boxes to the door to his office, Botch thought, *If it's Debbie, then she's probably screwing the floor guard—what was his name? Ciro*, he recalled. She had said once she liked uniformed men. Botch was suddenly surprised, now that he thought of it, how much he knew about Ciro, and detested him. Ciro thought he was God's gift to women. *How could an endearing woman like Debbie fall for such a piece of crap! And she's in there, doing him in my office!* Was this some kind of perverse revenge for him having ended the relationship, unable—no, that wasn't true—*unwilling* to commit? And why shouldn't a kindly woman like Debbie move on? *Be calm; don't allow your anger to get the best of you. Be a man. Yeah, be a man —and catch the bitch red-handed! That way the anger will kill any remaining feelings you have for her, and you can tell yourself that she was the one who really ended the relationship. It'll be all her fault then.* Of course, there was also the fact that the opportunity was presenting itself to smack the shit out of her new lover. Botch used the light from the phone to locate the seam of the door that opened into his office. Closing the cell phone, he peered unnoticed into his office. What he saw was neither Debbie nor Ciro, but three junior FBI agents who reported directly to him.

Botch, at first relieved, began wondering what they were doing in his private office on a Sunday without him there. FBI Agents Gary Ross, Mike Smith and Rich Pagano were probably setting him up for a practical joke in retaliation for the one he'd played on them the week before. They'd gotten pretty pissed at him for his taking Vick's Vapor Rub and putting it on the doorknob to the men's room. After getting it on their hands and then on their privates when they took a leak, they complained the entire rest of the day about the burning. It hadn't taken much detective work to ascertain that Botch, the office practical joker, had been behind it. In fact, everyone on the floor but Botch's three agents had been in on it. *So,* Botch reasoned, *here was a revenge plot unfolding, and he was going to hear all about it without them knowing.* Botch exchanged an ear for his eye to pick up the conversation.

Agent Ross: "Alright, let's get down to business." Gary Ross went on about a Mafia big shot Botch had heard of through his friend, Mack, named Jerry 'Sweaters' Cannistraci. The gangster had gotten his nickname from his early days when he was known for wearing outlandishly garish sweaters at kills. Only one man ever had the balls to comment about Sweaters' sweaters and remained alive to tell the story. "There'll be four to six million in cash in the apartment. The Dominicans have been profiting heavily from drug sales in their part of the city, and Sweaters has been trying to gain their trust so he could move in on their business."

Agent Smith interrupted. "Sweaters may be a made man, but from what I hear, he doesn't have that kind of juice. He was more into numbers, prostitution and porn."

"True," Gary retorted. "And everyone above and below him thinks he's an asshole. That's why he needs to swing this deal and find out who the Dominican supplier is—so he can cut the Dominicans out and command more money, power and respect."

Botch, listening to his junior agents' conversation, wondered why the three hadn't informed him about the investigation. Had they gone over his head? And if so, why? If, indeed, they'd skipped over him, then his boss would have to be in charge of the investigation. *Maybe they've discovered my slipping in and out of the office?* he thought suddenly.

Botch squelched his fears and, with the greatest of care, put an eye back to the crack. He could just barely make out Gary shifting through some papers in a brown manila folder. What wasn't clear was whether the folder was Botch's.

"Here's the layout to the apartment where the cash is. I got it from Joey Van Gogh—you know, 'Joey V.' as he's now known. He won't reveal the exact location, however, until he brings us there."

Rich looked puzzled. "Joey Van Gogh? What kind of name is that?"

Gary slipped a picture out of the folder and showed it to Rich. "Joey V. was the guy I mentioned who commented on Jerry Sweaters' sweaters and remained alive. Sweaters, instead of killing him, made an example of him by cutting part of his ear off with a letter opener. After that people took to calling the man Joey Van Gogh, because of the ear. Now he's called 'Joey V.' for short."

Mike grabbed the pictures. "So this Joey V.—what's his part in this again?"

Gary grinned slyly. "He'll be delivering Sweaters' 'buy-in offer' money. He thinks he's working with the FBI, and that we're going to relocate him and his family through the Witness Protection Program afterwards. Once he brings us to the apartment where the cash is and gets us in, we won't need him anymore. After that, he's a liability, but don't shoot Joey V. until *after* we get into the apartment. Joey's the only one who has the Domincans' trust, knows exactly where their apartment is located, and where the drug money is kept. Guys, once we enter the apartment, things are likely to go wild. This has the potential of a blood bath. We have to fine tune this plan, so we don't get our asses shot off. Joey figures there could be as many as eight armed Dominicans in and around the apartment."

Gary continued: "There's a hidden chamber built somewhere into this room. I'm told you couldn't find the door to it unless you already knew where it was, it's so well concealed—like the one our fearless leader, Bartolata, has."

"What do you mean?" Mike asked, confused.

Gary pointed directly towards Botch. "See that bulletin board over there?" Botch, in panic, drew his head abruptly back. "Behind it is a door to a supply room. That's why Bartolata never went for a bigger office. He can cut out anytime without anyone knowing. I never noticed the door until one day I saw him go into his office and tell his secretary he was not to be disturbed. I stood there for about twenty minutes, then got tired of waiting. After convincing the secretary that our boss would not be pleased by not receiving some critical information he had requested, we knocked on the door together. When he didn't answer, I tried to open it, but it was locked. I told his secretary to save her job by going out for some coffee, while I figured a way in. It wasn't hard to pick the lock, and when I walked in, he wasn't there! I knew he couldn't have gotten by me and only after searching very carefully did I noticed the seam in the wall along a bulletin board edge."

Mike walked towards the board. "That old weasel." Botch froze as Mike reached forward to try and open the door.

Gary, however, waved Mike back. "It just goes to a storage room. Let's not get side-tracked."

Mike returned behind Botch's desk and stretched out regally in his boss's chair.

"Like I was saying," Gary continued, "there's a hidden compartment in the Dominican apartment, and behind it is a well-armed guard sitting on millions in cash. If we can get that far, all we have to do is pry open the door, off the guard, grab the cash and be gone. Then we sit on it a few months to let it all blow over, and discretely quit the force, one at a time."

The two other agents nodded in agreement, sinister grins distorting their faces.

"Alright, before we begin to work out the details, remember, if one of us goes down, his part in the game's over. No hard feelings, but no hospital. We finish him off and bring the body with us so there's no evidence. Agreed?"

Each conspirator bumped a fist against the others' as if toasting.

Botch ran his fingers through his hair in amazement, thinking, *I can't believe these guys are dirty.*

Botch listened awhile longer as the three fleshed out the details of their plan. After an hour or so, he had heard enough. Using the light from his cell phone to locate the door to the hallway, he reached for the doorknob as the phone lid snapped shut. The phone immediately began beeping to indicate a message waiting. Botch quickly turned the doorknob and walked out into the hall, trying desperately to muffle the sound by placing the chirruping phone against his flat stomach under his clothes as he checked the hallway. He was imagining Gary in the next room saying, *Did you hear that?* when he heard Rich, from behind both doors yelling, "It came from the storage room!"

The trio tried to force door open, but not knowing the secret to opening it, couldn't make it budge.

As Gary yelled, "Go through the secretary's office!" Botch bolted silently down the hallway and into the back stairwell. If they caught up with him, the three-to-one odds would be iffy at best.

He made it down to the second floor stairwell, turned, opened the door, ran into the second floor hallway and slammed into someone exiting an office. Both fell clumsily to the floor. Botch jumped up to continue running when he realized it was Debbie, cleaning lady and ex-girlfriend. He gallantly helped her up, his pounding heart suddenly heightened by the urge to wrap his arms around her and kiss her. Instead, he ended up apologizing over and over like a schoolboy, asking if she was alright, and if she was hurt anywhere. If the three conspiring agents happened on them, he would play it cool, like he was there to see Debbie. Debbie looked at him with her big brown eyes, suggestively rearranging her hair while trying to hide her escaping happiness at seeing him again. "Just like old times. You knock me down and I get back up," she said.

Botch, embarrassed, fumbled with his hands while trying to decide whether to hug her or shake her hand, finally blurting out, "Ouch! I deserved that." The look in her eyes cautioned him about showing any deeper feelings, for fear of conveying further false hopes. Despite the renewed ardor, he knew he would be no more able to commit to her now than before, even with the powerful combination of loneliness and desire that was coursing through his body at the moment. *Some men have the ability, others don't*, he reasoned. Botch had been married once and, in his mind, it had proven more than any man should ever have to endure.

Both hesitated, trying to sort though the bewildering array of wild, electric-like feelings sparking between them, when Botch overheard the security guard, who had let him into the building earlier, talking into his radio. Between crackles, Botch could plainly hear, "Mr. Bartolata went upstairs something over a half hour ago."

Botch dragged Debbie along with him back into the stairwell and further downstairs, telling her, "I'll explain later. Just go along with me on this. Please. It's a matter of life and death."

Debbie instantly took what Botch had said totally different than it was meant. Giving him a big smile, she willingly followed.

Whether Botch was ardently asking for another chance or not, Debbie had always rather liked playing sidekick to his practical jokes, being the straight one, not only for the joke, but also as a foil against their mutually secret tryst. They had been so close to making it together. So very close. All Botch had to do was take the plunge; she had promised him over and over he wouldn't regret it.

Hand-in-hand, Botch led her out the first floor stairwell door and said aloud, hoping if any of the three outlaw agents were anywhere nearby, they would overhear him: "The dinner reservation is for 8 o'clock. I'll pick you up at your house."

Debbie nodded, obligingly going along with the charade. "Perfect."

"Great! See you later, then!" Botch gave her a quick kiss and watched as Debbie walked off in a daze, biting her lip, wondering what just transpired.

24

Botch's eyes darted left then right, and noticed a movement near the elevator bank. Putting on a look of surprise, Botch announced, "Hey, it's Sunday. What are you doing here?"

Gary, breathless, stopped mid-stride and eyed Botch suspiciously. Then, catching his breath and smoothing his clothes, he responded with raised eyebrows and a grin at seeing a cleaning lady walking down the hall, "Just catching up on a few things, boss. How about you?"

Botch tried to unobtrusively scan the area for any sign of the other two agents. "Me? Just catching up on a few things, too," he said, cavalierly nodding down the hall in Debbie's direction.

Gary grinned. "Starting it up again, are you? Why don't you stop stringing the poor girl along and make an honest woman out of her?"

"Do me a favor," Botch countered, "and stop putting in Sunday hours. Next thing, they'll be demanding I haul my ass in to supervise you, and, frankly, I like my weekends free. Go home. I'll see you tomorrow." Botch turned and walked through the entry area and out the large front door.

Mike stepped from the shadows into the light. "Do you believe the man?" he asked warily.

Gary stared at the front door that Botch had exited. "He's pretty crafty, but it's not hard to believe he wants to tap the girl again. I don't think he knows anything. The noise we heard must have been the floor guard walking by."

Rich appeared from another dark corner across the room. "I wish I felt as convinced as you two."

Number One Bestseller

CHAPTER 4

Botch drove towards Farrell's Bar, wondering what to do with the information he'd just acquired. He'd have to contact his supervisor, Walter Steiner, to feel him out and see if Walter was in bed with the three agents. Botch really had no idea how far up this cancer in the bureau might go.

He reached for his cell phone and dialed the Midget Bar, where Walter could be counted on to be on any Sunday, blind drunk and gambling away his monthly paycheck.

Botch used to hang out with Walter, the two having started work for the bureau at the same time. Walter, aggressive and ambitious, was quickly promoted above Botch. It looked as if Walter's life was going to take off...until Walter's wife died and the man fell into a bottle. These days, Walter barely went through the motions of living, and while Botch continued to help his supervisor keep it together at work, he refused to be the man's nursemaid the rest of the time.

The bartender called Walter to the phone.

Walter spit out a surprisingly comprehensible, "Hello?"

"Walter, it's me, Botch."

"Aw, fuck. Listen. I promise you I'll return the money you loaned me. It's just that, well, Lady Luck's been down on me lately. But my luck's gonna change. I can feel it in my bones." Botch heard muffled coughing, and counted the seconds while Walter took a long draught of something—anything—alcoholic. "That *is* why you're calling me on a Sunday, isn't it? Say, where are you? Why don't you come by for a drink, ol' buddie?" Botch could hear the booze kick in, but mostly was surprised at how sober Walter could sound even when flat out drunk.

"I can't," Botch replied. "I was wondering...well, I stopped by the office and found Gary, Mike and Rich working, and I'm thinking, hey, I'm their supervisor, but they're getting the overtime, and I'm not! Now why is that, Walter? What have I done to get on your shit list?"

"You called to break my balls about some overtime pay on a Sunday? Yeah, well, I know they're working overtime, and, yeah, I didn't ask you about it, one, because you never work on weekends, and two, if you did, I figure you'd be in your office sleeping on the job." Walter cursed angrily at himself for answering the phone. Botch was fishing for something, and Walter didn't like being fished.

Botch, at the same time, was thinking that if Walter was involved, drunk or not, Walter was an expert at concealing information, even to his buddy and benefactor, Botch. "Walter, I'm just joking. Don't get your skirt in a bunch."

"Man," Walter said, obviously relieved, "even after all these years, I still fall for your bullshit. Why can't I get you to work regular hours?"

"That hurts, Walter. Here I am, breaking my ass day in and day out for you and you assume I'm jerking off."

"Investigating a new gin mill doesn't mean you're working."

"What's that? You're breaking up. Can't hear you, Walter." Botch retorted playfully.

"Yeah, bullshit! See you tomorrow," Walter growled and hung up.

Botch thought a moment. Could Walter have enough brain left after all the heavy drinking to be part of such a scheme? Walter was heavy into the bookies and sorely needed money. Still, Botch liked Walter because he wasn't like most FBI supervisors who, as they moved up, put their fellow co-workers down for the very same offenses they were guilty of during their climb. He may be a hopeless alcoholic, but he was fair, and never forgot where he came from. The problem was that Walter was showing up at work these days with alcohol coming out of his pores. Seasoned agents called his condition 'soaked'—his mornings were mostly spent waiting for a couple of shots at lunch to get shit-faced again. Given his condition, if Walter was involved, Botch wouldn't be able to believe anything he said or help him.

Botch drove faster, his head pounding as he rethought his options. He finally decided he needed to let go of the whole thing until he could talk it over with Mack and Andre. Botch forced himself to think of something else—anything—like what years the cars on the freeway in front of him were built. One was a Ford, maybe an '85 or '86. He started to feel better and moved on to another car, a 1990 Mercury. He knew that one because Debbie drove one just like it. *Damn that Debbie! Always showing up in my thoughts. I don't want to think of her, either, right now!*

Botch tried returning to guessing car years but this time it didn't work. He just couldn't stop thinking about Debbie. He'd dumped her once, and would do just about anything not to hurt her again, except, of course, the reality was that earlier today he'd used her to save his own ass. He also hated the thought of giving up being a bachelor. *Okay, if I can't stop thinking about her, then maybe I should stop trying so hard to stop thinking about her and see where that line of insanity goes.*

Botch had had a lot of women in his time, but it always left him feeling empty. Worse, he hadn't, in innumerable years, run into a woman like Debbie who could make him laugh! That one kiss from Debbie today had momentarily wiped away the empty feeling he struggled with day in and day out, and now he simply missed her...and, yes, loved her.

He was always careful to regard his post-divorce bachelorhood as the perfect life: coming and going as he pleased, not having to answer to anyone, lounging around in his underwear, drinking beer, watching movies, while the phone rang off the hook. After the divorce, he'd spent a couple of months dating like he was in his early twenties, coming home with a different, willing woman every night. The thrill of undressing them like one after another Christmas present, and exploring their bodies like Columbus did America, simply grew tiring after awhile. He started staying home, alone.

Being alone, of course, sucked, too, but at least he had Mack, who was also flying solo. Still, when the parties were over and he went home, the laughs with Mack didn't fill the aching void inside him for long. This evening, Botch discovered yet again that Debbie did.

He knew now that continuing to live without her would be like living in a balloon, floating around with no direction or purpose. She was the one person he felt he could let hold the string. He could happily float *with* her anywhere that the wind took them. Debbie never let him fly too high before she brought him back down to earth, but at the same time, she never sucked all the air out of him like many women in a 'relationship' were wont to do. He knew how destructive he could be to himself, and she had a way of making him stop and open up. He wondered how many more chances she would give him and began reminiscing about the first day he met her.

When he first saw her smile—happy, gentle and caring—both his body and heart twinged; he knew he desired her, but her response to him seemed the same as it was to everyone else: sympathy for another wretched human, and little more.

He figured he didn't stand a chance with her, if only because of her stunning beauty, and, adding their age and cultural differences, it was strike three, you're out! When the other agents talked about her, Botch would put in his own two cents, and they would as likely look at him and say, "No offense, but you're more AARP material, Botch. Forget her!"

Clamming up, he listened with silent rage when the talk turned to the various sexual positions in which they imagined engaging the 'hot' but lowly Latin cleaning lady. When, later, a contest was announced, with bets as to who would be the first to bang her, he vehemently objected. They, however, just laughed at him, and they were right about one thing: He was an old fool and didn't have a chance with her. But that, paradoxically, was what ended up taking off the usual pressure of finding a way to get to know her.

Botch recalled striking up a conversation one afternoon when she caught him in the stairwell trying to sneak out. Born in Cuba, she'd immigrated with her parents to the United States when she was seven. She actually had a better command of English than he did, and was going to school to become a nurse. The more friendly time he spent with her, the closer they became, and he soon realized she was more than special. If he couldn't have her, at least he could protect her from the idiots at work.

Then came the day he made a stupid bet with her and she'd accepted. The penalty: The loser had to take the winner to dinner. The bet didn't matter beyond that she'd accepted it; he'd already decided to lose and promptly did.

They spent several wonderful hours at a cozy, quaint, upscale restaurant talking about life's myriad disappointments and each other's hopes for the future. She was nothing less than stunning that night in her short, black dress and heels. In counterpoint, she spoke mostly of the struggles of being a single mother. She had married young. When she found out she was pregnant—she, the classic, poor, child-bride, and him, the scared, kid-husband with no employment prospects—the guy ended up walking out on her and their daughter, Evie. She started to cry when Botch asked about Evie and Evie's father, whom she never heard from again. Botch remembered sliding around the booth and putting his arm around her to console her. It was when he touched her that he realized how much he cared for her. Later, he said, "Give me what you have on the guy. I'll track him down, and we'll set you up for child support and alimony. After all, I *am* FBI!"

Debbie looked at him askance, then smiled. "That's about the nicest thing anyone's ever said to me."

Botch's cheeks burned red, and he stared into the swirling vortex of the drink he was rolling between his hands. "It's not easy protecting you from all the animals in that office," he mumbled.

Debbie's smile softened and widened. "Don't worry about them. When I hear them talking about me, it reminds me of my ex, and that's enough to turn me off. But you're different." She closed her eyes, leaned towards Botch and delicately touched her lips to his. A moment later she broke the connection and, staring into his eyes, whispered: "*El amore es ciego*. I'll be right back," she said, as she got up and headed for the ladies' room.

Botch was stunned and bewildered. Did what he thought happen *really* happen? Did she just kiss him? And didn't the Spanish phrase include something about love? A boyish smile crept across his face while a voice in the back of his head confirmed, *yes, yes, 'the real thing.'* Botch was gazing into unfocused space when Debbie reappeared. The voice of Frank Sinatra was singing "The Way You Look Tonight" in the background. He would never forget that moment.

As Debbie approached the table, Botch cleared his throat. "You look absolutely...gorgeous."

She blushed, thanked him, and sat closer. Pouting slightly, she shrugged her delicately-curved, mocha-brown shoulders. "I like this music, but can't place the singer."

Botch, stunned by her admission, jokingly clutched his heart and said, "You don't know 'The Crooner,' 'Ol' Blue Eyes?' Me, I'm Italian. You might just as well take the knife on your napkin and plunge it into my heart!" Botch reached for her hand, but instead of directing it towards the table knife, led her up and over to the jukebox. Together they chose some Sinatra numbers. Together, they cheek-danced, later laughing, hugging and sipping drinks until the owner of the establishment came out from the kitchen, and, catching Botch's eye, faked a wide yawn. Botch looked at his watch. "Oh, shit, it's four o'clock! I forgot about you having to get home to Evie!"

As they got up, Debbie slipped her arm in his, leaned her head against his shoulder and whispered, "I hope I'm not being too bold, but I told my sister I would pick Evie up later this afternoon." She hesitated. "That's okay, isn't it?"

Botch briefly searched her eyes, then let himself say, "That's great. We can go to my place then." It just rolled off his tongue like water off a duck.

Debbie laughed. "Thank God. I was starting to wonder if you were gay."

"Gay?" Botch shot out. "Gay? Never! I just figured you were so far out of my league..."

They drove the cool, damp, early-morning streets back to Botch's apartment. It was all of three p.m. before they finally disentangled their naked, sweating, fully-satisfied bodies. Botch offered her a shirt of his and they shared rich, aromatic afternoon coffee together. Neither said anything, and instead, entwined fingers, occasionally stealing lover's glances.

The first year with Debbie proved tough. They didn't want their relationship to be known at the office, but the way they acted around each other made it obvious, and Botch's jealousy reared its ugly head whenever anyone talked lowly of Debbie, or, for that matter, whenever he saw her talking to another man.

Debbie appeared the same to him whether talking to other men or in his arms —warm, smiling, unwaveringly happy—which made her even more irresistible, and made him feel even more jealous. He couldn't concentrate on his work. He wanted her desperately, and she knew it, but there was something he couldn't put his finger on that kept them from fully consummating their love. Debbie took to calling it 'commitment.'

The next couple of months were filled with on-again, off-again battles, with Botch reluctantly acknowledging it *was* an issue of commitment, but never quite getting 'it.' Perhaps being so badly burned once had left a scar on his heart that left him more confident when alone. Then again, his other problem with commitment was Debbie's fourteen-year-old daughter, Evie, whom he loved dearly, but who, in their present arrangement, he could leave and go back to the solitude of his own apartment. The thought of her coming home someday in the near future with a loser boyfriend put his stomach in knots. He wouldn't be able to distance himself if he were 'committed.'

At first, the idea of being a father and caring for the two women intrigued him. The trouble was that underneath his rough, New York exterior, he was still a big kid, and the thought of being a husband again, and also step-father to Evie, terrified him. He needed more time, and he knew it, but as his and Debbie's relationship escalated, he reasoned that time might not be an option, and slowly became his own devil, questioning himself relentlessly and without mercy. The more he questioned, the more he realized how unhappy and lonely he still was in the end. *Is this another of my quick-fix schemes leading back, after a time, to the same, ugly place?* What would happen when, like with his ex-wife and every girlfriend since, the time came when she simply didn't invite him back? Whatever it was he desperately needed, it continued to elude him, and instead of turning to Debbie, he turned to his old buddies and drink.

Botch's cell phone rang and he jumped. He looked at the number and panicked even more. It was Debbie's. She was probably wondering what all the stuff at the office was about…and what could he say? "Debbie, I love you dearly, but I can't talk to you just now?"

In frustration, he let her call go to voice mail; he would listen to it later. If it was Debbie telling him she wanted and needed him, he couldn't handle it right now. If it was her telling him to fuck off, he didn't want to hear that right now, either. Botch shook his head, trying desperately to clear his thoughts. *Look at you. You're still the same, immature asshole you've always been*, the 'responsible' voice in his head said without mercy. Botch nodded agreeably and went back to thinking of Gary, Rich and Mike. It was a whole lot easier than thinking about Debbie right now.

He could imagine the upcoming scenario: Mack and Andre would agree to help him. In fact, the thought of screwing over Jerry Sweaters and three rogue FBI agents was something that Mack would undoubtedly love. Suddenly Botch's hundred-mile-an-hour thoughts turned to Jerry Sweaters. Mack had never confided, even to his closest friends, what happened between him and Jerry Sweaters. Mack always tiptoed around this secret part of his past, careful to never let it knowingly slip out. However, whenever Mack got drunk, he would quickly fall into talking about how he planned to take out Sweaters "when the time was right." Mack acted as if it didn't matter why he wanted Sweaters so bad, but Botch knew whatever it was, it was eating Mack up from inside.

At first, Botch and Andre attributed it to lingering PTSD from Viet Nam. Mack *had* suffered badly from post-traumatic stress disorder, but seemed to have eventually reached a point where he was able to suppress his anger and function "normally" in society. Whatever had happened between him and Sweaters had certainly cost Mack his marriage to Annie, the girl who, when they were younger, had saved his face from certain disfigurement. These days, Mack treated her like she was dead in his eyes, but both Botch and Andre knew that deep down Mack still loved her dearly.

Botch had once tried to talk to Mack about it, telling him "time heals all wounds."

Mack had looked up from his drink and said coldly, "You like old sayings, do you? Well, here's one: 'A friendship is like fine china. You can break it in two and glue it back together, but there will always be a crack.'"

Botch had thought long about that. Irrespective of whether Mack was referring to his relationship with Botch, Anne or Sweaters, it boded ill. "Got you," Botch had replied. "I'll not bring it up again." And he never did. That was the first time Mack had put up a wall between them. Botch reflected pensively back to that day when he'd figured he'd lost his friendship with Mack, then Botch's cell phone rang. Debbie was calling a second time, and, still the coward, Botch let it go again to voice mail. He looked at the bumper sticker on the car in front of him. It said, "The College of Vietnam 67-69." *I Got to get that for Mack*, he thought, then went into a trance thinking of some of his own experiences in 'Nam. There were more than enough to fill an entire book.

Number One Bestseller

CHAPTER 5

By the time Andre, Mack and Botch had reached their twenties, the Bronx was no longer theirs. The area was bracing for race riots, while the rest of the US braced for the next in the series of escalations in the bitter Vietnam War. Andre grew tired of not being able to find a job and joined the Army. Botch got drafted through the lottery. Mack often talked about how his claw marks could still be seen in the neighborhood sidewalk as they dragged him off to the waiting Army truck.

Mack tried every different way he could think of to stay out. His most colorful one was dating a cantankerous girl who worked at the Draft Board, whom he enticed into delaying his papers from getting sent further up the chain. They lived together—"sort of"—the two together staying high on uppers she had obtained to lose weight. One day, after sleeping for the first time in days, he looked in horror at the heifer snoring away next to him and decided he couldn't continue strung out day after day like this. Gathering his clothes, he up and left. His orders to report to Fort Bragg came two weeks later.

The "Three Musketeers" finished basic training together then found themselves separated a week later in Vietnam. Mack was posted to a forward infantry unit where the average life span in combat was fifteen seconds. He unceremoniously tried bucking the system, taking a stance as a conscientious objector until he realized, objector or not, they were going to put him forward and he was still going to be shot at. In the end, it proved more noble to be alive, fighting for his life, than objecting, dead. A week later, for his twenty-first birthday, he was shot in the back during an ambush.

Andre's first day in Vietnam began with tumbling out of a recon chopper with two other grunts. All had brand-new uniforms. While they stood trying to figure out where the hell they were, the area started taking on mortar rounds. Andre dove into a muddy ditch. The other two hesitated, concerned about getting their new uniforms dirty. Minutes later, when Andre struggled his way out of the ditch, wiping the wet mud off his face and clothes, it was to see two shredded bodies lying before him on the ground. One was lifeless. The other was just alive enough to wince and say, "Welcome to 'Nam," before joining his companion in death.

Andre heard about Mack being shot and finagled a pass between firefights to search for his old buddy in a nearby field hospital located just behind front lines. When he at last located the tent where Mack was, he rolled up his pants, secured a sheet around his waist, heisted a nurse's cap—and her lipstick—and walked into the tent full of soldiers swinging his hips and asking in a high-pitched voice, "Where's my big boy, Mack?"

Mack, startled at first, laughed loudly. Andre sauntered over to Mack's bed to unending cat-calls and whistles, and gave Mack a big, wet kiss. The ward went crazy, all except one guy with eyes as big as saucers, who watched it all like a buzzard sizing up his prey. Mack, sputtering, red-faced and laughing even harder with lipstick smeared all over his face from the exuberant kiss, muttered, "Oh, I'm gonna get you for this, darling!" The only soldier not roaring with laughter, "Saucer Eyes," pulled out a bayonet from beneath his pillow and grunted, "Hey, Mack, this creep fucking with you?"

Mack jumped up and placed himself between the man and Andre, pleading, "Bobby! Relax! It's alright! He's my friend from the real world! Put the blade away. We're in a hospital, not in the field!"

Bobby slid the bayonet back under his pillow and closed his eyes, laying still as death. Andre whispered from behind into Mack's ear, "Nice friends you've got here."

Mack sucked his breath in through clenched teeth. "It's 'Nam, man. Hey, you got some?"

Andre, still dressed in drag, replied nonchalantly, "Have I got some for you, big boy? Let's just get out of here and..." nodding towards the open tent flap. The hooping and hollering hit a high, then receded as they walked away.

The two found a couple of boxes in the sun near the dusty main road where they sat in silence, watching truckloads of soldiers coming and going. Andre shed the makeshift costume, wiped the lipstick off his face, and lit the first two of the many joints he had brought. Mack was already quaffing down a bottle of bathtub vodka he had bartered that week for a half-pack of American cigarettes. Together, they smoked, drank and talked through the afternoon into evening and finally night. Waking side-by-side on the ground the next day, Andre offered Mack the dregs from the otherwise empty bottle. "I hear Botch is somewhere near Long Bein. Too bad you're hurt and can't travel. We could cheer up the poor bastard."

Mack grinned affably. "Shit, I've been fine for weeks, now. I'm just not in any rush to get back into battle."

Asking around, they determined that Botch was billeted in a heavily fortified, concrete bunker complex a considerable distance back from the front lines. It took most of the day to make their way there, but when they walked in, they saw Botch in a makeshift hot tub with a nubile, topless, Vietnamese girl. Botch, his back to his two best friends, was complaining to the girl that the water wasn't hot enough.

Andre looked at Mack. "Do you believe this? We're out getting our asses shot off and this prick's complaining about the hotel service at the Concrete Club Med!"

Botch, recognizing Andre's voice, looked back at his two grinning friends. "What the fuck! How the hell did you two sick bastards find me?" Botch jumped out of the pool, naked and dripping wet, to shake their hands.

"We just followed the line of waiters, you sorry sack of shit!"

Botch hugged them both, ordering the girl, "Cocktails for my friends."

Mack eyed the girl as she exited the tub and walked, enticingly naked, over to a makeshift wet bar. Flipping his thumb her way, Mack braved, "So, what's her name?"

"Hop On," Botch replied with a shit-eating grin. The girl, overhearing her nickname, giggled and nodded politely.

"Figures," Mack and Andre replied together.

The three sat together around a makeshift table of spent cartridge boxes, with Hop On serving, and drank and smoked more of Andre's stash till thoroughly drunk, high and happy. Mack pointed at Botch and said to Andre: "This is the guy who unfailingly falls into a tub of shit and comes up with a gold watch. So, tell us, Botch, how did you get this gig?"

Botch explained how, during basic training, his group had been asked if anyone had any technical skills. "I raised my hand and they put me in communications."

Mack frowned, "Technical skills? You can't use a stapler. What technical skills do you have?"

Botch chuckled, partly from the thought and partly from the effects of the combined alcohol and pot. "Remember St. Helena High School? Well, before we got kicked out, I was the AV guy—you know, the audio-visual technician."

Mack coughed out the smoke he had been holding in his lungs and, half-choking, asked with disbelief, "They accepted that as 'skill'?"

"Hey, they didn't ask for details, so I figured, 'What the fuck.' They took me without comment," adding, "Taught me communications and intelligence."

"That's a first: Botch and intelligence in the same sentence," Andre laughed.

"Still, you gotta admit he's smart enough to get out of the firefight shit!" Mack said with admiration.

Botch was immediately on the defensive: "Hey, I've seen action. We were under mortar attack here once. It hasn't always been a tea party. Some of the mortar rounds hit as close as that ridge over there."

Mack and Andre squinted out the window, searching for the ridge in the direction in which Botch was pointing, Andre finally nodding melodramatically. "Ohh! That ridge!" The ridge, if indeed it was one, was at least ten miles away, and showed no sign of having been shelled. Each looked at the other, then broke out in fits of laughter.

Mack and Andre stayed with Botch for two days, talking about the good ol' days in the Bronx and each one's future plans for when the war was over. It was Mack, struggling hard to keep a straight face, who suggested they make a pact that, if all three somehow survived, they'd join the police force and continue the fight together for justice and the American way. The suggestion got a big laugh, followed by a longer, poignant silence.

Near the middle of the second day, Andre reminded Botch that their passes were almost over, and that he and Mack needed to head back to avoid being AWOL—absent without leave. Botch looked at his watch and assured them he had a chopper pilot friend who owed him a favor, so they could stay another day, which Mack and Andre gladly did.

The next day, Botch requisitioned a Jeep and drove his two friends to the nearby airfield decorated with line after line of waiting choppers. Mack and Andre sat in the Jeep while Botch walked from chopper to chopper, talking to the pilots. "I guess his 'friend' isn't here," Andre offered with a mixture of concern and chagrin.

Mack, annoyed, retorted, "You kidding? Botch's always full of shit: there never was a 'chopper pilot friend.' He just said that to get us to stay another day."

Near the end of the chopper line, they saw, with relief, Botch shake hands with a pilot, and then wave for them to come. The 'copter coughed, flashed, spit out a cloud of oily smoke and began revving up noisily, creating a huge dust-cloud through which Mack and Andre passed, Botch yelling over the din, "He'll take you to Cui Chi!"

Botch slapped his two best friends on the back as they jumped aboard and joined a squad of soldiers in full field gear, helmets strapped on, black grease-paint beneath their eyes, guns at the ready, grim looks on their faces. Botch back-stepped out of the dust, smiled and saluted as they rose and flew off. Mack and Andre waved back to Botch, who, in the distance was trying to light a joint, only to have it blown out of his mouth from the backwash.

After several minutes of flight, the pilot yelled back, "Welcome to Air Vietnam! Your buddy down there said you're both excellent M-60 gunners."

Mack and Andre gave each other a non-committal look and shrugged their shoulders. "Yeah. Guess so," Mack offered the pilot in return.

The co-pilot pointed to two mounted machine guns, one on either side of the chopper, and yelled, "Strap yourselves in and man the guns."

Andre, never having been in a gunners harness or, for that matter, shot an M-60, hesitated, yelling at the nervous, 18-year-old infantry lieutenant seated next to him, "So where's your regular gunners?"

The lieutenant smiled weakly and yelled back, "The previous two lasted a week—a longevity record for us."

Mack, noticing they were going in the opposite direction of where his field hospital or Andre's unit were located, turned and yelled loudly forward, "Hey, aren't we going to Cui Chi?"

The pilot laughed nervously. "Yeah, on the way back from a little mission."

The infantry lieutenant appeared to draw courage from the whole practical joke, and joined in: "We were going to wait for replacements, but as your buddy said how good you both are with M-60s, we figured we could take care of a little business on the way. You know, do some damage, and then drop you guys off on the way back."

Andre looked at Mack and yelled, "Fucking Botch!" to which Mack nodded his assent.

Each got up and strapped himself into his respective gunner's harness, just in time for the metallic ping of bullets hitting the chopper to spur them to action. Mack and Andre started firing back with the M-60s. Never having experienced the aggressive recoil of the weapon, both lost his balance and ended up free-swinging back and forth, in and out of the chopper, much to the infantrymen's amusement. Laughing at their gunners' ability to joke in the face of certain death, the lieutenant and another infantryman hauled the two back into the chopper between enemy gun bursts. To everyone's surprise—and relief—Mack and Andre proved excellent marksmen, and together, exactly the kind of deadly force needed against the enemy. Hovering just above ground, the duo rained cover fire while the lieutenant and his platoon offloaded, then the chopper rose furiously, and headed off in the opposite direction, eventually landing at Cui Chi.

A lieutenant at Cui Chi provided transportation for Mack back to the field hospital and pulled rank to grab Andre, the now legendary M-60 gunner, to assist in a few days "cleaning tunnels" in Cui Cui.

What sounded like janitorial relief duty turned out to be the most dangerous assignment of Andre's tour in 'Nam. Andre was six-foot-two, and climbing into tunnels built for men not much bigger than a child, flashlight in one hand, gun at the ready in the other, was difficult, at best. Andre nonetheless agreed to do it when informed he would get a week off battlefield duty for every tunnel he "cleaned." Over the next several days, he came to realize that the most dangerous part was that once he entered a tunnel, he was just big enough that he couldn't back out without someone behind to pull him out.

Andre heard stories every night about this or that soldier, who climbed in, got stuck and was unable to get out. An enemy soldier, hiding in one of the side tunnels, would shoot the soldier who was supposed to pull him out and to discourage future "cleaning," would set the soldier stuck in the hole on fire.

Fear began to overtake Andre each time he climbed into a tunnel. The fear, however, was mitigated by one less week of battlefield duty each time he returned alive. One day, following his sergeant into a tunnel, Andre was amazed when it opened into an vast, underground Viet Cong hospital. The sergeant yelled in English for no one to move. Doctors, medics and the several nurses froze, looking at each other in confusion, until one of the wounded lifted an arm. Whether in a gesture of greeting, or in preparation to defend himself, no one would never know. The sergeant began raining bullets in every direction, killing everyone—doctors, medics, nurses, patients, and damn-near Andre in the process. Andre looked on with horror, and never went into a tunnel again.

CHAPTER 6

Meanwhile, Mack had his own cross to bear. Several months after returning to the field hospital, he was determined fit for duty and sent to Korea for R & R in anticipation of returning to 'Nam. While there, Mack met and fell in love with a Korean girl, eventually ending up AWOL. The relationship ended tragically and Mack slipped into a deep depression. When he finally got up the nerve to go back to the Army to face charges, he really didn't care about the Army, himself or anything else. After being transported back to his unit, he was told they had lost his paper-work and didn't even know he had been gone. In a sudden, unexpected reversal, Mack began volunteering for every hazardous assignment offered. Lost, with no idea where or how to find himself, Mack was looking to end his now miserable life.

As it turned out, during one such high-risk mission, he incurred a minor shrapnel wound which put him back in the hospital, got him another Purple Heart and, for bravery in the line of fire, several bronze and silver stars. This time when he recovered, he was sent to the rear: no more opportunities to die gloriously in action, no more action at all, just mountains of food to prepare and endless lines of tired soldiers who needed to fill their stomachs in anticipation of another day of fighting.

Mack's time working the mess halls turned out to be the happiest in his military career. Anything to stop the kill-or-be-killed routine and give him time to get his head back together. Their tours rapidly coming to an end, both Botch and Andre had been given the choice of doing two more weeks in 'Nam or six months back in the States. They opted together for six months stateside at Fort Bragg, North Carolina. Mack actually got his final orders several weeks ahead of Andre, and headed for what he prayed to be the relative sanity and safety of the Bronx.

At the Los Angeles airport, Mack came across three highly-decorated Army Special Ops men in uniform. When asked where he was headed, Mack replied wistfully, "Home...the Bronx."

"Been there, done that," replied one. "It's not the home you left, man. You're a killing machine now, and, trust us, they don't want killing machines. Join us. We're on our way to fight the Sudanese rebels."

"Nah, but thanks, guys," replied Mack. "Mercenary work's not for me," and he walked briskly on, the three soldiers hefting their duffle bags onto their broad, muscled shoulders and following at a distance in his wake. As Mack walked, he began to wonder if, based on what he was hearing, life in the Bronx would be as different as the soldiers had said.

Two flagrantly dressed hippies eyed Mack as he approached. One bumped into Mack's uniformed shoulder and yelled loud enough for everyone, including the nearby soldiers, to hear, "Baby killer!" Mack ignored them, and their later cries for help, when the two got the shit kicked out of them by the trailing soldiers.

"The Bronx won't be the same!" one yelled to Mack who continued walking out the lobby doors.

CHAPTER 7

Back in the Bronx, Mack threw his duffle up onto his shoulder and walked around the old neighborhood looking at different places where he'd hung out before service, trying in vain to soak up some good memories in a futile attempt to push out the bad ones he'd acquired during the war. Unfortunately, like his buddies at the airport foretold, things *had* changed in the two years he'd been away.

The old neighborhood looked depressingly run down. Most of the faces in the neighborhood had changed, and of the few he recognized, none recognized him back.

"Great," he said to himself under his breath, "Couldn't wait to get back. Now first day back and I'm wondering about how my friends in 'Nam are doing." He stopped for a drink at a favorite hangout, The Gin Mill, where he was greeted by his old friend, Babe, who was still bartending there. In between covering the bar, Babe and Mack recounted person after person Mack had known, all of whom, according to Babe, had moved on or died. While towel-drying the last of the glasses, Babe looked over at a suddenly silent Mack who seemed as if in a trance with what looked like pure, unadulterated rage roiling in his eyes.

"Mack!" Babe yelled.

Mack jumped, snapping back, his eyes still half-glazed, his face suddenly contorted into an evil smile. Mack toasted his bartender-friend as tears streamed from his eyes. His speech slurred as if drunk, Mack began relating how easy it had become for him to kill. Babe listened attentively, but stared nervously at Mack when Mack began listing person after person he'd killed.

Suddenly Mack switched from uncaring murderer back to friendly inquirer: "So what's the deal, Babe? Did you eventually buy this dump from the Millers?"

Babe, taken even more aback, said distantly, "No, I just work here, Mack." Then he leaned forward across the bar until his lips were next to Mack's ear and whispered, "Jerry Sweaters bought it."

Mack seemed to have to struggle to hold onto his re-acquired presence, grunting loudly, "Who'd you say?"

"Shhh! Sweaters! You know who I'm talking about, Mack." Babe pushed his nose to the side with a finger to signal to Mack that Sweaters was part of the local mob. "He came in one day, and," Babe snapped his fingers, "just like that said the management had changed, but, if I kept my nose out of his business and ran the bar like I did before, I'd always have a job here. That's him over at the end of the bar." Babe tipped a finger towards the door.

Mack followed Babe's finger to where, sitting in the darkness, he could just make out a heavy-set man surrounded by several others. Sweaters appeared to be nursing in one hand what looked like a tumbler of whisky and rocks, a dusty bottle in the other.

"I remember Jerry," Mack said. "Man, has he ever gotten fat!" Before Babe could stop him, Mack continued, "'Sweaters?' What kind of stupid name is that?" Babe shook his head hopelessly, and at a signal from Sweaters, walked down the bar. Sweaters said something to Babe, Babe nodded, and walked back to Mack. "Sweaters wants to know if you'd like another drink," said Babe, adding, "On the house."

"Sure," Mack said, holding his current drink up and tipping it towards Sweaters, in the process sloshing most of its amber contents onto the bar.

"Hey, Mack!" Sweaters acknowledged from the other end of the bar. "I hear you're one tough 'Nam hero. You ever need a job, let me know. I like to help boys who've risked their lives in service to this country and have just returned home."

Mack didn't answer. Instead, he downed the proffered drink in one gulp and said goodbye. Getting clumsily up off the stool and staggering to the door past Sweaters and his men, Mack pausing momentarily to slur, in barely discernable words, "I'm nobody's lap dog…Sir!" and left. Sweaters' men turned to follow, but Sweaters waved a hand lazily and stopped them. "Forget it! I may have use of him someday. That was his one free pass."

The rest of the month, Mack spent every afternoon, evening and night at the The Gin Mill getting piss-eyed drunk. Sweaters never returned, though Mack noted that one of his henchmen came every midnight, like clockwork, to check the books and collect the profits from the day before.

"Mack, what the hell are you doing?" Babe asked one evening. "You're going to be a whiskey-stick before you're twenty-five."

Mack replied, despondent, "I know, Babe. And you're right, but getting drunk seems to be the only way I can get any sleep. It's the nightmares…"

Concerned, Babe interrupted: "So, how's the job search going?"

"Not many places consider killing a job skill. Give me another drink, okay?"

Babe looked towards the door to see Andre walk in.

"Jesus, God! Another blast from the past!" Mack blurted, swaying on his stool, as he reached out a hand toward his tall, lanky friend.

Andre, grinning, started towards Mack, but stopped short, eyeing the slovenly drunk in front of him. Andre looked quizzically at Babe. With a broad, sweeping gesture, Babe said, "Be my guest, Andre."

Mack, who looked as if beginning to doze off, suddenly started and looked, blearily-eyed, into the handsome black face he knew so well. Standing with difficulty, Mack gave Andre a bear-hug. "What the fuck took you so long to get here?"

They toasted making it back alive, and then Andre informed Mack that Botch would be arriving next week. Mack, smiling the biggest, genuine grin Babe could recall seeing on the man's face since he'd returned home, nudged Andre's shoulder and the two promptly got stinking drunk.

Andre mostly listened; for Andre, *not* talking was more healing. The less he had to relive his own horrors, the better.

The bar got crowded as the evening progressed and they got drunker, singing boisterously and generally annoying everyone there. Even so, none there would say a word as, fascinated, they watched the initial healing take place. That, and no one wanted to risk getting the crap kicked out of them in a drunken brawl with the former legend of the Bronx and his best friend.

Near midnight, Jerry Sweaters and the two musclemen who had volunteered to 'walk Mack home' the first night of Mack's return, sat quietly at their end of the bar next to the entrance. Mack and Andre were laughing and joking boisterously, and Babe, against his better judgment, was drinking with them. Mack was starting to remember what it felt like to be happy, to be able to talk freely, to feel safe, surrounded by close friends who weren't likely to suddenly die on him.

Mack had just put his arm around Andre, when a voice from the other end of the bar yelled out. "What's this nigger doing in here?" It was as if a prison cell door clanged loudly shut, stopping all conversation in midsentence. Mack tensed and glared in the direction of the yell, and saw Jerry Sweaters with his right hand man, Twisted Ray, and a huge roughneck called Buddha. Buddha lifted his heavy bulk and stood tall between the two separate parties.

"Did you say something, lard-ass?" Andre offered.

Buddha, sloshing his weight ponderously from side to side, walked towards Mack and Andre like a Sumo wrestler eager to crush anything stupid enough to stand in his way. He stopped just past Mack, immediately in front of Andre. "You heard me, moulie. I called you a nig…"

Andre sucked in a short breath, closed his eyes, and stabbed his extended fingers into Buddha's throat before the man could finish the sentence. It happened so quick, witnesses would later argue whether Andre had done anything at all. Buddha, however, grabbed his throat, wide-eyed, trying unsuccessfully to gasp for air. Andre casually extended himself to his full height and, in another, almost imperceptible, lighting-like strike, kneed the hulk in the crotch, sending the fat man to the floor with an ear-bursting thud.

At Jerry Sweaters' signal, Twisted Ray pulled out a revolver and ran over to help Buddha, but halfway there Mack had kicked a barstool in front of Ray, tripping the gunman flat onto the floor next to Buddha, both arms outstretched. In a flash, Mack struck Ray's gun hand with the heel of his shoed foot and grabbed the escaping gun in one hand and Ray's ear in the other, twisting Ray's ear as hard as he could. Ray groaned and flailed about trying to grab Mack's hands, but Mack already had the barrel of the gun at Ray's temple. "I'm sorry, sir. Did your friend on the ground beside you say something to my friend, here?"

Jerry Sweaters, acting as if nothing had happened, walked lazily towards them. Mack slid the barrel of Ray's gun liquidly from Ray's temple to Sweaters' forehead. Things were, like combat, going too far too fast, Mack realized, even from within his drunken fog. It wasn't smart to point a gun at a made man. Mack looked over at Andre, who was forcing Buddha's head down on the floor with one foot, and slowly lowered the gun. "I'm sorry, sir. Are these two with you?"

Sweaters snorted softly at how easily the two vets had disabled his best. "Unfortunately, yes," he replied. Mack gave Andre a barely perceptible nod. Mack released Ray's ear and Andre let up on Buddha's face. Ray got up and, embarrassed, brushed himself off, vociferously demanding a piece of Mack in return, but Sweaters waved him off.

"No hard feelings," Mack said nonchalantly to Ray. Ray squared his shoulders menacingly, then walked back to other end of the bar, nursing his injured pride.

In the meantime, Buddha was having difficulty getting to his feet. Everyone watched the fat man's comically unsuccessful efforts, until Sweaters, disgusted, reached down and jerked the man up, then shoved him towards the door, ordering him to wait in the car.

Sweaters surveyed Mack and Andre, then asked Mack, "So, have you thought about my offer? I mean, look at you. The world doesn't need another…"

"Another what?" Andre cut in threateningly.

Sweaters stared at the two awhile, then scowled. "Well let me know," he said, and walked out the front door, grabbing Ray's elbow on the way. Ray yanked his elbow angrily out of Sweater's grip and growled, "What was that all about?"

Sweaters looked down the bar towards Mack and Andre, who had resumed talking, joking, and drinking, and said, "I asked them if they wanted to work for me."

"Jesus, Sweaters. You don't want to deal with no niggers. And the Irish one! I'm not done with him yet!"

Sweaters studied his manicured nails for a moment, then looked Ray coldly in the eyes. "You'll do what I tell you to do, Ray, and no more."

A week later, Mack began working as an enforcer—tracking receipts from the bar and collecting unpaid debts for Sweaters.

Years later, after his divorce, Mack became a silent partner in his own bar across town, naming it Farrell's Bar after a favorite hang out from when he, Andre and Botch were younger. The building looked quite similar on the outside, but the days of packing crowds of people into bars had gone. In an effort to keep his mind off the painful divorce he slowly and completely renovated it.

The mahogany bar Mack was adamantly insistent about made the place appear upscale for the neighborhood. That, and the ladies room being as nice as a grand hotel's. Mack's philosophy was if women felt welcome, they'd come back, and where there were women, there'd eventually be two or three times as many men. Amazingly, his strategy worked.

Soon a modern kitchen was added, the pool tables were replaced by booths, and, with Mack's experience working as a cook in the military, the place quickly developed a reputation for pleasant food and conversation. Botch, being half-Italian, contributed suggestions to improve the menu, and, in time, fancied himself a culinary expert.

Botch, clutching the steering wheel, forced himself to snap out of yet another of the seemingly endless trances. It was hard to believe that thirty years had gone by, and even more ironic that he, Andre and Mack had ended up together in law enforcement as they had agreed in 'Nam.

Botch drove into the overflow parking lot behind Farrell's Bar, and entered through the back door. Walking through the kitchen and into the large, one-room bar, he spotted Mack talking to some customers. As he walked by, Botch blurted out to Babe, "One beer," and immediately afterward to Mack, "We gotta' talk."

"Grab a booth," Mack responded, "I'll be right there."

Mack made a drink for himself, opened a bottle of beer for his friend, and, carrying each in hand, sidled over to where Botch was sitting. "So. What's up?" he asked.

Botch explained what he'd overhead while hiding in the supply room and how he'd escaped his three turned underlings with Debbie's help.

Mack took it in calmly. "Did you take it to your boss, the lush? What's his name? Steiner?"

"I did, but I can't tell if he's in on it or not. I don't think he's part of it, Mack, but he's so damn cautious, even drunk, he wouldn't let on one way or the other."

"Andre's on his way," Mack stated.

Botch gave a sigh of relief. "Good. That's why I'm here: to get your and Andre's take on it and ask for your help."

"Well then, let's you and me throw a few back and try to figure out as much as we can while we wait," Mack suggested, interjecting, "but I need to talk with the kitchen staff, for just a moment. I want to be sure we're ready for the second half of the Jets game that's about to begin. You ponder and I'll be right back."

"Yeah, and what's with those guys in the kitchen, anyway?" Botch asked quizzically. "They looked at me weird when I walked through."

Mack let out a belly-laugh, "Maybe it's because I told them you're an immigration officer. When one of them saw the government plates on your car as you drove around back, they all got nervous. Then I told them you're gay and have had your eyes on one of them."

"Nice. Do you always scare your workers into submission with threats of deportation and unwanted sexual advance?" Botch barbed his reply, shaking his head in disbelief.

"Nope," Mack replied, getting up. "Just when you come."

While Mack made his side-trip into the increasingly noisy kitchen, Botch got up, walked back to the bar and greeted Babe. Botch surveyed the packed bar, where everyone was eagerly waiting for the second half of the Jets game to begin. Aside from Babe, Botch didn't recognize anyone.

Botch thought briefly about all the people he could remember from before his 'Nam days that used to frequent the bar. Now they were all married, stayed home with their family, took the cure, or had died.

The front door suddenly swung open and Botch yelled above the increasing din towards an advancing Andre, "Get the moulie a drink!"

The crowd immediately quieted. Andre stopped and looked around suspiciously. "What exactly is a 'moulie,' and who here says I'm one?" he ventured.

A hundred or so sets of eyes turned to Botch as he worked his way forward to stand chest-to-chest against the much taller black man. "It's short for moulignon, and that's Italian for 'eggplant'," Botch said, staring at the middle of Andre's chest.

People moved away as the two squared off. Andre frowned, then replied pompously, "I'm sorry, little man. I can speak a lot of different languages: Russian, Arabic, French, Korean, but I never learned gutter Italian..."

The crowd drew in a single breath as Botch interrupted, "Don't forget Ebonics."

"Like I was saying," Andre continued menacingly, "Italian is a beautiful language. It's the gutter dialect I object to."

Andre looked at Babe and commanded, "Back up my guinea-friend here."

Botch gestured to Andre to grab the drinks and bring them over to a corner booth reserved for Mack and his closest friends, and slid into the seat. Andre slid in next to him. The crowd milled about nervously. "What the hell was that all about?" someone finally asked the smiling bartender, to which Babe snorted, "They've been doing that skit for years. They think it's funny."

Andre, relaxing, looked around, "Where's Mack?"

Botch nodded towards the kitchen. "Here he comes," he replied, and Mack slid in next to his two friends and colleagues.

Andre politely inquired how Nick was.

"Sore, but okay, after popping a few pain pills. He's on his way over."

Botch looked confused. "What happened to Nick?"

Mack gestured with his thumb towards Andre. "My son got a beating this morning from one of Andre's boys."

"He's not one of my boys anymore," Andre replied sourly.

"So? What happened?" Botch asked, looking from Mack to Andre and back, knowing Mack's protectiveness surrounding anything family.

Mack cut Botch short. "Nick'll tell you when he gets here. For now, Andre, I want Botch to tell you what he just told me." Mack looked up suddenly. "Wait, here comes Nick now!"

Nick limped across the floor looking for the loudest group in the bar, expecting to find his father in the center, which he did. Nick ambled over, letting out a sigh of relief, and he eased himself down. "What's the occasion that you're all here together on a Sunday? The game?"

Mack snapped, "No! Business!" as Botch asked Nick what had happened to him. Nick started to answer, but Mack cut him short. "I said, he'll tell you later." Turning to Botch, Mack commanded, "Tell Andre what you overheard today…"

Nick sat up, rigid, pissed with his father, and grumbled, "What the hell, Dad! What do I have to do to break into the conversation here? Die?"

Ignoring Nick, Botch quickly summarized what he'd heard earlier in his office at the FBI building.

"How much money?!" Andre asked, leaning forward on the edge of his seat.

Botch answered curtly, annoyed at having to repeat himself. "You heard me. Four to six mil. Maybe more."

Mack and Andre looked at each other with raised eyebrows. Andre returned his attention to Botch. "What are you planning on doing about it?"

Botch shrugged. "That's why I came to you guys, because I don't know how deep it goes at the bureau."

Mack cleared his throat. "I think what Andre's asking is what you're planning on doing with the money, if *you* got hold of it?"

"It's drug money! I'd have to turn it in," Botch said, matter-of-factly.

"So, what you want us to do is risk getting killed to help you return six million dollars into the outstretched hands of a bunch of dirty politicians, who will use it for their own personal gain?" Andre replied, as if he'd rehearsed the answer for use at just this moment.

"Andre's right," Mack agreed. "We're talking the very same government that sent us all to 'Nam to get our asses shot off while conveniently forgiving the draft dodgers that went to Canada to become rich doctors! Pleeeeeeese!"

"So what are you saying?" Botch asked, innocent as always to the end.

"I think they're saying six mil would be a nice retirement plan," Nick blurted out, frustrated with Botch's dumbness.

Botch grinned, "'From the mouths of babes.' To tell the truth, it *did* cross my mind, I just felt guilty about thinking it. I mean, how many summers do we have left? I don't want to end up in some nursing home wondering, 'What if...'" Botch raised his glass. "Okay, then, let's come up with a plan to take this dirty money off the streets, and apply it to a truly worthy cause: us." All tapped glasses together including Nick.

"Wait just a moment. You're not in this, Nick," Mack quickly added "You're too young and pretty for prison, should this blow up in our faces."

"Oh, I'm in, Dad. I'm not a child, and with cash like that, I wouldn't have to grow up bitter like you guys."

Botch looked at Mack, paused, then shrugged. "The kid's got a point, Mack."

Mack looked from one determined face to another and decided to drop it. Then, as if on second thought, he looked his son squarely in the eyes and ordered, "Okay, Nick, but you do whatever we fucking tell you! Got it?"

Nick put his right hand on his heart. "I promise, Dad. No fuck ups."

Andre laughed, clapped Nick on the back, and the four started planning how to heist the money from Gary, Rich and Mike. As they talked, they drank, and as they drank, the free-flowing liquor eventually directed the discussion elsewhere.

Andre yelled out something clearly not in English.

"What's that, Russian?" Nick asked, surprised.

"Actually, yes, it was," Andre proudly replied. "And damned near native-perfect Russian, if I say so myself."

Nick was impressed. "But why Russian? How come you never learned Spanish? That would be a lot more practical here."

It was Botch's turn to laugh, but, "Oh shit," was all he ventured.

Mack raised his eyebrows, "Here we go."

Nick looked around at the circle of Cheshire grins about him. "What did I say? What's so bad about speaking Spanish? I mean you all grew up in the Bronx and many of your 'friends' are Spanish-speaking."

Andre winced. "I didn't learn Spanish because I chose to do what *I* want to do, not what people expected of me! Speaking Spanish would have made me typical and growing up as a black kid in the Bronx, I wanted to be special. SO, FUCK SPANISH!"

Nick, astonished at the vindictiveness in Andre's remark, said sheepishly, "Andre, I'm sorry. I didn't know that you would take what I said as an insult. It wasn't meant to be one!"

Mack and Botch continued laughing at Nick's discomfort.

Andre swirled his drink, looked angrily at the three as they continued laughing, and said, "Fuck you guys," and then started to laugh also. Tapping his glass to Nick's, he added, "Don't sweat it, kid. Sometimes I just overreact."

Nick gladly added his smile to the group's. "That's cool, Andre," he said, but he still felt uneasy and began searching for a way to change the subject. "So, assuming we get hold of this money, what would we do with it?"

Mack raised a hand like he was back in first grade. "Let me go first, because my answer might change yours. Ironically, I spoke to Tommy Chang last night. Marisol's is for sale. If we came up with half, he'd do the other half."

Nick's forehead tightened into a frown as he tried to remember where he had heard that name. "Isn't that the resort you guys go to every year? In the Canary Islands?"

"Technically, it's on La Palma Island. So, you remember us taking you there once as a kid?" Mack asked with enthusiasm. "It had a different name back then," he added.

Andre joked, "Your father's been going there the last several years to write his book."

Now it was Botch's turn to laugh. "Yeah, in five years he's written ten pages—the rest of the time he's been busy, avoiding getting sober."

Nick sat bolt upright. "What's this about a book, Dad?"

Mack boasted, "I'm going to call it 'Number One Best Seller.' I figure people would fall for the title even if the story sucks."

"Seriously, Mack," Andre interjected. "Are you proposing we buy Marisol's? Is it really for sale?"

Mack nodded affirmatively. "That's what Tommy Chang says."

Botch suddenly went glassy-eyed: "Now *that* would be my idea of retiring..."

Andre scratched his head. "I'd have to talk to Joyce, but I know she'd like spending winters outside of New York. Oh, the hell with asking Joyce. Count me in."

"I'm in, too," piped in Botch and Nick.

"Okay," Mack responded. "I'll talk to Chang. Now all we gotta' do is get the money."

"Isn't Tommy Chang a big-time, international businessman? Why would he need us?" Nick asked in rapid-fire succession.

"Good questions, kid. He told me he wants to retire, but he couldn't manage a resort the size of Marisol's without help. He said he wants to enjoy his retirement years with a few 'trusted' friends—us—but he knows we wouldn't feel right if we weren't paying our way. So he asked me if we three—four now—would someway like to become equal partners. Personally, I liked the idea of helping run the place instead of sitting around here getting fat, drunk and shot at."

A loud cheer filled the bar. The four looked up at a large-screen corner TV just in time to see the Jets take the field after half-time. "Hell, I completely forgot about the game. Can you read the score? I must be going blind in my old age!"

"It's not old age, Dad, it's the booze. It's ten to three, Jets." Nick said with authority. The Jets star quarterback was warming up in the background. Nick watched intently. "You know, this quarterback might take them all the way this year."

"Or the guy might not see the end of the week," Andre growled.

"What?" three voices asked in unison.

Andre, his ruffle up, explained: "He's been slapping his girlfriend, my daughter, Tina, around again this week like he's done in the past. Couple nights ago, I get a call from the neighbors. They say the two are going at it loud and hard, and they heard him threaten to hit her if she didn't shut up. They said she left to stay with some friends. I had just decided to hunt him down, out-of-uniform, and break his fucking legs, when I realized he'd be out-of-town playing this game. Then I figured I would wait till he got back home from this game. I'd have a better shot of getting away with it if I could catch him alone somewhere at night. That was my rather hasty plan anyway."

Botch tried to calm Andre. "I understand your anger, but you got to act smarter, Andre. The guy's a football super-star, for God's sake! He's always surrounded by press or admirers. Call in some favors and have him locked up for a few days, or at least wait for a more opportune time to give him an informal thrashing."

Andre muttered something indecipherable. "...if *I* were to arrest him or in any way do in his career, my daughter would never speak to me again."

"Then listen to Botch, Andre." Mack said. "Let things die down, and *we'll* pay Amazing a visit for you."

"Alright, alright. I'm too drunk right now to do anything tonight."

Nick looked at Mack as if asking *how come you didn't tell me Tina was going out with Amazing Jones?*

Mack caught the look and replied, "I was gonna tell you at the game. We had tickets right on the side line. My neighbor's son is a big shot and got us the tickets, but someone here has the kidneys of a teenage girl."

Several chuckles later, they all turned to watch the game. The announcer was raving about the Jets' star quarterback, Amazing Jones. The view suddenly flashed to a reporter asking Amazing how he felt about being fined by the NFL for showboating and giving the crowd in Denver the finger. With his usual, cocky, celebrity smile, Amazing replied, "Man, that don't mean nothing. The Commissioner can kiss my ass. 'Oh, oh! Someone get my checkbook. I feel another fine coming.' I'm my own man, see? I do things the way I want. I'm the best thing that ever happened to this club and this game, and the fans out there know it!"

A second reporter asked, "Amazing, what happened in the first half, that you only scored fourteen points?" This time, Amazing responded arrogantly. "Hey, I can't throw the ball and catch it, too. *Some* people don't wake up until the second half. Just you watch: I'm ready to light the house up with another thirty-five points at the least."

Mack looked at Andre. "Listen to him! How insulting, talking about his teammates as having to 'wake up' and making it sound like he scored all the points himself. I may be a Jets fan, but I'm inclined to make that informal visit to meet the jerk on Andre's behalf tonight. What an obnoxious bastard!"

Andre let out a deep sigh. "He's actually been beating Tina for some time now, but I got sucked into the fame and fortune thing. Why does such a great quarterback, who has the world by the balls, have to beat on a defenseless woman?"

Botch whispered to Nick, "Tina's anything but defenseless, but look at the size of Amazing's arms! If he's beating her, it'll only be a matter of time before he does her in, accidently or on purpose."

After the game was long over and the bar empty, Mack's inebriated face suddenly lit up: "I think I just got an idea how to pull this job off."

"Good," said Botch, struggling to awaken from his own drunken stupor. "I'm still trying to figure out how I could condone possibly getting killed, or worse yet, locked up indefinitely for stealing drug-money."

Mack looked up pensively at the electronic snow on the TV screen nearest him. "You mean, taking money from those three scumbag agents and Sweaters' men? When I vowed to protect and serve, it didn't include their kind. I know of at least twenty murders Sweaters was responsible for from back when I first worked for him. I personally suggest taking him and all his scumbags out in the process. It would be a service to humanity."

"What about your boy, Joey V.?" Botch asked carefully.

Mack frowned. "That ain't the guy I was friends with back in the old days. His last name then was Bisignano with a 'B,' not a 'V'."

"When was the last time you saw him?" Botch asked.

"Maybe four or five years ago."

Botch, confident in his information, continued to press. "Well, I'm telling you now, Mack, he's still your old buddy. The only good apple in that whole bunch is Joey V. Remember, he thinks he's working with the Bureau to expose both Sweaters and the drug ring in return for witness protection for himself and his family. The three agents will need to keep him alive to locate and get into the drug-lords' apartment. If we can make our entrance there in time, we should be able to honor the agreement he thinks he's negotiated."

Mack nodded approval and proceeded to tell his three compatriots about his blossoming idea, allowing each to add his input. When finished, they sat silently, trying to anticipate problems.

"Sounds like it could actually work," Andre said, breaking the silence after going over it for the hundredth time in his head.

"It does," Botch agreed. "But then we're all drunk right now. Let's work some more on it when we're sober, before we make a final decision."

CHAPTER 8

Joey V. pulled his Classic, cherry-red, 1967 Chevy Impala into the driveway of Jerry Sweaters' mansion in West Hampton, got out and looked around the lavish structure and immaculate grounds, silently wowing inside. "Jeeze, how much is this guy worth?" escaped his lips, despite every attempt to keep the thought to himself.

Walking around the back of the house, he was dazzled by the beautiful, 180-degree view of the ocean and stopped, breathless, to take it all in. Then he heard the voice of his boss, Jerry Sweaters. "What the fuck took you so long?"

Joey felt good, immersed momentarily in the beauty of the ocean, only to get sucked back into his miserable life under Sweaters. "The L.I.E. was one big parking lot. I ended up having to use the service road."

"Shut up and sit down," Sweaters barked. "We've been working through this Dominican connection shit." Then Sweaters yelled over at one of two, lithe young girls lounging by the pool to go inside and bring everyone outside.

Out walked Twisted Ray, Joe Buddha, Fortunate Phil and Sweaters' two nephews, Sal and Dom. The first three were trusted lieutenants. The latter two, Sweaters had taken under his wing because they were family, but he could barely tolerate their laziness and stupidity. The only one that acknowledged Joey V. was Phil. Joey V. didn't think of Phil as one of the 'bad guys,' but Phil was being moved up the ranks under Jerry Sweaters' tutelage, most probably to replace Joey V. The fact was, Sweaters had tired of Joey's wanting to stay strictly in book-making, and Joey knew it.

After everyone had gathered, the two girls returned to sunbathing on the other side of the pool and Sweaters started explaining what he expected from the upcoming drug deal with the Dominicans, all the while staring coldly at Joey V. "The Dominicans have grown to know and trust you, Joey. Tonight, I want you to dazzle them with bullshit and find out who their supplier is. Then I can cut them out and deal direct."

"What, are you kidding, Sweaters? They're not going to tell me their supplier!" Joey V. cried indignantly.

Sweaters spoke slowly, emphasizing every word. "You'll *make* it happen, Joey. Or else. I'm sending Ray here with you to make sure it happens. You'll be carrying a million of my money as a token buy in, so if you get the idea that you've hit the lottery and try to make off with it, ask yourself how your wife will look in black. Let me say that again, so we're all clear: If anything *at all* goes wrong, it's gonna be on you. By the way, how old is that gorgeous daughter of yours now?"

"Seventeen," Joey V. reluctantly volunteered.

"Just the way I like 'em. I'm planning a new porn film and I'm in the market for a new bimbo. Get my drift, Joey?"

Holding back his fear and rage, Joey replied with careful civility, "I hear you, boss."

Twisted Ray laughed and patted the gun he carried under his jacket. "Don't worry, Joey. Everything will be fine. I'll make sure of it!"

Sweaters, satisfied, turned a fatherly gaze to Fortunate Phil. "You're going to sit this one out." Sweaters' face re-hardened as he shifted from Phil to Buddha. "Buddha, I want you and the idiot twins here, to accompany Joey and Ray."

Sal and Dom had broken from the group and were already hitting the buffet table, unaware that Sweaters was talking about them. Sweaters scowled, shook his head, then looked caringly at Joey V. "You should eat, Joey. It's going to be a long night."

Joey walked over to the buffet table, grabbed a hamburger and some potato salad, and sat down near one of the two girls. She took off her sunglasses, looked him over, then smiled sweetly at him before putting her sunglasses back on, unsnapping her top and returning to her tan. *She's a stunner*, thought Joey, *just like all of Sweaters' girls. I wonder how long she'll last?*

It was the view of the ocean behind her, however, that called. Seagulls cried as waves crashed against the shore. *For which of us are they crying today?* Joey wondered in a moment of insight.

Joey let his mind wander. The more he thought about his life, the more he longed to be able to get through one day without fear and one night with a clear conscience. Before him loomed the all-or-nothing double-cross he had secretly engineered with the FBI. The fact that he could be killed by Twisted Ray at any moment wasn't what really worried him. It was knowing the danger that his family would be in if *anything* went wrong. He knew Sweaters would make good on his promise to abduct his daughter and that she'd end up used and abused, another junky appearing in a long line of Sweaters' porn movies until she was used up.

Then Sweaters would toss her away for the next in line. Joey's mind leaped wildly from one disastrous scenario to another, and he began second guessing himself. *What should I do if…*

Sweaters suddenly yelled at him, "You gonna eat or not?"

A wave of nausea gripped Joey V.'s stomach, and a sickly sheen of perspiration began wetting his brow. He felt lightheaded. A drop of sweat worked its way down his face. "I…I had a big breakfast."

Sweaters laughed, "What did you have? A shit omelet or something, because you look like it just fell through your ass!" Everyone laughed uncomfortably.

"I'll be fine."

"You better be, for you and your whole family's sake!" emphasized Sweaters.

Joey V. looked at Sweaters, Twisted Ray and Joe Buddha as they pointed and laughed at him. Oddly, the harassment made him feel stronger. Now he had to do it. There was no turning back. He had to make the change or he'd eventually end up being killed anyway. The three FBI agents had promised if he helped them, they would put Sweaters and his crew away for life, and Joey and his family would get new identities in the oh-so-welcome Witness Protection Program. This was his one chance at a new life. And just as it was coming into reach, Sweaters had to assign Twisted Ray to go with him. That opened up a big can of worms.

Twisted Ray had been Sweaters' right hand hitman for years. They started out together as teenagers shaking down local merchants, then moved as a team to shaking down individual drug dealers and loan sharks. That's when Sweaters' uncle, a big shot in the mob, intervened, and Sweaters became a made man. From then on, Sweaters and Ray advanced, side-by-side, to outright murder, eventually becoming wealthy enough to subcontract out the killings. Twisted Ray still did one every once in a while, as he put it, 'so as not to get soft.' Then Sweaters moved into the more lucrative and much safer prostitution business.

Even that, however, wasn't enough. For a "hobby," he developed his own porn industry, in which he personally directed the movies, enjoying rehearsing the sex scenes with the girls. Recently, he had begun scouting out newer, younger flesh, getting them hooked on drugs, putting them in his movies until they burned out, and disposing of them afterwards. Although feared, there was something about Sweaters that didn't garner respect even from his own. Sweaters felt a desperate need to identify the Dominicans' supplier. If he could make the connection, he would score big. Then maybe his men would respect him and his bosses would admit him to their exclusive group to go 'big time', as the saying went.

Joey V. was no saint, but he wasn't evil, at least, not like Sweaters. Like Twisted Ray, Joey knew Sweaters from when they were kids, but it was Joey's older brother who had first befriended Sweaters, and who had proven equally cruel. Most nights, after 'work,' his brother would get piss-assed drunk, go home and beat on Joey. One day, Joey's brother disappeared; Joey never saw him again, which suited him just fine. It was assumed that someone from his brother's dark past had done the man in, but no one really knew, or if they did, they were careful never to discuss it around Joey.

After Joey's brother disappeared, Sweaters recruited Joey to take over his brother's collecting job. Joey, quickly tiring of the constant danger, moved out of collecting and into book-making. *How bad could taking book be, if so many of the city fathers were guilty of making bets?* Still, Joey thought often of going to the cops when the muscle end of the collection of payments grew more violent, but, hell, many of the cops, even FBI like Walter Steiner, Botch's boss, were regular clients.

Then things changed. Mack left Sweaters' gang and became a cop, and because Joey, for awhile, had been close to him, Sweaters took renewed interest in Joey, frequently venting his anger over Mack's defection on Joey. Sweaters, however, eventually came to look at Joey as a leech, albeit a useful one, a wild card he could use against Mack, if and when he had to. That's when Sweaters started pushing Joey V. into drug dealing, irrespective of how much Joey protested.

Twisted Ray, on the other hand, hated how Sweaters had always protected Joey, feeling that Joey was little more than a sniveling weakling, hiding behind his brother's ghost. Ray took a big bite of hamburger and smirked, happy that Sweaters was at last seeing Joey for the worm that he was.

Joey, in the meantime, had withdrawn to the far end of the pool figuring and refiguring the odds of his surviving the upcoming night. Even if he silently recanted and refused to play ball with the FBI, Ray, once everything was over, would undoubtedly take him into a dark alley and put a bullet through his head. All Twisted Ray need do was tell Sweaters that Joey V. had tried to run with Sweaters' money.

CHAPTER 9

It was time. The five Sweaters' men loaded into Joey V.'s Impala and headed out of Sweaters' driveway towards the L.I.E. to the Bronx. The FBI had bugged Joey's car, so Joey kept the in-car discussion away from any hint of the actual location of the Dominican apartment. If the FBI uncovered the exact location, they might decide they didn't need Joey any longer, and, by his thinking, that could quite possibly result in loss of the relocation deal, followed by his, his wife's and his daughter's lives in that order.

Joey V. drove and Twisted Ray rode shotgun. Buddha positioned himself directly behind Joey V. with Sal and Dom behind Ray. Buddha immediately started complaining about it being too tight in the back seat, asking Ray if he would switch seats. Ray, incensed, snarled, "Are you fucking kidding? What? I'm supposed to be uncomfortable in the back because you don't know when to stop eating, you fat bastard? Why don't you do yourself a favor and eat your hands next meal. Then you won't be able to shovel so much food down your throat."

Sal and Dom suppressed chuckles.

"Hey, fuck you, Ray! I was just asking," Buddha whined.

Ray turned and looked directly back at Buddha. "Look at you, sweating up a storm. You and that sorry wife of yours are a disgrace to humanity. Hey, why don't we stop at the asshole store on the way, because, God knows, you and your wife both need an extra one the way you two pack in the food!"

Sal and Dom's suppressed chuckles escaped this time, filling the car's interior with hysterical laughter.

Buddha stared at the back of Ray's headrest, apparently in deep thought. Then he snapped, "Asshole store? The one that's been handed down from generation to generation in your family? Do me a favor: Leave my Angie out of this!"

"Oh yeah, sweet Angie. That fucking heifer of yours wanted me to do her. Imagine that! She's so fat, me and her together would make a threesome!" Ray, Sal

59

and Dom guffawed loudly.

"That's enough!" roared Buddha.

"Yeah, she's definitely more than enough…"

"Fuck you, Ray." Buddha said venomously. "Fuck you."

Sal and Dom, sensing a shift from sarcasm to anger, stopped laughing, caught their breaths, and, not knowing what might happen next, squeezed into the corner of the back seat as far away from Buddha as possible.

Perfect, thought Joey. It was now time to put his own plan into action. Joey V. began to talk louder so Gary and the other FBI agents would overhear him. He needed to feed them just enough information to get them into the area so they could spot his car and follow him to the apartment. Joey V. had done his homework earlier, and had a way that, he hoped, would work without drawing suspicion from Twisted Ray.

"Ray, we have to stop at Enzo's Restaurant."

"What the fuck for?" asked Twisted Ray suspiciously, moving his malevolent gaze from Buddha to Joey V.

"The Dominicans are more cautious lately, what with this big deal and all. I need to let them know we're in the area so they can watch us."

"Why Enzo's?" Ray inquired, a little more at ease.

"I'm supposed to call from any one of Enzo public phones: ring three times and hang up. That's the pre-arranged signal that everything's okay. After that, they'll call out their scouts to make sure we're not bringing an army."

"Clever bastards," Ray responded, adding quickly, "I'd have done the same."

Like hell you would, shit for brains, Joey V. thought, still worried. If the FBI agent listening to them didn't happen to know where Enzo's was, then he was fucked. He talked slowly and loudly for the hidden microphone to pick up: "We're almost there now. It's at Williamsbridge Rd. and Neill Avenue."

Ray looked askance at Joey V. "What the fuck's the matter with you? I'm not deaf and I'm not an idiot. I've been there plenty of times before. Joey, I swear if I see anything I don't like going on at Enzo's, I'll beat you like a rented mule, and *then* kill you."

Joey tried to seem unimpressed. "Yeah, yeah, yeah," he said casually, while shaking in his shoes.

FBI agents Rich Pagano, driver, and Mike Smith, front seat passenger, had no problem overhearing the message and confirming that Joey V.'s car was indeed on its way to the stated intersection. Well behind Joey V., hidden within the traffic on the L.I.E., Agent Smith called the third conspirator, Agent Gary Ross, who was waiting in the city. Ross told his two comrades to push forward, code three, and get into position ahead at the place Joey V. had indicated. Pagano pulled out a cherry light, slapped it onto the top of the car, and hit the siren.

Joey V. looked in his side view mirror at the whirling red light and worried that the three had somehow used the vast resources of the FBI to figure out the actual apartment location. As the screaming car passed, he thought he recognized one of the agents—Smith, if he recalled correctly—he'd been dealing with. In the seat beside Joey, Ray quietly removed his gun from its shoulder holster.

At first, Joey, like the rest of the Impala's occupants, thought the car overtaking them, lights flashing, siren wailing, might be for them. However, the car passed quickly by without the occupants so much as looking at the Impala and in seconds disappeared into the yielding traffic ahead. Ray followed the car with squinted eyes until it disappeared, saying to Joey V. as the gun disappeared, "That's what you need: a siren for this sorry piece of shit," as they moved along in the traffic which had, because of the 'police' car, now slowed to a crawl.

"This is a real car, pal. I've seen your 'hey, look at me I'm a bitch' car'," Joey V. responded defensively, relieved to no longer see Ray's gun out. "Everyone knows your Lexus is for a man who wishes he had a pussy."

Buddha, Sal and Dom laughed defiantly at Ray this time.

Ray, instantly furious, swung a fist in a backhanded arc at Sal and Dom in the back seat. "Who the fuck you laughing at?" he asked, the rage obvious in his reddened face.

Sal and Dom sobered up, Dom trying unsuccessfully to hide a final snicker. Ray swung again, this time gun in hand, hitting the metal window molding. From the sound of the crunch, everyone knew Ray had broken a finger or two, but Ray was too macho to admit it. Stuffing the gun indelicately back into its holster, Ray leaned forward and unzipped an athletic bag he had brought with him that was lying next to his feet in the passenger well, and pulled out a razor-blade box cutter, saying to Joey V., "At least my car is intact," as he sliced an X in the header panel above the driver.

A piece of the material flapped loose and hit Joey in the head. "Smart! Real smart, asshole!"

Ray held the box cutter awkwardly in his hurt hand up against Joey V.'s good ear and threatened, "If you don't shut up and drive, I'll make sure you never wear sunglasses again." Ray laughed at his own joke, then looked back to see if Buddha was laughing. Buddha smiled until Ray turned back around, and then mouthed the words, "Fucking asshole," while shaking his head from side to side.

Ray, as if psychic, turned around, catching Buddha still mouthing the expletive, and immediately began fuming more. Joey V. knew when Twisted Ray got worked up like this, there was no room to push him further. For years, Sweaters had carefully controlled Ray when he was around Joey and hungry for blood, but Joey V. didn't have Sweaters' protection anymore. They were nearing the bridge, so Joey slowed, giving the FBI, wherever they were, as much time as possible to position themselves near Enzo's.

A few minutes later, Joey pulled the car into the back parking lot of Enzo's, realizing this might very well be the last place he would visit in this lifetime. Joey looked to the side and back of the car, saying, "You stay here. I'm going inside to call the Dominicans."

"I'll go with you," Ray immediately demanded.

"Why are you so anxious to screw everything up? You're so fucking on edge, it's going to be your fault if we lose Sweaters' million. I told you I needed to go inside and make the call. You wait here. I'll be right back," Joey V. scanned the parking lot for the FBI. They should be positioned all around the parking area by now, watching, waiting to act as soon as he identified the apartment building. Yet, even if they suddenly rounded the car, Ray would still have enough time to put at least one bullet in Joey V.'s head.

Ray taunted Joey. "What's with you? You're sweating like a pig. Is the little girl nervous?"

"I'm fine," was all Joey could eke out.

"I'm worried about your health, Joey," Ray said sarcastically, after telling the others to stay put, adding, "Joey and I'll be right back," as he slipped out his gun and climbed out the passenger door.

Joey V. sighed, reluctantly opening the driver's door and exiting. He looked around nervously. He still didn't see anyone or anything that hinted at FBI presence. *Maybe the agents were racing off on a sudden, more urgent call when they passed our car earlier? Maybe they figured out where the apartment was, and were hitting it now, stringing him and Sweaters' gang along to finish them off as a group. That would look good in the newspapers. Maybe..."*

Joey V. led Twisted Ray to the back door of the restaurant, the barrel of Ray's gun poking Joey's ribs irritatingly. *Where was the FBI? Why weren't they moving in? This would be a perfect time. Maybe the microphone in the car hadn't worked after all—that was possible. Hell, just about anything was possible.*

Inside, the popular restaurant was jam-packed, forcing Ray to quickly conceal his weapon. Hoping to put some distance between himself and Ray, Joey V. chose the middle of the five public phone booths to call from. Ray, however, followed him, and leaned against the door of the booth, pressing his ear against the glass.

Caught in his own lie, Joey tried desperately to figure out what to do next. He had to think of a number—any number—that he could ring three times without anyone picking up. Then it came to him: His sister, after months of bitching about how tired she was living in the same house for twenty years, had badgered her husband into buying a bigger one. They would have just completed the move and her old phone number would still be working at the vacated house.

Joey V. dropped in a coin and dialed the number, trying to keep his hands from shaking. The phone rang twice, then a woman answered, "Hello?"

Joey panicked and hung up. Ray from the other side of the glass, said, "Hey, I thought I heard someone answer."

Joey V. opened the door, forcing Ray to the side, and responded, "No one answered. Now, we can safely proceed."

Ray shrugged, accepting the explanation, and Joey breathed a sigh of relief as they headed back towards the door. Then the middle booth phone rang. Ray shoved his way back and grabbed the phone handle, knocking Joey V. to the side in his haste. A female voice said, "Hello? Did you just call me and hang up?"

"Yeah, that was me. I've been holding my dick waiting for you to call back," Ray responded in an oily voice.

The woman, appalled, hung up, and Ray pushed his way out of the phone booth. "You want to tell me what the fuck is going on?" he whispered, shoving his gun this time into Joey V.'s lower back.

Joey blanched. "I...I don't get it, They called back? Ray. That's...well, that's the signal that something's wrong. They must have a spotter here who saw you come in with me and..."

Ray pressed with the gun harder into the small of Joey's back. "To the car! Now!"

Earlier, while Joey V. and Ray were entering Enzo's Restaurant, Buddha climbed out of the too-packed backseat to stretch and have a smoke. Sal and Dom stayed inside. As he walked towards the front of the car and lit up, the car parked in the row in front turned on its headlamps and roared to life. Jerking forward, it rammed straight into the front of Joey V.'s Impala. Buddha, to avoid being hit, threw himself on top of an adjacent Cadillac. Sal and Dom bounced forward and back inside the Impala like rubber balls. Buddha slid off the Cadillac, drew his gun and hollered, "What da' fuck?"

Out of the offending car climbed FBI Agent Ross, wearing a purple valet jacket and stuttering, "Yourrr...nottt...suppposed...to be pa-pa-parked there!"

Buddha, enraged, nonetheless put away the gun and yelled back, "And that's how you ask me to move it, you fucking retard?"

Ross stuttered again, "Fu-fu-fu-fuck you...you guinea prick!"

"What did you say?" Buddha demanded, unable to believe the valet's impertinence. Shifting his bulk towards the Impala's open passenger window, Buddha reached into Twisted Ray's open athletic bag and pulled out a bat. "You think you're fucked up now? Just wait..." Buddha threatened, lumbering forward.

Sal and Dom shakily exited the car from the other side. "We don't have time for this, Buddha. Stop, or Ray will be pissed!"

Buddha yelled at Sal and Dom over the top of car. "Fuck you two and fuck Ray. I need to teach this asshole a thing or two about being a valet!"

Sal and Dom stood helpless as Buddha approached the valet, bat swaying loosely from atop Buddha's huge shoulder. Suddenly, from out of the darkness, FBI Agents Smith and Pagano appeared behind Sal and Dom, guns drawn, forcing the twins halfway back into the car, to the two wanna-be gangsters complete and utter surprise, popping a silenced round into each one's temple.

Buddha, recognizing the sound of silenced gunfire, turned and watched with horror as the two agents shoved Sal and Dom's lifeless bodies into the back seat of the Impala. As if from a distance, Buddha saw himself, in slow motion, drop the bat and go for his gun. At the same time, he saw the valet draw and point a silenced gun at him. Buddha, abruptly returning to present time, dropped to his knees and raised his huge hands, dropping the gun to the ground, and began begging his assailant not to kill him.

Ross smiled coldly and stuttered, "Ss-ss-sorry...asshole," and pumped a round into Buddha's right eye, killing him instantly. Together, the three agents dragged Buddha's massive body to the restaurant dumpster, struggled mightily to hoist him up, and dropped him into it.

Rich, exhausted, sighed. "Let's leave the other two where they are in the car for the moment."

Back inside the restaurant, Joey V. was heading for the door with Twisted Ray's gun rammed painfully against him.

Ray looked around cautiously, and, assured that no one in the restaurant was paying them undue attention, growled, "Get the fuck outside," and shoved Joey V. through the doors out into the back parking lot.

Ray scanned around. "Now, where the hell did those assholes go?" he said, looking at what appeared from the distance to be an empty space where the Impala, minutes before, had been parked.

Joey V.'s gaze was following Ray's around the dark parking lot, when Agent Ross walked up to the two, still wearing the purple valet jacket. "Can I help you, gentlemen? Do you have your ticket?" he asked without the slightest hint of a stutter.

"We're...ah...looking for some friends in a red, '67 Chevy Impala. They were supposed to...join us here for dinner," Ray replied, looking past the valet and continuing to survey the lot.

The valet looked Twisted Ray directly in the eyes. "Well, that makes perfect sense. If they're real men, they wouldn't be driving a Lexus!"

Ray's eyes darted to the insolent valet. *How did he...*

"Hey! Just kidding, man! I know the car. A guy who had just a little—well, actually, a lot—too much, accidently hit the car while pulling out. I moved the Impala further down, back there." The valet pointed towards the far corner of the parking lot.

Ray nudged Joey V. forward with the tip of his gun in the direction the valet had pointed. "Move," he whispered to Joey V., shoving him past Ross as if the valet wasn't there. Joey V.'s car soon appeared in the distance, its front end crumpled. "I swear, Joey, if you've made a separate deal with the Dominicans, you or both of us are going to die," said Ray when he didn't see Buddha waiting in the car.

The next moment, they heard the word, "Freeze!" coming from every direction.

Joey V. was stunned. Ray was actually relieved. "Freeze," was a police, rather than a gangland term, and if these were indeed police, all they could get him on was gun possession.

Agent Ross, taking the lead, yelled from behind, "Drop your weapon," to which Ray did just that, raising his hands slowly and confidently, as if he'd been through this before.

Ray turned to face his antagonist, and, with a smug smile, said, "So what's the problem?"

Ross yelled louder, "On your knees! Both of you! Hands above your heads!"

Ray and Joey V. complied, Joey V. feeling for the first time in several hours as if he might end up getting his wish for a new life after all.

Ray, ever the professional, kept talking: "Hey, man, you got this all wrong. This guy here—he's a buddy of mine. I was just breaking his balls, friend to friend, you know, nothing else. Look! See my finger. See?" Ray slowly held out his hand to show his swollen, discolored trigger finger. "I couldn't have pulled the trigger even if I wanted to."

Agent Ross walked over, picked up Ray's gun, and then grabbed Ray's swollen trigger finger and abruptly twisted it until it cracked loudly. Ray yelped. The agent immediately sliced Ray hard across the face, and Ray crumpled into a heap on the ground. "Now you got a matching, broken face," Ross said. Then he turned his attention to Joey V.

Joey's first thoughts at seeing the agent strike Ray, were of relief and pleasure, but the cold expression on the agent's face made him quickly change his mind, and all the nagging worries returned once again, but this time in greater force. *Would they do the same to him after he showed them where the apartment was?*

To his relief, Agent Ross, or Gary, the name he had asked Joey to use, enlisted

Joey V. to help drag Ray's limp body over to Joey's car. Agent Smith placed the muzzle of a silenced pistol to Ray's temple and began to squeeze the trigger, but Gary whispered, "not yet," and Mike reluctantly put the gun away. Instead, they stuffed Ray into the back seat of the car between the dead twins, handcuffing Ray's limp hands, one to Sal and one to Dom.

"Where's Sweaters' front money?" Gary demanded of Joey V.

"In a duffel bag in the trunk," Joey replied, glad to be joining the 'good guys' properly at last.

Gary opened the trunk, pulled out the bag, checked it briefly to make certain the money was there, then tossed the bag through the Impala's passenger window onto the front seat. Rich Pagano suddenly drove up next to them. "Pick up the girls and then follow us," Gary ordered, jumping into the passenger seat of Joey V.'s car, signaling for Joey to get in and drive.

Joey climbed in and looked at Gary quizzically. "What girls...and what did you do to my car?"

"Don't worry, just drive. Follow Rich and Mike around to the front of the restaurant."

Joey V. inserted and turned the key. Despite the damage to the front end, the car roared to life. Driving slowly in front of the restaurant, Joey V. watched intently as two gorgeous stiletto-heeled girls dressed in spaghetti-strap, black micro-mini dresses, slipped into the backseat of the car in front. "Wow, female agents! And I really like those 'uniforms.' Why couldn't they come with us?" Joey V. quipped.

Gary ignored him and asked instead, "How far is it to the apartment?"

"Five minutes tops," Joey V. answered.

"Alright, pull around my friends' car and lead the way." Gary said, all business.

Joey V. drove off, the other car following close behind. As he drove, he glanced over at Gary, and, in the corner of his eye, noticed a pool of dark blood on the back seat next to one of the twins. Nodding towards the back, he asked, "What happened to him?" He could just make out one side of Dom's face missing.

"He didn't want to play ball," Gary replied coldly.

Joey V., as unobtrusively as possible, adjusted his rearview mirror to check the other side of the back seat. He just could make out Ray in the middle, with what was left of the other twin's head resting on Ray's shoulder. "I guess his brother wasn't much of a player, either."

Gary shook his head. "No, he wasn't. You, on the other hand, want to play ball, don't you?"

Joey V. gulped. "I always play ball with the 'good guys,' yeah." The 'good guys,' however, were different than he'd expected. In fact, they didn't seem much different in demeanor than Twisted Ray. He was going to have to learn the game quick or he wouldn't have a chance at surviving the next couple of hours in the presence of the murderous Dominican gang, headed by that total wack-job, 'Loco' Paez.

Number One Bestseller

CHAPTER 10

Born in the hills of Santa Barbara de Samana in the Dominican Republic, Juan "Loco" Paez was one of six boys being constantly abused by a constantly drunken father. Given the situation, the chances of Juan turning out good were slim from the start. Juan hated his father intensely, suspecting him of having killed his mother either directly or indirectly during one of the old man's innumerable fits of rage.

One day, Juan's younger brother, Miguel, happened to be standing near the father, who, in a drunken frenzy, slashed Miguel's face with a broken bottle. Little Miguel, screaming, held his torn and bleeding face in his hands, while Juan, fifteen at the time, looked on in horror as their father raised the broken bottle to strike again. Without thinking, "Loco" grabbed the nearest thing he could find, a kitchen cleaver, and began hitting his father, stopping only when the cleaver embedded so firmly and unyieldingly in his father's chest he couldn't pull it out. Later that night, Miguel, Hiram and Juan together dragged the limp body through the town, tossing it down a hill into the refuse heap where the shanty town disposed of its collective offal. Juan's principal memory of the event was that it had been strangely difficult to tell where the shanty town ended and the dump began.

Word quickly got out about the missing man, with "Loco" claiming the kill. The boy immediately began enjoying a new role as the tough leader of his family —a man to be feared and respected. After his first taste of power, Juan, now Loco Paez, thirsted for more. By the time he was twenty-one, he had saved enough money from organizing and running the shanty town's dark-side businesses to catch a flight to New York, where he found and paid a local Puerto Rican girl with American citizenship to marry him.

With his wife's help, he landed a job with the US Post Office. The long string of incompetent bosses with menial attitudes towards their employees, however, proved too much for him. It was time for him to be back in charge.

69

In a couple months, Loco Paez had organized and was running the largest stolen car ring on the East Coast. He quickly made enough money to bring Miguel and Hiram to New York, and enlisted them into the "family" business.

Next Loco brought over his two younger brothers, Angel and Jorge, the two finding a welcome place in New York City's slum-drug culture. Always high on one drug or another, Loco used them as watchdogs, so he wouldn't have to see or hear them, but soon they began paying their own way by organizing the local drug trade. Through their diligence, drug trafficking soon became more lucrative than stolen cars.

Loco Paez then brought over his oldest brother, Ralph, whom he began grooming to be his successor. Ralph was ambitious, loyal and had a knack for figuring out ways to invest their illegal money profitably in legitimate businesses. Ralph quickly became the family "lawyer" and head of the family's rapidly enlarging, money-laundering operation.

Julio, Gilbert and Jesus were the last to be brought over. Half brothers, they nonetheless established themselves in the family business, though in the end, they paid more respect to Loco's two main business associates, Hector and Ramon, than to Loco. Loco had long ago recruited Hector and Ramon, though not really family, into the business. Thus began the Dominicans.

Joey and Gary pulled up to the Dominican apartment house in Washington Heights, with Agents Smith and Pagano and the girls close behind. Joey V. pointed. "That's the building."

The Dominican lair was located in a four-story walk-up. Gary directed the two cars half-way up the block, just out of line-of-sight, and parked.

Gary looked back at Twisted Ray, pronouncing, "He'll be out for quite a while yet," then turned back to Joey V. adding, "You got something to cover them?"

"There's a blanket in the trunk," Joey replied, exiting the car, grabbing the blanket and climbing into the blood-spattered backseat area. Joey noticed Gary glancing repeatedly out the back window as, together, they covered Ray, Sal and Dom.

"What the hell?" Gary suddenly bellowed, seeing Smith and Pagano get out of their car and begin walking towards the Dominican apartment building. Gary slipped out and indicated wildly with his hands for his associates to get back into their car and pull alongside his.

"What the fuck were you doing back there?" Gary complained through the window as Smith pulled up and stopped.

"Checking out the building."

"Why not just get out and tell them we're coming?" Gary responded vehemently, adding suspiciously in his next breath as he fingered his concealed weapon, "And how exactly did you know that was the building?"

"Your car is wired," Smith answered smugly, pointing at Joey V.'s car.

"Yeah, well, find a spot just ahead of us, and stay in the car and wait for my orders!" Gary snapped.

As Smith rolled the car slowly forward in search of a parking place, Joey V. ran over the layout again with Gary: "The apartment is on the third floor, facing the street. It's the last door on the right off the stairway at the end of the hall. Outside the building, they'll have a guy at the front door to check people coming in and out of the building. If you can't name a Dominican in the building you won't live to try a second time."

Gary interrupted, "The girls have the name you gave us."

Joey V. nodded, continuing, "The guy at the door will be Hector. If he sees anything out of the ordinary, he'll yell up to Gilbert. Gilbert will be on the fire escape by the hallway next to the door leading to their apartment. Follow me so far?"

"Yeah, I got it," Gary said, adding, "and on the other side of the window, in the hallway, will be two more guys guarding the apartment door, right?"

"Yeah, so if Hector yells up to Gilbert, then Gilbert warns the two in the hallway and they're ready for war. So what's your plan? Where are all the other agents?" Joey V. asked, glancing around at the silent, dark neighborhood outside.

Gary hissed curtly, "Don't worry about our part of the plan. Just stick to me. Trust me, all the agents we need are already here." Gary got out of the car and walked up to where Mike Smith had parked. Gary pointed to a taller building across the street. "Take your position on that roof. This place is set up like most drug dens we've been trained on. I suspect the Dominicans will have two spotters posted on their own roof, undoubtedly armed, so don't let yourself be seen."

After a quick radio check, Agent Rich Pagano replied confidently, "No problem," and removed himself and a valise from out of the car, withdrawing from the valise the parts of a perfectly-machined, custom-made, high-powered rifle including telescopic night scope, silencer and a handful of custom-made bullets. Rich assembled the unit and slid it into a black velvet gun sleeve. Walking past Gary, Rich looked briefly back to say, "I'll call you when I'm in position."

Gary nodded, and then told Agent Smith to work his way onto the roof of the building immediately adjacent and attached to the Dominican building. After a quick equipment and radio check, the second agent disappeared into the night. Gary herded the girls out of the car and over to Joey V.'s car.

"If I knew that FBI agents looked like this, I would have applied for a job," Joey V. said. Looking at the first of the two girls, he offered a friendly hand and hello.

The two girls exchanged petrified looks. Each nodded uncomprehendingly back at Joey V. with nervous smiles. Joey, confused, pointed a thumb over his shoulder at the two girls, and asked, "What's with...?"

Gary cut in, "I told you, don't fucking interfere with official bureau business! You just do exactly as I tell you. No more questions, got it?"

"Yeah, yeah, I got it. Relax and..."

In fact, Gary had last week picked up the two girls, both young, illegal, South American immigrants working the New York streets, during a joint FBI-Immigration Department sweep. Given the choice of deportation in chains along with any family and relatives, or continuing their trade in the Big Apple after doing a job for the bureau, each gladly complied. The girls, both in their mid-teens, but clearly as tough and sophisticated as adults in experience, were further pleased to hear they would each receive a $500, clingy, black, name-brand micro-mini dress with matching black heels, theirs to keep after the job. Gary handed one girl a small walkie-talkie and explained, in Spanish, to be ready to go on Agent Pagano's command. All they had to do was walk seductively together up to the entrance of the building, where he and Joey V. would be waiting. If anyone, outside or inside, should stop or challenge them, they were to flash a smile and say, "Loco." Once inside, they were to go directly up the stairs to the roof and hang out with anyone who happened to be up there. That was it. The girls nodded affirmatively and smiled at each other, enjoying being part of a covert operation targeting someone other than themselves.

Meanwhile, Agent Smith had reached the top of the building directly connected to the Dominican house and called in to let Gary know. A moment later, Pagano did the same.

Gary turned to Joey V. "You got the money?"

"It's all here in the sports bag. You checked it yourself."

"Okay. Let's go!" Gary said with determination, trading his shoulder holster for a metal flashlight in a clip belt holder, and palming something into a small slit on the inside of the holder. Ready, Joey and the agent started walking across the dark, damp street towards the Dominican house, the girls looking troubled, but following directly behind.

Gary spun around abruptly. "No, you dumb bitches!" Then, switching to Spanish, he pointed, reminding them to go back to the car and wait until Agent Pagano called them on their walkie-talkie and told them to go. The lead girl, realizing her error and that the only thing that stood between them and certain deportation was doing their part correctly, nodded affirmatively, then grabbed her friend's arm and led her back into the shadows, all the while reprimanding her sternly in Spanish. Gary and Joey V. continued down the street, Gary cursing bilingually under his breath.

On the roof of the Dominican house, the pothead twins, Angel and Jorge, stood cradling their custom-made assault rifles while passing another joint. Angel, eyes completely dilated, said, "Hey, man. Didja see that flash of light on the top of the building next door?"

Jorge, with a stoned grin on his face, chuckled. "Man, you're really wasted, Angel. Ain't nothin' over there but darkness."

"No, man, like I saw somethin' flash for just a moment," Angel replied, unable to focus on the place where moments ago he thought he'd seen the flash. He laid his assault rifle against the low brick divider separating the two adjacent buildings and climbed over. Peering curiously around a large chimney, he turned right into Agent Smith's waiting gun. The agent fired a single, silenced round, knocking Angel solidly against the chimney. Jorge, hearing the round ricochet off the chimney, lifted his rifle to shoot, not hearing the muted spit of the rifle from across the street. Jorge jerked and fell dead, face first onto the tar floor.

Gary and Joey V. continued walking towards the front steps of the Dominicans' building, Joey V. nervously greeting the guard there. "*Hector, como esta?*"

Hector, having already pulled his gun half-way out of its holster, hesitated. "Hey, Joey. Who's dat wit' chu, huh? Where's Phil?"

"I'm here for Loco. This guy's cool. Phil couldn't come. His mother just died," Joey V. answered calmly.

Hector said a short prayer in Spanish while he made the sign of the cross. Then, looking up towards the fire escape, he yelled, "Two coming up!"

Up on the fire escape, Gilbert banged the flat of his hand against the window and put up two fingers to advise the two men standing guard in front of the apartment door that two "visitors" were about to be admitted to the building.

Back on the street, the building entrance buzzer went off and Hector pushed the door open. Pointing to Gary, he said, "You first."

Gary walked into the vestibule. Hector immediately tapped him on the shoulder with a gun. Then, looking back over his shoulder, Hector said, "You next, Joey, aftah I check out dis' guy," locking the outer door with Joey V. outside.

"Raise yo' handz," Hector ordered, pointing his gun at Gary's forehead. Hector reached to the side, grabbed a metal detector with his free hand and began scanning for weapons. The wand squawked over the agent's right hip. Hector jumped back ready to shoot. "Easy, man. It's just a flash light," Gary said, pulling the flashlight within it's holster from his belt and showing it to Hector. Hector, spooked, eyed it suspiciously as Gary turned it over for him to inspect.

"Geeze, man! Ya' almost died over a fuckin' flashlight!" he snapped, signaling the agent to put it away while lowering his weapon and unlocking the outside door.

"Okay, Joey. You next," Hector said, waving Joey V. into the foyer and grabbing the duffle bag. After searching it thoroughly, Hector smiled. "Looks like yah boss's business is about to expand," he quipped as he finished wanding Joey quickly over.

Finding nothing metallic on Joey V., Hector visibly relaxed. "Joey, yah late. You of all people should know dah boss hates late."

"Hell, I'll just blame it on you."

"Hey, don't even kid 'bout dat!" Hector retorted gruffly.

"Easy. Easy. Just kidding," Joey laughed, trying to lighten the situation while waiting for the man to pass them on through a second door and into the apartment hallway.

Hector shook his head from side to side. "Dat ain't funny. Paez iz a friend, but when it comes tah business, he don' joke or play none." Hector stepped outside and signaled up to Gilbert to hit the buzzer for the inner door. The message was further relayed to the guys standing outside the apartment who instantly relayed it to someone inside the apartment, and a second buzz-click sounded in the foyer next to the inner door below.

The moment the click sounded, Joey V. shoved the inner door open, while Gary knocked the gun from Hector's hand, grabbed the Dominican and dragged him through, having magically retrieved a thin, ten-inch-long, hardened plastic knife from the slit in the flashlight holder. Pressing the blade firmly against Hector's throat, Gary instructed, "Don't let the plastic fool you. This'll kill you just as dead as steel will." Joey V. retrieved Hector's weapon from the floor. Hector started to raise a hand to his neck, but stopped when he felt the edge of the knife bite into his flesh. "How many in the apartment?" Gary continued coldly.

Hector, starting to bleed, gasped, "Foah."

Gary pushed him against the wall and repositioned the blade of the knife across the base of Hector's windpipe. "Is that including the guy in the secret back room?"

Hector's eyes widened and he croaked, "Okay, five. I forgot…"

Gary revealed a handkerchief. "Now, that wasn't so hard was it?" he asked. Hector reached thankfully for the handkerchief to staunch the slow flow of blood from his neck.

"No, but Paez…He gonna kill me…*after* he kills you two!"

"No, I promise you, he won't," Gary said, slashing the knife across Hector's windpipe, then plunging the tip of the blade from underneath Hector's chin up into the man's uncomprehending brain. Gary caught the lifeless body and directed it against the wall. Then, opening the outside door of the building, Gary signaled

Agent Pagano across the street with the flashlight.

Joey V. stood holding the inner door open, watching in shocked silence as Gary dragged Hector's body through the door and into the hallway where he stuffed it under the staircase. "What the fuck..." Joey finally burst out.

Gary, cheetah-fast, whipped the point of his knife against Joey V.'s temple and grunted through his teeth, "Didn't I tell you to stop with the questions?"

"Yeah!" Joey V. gasped, totally stunned. If these guys were FBI, then they were playing unusually tough and dirty. And if they were phony—if this was all a setup—his usefulness would be very short-lived.

Rich Pagano had, in the meantime, made the call to the girls, who walked jauntily across the street and up to the front door of the Dominican building. Gilbert looked down from the fire escape, noticing the two girls as Gary planned. Knocking on the window to Ramon and Julio in the hallway, he mouthed, "Check this out," pointing below to the two classy girls standing in front of the doorway, waiting.

Ramon and Julio pressed their faces against the window as Gilbert mouthed, "We having a party?" Ramon and Julio shrugged their shoulders, then smiled and shook their heads affirmatively in hopeful anticipation.

Ramon cupped his hands on his chest in reference to the size of one girl's breasts. While Gilbert laughingly nodded in agreement, Gary, below, opened the front door, grabbed the girls by their arms, and jerked them in, sticking his hand out just far enough to give a thumbs up to Gilbert.

Gilbert fell for it and gave the signal to open the inner door, though Joey V. was already holding it open, and the two ladies were pulled into the hallway. Gary reached into the duffle bag, grabbed out a couple of stacks of bills, gave a stack to each girl and instructed them in Spanish to go as instructed up to the roof. As they walked up the stairway, Gary reminded them to walk sexily. The two girls giggled and wiggled their asses playfully as they walked up the stairs. Gary and Joey V. followed silently at a distance. As the two girls reached the third floor where the Dominican's apartment was, Gary shoved an arm in front of Joey V., abruptly stopping him.

The girls surveyed the third floor hall and smiled at Ramon and Julio, who immediately began waving them over to join them. This was their moment. Once the big-wigs in the apartment got hold of these girls, Ramon and Julio wouldn't have any further chance with them.

The girls ignored the two men and continued up the next flight of stairs, moving slowly and, as instructed, sexily. Curious, Ramon and Julio slipped over to the stairway to peer under the short skirts of the two invitingly-swaying derrieres before they disappeared. Looking at each other, then at the door to the apartment they were supposed to be guarding, then back at each other, both simultaneously said, "Fuck it," and ran up after the girls. Leaping the stairs three at a time, on the next floor, instead of the two girls, a man was standing there with a silenced sniper rifle pointed directly at them. "FBI! Drop the weapons! You're surrounded!" Agent Smith commanded in a low, but firm voice.

The two stunned Dominican guards looked furtively left and right, and then sadly up the stairs at the two inviting asses disappearing once again from their view. One, then the other of the guards squatted and laid down his weapon. Smith walked forward, kicked the weapons aside, then rammed the point of his rifle up hard underneath first one and then the other's chin as he pat-searched each for other weapons. Convinced they had none, Mike Smith backed off and ordered the two to turn around and head back down to the third floor. On the way, the agent snatched their two rifles up off the floor.

Back on the third floor and outside the window, Gilbert had watched the two guards fly up the stairs after the girls and looked down outside anxiously towards the building front door. While Hector had given him a thumbs up, he hadn't come fully out like he was supposed to, and having resumed his position, given him the required signal that Joey V. and his assistant were on their way up the stairs. On the other hand, Gilbert knew Hector liked to bullshit with Joey V. In the end, however, it was the fact that Hector hadn't detained or tried to hit on the two girls that made him most suspicious. Making a fatal command decision, Gilbert began to open the window. Agent Pagano, watching closely from across the street, placed a carefully aimed bullet cleanly through Gilbert's exposed temple.

Mike Smith ushered the two guards down to the third floor where Gary Ross and Joey V. were now waiting. Mike offered Gary one of their prisoner's weapons. Gary, in turn, showed Mike the 45-caliber automatic he took from Hector. "But I won't be able to get into the apartment if I show either," Gary retorted, declining the rifle and slipping the handgun into a jacket pocket.

In the meantime, the two girls had finished working their way to the roof and pushed open the roof door. Standing on the roof, in their sexy outfits, in the cold of night, one girl, shivering, asked the other in Spanish, "Now wh..." but before she could finish the sentence, she jerked backwards and fell to the rooftop floor. The second girl, noticing her girlfriend suddenly covered in blood, screamed wildly, only to meet the same fate an instant later.

Joey V. asked Mike, already knowing the answer he'd get, if he could please have one of the assault rifles. "Don't worry, we'll protect you," Agents Smith and Ross said sarcastically at the same time.

Together, the five approached the door of the Dominican's apartment, where Ramon paused just long enough to taunt Joey V., "You'll never get away with this.

You know Paez. He's gonna kill you and all your…friends here."

"Then he's going to have to get in line, Ramon," Joey V. replied, gulping, now completely demoralized. Gary pulled the automatic out of his jacket pocket and applied the tip of the barrel to the back of Ramon's head, whispering in Spanish, "Shut your mouth. All you have to do is help get us in. If you get us in, no one has to die."

Ramon, however, suspected otherwise, having glanced hopefully out the window only to see Gilbert's bloodied face plastered up against the glass, a single small hole in the glass where an eye should have been.

Gary whispered to Mike, "Stay in the background. When it's your time to enter, spray the left side of the room. Kill everyone there…"

Mike nodded. Then Gary instructed Ramon and Julio: "You two go up to the door and get them to open it. Then back off, let Joey and me in, and remain in the doorway. If you try to go any further in, or to shut the door, me and my two friends here will shred you both to pieces. Got it?"

Ramon and Julio, sufficiently mollified and sweating profusely, nodded their understanding.

On Gary's signal, Ramon and Julio moved up to the door. Ramon knocked. A voice from behind the door yelled back, "What?"

"It's Ramon. I got Joey V. and his partner here." A bloodshot eye looked through the peephole, then the door opened. On the other side of the door, Ralph grumbled, "What good is a fucking peephole if all I can see is your two fat, ugly faces?"

Ramon and Julio stepped just aside the doorway and stopped as instructed, parting to let Joey V. and Gary slip in.

Inside, Joey V. held up the bag and said merrily, "Paez, how are you? I have the money, as promised."

Gary checked out Loco Paez thinking, *This sloppy-looking piece of shit is the boss?* Loco greeted Joey V. in a thick Spanish accent, "How are you, my friend? And who is this with you?"

Gary interjected in Spanish before Joey V. could answer. "I'm here in place of Phil. His mother died."

Loco's eyebrows raised. "Very sick, was she?"

"Yeah, for a short while."

"That's a shame," Loco said sadly, turning his attention back to Joey V.

The brief exchange had given Gary the opportunity to scope out the room. Ralph, who had answered the door, was returning to the kitchen on Gary's left. Loco stood between Gary and Ralph, to the left of a long, perpendicular, white leather couch. A girl was decked out, legs spread awkwardly, in the middle of the couch, apparently passed out. To the right of the girl was Miguel, sporting the telltale facial scar across his face that made him look like he had been stitched back together with a sewing machine. Hiram stood to Miguel's right, a cross tattooed boldly from his forehead to the top of his bald head.

Looking Joey V.'s companion in the eyes, Loco Paez offered, "Damn shame, losing his mother like that, especially since that would mean that the poor fucker lost her twice."

Joey V., confused, looked from Gary to Paez, "What do you mean 'twice'?"

Loco Paez had by then noticed Ramon and Julio looking down at the floor, neither entering nor shutting the door as might be expected. Taking a long drag on his cigarillo, Loco suddenly whipped a gun from off the glass coffee table and swung it around towards his visitors. "Don't remember her first wake, eh, Joey? No? Well, about a year ago *my* mother-in-law died and Phil's mother was decked out dead in the next room. Ring a bell?"

Everyone froze. Joey V.'s heart raced, then he calmed himself and responded coolly, "Yeah, I remember something like that, but that wasn't Phil's mother, it was his mother-in-law."

Paez, shifting the point of the automatic back and forth between Joey V. and Gary, crooked his head towards his brother, Ralph. "Ralph, go ask Gilbert what family member of Phil's was laid out the same day as my mother-in-law." Then, as an aside, he smiled and hissed at Joey V. "Gilbert accompanied me to the funeral."

Ralph sauntered into the kitchen and opened up the window, yelling, "Gilbert!" After a few moments, Ralph yelled again, then pressed his head against the metal grating to see why Gilbert hadn't answered from the nearby fire escape. Looking momentarily back toward the apartment door, Ralph, from his new vantage, noticed an armed man standing well behind Ramon and Julio. Ralph opened his mouth to warn, but instead of words, a gush of blood burst out and he fell to the floor gagging.

In the building across the street, Agent Pagano exhaled. It had been a bad angle from across the street but, sensing trouble, he had taken the shot through the kitchen window bars and was already targeting the next gang member further inside the room. The bullet that felled Ralph in the meantime thudded into the inside kitchen wall.

Joey V. gasped as the bullet ripped an exit hole in the dry wall and hit Paez's forearm, knocking the pistol from the gang leader's hand and flinging it high into the air. A second shot from outside hit Hiram, just to Gary's right. Gary reacted instantly, snatching Paez's gun from the air and using it to shoot Miguel dead onto the couch. Feeling the weight of the man on her, the girl on the couch started and began screaming, covering her ears with her hands and stamping her feet.

Mike hit Ramon from behind with the butt of his automatic rifle, pushing him into the apartment as a shield. Then Mike rolled to the floor and dropped Julio in a volley of bullets.

Ramon flew forward, knocking Joey V. off balance and onto the glass coffee table. The explosive crash of their combined weight shattered the glass top, sending shards of glass flying throughout the room.

Loco Paez stood stunned. One moment he was squeezing off a shot at the traitor and his companion, the next he was holding his shattered, bleeding forearm, his gun now in Joey V.'s companion's hands pointed at him. Gary braced Paez's gun with both hands and shot the man cleanly between the eyes.

Mike Smith, automatic at ready, called to Gary, "That all of them?"

Gary, the smoking gun still pointed at where Loco Paez had been standing a moment before, motioned with his head towards a doorway across the room on the far right. "Check the bedroom."

Mike got up, approached the door cautiously from the side, and kicked it open, shattering the door jam. Dashing inside, Mike returned a moment later, cradling his weapon like a baby in his arms. "It's clear. I think we got them all."

The girl on the couch continued screaming hysterically, until Mike, mimicking her screaming, swung the barrel of his automatic rifle close to her face and barked, "Shut the fuck up!" The woman immediately silenced.

"Leave her," Gary snarled. "We don't have time for her," then continued, "Get him," pointing to Ramon who was lying motionless atop Joey.

When Mike didn't divert his attention from the woman as ordered, Gary walked over to Ramon and demanded: "Ramon, get up...I know you weren't hit."

Mike swept the point of his automatic rifle around the room at the lifeless bodies scattered about. "We better finish this quick so we can leave before the NYPD gets here."

Gary tried once again to get Ramon's attention. "I asked you once, nicely, Ramon," and Gary promptly shot Ramon in the knee. Ramon let out a shriek and grabbed his knee. As the man rolled off Joey V., Gary snarled at him, "Don't try playing possum with me. Stand up!"

Ramon, braced against the sofa and pulled himself shakily up onto one leg, the blood draining out of his face and flowing freely from his shattered other knee.

Joey V. didn't move. Gary, pointing his gun at Joey V.'s head, checked Joey V. with his other hand, surprised at the amount of bright red blood on his hand as he withdrew it. "This one's not playing possum," Gary declared. "Call Rich over here. Now!"

Mike did as instructed, then, together, the two moved the sofa aside, and began looking for marks of a hidden door, behind which at least one more of

Paez's men and millions of dollars lay waiting for them. Both felt all around the area for an indention, latch or button.

While they were searching, Rich Pagano entered the apartment with an empty duffle bag, and paused to gasp at the carnage.

Mike and Gary, startled, turned reflexively, pointing their guns at Rich. Gary shook his head, "Nice way to get your ass blown off, stupid. Come in...and shut the goddamn door!"

CHAPTER 11

Having located the outline of a hidden door within the wall without finding any indication of a release mechanism, Gary, Mike and Rich stood Ramon in front of the area. Gary pointed a gun at Ramon's crotch. "If you don't convince your friend behind this door to open it in the next five seconds, you're going to be childless and maybe die a painful death. Neither you nor the girl need die."

Eyeing the bodies scattered throughout the room, Ramon yelled in Spanish, "Hey! Jesus! It's me, Ramon! You and I are the only ones left. They had a fight and all killed each other. Grab the shit and let's get out of here before the cops come."

A muffled yell echoed in Spanish from behind the wall, "Where is Paez?"

"Killed, man," yelled Ramon. "It's just you and me now."

Jesus could hear sirens outside. If he stayed in the room with the drugs and the money he figured he'd be in jail for life, if lucky, or, more likely, convulsing in a gas chamber, if the state decided to make an example of him. Saying to himself aloud in English, "Fuck this," Jesus ripped open a bag of cocaine, shoved his face into the fluffy white powder, and drew in a big breath through his nose. His heart began racing as he wedged the butt of his assault rifle firmly against his shoulder and started shooting wildly through the door.

Bullets ripped through Ramon's shuddering body, flinging pieces across the room and onto the far wall, splattering it with red. Gary dove to the floor, Rich and Mike diving to either side of Gary.

Jesus kept shooting, sending wood splinters all over the room, blasting an ever enlarging hole in the wall. When the hole was big enough, Jesus jumped through, shooting in every direction. Tripping over the three agents and landing on top of them, Jesus rolled to his side and rose unsteadily onto his feet in a single motion.

Aiming the hot assault rifle at Gary, Mike and Rich, who were trying to get up off the floor as fast as they could, Jesus, wild-eyed, knew they wouldn't be able to lift their guns in time, and smugly quoted a line from his favorite movie, *Scarface*: "Say hello to my little friend."

Jesus braced and pulled the trigger. To everyone's surprise nothing happened.

Looking down at the spent rifle, then up at the three men advancing towards him, Jesus gave a nervous laugh. Gary leveled Paez's automatic at Jesus's head and said, "You like movie lines? Remember *The Matrix*? 'Dodge this,'" he said. Jesus' eyes focused momentarily on the flashing muzzle of the gun less than a foot away. The next moment he was flying backwards, hitting the floor dead.

Gary, Mike and Rich peeked into the secret closet, cautiously entering through the hole Jesus had created with his weapon. On the right, three-inch-thick stacks of greenbacks were piled, one on top of another, from floor to ceiling. On the left, neatly-tied bags of cocaine were similarly stacked, except for the one Jesus had buried his face in. Gary tossed his gun aside and slapped a fist into the other. "Jackpot!" he yelled in triumph.

Rich walked up to the window overlooking the street. "There's cops all around the place. They're about to break in the front door of the building below."

Gary, frustrated at seeing the millions, at last, piled high before him, but no time to collect it, grabbed his gun. "Shit! We have to stall them. Quick, put on your identification badges and help me move this picture in front of the hole in the wall. Rich, shove the sofa up against the picture. Now! We've no time to lose!" Turning to Rich, Gary continued: "Open the apartment door and stay there! When the cops appear, insist this is our crime scene and that we want nothing disturbed. Hurry!"

Agent Pagano walked towards the open door, stopping momentarily in the center of the room to survey the chaos. "What about the girl?" he asked.

"I'll take care of her," Gary said, reaching to pull out his plastic knife while making his way through bodies and rubble toward her. The girl, awakening from the horror of what she had been watching transpire, jumped up and darted for the door. Agent Pagano dropped his rifle and ran forward to catch her, stopping suddenly in the doorway, finding himself looking directly into the barrels of Mack and Andre's guns. A crowd of uniformed cops stood wide-eyed and open-mouthed behind Mack and Andre, their weapons also pointed directly at him.

CHAPTER 12

Rich Pagano was barely able to squeak, "FBI, don't shoot!" while he reflexively lifted his hands in the air, gesturing with his eyes towards the identification badge he held in his right hand.

"Arrest him," Mack ordered the two officers nearest behind him.

Rich protested. "I'm FBI! Federal matters take precedence. This is our crime scene and…"

Andre interrupted, "Who's with you?"

Gary Ross yelled from inside, "Agents Ross and Smith! Stay out! Don't lay a foot on our crime scene. We're coming out; tell your Boy Scouts not to shoot."

Andre yelled back, "Do everyone here a favor: Put down your weapons, and put your hands in the air, identification badges up where we can see them!"

Mike Smith walked out first, hands high, followed by Gary Ross. Andre didn't even look at their badges; instead, as the man passed, he grabbed Mike's wrists, rolled them back behind the man and snapped on cuffs. Gary, startled when Mack prepared to do the same to him, asserted, "Hey, we've got this under control. This is an FBI investigation, so stay the fuck out."

Mack threw Gary face against the hallway wall, jerked Gary's hands roughly behind and cuffed him.

"What the fuck…" Gary exclaimed in anger. "I told you, we're FBI, asshole! Look at my badge."

Mack rammed Gary harder against the wall and began frisking him. Prying the plastic knife from Gary's hand, Mack held it up to the light. Wet blood dripped down Mack's hand. "Not standard bureau issue, if you are, indeed, an agent as you claim. I'm going to call your office, and until someone comes here and personally confirms that you're who you say and this is your crime scene, you're ours."

Andre nodded his assent, adding, "Put them in the bathroom. It's the only place not covered in blood. And you," he pointed at an officer," "watch them carefully."

The policeman dragged the three dour-faced agents into the large bathroom and, standing menacingly over them, closed the bathroom door.

"Shut the apartment door and wait outside. Don't let anyone in unless I tell you to," Andre ordered the remaining officers, "and I mean no one! I don't care if it's fucking J. Edgar Hoover back from the dead wearing a skirt and pumps, get me?"

After assuring the bathroom door was shut, Mack began walking from body to body, at last locating Joey V., draped face down over the coffee table frame, hundreds of glass shards mixed with blood underneath. Checking for a neck pulse, Mack said with relief to Andre, "He's alive."

"How bad is he?" Andre said softly, knowing Mack's awakening affection for Joey.

"I don't know. With all the broken glass, I'm afraid to lift him. What do you think we should do?"

Joey V. twitched, then gasped, "How about getting me to a hospital?"

Mack squatted, trying unsuccessfully to see Joey's face. "Keep your voice down, you dope," he whispered. "How badly hurt are you?"

Joey V. exhaled slowly, "I'll live, I think, but you gotta lift me out of this glass frame. The glass is poking into me from every direction."

"Yeah," Mack sighed, "but there's something else we got to do first."

Joey V. exhaled, his blood-dripping face inches from the mess of broken glass beneath the table. "Let me guess—the money," Joey sighed.

"That's right, the money," Mack echoed quietly back. "Where is it, Joey? Where's the secret room with the money?"

Joey V. tried to point but had to stop from the pain. "Sorry, Mack, but I guess you'll have to pull me out first after all."

Mack and Andre positioned themselves on either side of Joey V. and carefully lifted him, to a string of suppressed groans. When they finally had Joey sitting on the couch, Mack frowned sickly and shook his head. Joey's bloodied face and torso were haloed by sparkling glass shards.

Joey V. winced as he lifted an arm and pointed towards the slightly askew wall-picture behind the couch. Mack and Andre quickly moved the couch with Joey V. still on it. As they did, the painting fell with a crash. Mack climbed through the ragged hole into the secret room and smiled. "Now we're talking."

After a quick survey, Mack exited backwards and returned to Joey V. "Take it easy. Don't move or make any noise. We'll get you to a hospital in just a few minutes."

"I think you'll want that, too." Joey said, painfully swinging his arm towards a sports bag lying on the floor. "A gift from Sweaters."

Mack broke into a big grin as he and Andre carried Joey V. into the bedroom and delicately set him on the bed. The two immediately began carefully picking out the worst of the shards.

"How'd you know where to find me?" Joey V. asked, in between grunts.

"We had your car bugged, too," Andre responded.

Finished, Mack handed Joey V. a couple of towels to stop the bleeding from the worst of the lacerations. Then Mack and Andre returned to the living room, righted the painting over the wall hole and moved the couch back, Mack collapsing resolutely onto the couch.

Andre called on his portable radio, alerting the policemen guarding the door that a crime scene unit and some morgue attendants would soon be coming.

The crime scene unit got there first, and Andre walked them around, pointing out pertinent evidence while the men measured, photographed and dusted.

Twenty minutes later, a professional-looking Nick dressed in a city morgue uniform pushed a hospital gurney through the apartment door. Nick looked around and whistled. "What a mess! Worse even than downstairs!"

"What happened to your assistant?" Andre asked, watching the crime scene unit work and pretending not to recognize Nick.

"Don't ask," he responded beneath his breath, continuing as he looked at the lieutenant in charge, "You guys done yet?"

Before the lieutenant could answer, Andre announced that the lieutenant was, indeed, done. The young officer, glancing back at Andre and, mustering all the authority he could muster from his short time with the police, said bluntly, "I'm sorry, Captain, but we're *not* done yet."

Andre gave the man a fierce look, pointed at his Captain's bars and commanded, "Are you trying to pull rank, lieutenant?"

The officer blushed. "Well...well...I mean, no, sir!"

"Well, then, you're done when I say you're done!" Andre snapped back. The red-faced officer apologized profusely, gathered his group and left.

Andre then turned his full attention to Nick. "So far, so good," he pronounced as he helped Nick roll the gurney towards the sofa. Nick looked at Mack sitting resolutely on the couch. "You plan on helping?"

"I've been doing a most important task: sitting on this sofa to make sure no one would move it. Now, however, I'm available," Mack replied, standing and adding, "You know, you make a good morgue attendant."

Nick snorted, and together the three moved the sofa and removed the painting. In the process, Nick asked his father, "So what happens when the real morgue truck pulls up?"

Mack shook his head. "These are the questions you should have asked back at Farrell's. But don't worry, I'm on it."

Andre grinned conspiratorially. "A friend at the morgue owes us a favor: We got his son out of a big jam. The real morgue attendant is on his way over, but..." Andre looked at his wristwatch, "he won't be able to get here for another forty minutes. Traffic," he concluded, smiling collusively.

Nick nodded and turned his attention to the room, starting when he noticed Joey V. in the next room seated on the corner of the bed, holding his head and side with two of several blood-soaked towels.

Mack, all business, commanded, "Nick! Unzip the body bag on the gurney."

The three men then proceeded to layer the money from the sports bag and from inside the secret room into the body bag, leaving the drugs. Then they carefully helped Joey V. into the bag on top of the money.

At Mack's signal, Andre walked over to the bathroom and opened the door, careful to make certain the policeman and three agents would see Mack and Nick zip the bag up over Joey V.'s bloodied face. "Don't bleed on the money," Mack whispered as he finished zipping. Nick assumed position at the far end of the gurney and began pushing it towards the apartment door.

Mack called on the radiophone. "You're up," he said, the only one in the room who knew it was Botch on the other end, then assisted Nick and gurney out of the apartment.

Satisfied that the first part of the plan was going well, Mack returned, and walked over to the three cuffed agents. "I contacted your boss, Mr. Bartolata. He's on his way over, so I suggest you sit tight and think about what you're going to tell him."

"This is bullshit! You could have confirmed our names over the phone!" Gary claimed angrily.

"True," Mack replied, "but your boss said he didn't know anything about this investigation, and wanted to talk with you personally to see what you were doing here."

As Mack walked away, Rich turned to Gary: "Is it me, or do all these guys look familiar?"

Gary, Rich and Mike looked at Mack, then shrugged their shoulders, wary but uncertain, cautious not to say anything that might tighten the noose Mack had just placed around their collective heads by calling in Botch.

Downstairs, Nick exited the building and worked his way through the crowd, maneuvering the gurney into a plain, windowless, white van, closing the van's back doors behind the gurney. After getting in, Nick drove a couple of blocks to a prearranged place and stopped.

Botch appeared, opened the passenger door and climbed in while Nick worked his way into the back and unzipped the body bag.

Botch looked briefly into the back of the van, to be surprised by Joey V. gasping for air. "Are you guys fucking crazy? I could hardly breathe in that bag!"

Nick laughed apologetically, "Actually, I left it open a crack down near your feet—just enough to not let you suffocate or even more importantly be seen. You're supposed to be dead, you know."

Joey V. gasped again, "Well, you came damn close to succeeding at what all the others almost did to me!"

"Stop bitching," Botch retorted. "You're alive, man! And your prospects are a damn sight better than only a short time ago. So, where are the keys to your car, Joey?" Joey V. climbed out of the body bag, groaning wearily. "Toss me your car keys, Joey," Botch ordered.

Joey V. rummaged around in a pocket and a second later tossed the keys at Botch, telling him where the car was parked.

A sudden knocking on the front window of the truck caused all three to jump. Standing next to the driver's door was Mack, carrying a limp girl in his arms.

"Who's this?" Botch asked, annoyed at being caught off-guard.

"She was in the apartment when this all went down. I found her a minute ago, stunned, outside a neighboring building. I figured that when those three rogue agents are let loose, their first order of business would be to make sure she doesn't see morning. Of the two, she's the only creditable witness to the crime," Mack replied, nodding momentarily at Joey V.

Nick stared at her as Mack awkwardly removed the matted hair covering her face. The woman looked dead.

"What's wrong with her?" Nick asked.

"She keeps slipping in and out. She's obviously on something."

Botch jumped out of the truck and helped Mack deck the girl out on the bed of money Joey V. had just relinquished. Botch and Mack, after instructing Nick to watch her, then said goodbye and headed back to the scene of the crime together. Once upstairs and inside the apartment, Botch approached Andre as if he didn't know him. "I'm Senior FBI Agent Bartolata, Captain. You called me?" Botch said, flashing his identification badge.

"Sorry to bother you, Agent Bartolata, but are these your men?" Andre asked, pointing to the three cuffed agents staring at him from the bathroom with a mixture of hatred and fear. Botch looked them over. All three avoided making eye contact with their boss.

"Yes," he said slowly. "They're all FBI agents assigned to me. What happened and why are they in cuffs?"

"Follow me," Andre said, taking Botch on a quick tour of the chaotic scene, stopping in the bedroom doorway where he and Botch could be seen but not hear by the three rogue agents. Andre whispered, "Where are the 'good' agents you promised?"

"On their way. Should be here any moment," he whispered back.

Andre whispered again. "We got the cash, but left the drugs."

Botch smiled. "I saw the cash. My heart's still pounding."

In the bathroom, Gary was trying to persuade the officer guarding them into taking off the cuffs. "Hey, the man said we're with him," Gary offered. "So uncuff us."

The policeman looked across the room at his boss, Andre, huddled in conversation with Botch. "*My* boss didn't say shit about uncuffing you!" the officer returned irresolutely.

"Fuckin' shit," mumbled Gary, turning and wishing he knew what the Captain was telling his boss.

Mack had split away from Botch as soon as they had reached the third floor landing. Continuing up the stairs to the roof to investigate reports by the neighbors of some additional action, he found four more bodies. The Dominicans would have had no reason to kill the two girls and their own spotters, yet Mack, hardened as he was, couldn't bring himself to believe the three agents had done it in cold blood. Suddenly filled with remorse, Mack chided himself for not coming up with a better plan that might have somehow saved the two young girls who had died with the majority of their lives still before them.

After radioing for assistance, Mack walked sullenly back downstairs to the apartment and, walking in, stared at the three men huddled in the bathroom, resolving never to forget what they'd done. Then he shook his head and said to the guard, "Uncuff them."

CHAPTER 13

Andre nodded and echoed, "Release them," continuing louder so all could overhear: "I guess you'll be taking over the investigation from here?"

"Not me. This mess is theirs," Botch said, flicking his head at the three agents eagerly awaiting release.

Gary, hands freed, glared momentarily at Mack and growled in a low voice, "This isn't over yet."

Botch's face flushed, furious at what he'd just overheard. "Don't add more to your already long list of fuck ups, Agent Ross. I don't know how you're going to explain this mess. I sure as hell can't."

Gary, Mike and Rich gave Mack stares to kill as they pushed by him. Mack, in response, blew each a kiss. Mike and Rich together lunged towards Mack, but Gary stopped them in flight, diverting them back towards the apartment door. "Not now," he whispered, turning to Mack and finishing with an evil-looking grin: "Not *yet*."

Botch herded his three subordinates to the door. "So you want to tell me what happened, before I hear it at your disciplinary hearing?"

Gary, Mike and Rich stopped abruptly; Gary threw Botch a murderous look.

Andre signaled the policeman just inside the apartment door and the remaining policemen outside the apartment to leave the building. Botch looked back at the bodies lying about the apartment and barked, "So tell me, hot shots, what the fuck really happened here?"

Gary Ross took the lead: "We...ah...got a tip and had to jump on it. There wasn't time to call you."

"The *three* of you did *all* this?" Botch asked incredulously, sweeping an arm around the room.

"Yeah, well, things got ugly fast." Swallowing hard, Gary continued, "What happened was..."

"Actually, I don't want to know. Like I said, this is your mess. You deal with it. I don't want the stink to rub off on me. And when you get your story straight put it in writing on my desk."

Botch shook his head and walked out of the apartment building with Andre and Mack behind him, careful to leave the three rogue agents alone in the apartment. Searching the crowd, Botch identified the senior FBI agents he had called in. "Agents Ross, Smith and Pagano are upstairs. Apartment 3C. Just walk right in. You'll know what to do," Botch said without emotion.

Upstairs, Gary surveyed the apartment and finding no one living who might overhear, quickly closed the apartment door. "I thought Bartolata was never going to leave. Quick! Get the duffle bags!" Rich scrambled for the bags as Gary and Mike moved the sofa and removed the painting. Looking through the hole, all three could see, to their complete surprise, that all of the money was gone. Gary screamed, "Those God-damned, cock-sucking cops! But when? How? They weren't carrying anything with them when they left. Shit! Shit! Shit! There's no time! We'll figure it out later! At least, let's grab the fuckin' cocaine so we don't have to walk away empty-handed!"

While the three conspirators frantically loaded the bags of cocaine into the duffel bags, the two agents Botch had sent up pushed open the door. Aghast at what they were witnessing, the two FBI agents stood frozen, jaws dropped, unable to speak while the three FBI agents before them continued stuffing the duffle bags with millions of dollars of street-narcotics. The two agents in the doorway said, simultaneously, "Wow, looks like you guys hit the mother load!"

Gary, surprised, then incensed, yelled back, "What the hell are you doing walking in on a crime scene!"

The two agents, neither of them fans of Agent Ross, responded, "Bartolata told us to walk right in, so if you got an issue with that, take it up with him."

The second agent looked around and said, "Holy shit! Look at this! There's bodies everywhere."

Moments later, more FBI agents were dashing through the door and looking disbelievingly about the apartment. Gary, appalled at their new situation, whispered to Mike and Rich, "Shit! We can't even take the drugs now."

While Botch talked with the increasing number of FBI agents appearing just outside the apartment building, Mack and Andre continued walking down the block, finally tumbling into the back of Nick's "mortuary" van. Joey V. was whining, "Can you believe this? They fucked up my other ear! At least, this time, I got the piece to sew back on." Joey opened a folded Dixie cup and glumly showed Mack the bloody piece of his "good" ear in it. "That is, if you get me to a hospital like you promised," Joey added, refolding the cup after seeing the looks of revulsion all about him.

Andre frowned. "You're supposed to be dead."

Joey V. frowned and, feigning deafness, asked Mack, "What did he say?"

Mack grabbed the Dixie cup from Joey's hand, unfolded it and yelled into it, "He said, 'Shut up, asshole'!"

Joey V. stared at Mack, then shook his head. "That's not funny, Mack."

"Joey, where's your car?" Mack asked, looking out the van's windshield as if expecting it to appear on command.

"Down the block, but your buddy, Botch, has the keys."

Mack thought a moment, then said to Nick, "Drive down the block."

Nick started the van and Mack climbed into the passenger seat. "There it is!" Mack said with a smile, pointing at the car as it began to appear. "I'd know that heap of Bondo anywhere."

Joey V. winced and, with his hand, protectively covered the shreds of what had been his good ear that were now laying in the bottom of the cup. "That hurts, Mack. It really does."

Nick pulled behind the car and stopped, while Mack attempted to contact Botch on his cell phone. "Botch?"

"Yeah?"

"It's Mack. You got Joey V.'s keys?"

"Yeah. And I can see you from where I am. Be right there."

Joey V. asked, "Why did he want my keys?"

Mack removed the bag of Sweaters' money from the body bag with the girl and the Dominicans' money in it. "To double check, just in case you tried a switch and left the real one with the money in the car. You didn't, so now we've got to get your car out of here in order to cover your ass. Like Andre said, you're supposed to be dead."

"There's a problem," Joey V. replied solemnly.

"What's that?"

"Dom and Sal are in the backseat, dead, and Twisted Ray is cuffed to them." "Ray's alive?" Mack asked, surprised, his facial muscles tensing.

"Last I saw him, he was." Joey V. replied, looking sadly at his car.

Mack and Joey V. heard the echoing clack of familiar footsteps against pavement and climbed out of the van, waiting while the silhouette of the person approached, and, moments later, became Botch. Botch held the keys to Joey V.'s car between his outstretched fingers as if they were spoiled food. "Here they are. Now let's get out of here," he said, tossing the keys in a silvery arc to Mack who caught them in mid-air.

"We have a little problem," Mack said and then told Botch about Ray and the two bodies.

Botch gave Mack a confirmatory look, "Yeah, I know! They were supposed to be left at Enzo's. Now *we'll* have to dump them—and fast," he added, "before anyone becomes the wiser."

Mack turned to the van and motioned for Nick to drive on. "See you at the bar, son."

Nick and Andre drove off in the van with the cash and the girl, while Botch continued: "First, let's make sure Ray is still out."

In the back seat of Joey V.'s car, Mack, Botch and Joey V. could just make out Ray, in the center, still covered by the blanket, moaning and threatening, "Someone's going to lose their family for this. I swear it! I swear it!"

Mack looked from Joey V. to Botch. "He's coming out of it. We need a club or something."

Botch nodded, turned, and started walking back towards his car across the street. Joey V., in the meantime, opened the passenger door to his car, took out the baseball bat and struck the groaning body beneath the blanket until, freshly bloodied, the body beneath the blanket went flaccid and silent.

Mack watched Joey V. vent his pent-up rage on the man who had planned to do the same to Joey V. before putting a bullet in Joey's head. Mack called out to Botch, "Forget it!" then continued, "Hey, Botch! I didn't know that was your car? I thought yours was the one over there." Mack pointed to another nondescript federal car parked further down the block.

"No, that's Agent Ross's car," Botch replied. "We all get the same model and color; you know the government."

"Can you guys get serious for a moment and talk about the cars later? Man, I got to get my ear fixed!" Joey V. interrupted.

Mack suddenly fell silent, then rummaged through his pants' pockets. "Wait," he said pulling out a set of car keys. "I took Gary's keys from his pocket when I frisked him. I figured it would provide us a bit more time to get away. Give me a hand!"

Using Botch's master handcuff key, the three freed Ray from Sal & Dom, and, rolling Ray in the blanket, transferred him into the trunk of Joey V.'s Impala. Then they hauled the bodies of Sal and Dom out of Joey V.'s car and transferred them into the trunk of Gary's agency car. Mack, between breaths, explained, "Something more for them to explain. I'll see you back at the bar after I dump Ray off at Enzo's and take Joey somewhere private to get his ear fixed."

CHAPTER 14

After assisting the other agents with the investigation while at the same time attempting to cover up their own involvement, FBI Agents Ross, Smith and Pagano walked in single file down the stairs and across the street. Gathering his companions closely around the company car, Gary, dumbfounded, asked, "What the fuck happened? We had the money practically in our hands until the local cops showed up. It was ours! Ours! We earned it!"

Mike sighed, "How could we have known? I mean how the fuck did *they* know? And how did they pull off whatever it was they pulled off?"

"This isn't over. We just got to figure it out," replied Gary, pulsing with righteous anger.

Rich's feelings were darker. "Yeah. Well, here's another twist…"

"What?" Gary rudely interrupted.

"Where's Joey V.'s car and the bodies?" Rich asked. "In this neighborhood they'll steal the fillings out of your teeth if you're caught napping."

"Shit, you're right!" exclaimed Gary, scanning the area futilely, while avidly turning out every pocket for the keys to their own car. "Well, if someone's taken it, they're going to be surprised when they look in the backseat!" Gary added half-heartedly. "This whole night doesn't make sense. And damn it! Where are my keys?"

Staring through the driver's window, he suddenly spotted them in the ignition. "I can't believe I left the keys in the car! By all rights, they should have taken this one, too!"

Mike opened the unlocked back door and got in. "Who would want this piece of shit? Besides, it's a government car—with government plates—and anyone with half a brain would likely recognize it as such and leave it alone," he remarked.

"I don't know," muttered Gary as he climbed into the driver's seat. Rich slammed the front passenger door and settled in beside Gary.

"It feels to me like we're caught in someone else's play," Rich added.

"I say we get out of here while we can," responded Gary, "We can work it all out in the morning."

CHAPTER 15

Mack drove Joey V.'s car, Joey V. sitting next to him and Twisted Ray stowed in the trunk. "Do you still want to go to the hospital?" Mack asked.

"Yeah, man. I mean, I don't want to end up looking like some kinda' freak!"

Joey V. looked sadly into the Dixie cup and suddenly realized the piece of his ear was missing. Frantically searching the seat, the creases and finally the floor, he yelled, "Un-fucking-believable!"

"What?" asked Mack, looking worriedly at his half-crazed passenger.

"I lost my ear!"

Mack pulled over. "Maybe it's just as well. The longer everyone thinks you're dead, the better. Sweaters would eventually find out if we went to a hospital anywhere in New York City."

Joey V. agreed reluctantly, then changed the subject to something more hopeful. "So, Mack. How did you know this deal was going down tonight?"

Mack cleared his throat. "I heard on the street something big was going on and your name kept coming up. That's why Andre and I bugged your car."

"I really believed those three FBI agents were legit. Hell, I bet my life on it!"

Mack nodded. "I know. Good thing we showed up when we did or you'd actually be dead. Put some music on in case our 'friend' in the back wakes up. I don't want him overhearing anything."

Joey V. turned on the radio and cranked up the volume. "Hey, I love this song!" Mack listened. The melody carried him back to a time when he and Joey V. were kids on a joyride in the country. Mack squinted, searching his brain for the name of the singer. "I know this guy's voice but I can't get it."

A genuine smile spread across Joey V.'s pained and careworn face. "I'll bet you a grand you can't remember his name."

"You're on!" Mack shouted, refocusing his attention on listening.

"You got to get it before the song ends," Joey V. added with mock seriousness.

"Yeah, yeah," Mack acquiesced, struggling harder to remember. "Wait! Wait! I know it! It's the guy from Talking Heads. Ahhh...David Byrne!"

"Damn, you're good!"

"Can't see him ever doing opera, but I've always loved his sound."

"I can't believe I owe you a grand," Joey V. mumbled, looking morosely into the empty Dixie cup.

Mack looked compassionately over at Joey V. "Get me a copy of the CD and we'll call it even, buddy."

Joey V. stared at his re-found friend. "Consider it done, Mack," he said with affection.

Mack laughed, remembering a game he and Joey V. used to play when working for Sweaters. In dangerous situations, Mack would stick out his right hand, fingers spread, palm down, to show Joey V. that it wasn't shaking. Eventually it became a contest. *Metal or Nerves* Joey V used to call it.

Joey laughed. "I couldn't beat you back then, and I still can't now," he said, placing his hand next to Mack's. *Damn! Not even the slightest shake*, Joey V. thought, staring at Mack's steady hand next to his own flapping like a just-caught fish. "PTSD, my ass! You still got ice in your veins, Mack."

Mack thought about that. *Between 'Nam and working homicide, I've grown so thick a skin hardly anything can rattle me anymore.*

Joey V. broke the reverie: "Watch out, Mack!"

Staring blankly at their side-by-side hands, Mack had forgotten the road. Jerking the steering wheel to the right to avoid a head-on collision with a honking, oncoming car, Mack felt a rush of never-completely-forgotten combat adrenaline ablaze in his veins. "*That* was as close to being rattled as I've been in a while," Mack exclaimed.

Joey V. snorted. "You still drive like shit."

Mack laughed nervously, and, finding his hand shaking, retrieved it and changed the subject: "So what are you going to do now, Joey?"

"I...I don't know," Joey V. stammered, suddenly somber. "Nothing's turning out like I expected. I thought I would be in the FBI Witness Protection Program by now, starting a new life. There were several times I was certain I was going to die. Now I don't know what to think."

"Well, you got one thing working for you, Joey: No one outside of our little group knows you're alive, not Sweaters, not those agents. You could run anytime you wish, and none of them would know you were gone."

"I don't know, Mack. Sweaters won't believe I'm dead until he kicks my dead body. Besides where would I go? I promised my family a new home, a new job, a new life. I can't do that by myself, and I'd always have to be looking over my shoulder. Not enough scratch to make it all happen, Mack."

Mack smiled. "Well, as it turns out, I've come into a little money."

Joey jumped on the remark. "Funny. You know, I was just thinking about all that money, too."

"Whoa, boy," Mack retorted. "Slow down a minute. Remember that *we* just stuck our necks out and saved *your* sorry ass."

"Hey, Mack, I had to give it a shot!" Joey V. blurted out, sorry he'd responded so quickly, hoping Mack wouldn't take offense. "But you *were* about to offer me something, right?"

"I was, but it will require you to do a little job for me."

"How much and how little? And for God's sake, please don't tell me I have to kill Sweaters to get it."

"No, but I'd appreciate it if you could deliver a 'physical' message to someone else for me." Joey listened attentively, eyes wide. "You've heard of Amazing Jones?"

"The quarterback for the Jets?"

Mack sighed, "No, Amazing Jones, my sister. Joey, you moron, how many people can there be in New York City with a name like that?"

"None except him, but I do know your sister," Joey V. taunted, smiling and rubbing his crotch.

"Funny. Real funny. Anyway, Jones and Andre's daughter, Tina, are a couple, and Andre's found out the guy's been slapping the shit out of her."

"Get out of here! And Andre hasn't killed the guy yet?"

Mack's eyebrows raised. "That's the point. If Andre had a go at him, it'd likely get emotional and Amazing would end up dead. I'm trying to get this taken care of for Andre, and I don't want *anyone* dead. Especially not now! I also don't want Tina to hear about it and trace it back to Andre."

"What do you want. How bad a beating? You want a finger or something?"

"He's still a kid, Joey. I just want to smarten him up."

"No problem! I'd have to bring in my cousin or brother, though. It'd take more than just me to do a job on an athlete like Amazing. My cousin and brother are the only ones I can trust with knowing I'm still alive." After a pause, Joey V. added, "I have to admit: I won't mind doing the job. I hate the obnoxious bastard, really. When he's not the center of attention, he's the rich, spoiled little brat—well, not so little really at six-foot-five. So when do I do it? It'll have to be quick. I don't like fucking with someone I can't beat up or outrun. Does Andre know about your plan?"

"No. I'd rather tell him when it's over…and the time's right."

Joey V. nodded. "Consider it done. And, by the way, how does it feel getting back at Sweaters after all these years? You've been waiting for a long time."

Mack shrugged his shoulders. "Getting him back? What are you talking about?"

"Hey, I know all about the shit he has on you."

"Seriously, I don't know what you're talking about, Joey."

Joey V. blurted out, "You know…the tape? Of Annie?"

"Leave that alone!" Mack growled, as all-too-familiar feelings of anger and hopelessness flooded him.

"Hey, no problem," Joey V. said timidly. "Just wanted you to know."

As he drove on, Mack tried not to think about what Joey V. had said, but couldn't stop the memories and reluctantly fell into reliving the incident yet again in gruesome detail.

CHAPTER 16

While Mack worked for Sweaters, he was careful to keep the fact that he, Andre and Botch planned to become cops from the mobster. Mack slowly lost his mean edge as memories of the war faded, though neither entirely went away. He soon had a beautiful wife, Annie, and a young son. Life was starting to make sense again.

Sweaters was, however, not ignorant of Mack's changing demeanor, or, later, of Mack's interest in becoming a police officer. Still, as outraged as Sweaters was at first, he couldn't get permission from his bosses to take Mack out. The consensus from above was that Mack represented, at the least, a source of inside information, and, if handled right, a future paid informant. Knowing Mack as he did, Sweaters didn't share his bosses' hopes for Mack, and would become furious at the mere mention of Mack's name. Mack had betrayed him and Sweaters wanted revenge. After some years, Sweaters finally got it.

Mack served as a narcotics detective before moving to homicide, which put him on an even faster track for a head-on collision with Sweaters, their delicate truce becoming a little *too* delicate. Initially, Mack carefully avoided going after Sweaters, because of possible repercussions, should Sweaters reveal their past association. Sweaters, on the other hand, was spending more and more time figuring out ways to make Mack's life miserable. It was at this point that Mack decided enough was enough.

Mack had been watching the Bronx become hell. Despite Mack's best efforts, friend after friend was being turned into a junkie, their women being forced into prostitution to pay for the habit. Everyday people's savings were being wiped out, and life in the Bronx seemed increasingly flavored with an omnipresent undertone of murder. And all of it, in Mack's mind, was linked to one man: Sweaters, who now lived in a private, well-guarded mansion in the Hamptons.

Mack had stared death in the face in 'Nam and he wasn't afraid of Sweaters.

He put in increasing hours at the station and on the street to put Sweaters away, but, with Sweaters' ever-growing resources, Mack could never make anything stick. The "game" quickly escalated into an obsession, and that's when it began affecting his marriage.

Mack loved Annie as much as a man like him could, and knew it was becoming progressively tougher for her to put up with the always present threat of the death of her husband, herself and, most importantly, their son. Mack had decided that after he nailed Sweaters, the threat would disappear and he could make everything right again with Annie. In fact, Mack, in one instance, came within an inch of nabbing Sweaters and that's when Mack's life caved in.

On that fateful morning, Mack woke late for work. He had to rush to get ready, throwing on a wrinkled shirt and tie as he ran to his car and started it up. Turning on the radio, a loud voice boomed out, momentarily startling him: "Hello, Mack!" Mack jammed on the brakes and fidgeted with the radio/tape player, trying to place who's voice it was, having heard it before. An unmarked cassette popped out.

Pushing it back in after inspecting it carefully and finding nothing that hinted as to the speaker, he heard, "I'm sure by now you recognize your old friend's voice." He did. It was Jerry Sweaters. The message went on. "I've left a gift for you in the glove box. I'm tiring of playing cat and mouse, Mack, so now the next move is yours. Either you back off, or everyone you know—your precinct, your friends, your wife, your son—will all get a gift like the one in your glove compartment. I only hope it will move you as much as it moved me in its making."

Mack reached over and opened the glove box. From the size and shape of the brown paper package, it could only be a video tape. Mack's stomach tightened. He pulled the car to the curb, turned it off, and ran back to the house. His first thought was that Annie had been kidnapped when she left for work earlier that morning.

Mack ran downstairs into the living room and, ripping off the brown paper cover, shoved the tape into the VCR. The TV lit up and began spewing out the "Good Morning Show." The VCR had accepted the tape, but for some reason, wouldn't play it.

Cursing, he ripped off the black duct tape that he had placed over the flashing "12:00PM" and began pressing buttons. Nothing appeared on the TV screen, though the tape *was* playing. Then he remembered he had to switch from TV to VCR. The moment he did, an amateurish picture of the interior of a dingy motel room appeared. The picture jerked back and forth around the room and then focused on a door. The door opened, and what he saw made him feel like he had been kneed in the groin. Disgusted, yet mesmerized, he watched his wife, Annie, giggling as she walked out of the bathroom, clad only in a black bra and panties, a naked man walking immediately behind her, undoing her bra. She stopped and waited while the bra dropped and the man behind her began fondling her breasts and kissing her on the neck. Mack strained to see who the man was, as the man proceeded to pull down her panties, which she kicked up into the air with a foot, laughing all the while. Then the two fell together onto the motel bed. The picture zoomed in on Annie, oblivious to the fact that she was being filmed, happily turning around to face her lover and ride him. Mack, heartbroken, turned off the VCR, fully aware that the man was not him.

Dry-retching, he hit the eject button once, then several more times, but this time the malevolent VCR wouldn't eject the tape. Then the rage hit. Mack grabbed the VCR with both hands, ripped it from its connections and threw it towards the wall. The VCR arced short, hit the floor instead and skidded across the room. Mack ran over to the still-intact player and ripped the tape out of the broken machine, then kicked in the VCR and TV set, stormed upstairs, grabbed some clothes from his and Annie's bedroom closet, and never returned. It had happened four years ago, but it still hurt like it was happening again.

Mack never told Annie why he left, wanting to spare her the humiliation. He still loved her, but now he also hated her. Not letting her know why he had abruptly left was the only way he knew to have her feel some of the hurt he felt without embarrassing her with the details.

He never went after Sweaters, refusing to put Annie and his son through what Sweaters had threatened. Sweaters would quietly hold the tape over him, realizing at the same time that, from that day forward, Mack would ruthlessly hunt him, and if Sweaters ever revealed the tape, would gladly kill him. Mack promised himself that when he retired, and Annie and Nick moved on, he would get his revenge. But not until then.

Mack did some investigating and eventually tracked down Annie's lover on the tape. The man was a lanky, randy, con-artist who swindled single, elderly ladies out of their life savings by exactly this *modus operandi*. Sweaters had used the man in a couple of his porn movies. Mack tracked him down to a small studio apartment in Jersey and together, Mack and Andre broke down the door, catching the felon filming a scene of himself having sex with an underage girl, ostensibly for yet another of Sweaters' porn films. Mack and Andre told the frightened girl to get dressed and leave, then beat the man into a coma. Mack never knew if he lived or died, but if he lived, they had made certain he would be in a wheelchair and unable to enjoy sex again.

Mack stared out the window deep in thought, remembering in painfully exquisite detail that particular chain of events in his life which he was always trying to forget. Then he snapped out of the grisly reverie to Joey V.'s continued talking.

"I know who can get you the original tape," Joey whispered.

Mack turned to Joey V. "What?"

Joey V. motioned with his thumb towards the trunk of the car. "That piece of shit in the back. He knows everything Sweaters is into. You would have to motivate him. The prick laughed when Sweaters threatened to put *my* daughter in one of his porn movies. Ray has a daughter of his own in college. I wonder how funny he would think it was if he thought Sweaters was contemplating doing the same to his daughter?"

Mack nodded slowly, "Right. What's her name? Lori? Lucy? Hard to believe, she's already in college. Shit, I'm getting old," Mack's voice trailed out into silence.

"How long has it been since you and Annie talked?" Joey chanced. "I mean talked *civilly*?"

"Oh, we're quite civil these days, but we haven't really spoken the whole four years. She's given up asking why I left. Nick still asks, and I keep putting him off."

"God, it seems like a hundred years ago when Annie started hanging around you," Joey V. reflected, watching Mack's face carefully. "You were coming out of your 'Nam funk and starting to enjoy life again."

Mack nodded listlessly. "You know what's really funny, Joey? In the beginning I think she liked you better than me."

"I thought the same thing, until she started putting me off. I mean all she would say was 'Bye'."

Mack laughed and confessed, "Hell, I guess I can tell you now…"

"What did you do?" Joey V. asked, enjoying drawing out the hurting friend who had so recently saved his life.

"I made a deal with Rose."

"You mean Rose, before she became my wife?" Joey V. asked, eyes widening.

Mack laughed, "One and the same, my earless friend. So anyway, Rose liked you, and she knew I liked Annie since I was a kid—ever since Annie defended me from Tiny's sister. Our paths didn't cross after that for years, but I never forgot her. Well, Rose and I decided to put an end to you and Annie as a couple before it got started." Joey V. smiled, listening to Mack baring his heart. "I had Rose go over and tell Annie a very, very, very, *very* crude joke, saying that you were spreading it around making Annie as the butt of the joke.

Joey V. asked, "Alright, what was the joke?"

"It's an old one: Why did God give women yeast infections?"

Joey V. grinned, "Yeah, I remember that one: So that they can know what it's like to live with an annoying cunt."

Mack frowned. "The joke was bad, but when you use what women refer to as the 'C' word, you're dead in their eyes. I've seen women who can curse like truckers cringe when they hear that word applied to themselves or other women."

Joey V. shook his head, "You sure cock-blocked me with her. Hell, you always did find a way to get what you wanted. The funny part is that if I had known you liked her so much, I would have stayed away. I mean, you were just as sick a bastard back then as you are now. Everyone knew not to stand in your way."

Mack shrugged. "Desperate times call for desperate measures. I figured if I told you I liked her, you might move in on her quicker. I just wanted a chance with her." Mack stared out the window, the soft, faraway look in his eyes broadcasting how much he still loved the woman.

"Will you ever forgive her?" Joey V. asked softly.

"To be honest, I don't know. Besides, a lot of time has passed. After what she and I've been through, I don't think she'd be interested in my bullshit anymore. The thing is, I find it hard now to trust *any* woman, so to trust the woman that made me feel that way seems like a lot to ask of both of us. Let's just drop it," Mack finally growled.

"Fine with me, Mack. So here's a more timely question for you: What do we do with Twisted Ray?"

Mack's face strained as if he were deep in thought. "You said something interesting earlier: 'How would he like it if it was his daughter?' I could kill Sweaters but he's a made man and the mob always gets its revenge so, instead, I want to see him suffer, and that means, to have him watch his empire crumble."

"Then first we should begin by losing Ray," Joey V. suggested.

"You're right. And Enzo's *was* the last place he was conscious," Mack added, turning the car abruptly at the next intersection.

Number One Bestseller

CHAPTER 17

The night was still strong when Joey V. rechecked the shirt he'd wrapped around his head and what little was left of his 'good' ear. "Hopefully the cops haven't found Buddha's body yet."

"Good point," Mack reflected.

A moment later they pulled cautiously in back of Enzo's. The parking lot was emptier than earlier, but there were still cars. The night owls inside would likely be nursing a last *cappuccino* with their *tiramisu*.

Mack and Joey got out of the car and walked around to the trunk. Opening it, Mack sighed. Twisted Ray was still out cold. Rummaging through Ray's pockets, he found the man's wallet and pulled out a picture of what could only be Ray's daughter. Palming the photo, Mack enlisted Joey V.'s help to drag Twisted Ray's body out of the trunk and dump it into the dumpster on top of Buddha's lifeless body.

Getting back into the car, Mack pulled out from Enzo's parking lot, checking constantly to make sure they hadn't been noticed.

Joey V., holding his aching head, asked, "So what's the picture for?"

"What's the one thing that can pit Ray against Sweaters?" Mack asked, in his next breath answering his own question. "His family, especially his daughter. I hate to stoop this low, but what if we had a sex tape of Ray's daughter and led Ray to believe that Sweaters made it?"

"*That* could start a war," Joey V. mused.

"Actually, the more I think about it, the sicker it sounds. Sorry I brought it up," Mack quickly added.

"Why?" Joey V. asked.

"Because the girl is innocent," Mack replied disgustedly.

Joey V. grimaced, then looked pensively over his shoulder out the passenger window. "You're right, of course. But think of all the lives these guys have ruined, and all the ones they're going to ruin in the future if they're not brought down." Joey V. gazed back at Mack with a determined look in his eyes.

Mack frowned, "I know, but it still doesn't sit right with me."

Joey V. shrugged his shoulders. "Hey, only a few of us would ever know about the tape. We're not going to broadcast it on the internet. When we get the desired results, we can destroy the tape. You know: desperate times."

Ten minutes later Mack and Joey V. were pulling up to the back lot of Farrell's Bar. "Joey, you should let your wife, Rose, know you're alive and that she probably won't see you for a couple of days."

"That won't go over well."

Mack laughed "Hell, Joey, she's probably already out cashing in your insurance policy."

After waiting a few minutes to be sure there was no one around, they got out of the car and wound their way through the night shadows to the back of the bar. Mack knocked his "secret" late-night knock. Botch answered.

Opening the door conspiratorially, Botch hesitated when he saw Joey V. standing behind Mack. Mack knew Botch wouldn't be pleased that he'd brought Joey V. and everything stopped while the three thought about what should happen next.

"Come on," Mack finally said. "What was I supposed to do?"

Botch reluctantly nodded, then opened the door for the two, staring angrily at Joey V. as the man walked past, mumbling, "I could come up with a few ideas."

Joey V. stopped to stare back at Botch. "Is there a problem?"

Not wanting to wait for Botch's answer, Mack nudged Joey V. the rest of the way inside. "Don't worry," Mack whispered to Joey V. as they walked into the back room of the bar. "Let me handle it."

Andre was sitting on a bar stool, counting out the stacks of money that they had successfully lifted earlier. Botch slid in to one side of the table reserved for Mack and his friends, and grabbed some money from the open body bag spread out on the table. Counting allowed him to ignore Joey V. altogether.

"How's the ear?" Andre asked without looking up.

"Don't ask. I lost the piece I had."

Mack looked around hastily, then turned to Botch. "Where's Nick?"

"In the kitchen with the girl. I think he's in love."

Mack breathed a sigh of relief. "So how did we do?"

"I'm happy enough. Doing the resort with Tommy Chang in the Canaries is out, though," Andre responded.

Mack's face twisted with surprise and disappointment. "Really? Why?"

"There are a lot of fifties and twenties, so it's most likely going to come to about four million." Andre swung around to face Mack. "And that includes the million from Sweaters."

Botch shook his head. "Close, but short."

"I always seem to come up 'close but short' of my dreams," Mack replied, running a hand through his hair downheartedly. Then he shrugged. "Well, at least we have enough for a good retirement."

"Definitely beats waiting for an SSI check." Andre added, smiling.

Botch raised his eye brows: "Not that there'd be anything left in Social Security to collect."

Joey V. gave a snort of disgust. "You guys just break my heart. Where's the bathroom?"

"Down the hall and to your right," Andre returned, trying his best not to laugh at the total inanity of their situation.

Mack looked at his friends, then walked into the kitchen. "Hey, Nick. How is she?" he asked, spotting the two together in a corner.

"She's scared, but I think she'll be okay. Her name is Shelby."

"Did you get through to her that she shouldn't go home for awhile? It's probably not safe."

Shelby looked up at Mack and said with attitude, "You can talk to me directly if you want. I speak English. I'm an American citizen. Just because I'm dark-skinned, don't assume…

"Whoa! Easy, sister," Mack interrupted with frank disdain. "It isn't that at all. I was worried about you still being stoned out of your face and not understanding clearly."

Shelby stood up, shifted her weight to one leg, thrust out a hip and looked Mack directly in the eyes: "I'm a student at John Jay College, not some crack-whore, if you're wondering. I was telling your son, Nick, here—who obviously doesn't get his open-mindedness from his father—that I went out for a couple of drinks at a downtown club with a classmate. She told me later in the ladies' room that she had met a guy and was going on to another club with him. I felt tired and decided to go home. I returned to the bar and finished my drink. That's when everything gets fuzzy. I remember a fat guy arguing with the bouncer.

"The fat man was claiming I was his sister. I think I tried to object, but I felt so woozy and my mouth so cottony, the words wouldn't come out. Next thing I knew, the room started spinning and the fat man grabbed me. I couldn't talk or walk. I think he told the bouncer I was underage and that he was going to sue them.

"The next thing I remember was lying in that apartment trying to fight off one of those animals—the one trying to take my dress off while the rest laughed. I somehow pushed him off and in the process fell onto the couch. I knew it was only a matter of seconds before I would pass out again. Then—I can't believe I'm saying this—thank God, those three other guys came in and started shooting. My relief, however, immediately changed to horror. I thought for sure they were going to kill me, too. So I made a run for it, figuring a quick death would be better than a long, slow one with them having their way with me, at least, that was until you guys showed up. To think I was originally planning on staying home, but was worried I might miss out on something..."

Mack listened at first, eventually giving up trying to decide if she was telling the truth, or if he even cared. "They probably slipped a drug in your drink. You girls should learn to never leave a drink unattended. Finish it or dump it—it's the only safe way. But whatever, it wouldn't be smart to go home tonight, Sharon."

"Shelby!" Nick and Shelby chorused defensively.

"Who were they? I mean the second bunch?" Shelby interjected, curiosity replacing her fear.

"They're three extremely dangerous men who think you can identify them," Mack said matter-of-factly.

Nick addressed Shelby softly, "You should let your classmate, and any family" adding awkwardly, "or boyfriends," finishing his sentence with, "know you're okay."

Shelby looked into Nick's eyes and smiled sweetly. "My family is in Pennsylvania, and not expecting to hear from me till next weekend. My classmate..."

Mack watched, ashamed at how desperate his son Nick looked sitting on the edge of his seat hovering over Shelby's every word, waiting expectantly to hear what she would say about a boyfriend. When she didn't, he cut Nick off from inquiring again. "Shelby! You hungry?"

Shelby started to answer in the affirmative, but Mack interrupted again. "Nick will go get you something, won't you, Nick?" Mack, ordering more than asking, turned abruptly and returned to the bar area.

Shelby, mouth agape and wordless, finally blurted out, "Straight to the point, your father."

"When he's trying to work out something in his mind, he can be rather curt. Otherwise he never shuts up," offered Nick. Shelby nodded and took a seat across from Nick.

"How about your mother? She still around?" Shelby asked, crossing one bare leg over another suggestively, watching to see Nick's reaction.

"They split up. The funny thing is, they were always great together, then one day they weren't. I never found out what happened, and I've given up trying to guess. Well, almost," Nick added, suddenly aware that he had been staring at her legs while talking. Nick stood, moved to the stove and began preparing breakfast.

Shelby swung her comely legs towards him and smiled, "Sounds like my parents, except the part about 'great together.' Fact is, my mother moved to Florida and left my father to raise me."

Nick was cooking omelets. Shelby watched his every move with interest. When the omelets began firming up, Nick yelled back to the men in the bar inquiring if they wanted some breakfast.

They yelled back in unison, "No!"

Shelby adjusted her dress. "I would get up and help you, but I'm not a hundred percent yet," she said.

Nick joked, "Let's be honest, here. You're a princess and you thought the stove in your kitchen was just a big cigarette lighter. I know your type."

Shelby smiled. "Actually, I'm a great cook. Remember, I'm part Italian," but she continued watching rather than helping. Nick tried to impress her by flipping one of the omelets into the air, both without success.

"I can't watch this anymore," Shelby groaned, got up, lost her balance, recovered and then lost it completely. Nick caught her gallantly in mid-fall.

"You see!" she said, looking up appreciatively into his eyes. "You didn't believe me! I'm still weak. Bring me over to the lighter—I mean stove," she joked, "and I'll give you a few pointers."

Nick slipped his arms around Shelby's waist and steadied her in front of the stove. "What did you expect? I'm Irish. Food to us is something to soak up alcohol."

Nick kept his arms around Shelby as she took over the cooking. In minutes, they were sitting at a steel prep table, eating together, talking, laughing and exchanging stories. The food helped Shelby feel more like herself.

Actually, she had been on her own in New York City for some time, and was finally beginning to make the adjustment—learning to become wary of anyone she didn't know well. The strange thing was how comfortable she was feeling around this total stranger, Nick. Things were happening fast—too fast, really—and she wanted to make sure she wasn't being held hostage again, this time by Nick's disarmingly smooth talk or that arrogant father of his.

"Nick," she said suddenly, "I appreciate all you, your father and his friends have done for me. I owe you my life, really, but I don't know anything about who you are and I'd like to go home now, please."

Nick could see the tears welling. "Whatever you want. I'll make you a deal. You can go home, but only if you let me take you."

Shelby smiled and sniffled, brushing the corners of her mascara-streaked eyelids dry. "Deal."

"Hey, dad!" Nick yelled.

Mack answered with a grunt from the other room.

"I'm taking Shelby home!"

Silence. Then Mack's familiar, gruff voice shot back through the air, but with a decidedly apprehensive edge to it: "Nick, I'm not..."

Nick, unsure if his father heard him correctly, took Shelby's hand and walked with her to the doorway, careful not to provide her a view of the end of the bar, where the three men would be busily counting the money. Mack stood up nervously, signaling to Nick to stop where he was and not bring her any further in.

"I don't think they got that good a look at her, what with her doped up and all the shooting. She'll be safe enough at her home tonight, don't you think?" asked Nick.

"I can't force her to stay here," Mack blurted out, hiding the stacks of bills behind his body. "Actually we could," Botch offered, looking from Nick to the partial outline of the woman clinging to Nick, and then back to Mack. "But, of course, we won't."

"Like I said, I don't recommend it, but if she's determined, then call a cab and escort her there," Mack ordered, staring at Nick and Shelby's enjoined hands, then darkly at Shelby as she emerged from the shadows, "and for God's sake, Nick, keep her in the kitchen!" As Nick and Shelby retreated, Mack continued. "When the cab gets here, take her to the back entrance to her apartment, if it has one, and wait to make sure she's safe. Then take the cab back here right away." He reached blindly behind him, then walked over to Nick, and offered his son a hundred-dollar bill from the foot-high pile of money he had been counting.

Botch frowned. "Our money's already dwindling."

Andre laughed. "Shut up and control your inner Jew."

Nick looked his father in the eye. "Maybe I won't be back 'right away'."

Mack rolled his eyes. "Whatever! Just be careful. If you stay at her place, keep your cell phone handy."

Nick scooped Shelby back into his arms and waved over his shoulder to the three men as he left. "See you later."

Andre and Botch made a loud smooching noise, then yelled so Shelby and Nick couldn't help but overhear, "Bye, bye, lover boy."

CHAPTER 18

Nick called the cab while Shelby fixed her makeup using the stainless steel door of the bar's commercial refrigerator as a mirror. Nick started to ask her a question, then paused, and instead watched her make herself up, fascinated.

"Ready?" he inquired after she'd finished. "The cab should be here by now."

"You know, Nick, I can't help but notice that your father and his friends are always joking no matter how serious the situation."

"That's them: The more serious, the more jokes. It's like a perpetual contest. I don't know if it's a 'Nam thing or them all being in law enforcement together. Either way, it's a 'never let them see you sweat' attitude."

"I get it," Shelby said, tossing her hair. "A macho thing. Well, I'd like to thank Mr. Macho for saving my life. I know I was a little short with him."

"Yeah, well, you heard him. He's kind of busy right now. You can thank him the next time you see him."

Shelby smiled. That was what she wanted to hear. It was tantamount to an admission that *Nick* wanted to see her again.

When the cab finally pulled up to Shelby's apartment building, Shelby nodded a quick, "Thank you," to Nick, smiled and, placing one hand on the door handle and the other on the seat, prepared to exit. Nick grasped her free hand, and asked her to wait a moment. Shelby paused, directing soft, doe-eyes back at him. "My father suggested I stay with...watch over you...for the night." Nick blurted out.

Shelby peered at him, slightly askance, while running her hand through her long hair. "You're so full of shit!" she said, relaxing back into the seat.

Nick involuntarily blushed. "It's true."

"Yeah...well...right. After the day I've been though, I don't want to be alone, so why don't you come on up with me, 'big boy,' and 'watch over me'."

Inside Shelby's darkened apartment, FBI Agent Rich Pagano heard the cab pull up and peeked carefully out the curtained window. He recognized the woman from the Dominicans' apartment exiting the cab. He slipped out his gun and screwed on a silencer. It needed to be quiet and quick. He hid himself, gun at ready, to the left of the apartment door, waiting for the woman to enter. It hadn't taken him that long to locate the woman's apartment, having her wallet in hand, and Gary wanted her eliminated.

Downstairs, Shelby exited the taxi and entered the vestibule of the building, Nick immediately behind her. Shelby started walking up the marble steps to the second door of the building, then turned towards Nick and said, "Don't think you're going to get lucky tonight."

Nick turned and pretended to walk dejectedly down the stairs. "Have a nice night," he mumbled.

Shelby stared in disbelief. "Hey…"

Nick ran back up the stairs two steps at a time. "Gottcha!" he said, stopping inches from her. "You should see your face," he added, with an ear-to-ear smile.

Shelby closed her open mouth, "Well, if there was the slightest chance you *might* have gotten lucky, there's certainly none now."

Nick frowned, "That's not funny, Shelby."

It was Shelby's turn to laugh. "Now who's got who?" she said, brushing the side of his face with her fingers. Both stared longingly into the other's eyes, waiting for the other to make the next move.

Shelby suddenly started rummaging around in her handbag. "Great! My keys are missing. Shit, so is my wallet!"

"You saved your makeup but not your wallet or keys?" Nick half-asked, half-stated.

"They must have fallen out. I was pretty out of it. Now I've lost my keys, my license and my credit cards!" she exclaimed with frustration. Nick held up an index finger, ran back down the stairs, through the front door, and yelled to get the driver's attention.

Rich, hearing a man yell outside, walked across the room to check what was going on. Keeping his gun aimed at the closed apartment door, he peeled the edge of the curtain back just enough to look below.

A man on the street was opening the passenger door of the cab. The man had paused a moment, half in and half out of the cab, then turned and ran back into the building, reappearing outside a moment later with the girl on his arm. "Fuck," was the only suitable word Rich could think of at the moment, as he watched the couple get back into the cab, and the cab drive away.

Inside the cab, Nick tried to cheer Shelby up. "We can replace all that stuff, but now I definitely think you should lay low somewhere safer."

"And where exactly do you suggest?" Shelby petitioned coyly.

"You could stay at...my place...as long as you want."

"That's sweet of you, Nick, but I still have to get some clothes and..."

Nick cut her off. "Don't worry. Let's go with new clothes for now, my treat. Maybe you can call your boyfriend and use his set of keys to get in later, when we know for certain it's safe."

Shelby looked out the window and watched as one after another dark building flew by. Then she seemed to come to a conclusion, smiled and said, "Thank you, Nick. I had a bad feeling there outside my apartment building. And don't worry, I'll pay you back for the clothes and 'stuff' I'll need."

Annoyed that Shelby had once again successfully evaded the question about a boyfriend, Nick said chivalrously, "Yeah, well, glad to help, and you don't have to pay me back."

Rich Pagano looked out the window and watched ruefully as the cab disappeared in the distance. Disassembling the silencer from his automatic weapon and fingering the safety back on, he tucked the pieces away, knocking a lamp off a nearby end table in anger, grunting, "I'll see you soon, bitch."

A half hour later, Nick pushed open the door to his apartment. Shelby hesitated, then peeked in and looked it over. "Nice place," she said, her woman's eyes spotting a tell-tale pile of dishes in the sink that indicated a bachelor lived here alone. "So tell me, why are guy's such slobs when it comes to the kitchen?"

"I...I was in a rush when I left?" Nick offered submissively.

"Yeah, sure." Shelby tossed her handbag on the couch and grinned. "I need a shower."

"Down the hall across from the...ah...disaster of a kitchen." Nick said.

"Do you have something I can wear to bed?"

"I'll get you something. Will a T-shirt do for tonight?"

Shelby smiled to herself as she sauntered down the hallway dreaming of a hot, steamy shower. "That'll be fine."

Nick dashed into his bedroom and started picking clothes up from the floor, sniffing each piece, tossing the ranker items into a corner and stuffing the rest into the dresser. He heard the bathroom door shut and moments later, the hiss of the shower. Re-surveying the room, this time with approval, he proceeded to make the bed. Finished, he riffled through his dresser inspecting different T-shirts until he finally found one that met muster. Walking to the bathroom door, he knocked and announced, "Night shirt, milady."

Shelby opened the bathroom door just enough to stick a wet hand out.

"It's the shortest, I mean best one I could find." Nick joked.

"Very funny," Shelby remarked, the hand and shirt disappearing through the crack in the door and the door shutting again. Nick retreated to the living room and began picking up empty beer bottles here and some mostly-empty pizza boxes there.

Shelby finally exited the bathroom, her bare feet padding softly on the hallway's bare wooden floor, to stop at the entrance to the living room where Nick was. "You weren't kidding when you said the shortest shirt," she joked, striking an exaggerated pose, out-stretching an arm against the upper portion of the entrance way, carefully displaying her petite, curvaceous, barely-clad body for Nick's inspection. Nick stared at her with a shocked, school-boy grin.

The T-shirt barely hid the firm tips of her delicately-rounded breasts, while its short length accented her shapely, smooth legs. Shelby walked invitingly over to Nick, pulled him up to her, gave him a quick hug and then, rising up on her toes, gave him a quick peck on the nose. "That's for 'watching over me'," she whispered. Directing Nick against the couch, she gave him a little shove and then reclined next to him, nuzzling her head into his muscular shoulder.

Looking up, she said coquettishly, "You're still not getting lucky," then closed her eyes and promptly fell asleep in his arms. Nick looked down at her as she slept in his arms, unable to stop thinking about how tantalizingly beautiful she looked. He ran a hand through her long, soft hair, and she nuzzled closer. She wasn't just 'young' beautiful, she was 'for a lifetime' beautiful, he thought, and let himself steep in the arousing pleasure of her soft skin, her warm body stretched against him. Resigning himself to breathing in her exotic, spicy scent, he started to drift off. Shelby sighed contentedly...then started snoring. Nick broke out in laughter, thinking of how he would tease her in the morning about it.

CHAPTER 19

Back at Farrell's bar, a bedraggled Joey V. shuffled out of the men's room with a white towel wrapped around his head. Mack, Andre and Botch looked up from the stacks of money and laughed. Joey V. stopped, annoyed. "Now what?"

"You look like Gunga Din." Mack cackled.

"Fuck you, guys. I washed the blood out of my hair and what's left of my ear started bleeding again."

Mack stopped laughing. "So, what are you drinking, Joey?"

"Vodka and cranberry," Joey V. answered warily.

Mack walked over to the bar and returned with a drink for Joey V. and refills for Botch and Andre. Joey V. sipped his drink, and began more closely inspecting the interior of the bar. "You've fixed the place up nice, Mack. Last time I was here was before you took it over, around the time of the Policemen's Widows' Charity Golf Tournament. You remember?"

"Yeah, sure. How could I forget? Things got pretty ugly."

Mack's comment caught Botch's attention. Turning towards Joey V., Botch said, "I haven't heard this one. What happened?"

"Mack and me," Joey V. began with a wry smile, "we went up to Split Rock Golf Course, for the first and only charity event I've ever been invited to, and let me tell you those golfers, their groupies and 'patrons,' boy, could they drink! At every hole there was a wet bar and at least two kegs of beer waiting. From the sixth hole on, I don't remember much. After the event, twenty or so cops came back here with us to continue partying. What I do remember is that, later that night, two guys wearing black, knitted hoods and sporting shotguns busted into the bar, yelling something like, 'Put up your hands!' followed by a loud 'boom' as one shotgun went off. Mack was in the back over there on the phone." Joey V. pointed towards a short row of pay phones near the back of the bar, clearly enjoying being the center of attention.

115

"Mack was on the guy before anyone could say 'What?' and smacked the guy across the side of his face with a five-iron. Then everyone woke up and jumped the other mutt. Next thing I knew, twenty drunken cops were swinging golf clubs at these guys and each other. Apparently, the two had a lookout outside. Smart chick, she flagged down a patrol car when she heard the melee and saw her two guys stumble out the front door, bleeding like a couple of stuck pigs. They ran as fast as they could right into the hands of the waiting patrolmen.

Looking back, I gotta' admit, those robbers had balls: Ten minutes later, the three were escorted back into the bar by the two cops, the lady demanding the patrolmen arrest everyone. The two startled patrolmen walked around, saying hello to everyone by first name, while the rowdy bunch of drunken cops were hiding their clubs. In seconds, it seemed like a big, friendly, retired cops reunion, though anyone watching would have wondered, what with all the blood and bruises. The two male criminals, at this point completely bewildered, ran out the front door, fearing another beating. The rookie patrolman looked at the juke box and, noticing a pool of blood flowing out from under it, and several golf club handles peeking from behind it, started to point this out to his partner, but his partner smartly told him to forget it and go wait in the car."

Joey took a long gulp from his drink, then continued.

"I'll never forget the look on the rookie's face. See the hole in the ceiling over there with the mannequin's arm sticking out holding the American flag? That's the hole from the robber's shotgun blast."

Joey V. paused for effect, allowing Mack to add with a chuckle, "Yeah, and a week later, a guy in a wheelchair came in trying to glom money off the bar. Someone called the cops and, you guessed it, the same two patrolmen ended up answering the call. While they were on their way, code three, my regular customers listened to the cripple's sad story for evening entertainment, then threw the guy, chair and all, out the door. The two cops arrived just in time to see the old man fly out the door. The rookie watched the whole thing, mouth agape, in complete shock. His partner just shook his head and said without emotion, 'Tough bar,' and the two drove off. You know, the next day that rookie transferred out of the Bronx."

The four buddies raised their drinks, saluted each other and, laughing raucously, continued with more stories. And the drunker they got, the more Joey V. and Botch seemed to get along, which made Mack feel more at ease.

After awhile, Botch piped up. "Mack, see if there's a fight or something on TV."

Mack reached behind the bar, located the remote, and with one button-push, turned on all the wall-mounted TVs scattered throughout the bar. Flipping through the various sports channels, they quickly realized that there was no action going on in the predawn hours.

Andre grunted, "Go back to channel two."

Mack reluctantly acquiesced, saying, "It's an old interview, Andre, and it's only going to piss you off."

On the TV screen appeared Amazing Jones, the quarterback who had repeatedly beaten Andre's daughter, Tina. Andre's face darkened, and his attitude turned ugly. "I haven't forgotten you, you slimy bastard. Your ass is mine!" he yelled at the television.

Amazing's image, impervious to Andre's threats, rambled on about how he was the greatest quarterback the world would ever see. Andre, getting hotter and even more bothered as he listened, pointed a drunken finger at the closest TV and yelled, "Listen, you fucking idiot! That's it! I'm going to stomp your head in. Now! Right now!"

Mack frowned. "Andre, you couldn't friggin' wipe your own ass in your current condition. Listen to me. I spoke to Joey here. He's going to take care of it."

"No," Andre growled through clinched teeth, "No, I want him for myself!"

All eyes turned to Mack. "Andre, you're too close to this. You'll wind up killing the kid."

Andre grinned drunkenly and swayed in his chair. "I thought you were trying to talk me out of this, Mack."

Mack, sensing an opening, continued. "Just think if Tina found out you killed him. She'd never forgive you. Besides which, cops don't do well in prison."

Andre grabbed a fist full of money from the stacks and shook his fist in front of them, blurting out, "You weren't too worried about prison when we took this money!"

"Well," Mack emphasized with a grin, "now that we have this money, isn't it worth staying out of jail so we can enjoy it?"

"Alright! Alright!" Andre said, throwing the bills at Mack. Then he leaned over towards Joey V. "I want you to put the fear of God in him, you hear? The fear of God!"

Joey V. looked up at the TV.

"So how much to take care of 'Me-Me'?" Mack asked Joey.

"You-You?" Botch exclaimed, confused. "What the hell is 'You-You'?"

Mack explained, "The only thing Amazing talks about is 'me' and 'me'."

Botch grunted, getting it at last. Holding up an empty glass, he muttered, "Jesus, Mack, it's the booze speaking. Speaking of which I need some more..."

Joey V. ignored the three, continuing to stare up at the screen. "I have to admit: I would like to teach the guy a lesson. Shit, I'll even throw in slapping his mother for naming him Amazing. I'm not that much of an ingrate to do it for free though, seeing that my friends have recently come into so much money."

Andre stiffened. "How much money are we talking?"

"Well, guys, I'd like a piece of the pie, being as I made it all happen in the first place."

"And how big a piece are you thinking?" asked Botch menacingly, suddenly surprising sober.

"Well, I heard about how you're short money for that place in the Canaries and I just happen to have a plan on how to make the pie bigger, stick it to Sweaters, and have enough left over to cut me in."

The bar went silent. Mack slid next to Joey V. and the other two leaned in closer. Looking from Botch to Andre and back to Joey V., Mack said in a clear, uninebriated voice, "You have our undivided attention."

CHAPTER 20

Joey V.'s plan was to bet their money on the next Jets game with the early line. Joey V. looked at a perplexed Mack as Botch and Andre explained: "The Jets are favored in the next game by fourteen points, right? So if we bet on the other team —the Buffalo Bills in this case—the Jets would have to win by fourteen points or more to block our payoff. We could insure that doesn't happen by teaching Amazing Jones his 'lesson' just before the game. If it works, we could double, even triple our money, because the Jets aren't that good without Amazing."

Joey V. smiled triumphantly. To his unexpected chagrin, Mack, Botch and Andre stared at him, poker-faced and silent. Andre finally broke the tension. "How good is the Jets back-up quarterback? I've only seen him a couple of times in pre-season games."

"That's the beauty of it," Joey V. replied. "In my business, I see all the scouting reports. He doesn't even get much practice time anymore; Amazing apparently allows no competition when it comes to the lime-light."

Botch was next. "How about third string?"

"He's a rookie. The only playing time he's ever seen is taking snaps for field goals. Word is, he has trouble grasping the system."

Joey V. continued. "Guys! The Jets are favored by fourteen points over Buffalo. That's high to start, and it's a division game. Buffalo always plays division games tough, so that line will come down to ten points soon, so if we want to do this, we would need to act fast. When we take out Amazing, don't be surprised if the line goes to three or ends up even. I'm telling you guys, it's a lock. We can't lose, and, if we spread all this loot around, we will cripple Sweaters' operation to boot."

All eyes shifted to Mack.

Mack appeared increasingly enthralled as he took it in. "How do you plan on spreading the action without drawing suspicion from Sweaters?"

119

"If you can get Twisted Ray upset enough at Sweaters like we talked about, Ray'll take the action just to watch it bite Sweaters in the ass."

Mack suddenly grinned. "I must admit, tripling our money and wiping out Sweaters at the same time sounds enticing, and listening to you, Joey, makes me feel like we've hit the mother-load at last."

"I was just thinking, Mack," Andre offered, "about what you said about us always falling just short of our dreams. That place in the Canaries—I can taste it. Maybe I'm too drunk to think straight, but I like Joey's plan. Actually getting to do what we've so often dreamed about makes perfect sense to me, in spite of the risks. If we retire with only what we have now, we'll end up spending the money on new livers in a year."

Mack slapped the table. "I'm in!"

Andre joined in, slapping the table immediately after Mack, "Why the hell not? Me too!"

Joey V. beamed.

Botch, however, shook his head in disagreement and held out. "We haven't had the money a full day yet, and you all want to piss it away on a bet. Alright, fine! I'm in, too! But I refuse to fucking slap the table like you two drunken assholes."

All eyes turned to Botch. "What?" Botch asked, both irritated and confused. Then it hit him: It was always 'all or nothing' with this group. Botch frowned, shrugged his shoulders and yelled, "Alright, alright! I'm in!" and slapped the table. Then he turned to Joey V. "Just stop saying it's a lock, okay? That's bad luck!"

Mack agreed. "Botch's right, Joey. I remember you saying that once years ago before a venture, and you ending up saying, 'I don't believe this! How could this have happened?' when everything didn't work out like you figured."

"Not this time," Joey V. snapped. "Look, guys, we only have a couple days to get everything in place. Looks like my demise is going to work for us, but be short-lived. I'll need to oversee this personally, with so much money being spread around. I'm thinking of going through Joe Nator. Can one of you get Sweaters off the street for a couple of days?"

Andre looked at Mack then at Joey V. "Yeah, we can come up with something." Then Andre asked, "This Nator guy, Joey. Where'd he get that name?"

Mack threw Joey V. a warning look, knowing the answer would upset Botch. Joey V., however, either didn't catch the signal or ignored it altogether. "He got the name because they say he donates all his money to the bookies. Get it? Joe Nator sounds like 'Donater'?"

Botch threw his hands in the air, "Oh fuck! This guy sounds like just the person we should trust all our money to!"

Joey V., suddenly getting what Mack had been unsuccessfully trying to signal to him, sighed and explained further. "Relax, Botch. It actually works in our favor, see? Joe Nator has been known as a high roller for years. He's got just the kind of loser credibility we need. He's had a long run of bad luck, but always pays his debts, so bookies always take his action. There's been rumors that he's come into some big family money, a rich aunt or something. That'll be us." Joey V. smiled nervously at Mack, hoping Mack would add support. When he didn't, Joey V. added, "Stop worrying. This is as good as it gets. We'll win. I guarantee it."

Mack's frown deepened. "Damn it, Joey, you just heard Botch. Try not to be so cocky. If any of Sweaters' men, or those rogue agents, were to catch wind of this, you and the rest of us would be dead meat. One thing I can guarantee is that if they get wind of what we're doing, they won't take it lying down."

The four conspirators searched each other's faces, then slapped their hands again on the table together. It was time to set the wheels in motion—as soon as they drank and toasted their plan a few more times to celebrate.

Number One Bestseller

CHAPTER 21

A few days later, Mack called Joey V. via cell phone. "I have the video of Twisted Ray's daughter," he said with reservation.

"How did you do it? Never mind that, how did you do it so fast?"

Mack frowned. "Don't ask. I feel sleazy about just having it. So what have you found out?"

"Ray's still in the medical wing at Einstein Hospital. He was more fucked up than I thought. He's out of intensive care now. Are you sure you can get Sweaters out of the picture long enough for me to make certain all the bookies accept the bets?"

"I have a friend at vice," offered Mack, "who owes me a big favor. He just arrested Sweaters on child porn charges. We know a judge who hates Sweaters and timed the arrest to when that judge was working. The judge was so disgusted with Sweaters he remanded him, refusing to even think of setting bail. Sweaters will be in the slammer for at least five days. That gives you Friday and the weekend to do your dirty work. After that they'll have to drop the charges."

"So what's next?" Joey V. asked.

"It's time for you to re-appear, Joey. I want you to go to the hospital and smooth over things with Twisted Ray. Get there about 3 o'clock. My friends from vice will be there waiting outside Ray's hospital room to assist you."

Joey V. acknowledged, hung up, re-wrapped his head in a bandage and went to visit Twisted Ray. Locating Ray's room, he paused at the door to nod to the two vice squad cops waiting outside the door just as Mack had said, and to gather his wits. A moment later walked nonchalantly into the room. "Ray! I just found out you're here. I thought you were dead!"

Ray looked up at Joey V. with disbelief. "Yeah, well, I thought you were dead. If not, I swore if I ever saw you again, I'd make sure you were." Ray turned his bandaged face away.

Joey V. looked stunned. "Ray! What the hell have I done to deserve that kind of welcome?"

Ray turned his face back toward Joey V., hatred blazing in his eyes. "I finally figured out the plan and that it was yours. Those guys outside of Enzo's were with you. What the fuck else should I think, asshole!"

"What? With me? Those guys shot off part of my other ear. A half inch more and I would have been minus a head!" Joey V. said, pointing at his bandaged head. "Hell, Ray, I just got out of the hospital myself."

Ray looked askance at Joey V. "Yeah? Well, I guess if you *had* taken the money, you wouldn't be here now. You'd be long gone and not gambling on me believing you." Twisted Ray's face untwisted slightly as he continued. "The thing is, Joey, I'm really not your problem. It's Sweaters you need to watch out for. You better hope *he* believes you. The prick hasn't called or come to see me. That's a bad sign."

"I tried to contact him in order to find out about you. He's in jail."

Ray, now genuinely puzzled, asked, "What for?"

"Something about child porn."

Ray frowned, "I told him not to get involved in that shit. So who's in charge in his absence?"

Joey V. shrugged his shoulders, "Phil, I guess."

Ray snapped to attention; Sweaters had been clearly favoring Phil lately. "Phil? That scumbag? He's a fucking moron, for God's sake. He didn't even tell me Sweaters was in jail! He's so far up Sweaters' ass, I see his head when Sweaters yawns. This is bullshit!" Twisted Ray put a bandaged hand to his bandaged head. "I should be the one in charge, but they want to keep me here until the dizzy spells stop. If I'm temporarily indisposed, it should be me choosing my temporary replacement. Fuck, I'm putting you in charge, Joey. Get me a phone so I can call Phil and let him know!"

Joey V. grimaced, "I don't know if I'm up to it, Ray."

"Nonsense, it'll be two or three days at the most. I want you to find out who did this to us."

"Speaking of which, what happened to the others, Ray?"

"All I know is that I woke up in a dumpster on top of Buddha's cold body. No word on Sal and Dom. I find it hard to believe, but now I'm wondering if maybe the twins cooked all this up. Nah, those two couldn't organize a sock drawer!" Twisted Ray paused momentarily and then added, "What do you think?"

"That would be the beauty of it," Joey V. replied. "Maybe they were really a lot smarter than anyone suspected and just playing dumb. They never liked Sweaters because of his condescending attitude towards them."

"See if anyone's seen or heard from them," Twisted Ray ordered.

"How about me putting Phil on it?" Joey V. suggested.

Ray smiled, "Hey, I like that, Phil taking orders from me through you. That'll piss him off. Give me the phone so I can set the idiot straight."

Joey V. handed Ray the phone. Ray dialed and was waiting for an answer when the two detectives, who'd been listening at the door for the right moment, walked in. Ray immediately hung up.

The detectives eyed Twisted Ray and then Joey V. up and down, then walked over to either side of Twisted Ray's bed. The first detective, acting the good cop, asked Ray compassionately, "How are you today, Ray? You remember me, Detective Ryder, and my pal here, Detective Cunningham?"

"What's wrong, Officer? Is your sister mad that I don't call her anymore?"

Detective Cunningham, acting the bad cop, interjected, "Funny, Ray, but not so funny from where I'm standing."

Ray watched while Detective Cunningham hooked up the VCR suspended underneath one arm to the back of the hospital TV. "Let's see if you find this funny. It's a documentary entitled 'How to Bang Little Girls.' You'll like it, Ray. So will your pal here, too, if he stays." Cunningham tossed a thumb at Joey V. who was watching Ray and the two detectives closely.

This time Ryder continued, "We have proof that you and your boss have been introducing underage girls to porn and prostitution. Look, we all know it's not your thing, Ray, so we're willing to cut a deal. Testify against Jerry Sweaters, and we'll make sure all the charges against you are dropped."

Ray looked from side to side at the two detectives, then laughed dryly, "Roll on Sweaters? Sure, why not? I rolled three times before I got off your sister! Anything I can do to help, just ask. Now, get the fuck out of my room before I call my lawyer and slap you with a law suit!"

Ryder looked up at the TV. "Just thought you might like to know a bit more about the kind of slime you're protecting." Cunningham reached into a coat pocket and pulled out a remote. Pushing the center button, the tape player sprang to life. On the TV a young girl and guy were having hot sex. Ray looked away and then back up at the screen, acting like it didn't interest him.

"Hey, could you guys leave the tape? I'm actually getting a chubby! Come on, Ryder, Cunningham—if you have something on me, arrest me," Ray demanded, staring at Ryder who was watching Twisted Ray.

Joey V., who was intently watching the tape, suddenly shouted, "Shit, Ray, I think you better see this."

Ray looked up at the TV and studied the girl, realizing it was his daughter dancing nude in front of some guy before she sat on his face.

"That God-damned motherfucker!" Ray grabbed for the remote while Detective Cunningham nonchalantly fumbled with the buttons, acting as if he was trying to turn it off while allowing the carnal scene to continue to unfold. The girl was now sitting on the man's pelvis, grinding away, facing the TV and rubbing her breasts with a look of drugged ecstasy on her face. Ray sat up with effort and grabbed the remote out of Detective Cunningham's hand, shutting the machine off.

"I hope you enjoyed that as much as the rest of us at the station did," Detective Cunningham responded laconically. "Hey, do you want to see it again, Ray? Or would you rather help us bring the asshole down?"

Ray, incensed, growled, "Where did you get that?"

"Pulled it out of Sweaters' car when we arrested him. Must be one of his favorites."

The two detectives began drilling Twisted Ray from both sides, trying to coerce him to agree to testify, while Joey V., unnoticed, walked over and popped out the tape.

Ray, fuming, yelled, "If you're not going to arrest me, I want you out! Now!"

Detective Ryder signaled to his partner, "Alright, Ray. We'll leave for now, but we'll be around, just in case you change your mind." Ryder watched Twisted Ray while Cunningham busied himself with disconnecting the VCR. Cunningham tossed Twisted Ray his card, and the two detectives left without speaking further.

Ray, enraged, lay shaking in his bed. Suddenly he raised both fists and slammed them down, sending the hospital tray and a stainless steel basin clanking loudly down across the floor. Looking up at Joey V., Twisted Ray spat to the side. "I should roll on that fucker. I really should."

"Think it out before you react, and while you're thinking, I have something that might cheer you up." Joey V. pulled the tape out from under his shirt. "Thought you might want to have this."

Ray grabbed for the tape, and held it tightly in both fists, slowly calming down. "Guess I misjudged you, Joey. You know, you're more reliable than any of the so-called friends around me these days. I can't believe I trusted that weasel, Sweaters, and like a brother, too!" Ray held the tape up as if he could see what it contained from the room light behind. "Thanks, Joey. I mean it."

Joey V. decided to seize the moment. "That was just a clip, Ray. Sweaters probably has the original tucked away somewhere in his house. With Sweaters in jail, I could get it for you, if you wanted me to, but I'd have to do it right away."

Ray looked up at the blank TV screen. "He's got a storage place in the North Hamptons—Wadding River—L.I.E. Exit 69. It's on the north shore. He calls the storage building his 'private cinema,' and keeps all the master tapes there. There's an extra key to the building in his desk at the club. Listen, Joey, I want you to

126

destroy every tape in his library, especially the one of my daughter! That should drive him crazy. Hey, fucking over Sweaters like this is making me feel better already...I know you have a daughter, too, Joey, so I trust you in this. The address and number of the storage unit are on the key."

Joey V. held back his roiling anger, remembering last week how Twisted Ray laughed when Sweaters threatened Joey, his wife and daughter. *Not so funny now, is it, you low-life scumbag,* Joey V. thought while with a straight face, he replied, "You can always count on me, Ray."

Number One Bestseller

CHAPTER 22

Joey V. exited the cab, waving a congenial 'hello' to the manager of the House of Mirth, Sweaters' private club, and proceeded to deftly pinch the key Twisted Ray had told him about. Key in hand, a congenial 'goodbye' to the same manager on the way out, and Joey was proceeding to the prearranged pick-up location where he exited the cab and nervously waited for Mack. When Mack showed up, the two drove off in Mack's car and Mack inquired sympathetically, "How did it go?"

"Okay," Joey V. replied, pleased to think that Mack really cared about him—and that he, Joey V., was now one of the good guys. "Ray bought it, hook, line and sinker."

Mack nodded, his concentration directed towards getting them to Long Island as quickly as possible. Sweaters was still in jail, but time was running out. Sweaters' lawyers were working overtime to spring him. Mack found the location of the storage building complex and pulled up to the gate.

Seeing neither guards nor cameras, Joey V. slipped into the guard shack and opened the electronic gate. Quickly scanning the inside perimeter and again not spotting anyone, he returned to the car.

"People actually pay good money to store valuable shit in these kind of low-security places?" Mack asked rhetorically.

Joey V. shrugged.

"Number 27," Mack said, driving slowly ahead through the gate, while both continued scouting anxiously in every direction.

"Left," Joey V. stated officiously, pointing to a numbered garage door in a long line of weathered, numbered garage doors. "That's the one!"

Mack pulled up and waited while Joey V. got out and, looking as if he owned the property, casually unlocked the lock with the key he'd heisted, and pulled open the garage door. "Wow, look at all these tapes! There's even a wide-screen TV,

VCR and Italian leather sofa! We can check the tapes out in style to make sure we get the right one."

Mack reluctantly got out of the car and joined Joey V. in the garage. There was no room for a car inside, the interior being stacked wall-to-wall with boxes, except for a floor-to-ceiling shelf in front, with rows and rows of unmarked tapes stacked upright. Joey V. turned on the TV and VCR player while Mack grabbed the first of the tapes and shoved it into the VCR slot. Joey V. sat lazily down on the sofa in front of the TV, waiting eagerly for Mack to hit the 'play' button. When nothing happened, Joey V. looked up to see Mack staring at him.

"What?" Joey V. asked with obvious exasperation, realizing as he said it that if there was a tape of Annie in the lot, Mack wouldn't want him to see it. Joey V. stood and said despondently, "I think I'll go check the boxes in back." As soon as Joey V. started to rummage through the boxes, Mack started screening the tapes, one after another. That's when he realized they were in order. Watching a neighborhood teen he knew, but couldn't quite place, stripping brazenly on the screen, he shouted, "Joey, what's this girl's name?"

Joey V. was back in a flash, eyes glued to the screen, lapping up every lewd scene. "Ah, yeah. That's Brenda," Joey V. said absently as he watched the usually modest girl gyrating a naked ass in front of the camera.

Mack turned it off.

"What are you doing? She wasn't doing anything except showing herself off. Hey, that Brenda's got some body, don't you think?" Joey V. was trying his best to defuse the situation, hoping Mack would ignore him and continue screening the rest of the tapes with him there.

Mack pointed at two tapes he had already scanned. "Those tapes had Alice and Angela on them. This one's of Brenda. The tape of Annie isn't here."

Joey V. examined the shelf. "Wait! Look! There's some tapes tucked in back of Alice and Angela. You can just barely see them from this angle."

Mack walked back to the shelf, positioned a box and stood on it to reach the specially marked tapes Joey V. had mentioned. Joey V., respecting Mack's modesty, reluctantly resumed searching through the boxes in back of the shelf. As he rummaged from box to box, Joey V. noticed how quiet Mack had gotten. Glancing quickly at the TV screen, Joey could just make out reflected in the glass Mack's anguished face, indicating he had found the tape of Annie.

Several difficult minutes went by while Mack watched the TV screen expressionlessly in silence. Imagining what Mack must be seeing from hearing the sounds, Joey V. reached over and pulled the plug on the VCR. "Mack," he whispered, "You don't need to relive it all over again, unless you really want to. You have the tape. Let's destroy it and get out of here."

Mack started as if awakening from a trance, angrily marched out of the garage, grabbed the nearest metal trash can and pulled it in close to the shelves. Mack plugged in the VCR, retrieved the tape of Annie, and tossed it along with as many others as would fit in the garbage can, while Joey located a can of lighter fluid next to an old barbeque grill and began dousing the tapes with the acrid-smelling liquid.

Together, they dragged the can away from the garage and out into the open. Joey V. lit a piece of paper and tossed it into the can. The can thumped, then exploded in a rolling ball of fire that ascended in an inky mushroom cloud high into the sky. The concussion pushed the two back into the garage, knocking many of the remaining tapes onto the garage floor. Mack and Joey watched as the flames from inside the can licked at the air and the inky black cloud continued to rise.

In a copse of trees just inside the front gate, the security guard, completing his rounds, spotted the column of smoke and quickly drove to where Mack and Joey V. were standing watching the blazing can. The two watched the guard get out of his car, revolver drawn and hand shaking. He approached cautiously, yelling, "What are you two doing?"

Mack flashed his police badge at the security guard, whose eyes widened. The guard slowly put away the weapon.

"We're here to investigate a complaint about toxic waste on the premises. I need you to tell us everything you know about the owners of this property. Do yourself a favor and don't try to protect the owner or his pals. These are serious charges. It's a police matter for the moment, but you know how it is with toxic waste—this could quickly become a federal matter, especially if there turns out to be any subterfuge involved."

The guard muttered sheepishly, "Officer, sir. I don' know nothing. Really, I don'. This is my first week on the job, honest to God!"

"What's your name?" Mack asked pulling out a notebook and pencil.

"Edward Zeale, sir," the man replied, looking frightened out of his wits.

Mack, eyebrows knit into a menacing frown, looked at Joey V. and asked, "Is that one of the names on the list?"

"No, sir," Joey V. replied. "None of the names begin with Z."

"Alright, Security Guard Edward Zeale, I believe you're telling the truth. If you want to stay out of trouble, I suggest you forget what you just saw and begin keeping a careful log of anything suspicious you see happening on this property from now on: Name, dates, everything. We'll be by later to see what you've found. Don't let anyone know about this investigation or things could go bad—really bad —for you. Understand?"

Edward's hands and legs were shaking. "No problem, sir. Whatever you say, sir. I surely don' want no trouble."

"Alright, then get back to your duties and let us continue our investigation. We'll stop by on our way out to let you know when we're finished here."

"Sure thing, sir. I'll keep out of your way, and alert you if anyone comes befor' I let 'em in, sir."

Joey V. and Mack watched the guard drive off. Joey looked at the greasy black ribbon snaking high into the air from the still-smoldering can. "You know, Mack, I think it's time we got out of here."

Returning to the garage, Joey V. reached for the garage-door handle, and in the process noticed a piece of clear plastic containing what looked like some dollar bills sticking out from behind the base of the shelves. Pushing several boxes aside, he pulled out a large garbage bag filled with money. Joey V. called for Mack, smiling, and mumbling under his breath, "Look, Mack: Icing on the cake!"

"What's that?" asked Mack morosely, watching what was left of the black smoke disappear into the air.

"Money!" Joey V. replied with relish.

"How much?" Mack responded with reawakened interest.

"Enough to cover a lot of rainy days and piss the hell off Sweaters when he discovers it's missing."

Mack sauntered over. "It's turning out to be a nice trip to the country after all," he said as he looked inside the bag at wad after wad, estimating the total to be in the hundreds of thousands in small bills. Mack's half-smile gave way to a hearty ear-to-ear grin as he helped Joey V. drag the heavy sack to the car. Minutes later, after rolling the still-smoldering garbage can back into the garage and smashing up the VCR, TV and the remaining tapes, they drove off.

Joey V. couldn't hold back: "Sweet Jesus, thank you! I can't believe we found all that money! Damn it, Mack! I'm almost convinced that it really *is* better to be on the side with the good guys!"

Mack stopped the car at the guard shack. "We're done, but we'll be back," he warned. "And I better not find out you've compromised this investigation by alerting any of those responsible, understand?"

The guard gulped and answered, "I won't, sir. I promise," as he opened the gate for them.

On the ride back, Joey V. couldn't shut up. "How much do you figure we took in, this money included," he asked.

"I know you're wondering where I stand on the money you found, Joey. Don't fret. It's all yours. Consider that your payment for taking care of Amazing."

"You're serious? Great! I can gather my family and leave town after taking care of Amazing then! Perfect!"

Mack frowned. "Hold on a second. Are you saying you're not going to bet this money on the game like you talked us into? The one that's a 'lock'?"

"You want me to bet my money, too?" Joey asked, astonished.

"See if this sounds familiar: 'We'll win, I guarantee it!' If you're telling the truth, Joey, how could you pass up doubling or tripling your money along with us?"

Joey V. reluctantly nodded. "Alright, alright. I hear you. I'll add it to yours when we get back."

Joey V. babbled on during the rest of the ride back to the Bronx, Mack mainly responding with grunted, one-word answers.

Finally running out of anything further to say, Joey V. asked, "What's up, Mack? You angry or something?"

"No. Why?" asked Mack with seeming concern.

"I've been talking to you for almost ten minutes and you've hardly said a word. It's just not like you."

Mack sighed and looked languidly out the window, "Whatever, Joey."

"You still thinking about that tape?"

Mack's lack of answer answered the question.

"Come on, Mack, just because you saw it today doesn't mean it happened again! You should be happy it's no longer hanging over your head. You're free!"

Mack hmmm'ed, adding, "I guess you're right. It's just I've waited so long for this moment, and now it all seems so...anti-climactic. I miss her, Joey, and secretly I've always wished that this would all somehow go away—like after a bad dream, I'd awaken and we'd be together again. Watching the tape and seeing that guy... now I'm pissed off and hurting again."

"That's the past, Mack; this is now. Listen, I tell you what. How about I try to find the guy in the tape? Maybe you can work some of your anger off on him?"

Mack answered distantly, "That's already been dealt with."

"Well, then, you'll have your revenge against Sweaters soon, so let it go. Move on, Mack."

As they crossed the Throggs Neck Bridge, both looked out his respective window at the sails of boats bobbing on the water. For a moment, each felt on top of the world. "When you really think about it," Joey V. offered, "this was a productive day, right? We took even more of Sweaters' money and destroyed his security blanket, too."

Mack nodded and grinned. "You're right, pal. There's nothing to stop me from getting him now."

Number One Bestseller

CHAPTER 23

"That's the Mack I know! Point the anger where it belongs! It's taken me most of my fifty years to get that right."

Mack chuckled at last. "Looking at the wrinkles on your face, Joey, they must be city years. Hey, remember when you and I first met? You must have been in your late twenties. I remember you wearing your guido outfit. You looked like John Travolta in *Saturday Night Fever*. I have to admit you were the sharpest-dressed kid in the neighborhood. Where'd you learn your style, Joey, your brother, Jay?"

It was Joey V.'s turn to quiet. "He's been gone twenty-five years now, Mack—I can't believe we came from the same mother and father. He was totally out of control from the day he was born. My parents were scared to death of him, you know? Me, too."

"You ain't shittin' there!" Mack interjected. "Jay was the closest thing I ever met to pure, well-dressed evil."

Listening, Joey V. reflected on the last time he had seen Jay. His brother had gone to his parents' house, as he usually did once a month, hitting them up for money and then hitting them for the hell of it. Joey did his best to avoid Jay, even though Jay, who worked for Sweaters, had gotten Joey a job with Sweaters, too. Seeing his mother with the red, slap-mark across her face, Joey had snapped and went in search of his father's gun, only to feel the end of a shotgun barrel cold against his temple.

"What were you thinkin' of doing just now, you little ass-wipe?" Jay growled.

Their mother pleaded, "Don't hurt him, Jay."

That was how a 'family conversation' went in those days.

Jay took his brother hostage and the next thing Joey knew he was at St. Raymond Cemetery, thinking he was going to be murdered there by his own brother. Jay kept the shotgun pointed at his brother as they approached a large

135

mausoleum with the name "Colombo" on it. He threw a bag of tools at his younger brother's feet.

Joey's heart began to race thinking that his brother couldn't summon up the courage to just shoot him and, instead, was about to lock him up, alive, in the mausoleum. Joey reluctantly took up the crowbar that had bounced out of the bag and pried open the door of the mausoleum. Turning to his demented brother, he begged shamelessly for his life: "Please, Jay. Not like this! Please!"

"Just get inside," Jay demanded, prodding him with the gun barrel. Joey reluctantly entered the tomb with Jay following close behind.

"Open it!" Jay demanded, pointing at a dusty sarcophagus. Joey's terror suddenly turned to panic. He couldn't believe that his brother was so sick as to want to seal him in a stone coffin with a long-dead body. "Don't do this Jay! Please!"

"Just hurry up, so we can get out of here!" his brother replied, feral-like wildness flashing in his eyes.

Joey, relieved when his brother uttered *we* and *get out of here* in the same sentence, watched in shocked silence as his brother placed the gun against a stone wall and pushed Joey aside, ordering, "Help me get this lid off!"

Joey's mind flooded once again with thoughts of being sequestered alive in the stone coffin, suffocating in the arms of a decaying corpse. His brother patted a pocketed automatic as a reminder, and said, "What? You want to die here?"

The two pushed the heavy stone lid until it thudded onto the floor, and broke into large, irregular chunks. Joey stepped back with no idea what to expect next, as Jay smashed the seal of the crumbling, inner wood casket and ripped it open. Inside were the remains of an elderly woman with a gorgeous diamond necklace about her neck and several gold rings flashing precious stones on her bone fingers. Jay ripped the necklace off the body and struggled to get the rings off her fingers. "Give me the metal clipper over there!" he yelled at his petrified brother.

Joey obliged, handing him the clippers, and watched, as Jay held one of the corpse's fingers up ready to clip it off. Joey ran out of the mausoleum and vomited unremittingly on the dank grass. The last words he heard from his brother's mouth were, "Where you gonna run, pussy?"

Mack, aware of Joey's mental struggle, broke the awkward silence. "That was the craziest thing your brother ever did, robbing the grave of the mother of one of the biggest crime bosses on the East Coast."

Joey V. slapped Mack on the back. "Yeah, well, we were all pretty crazy back then. You hardly knew me, yet you went out on a limb to convince everyone that I wasn't with my brother that night."

"I was actually killing two birds with one stone. That independent scumbag,

Renny, was going around the neighborhood back then, robbing the elderly and the handicapped. I convinced everyone that Renny was the one with your brother, and no one's seen or heard from him or your brother since. I should have let them think it was you, then I wouldn't have to keep saving your ass all the time like I do."

Mack pulled up in back of Farrell's, turned off the car and sat for a minute staring in silence down at his hands in his lap. "You know the funny part?" he blurted out.

"What's that?" Joey asked, looking back at Mack with pale face and reddened eyes.

"I've been beat up, shot at, wounded, and faced death in countless situations, and none of it ever hurt as much as this shit with Annie."

Joey V. seemed to awaken, the color returning to his face. "You act like you're all alone and less of a man for having feelings for her. Well, you're not the only one who's felt this way and you're not any less of a man for it. Don't you remember your history classes, man?" Joey V. asked, forming a triangle with his fingers and placing them over his crotch. "*This* little thing between a woman's legs has toppled more empires than any other force. Napoleon and Josephine, Anthony and Cleopatra, Mark Anthony and Jennifer Lopez. Countless others throughout history have suffered no differently than you're suffering now, yet you think you're the only one. Smarten up, Mack."

"I guess you're right, Joey. Let's go inside and I promise not to whine for at least another minute or two," Mack vowed, climbing out of the car. Joey V. slid over into the driver's seat.

Mack stood, staring down at Joey V., hands on hips. "What are you thinking of doing now?"

"I need to borrow your car to go see my brother, Chris, and give him some of this money to bet. I'll do the rest of the money tomorrow with Joe Nator."

Mack, interest piqued, replied smartly, "Just don't smack my car up like you did yours. Right now *I* need a cold beer for breakfast, and tomorrow—shit, in a couple of hours—we should find out what those three rogue agents are up to."

Joey V. stared blankly at Mack, so Mack explained. "Botch took a couple of days off from work, but has been watching the bureau building. He hasn't seen his boss or the three agents since we took the money."

"Didn't he think taking time off right now might look a little suspicious?"

"That's what I thought, but what could I do? He's a big boy and it was his call."

"Hey, Mack, did you ever wonder if this whole thing was really an internal sting operation to get at *us*? Or perhaps your buddy, Botch, has set this whole thing up for us to take the fall? Or maybe…"

"Enough!" Mack complained. "It's bad enough, I have to listen to Botch and all of *his* conspiracy theories!"

Joey V. shrugged his shoulders and a moment later screeched out in a hail of rocks. Mack watched as Joey V. drove off, thinking briefly but seriously about Joey V.'s suspicions, dismissing them, in the end, with a nervous laugh. Turning toward the bar door, he reached into his pockets for his keys, thinking about a much bigger and infinitely more complex conspiracy that had suddenly occurred to him.

CHAPTER 24

Friday at FBI Headquarters was total mayhem. Botch's boss, Walter Steiner, burst into his subordinate's office and demanded snidely, "So how was your 'vacation,' Botch?"

Botch, feet on the corner of his desk, looked up from a stack of official papers in hand. "I take it by the dulcet tone of your voice there's a problem, Walter?"

"I've left messages for you everywhere, but you never got back to me."

Botch, frazzled from lack of sleep, snapped back, "Hence the term 'vacation'."

Ignoring the barb, Walter continued, "Are you then aware of what's been happening while you've been conveniently 'on vacation'?"

"Walter?" Botch said languidly. "I don't feel like dancing this morning. How about you do us both a favor and tell me."

Walter, infuriated by Botch's continued lack of respect, dumped: "Well, your three men apparently tried to break up a major drug ring with strong terrorist ties. The operative word here is 'tried'."

Botch listened patiently. Walter was already building a story to justify the Dominican debacle working its way through the bureau, by adding in a terrorist angle.

"Oh, really?" Botch replied sarcastically as he sat back, touching his fingertips together as if in prayer, his swivel chair squeaking as he rocked.

Mouth open, Walter was about to let loose a string of expletives when he was interrupted by a knock at Botch's door. He snapped his mouth shut, turned and opened the door, waving in agent Gary Ross. "Come in and you, too, Pagano, Smith."

The two agents slithered behind Ross, trying unsuccessfully to disappear into the woodwork.

Botch gestured magnanimously towards the couch while Walter paced back and forth eyeing the four suspiciously. He abruptly stopped pacing and resumed:

"Like I was saying, your men tried to single-handedly raid a major East Coast drug ring called the Dominicans. These three seized millions in cocaine after interrupting what some here believe to be a meeting between the Dominicans and some domestic terrorists. This is big, men. You," he said, pointing at Ross, Smith and Pagano, "are all up for commendations. What the bureau is not mentioning, for publicity's sake, is that the apartment was a fucking bloodbath without a single terrorist left alive to interrogate!"

Gary watched Walters' mouth move, all the while thinking how capable the bureau was at spinning things to fit its desired public image. Commendations? Shit! What the three wanted was the missing millions in cash. Gary looked up with a pained expression on his face to see Rich Pagano trying to catch his attention. Pagano motioned behind Gary's head.

Gary, faking a yawn, turned and studied a large, wood-framed photograph hanging on the wall. In it, Botch, Mack and Andre were wearing Hawaiian-print shirts, sitting at a Tiki-bar, toasting whomever had taken the photo. Gary turned and stared at Botch in amazement.

Walter, noticing that no one was listening to him, spoke louder. "I'm not keeping you from your beauty rest, am I, Agent Ross?"

"No, sir," Gary responded, eyes vacillating between Walter and Botch. "It's just that it's been another busy night."

"Well, despite the mess—and not letting me know what you were planning," Walter suddenly smiled, "good job! Now get back to work, ingrates."

As he turned to leave, Gary inserted, "Hey, Walter, I'm going to take Rich and Mike out for a cup of celebratory coffee."

"Sure," answered Walter, appeased to be acknowledged, if only after the whole operation was concluded. "And get me one—black, one sugar—while you're at it."

As the three sauntered out, Walter turned to Botch to continue reprimanding him. "It's one thing to keep me, your direct supervisor, in the dark, but it looks to me like you're losing touch with your own men. They kept you out of the loop, didn't they? They obviously don't respect you, nor you me. Maybe it's time to retire while you still can. I'm saying this as a friend, Botch, because it's too late in your career to be making messes like this."

Botch forced himself to think before rising to Walter's bait. He thought of all the political ass-kissing his lush of a 'supervisor' had had to do to get and hold onto his position, and how many times Botch had covered for him. For the man to stand there and shovel out ignorant accusations didn't sit well, especially since Botch could smell the booze wafting off Walter from ten feet away. "Let me ask you something, Walter. Did they contact *you*?"

"Come to think of it, no," a puzzled Walter replied.

"I was on vacation, remember?"

"Yeah, so what are you saying?"

"I'm saying that, as I was away, they should have reported directly to you."

"Well?" Walter was at a loss for words and suddenly desperate for a drink.

"Well, what? Obviously they have no respect for *you,* Walter! And apparently, neither does the bureau. By the way, you're several years closer to retirement than me. Maybe *you* should think seriously about retiring while you're still sober enough to."

Walter began to object, but Botch cut angrily in. "And one last thing: You smell like scotch, and, I might add, as a friend, to everyone within a mile of you."

Walter staggered, as if slapped. "How dare you accuse me of being an alcoholic! That's my...my heart medicine, you insensitive prick!" Walter said, turning abruptly and storming out of Botch's office, adding as he exited, "And everyone knows it!"

It troubled Botch deeply to put Walter in his place, but he needed to shut him up and get him off his back. *Everyone knows it. Right,* Botch thought.

Outside the FBI building, Gary, Mike and Rich walked around the corner and huddled just outside the local coffee dive. "So now what's the plan? I take it you think Botch is setting us up," Mike Smith offered as Gary Ross signaled through the coffee shop window for four cups of coffee.

Gary looked grim. "Setting us up, yes, but for what? He could have done anything he wanted to us the other day, but he didn't." The waitress signaled back though the glass that the coffees were ready to pick up.

"I say we take the scumbag out. Tonight," Rich concluded.

Gary looked around anxiously to make certain that no one had overheard the man's remark. "Calm down, Rich. First, we've got to figure out where the money is, and we need to do it while watching every move Botch makes." Gary entered the coffee shop, picked up and paid for the four coffees, and herded the group back toward the FBI building.

Rich stopped. "When we were at the Dominican apartment, I knew I'd seen those cops before. Even the morgue attendant looked familiar, despite Botch acting like he didn't know any of them. Then, there they all are in the photograph in Botch's office together! I say Botch is one slick bastard, and after we get our money, he's mine."

"Fine, fine, but the important thing right now is to stay focused on how to reclaim the money," Gary said sternly.

Mike tossed in, "Me, I'm still trying to figure out *how* and *when* they moved the money. I mean, we were right there! I don't remember seeing anyone carrying bags of money in or out. Everyone else was dead except the girl, and she ran out holding just a purse."

Rich nodded his assent. "It's a good thing her wallet fell out. I'm just waiting for her to return to her apartment. Then we'll have one less loose end to worry about."

Mike suddenly started. The others stared at him. Slowly he proffered, "Joey V. left in a body bag."

Gary snapped his fingers! "That's it! They put the money in the body bag with Joey V.'s body!"

"You know, there's a rumor going around that the morgue has misplaced Joey V.'s body," Rich added, reaching desperately to put everything together.

Gary frowned. "Yeah, but we all saw the body. The guy looked pretty dead to me."

Rich frowned. "Yes, but none of *us* actually checked his pulse."

Gary considered. "True, but I don't think that slimy little weasel could be *that* good an actor."

Mike agreed. "I can't imagine him having the balls to double-cross us. I mean, he really believed we were legit. He needed our help to disappear and start a new life or he was a dead man."

"Well," Gary replied, "he had the balls to enter that apartment, knowing there was a damn good chance he'd never walk out. Still, I can't believe he's still alive. It's more likely they dumped his body somewhere and hauled off the cash."

"Well, let's find out if his body's been located, or he's been spotted anywhere. That's what the bureau does best, right?" Rich laughed.

Gary shushed him, saying quietly to the other two, "Listen, I found out that Twisted Ray is in Einstein Hospital. He was in Joey V.'s car last we saw, handcuffed to those two stiffs. I say we pay him a visit and see how he got out of the cuffs. It might shed more light on all this. Botch might know, of course, but after this morning's talk, I'd prefer prying it out of Ray."

CHAPTER 25

By noon, Gary Ross, the acknowledged leader of the threesome, had checked out his usual company car, gathered his two fellow agents, Mike Smith and Rich Pagano, and the three were weaving their way through the maze of traffic to Einstein Hospital.

Gary, driving, cleared his head of all extraneous thoughts. The only thing that mattered right now was locating Twisted Ray and finding out what happened to the money.

The four towers of Einstein Hospital quickly dominated the bright blue-grey sky. Gary pulled the car into the semi-circular driveway, taking the closest visitor parking spot. Getting out, they walked together towards the large, automatic-opening front doors of the hospital. "No wonder health insurance is out of sight," Rich added as they entered the foyer of what looked more like a five-star hotel lobby, complete with concierge.

Gary stepped up to the clerk sitting behind the large, curved mahogany desk, flashed his FBI badge and asked for Twisted Ray's room. The clerk instantly obliged and pointed towards the wing elevators.

On the sixteenth floor, two of Sweaters' goons, dressed in black Armani sweat suits, sat lazily reading newspapers on either side of Twisted Ray's hospital room door. Both instantly dropped the papers, stood and tried to block the trio's entry. Gary flashed his FBI identification, saying simply, "Federal agents. Step aside."

The two men looked at each other, unsure what to do. Mike and Rich stepped up, shoulder-to-shoulder with the two guards, and flashed their identification cards. This time the guards stepped aside, one visibly relaxing a hand that had reflexively slipped inside his running jacket.

"Good boys," said Gary, pushing his way past the guards, Rich and Mike following on his heels. Once through the door, Rich paused to look the two guards sternly in the eyes. "You. Wait outside," he said gruffly closing the door in their faces.

Ray was standing at the side of his bed, dressing. "Nice of the FBI to send the goodwill team on my last day in the hospital."

Rich placed himself in front of the door and crossed his arms. "Sit down and shut up!"

Ray slowly backed into the wheelchair waiting to take him out to the front of the hospital. Looking anxiously from agent to agent, he said, "Okay, I can play hardball, too. I've nothing to say to you or anybody else. I stay out of Sweaters' porn business, so unless you've got something else on me, you're holding me up." He reached slowly and cautiously for the call button cord, careful to make sure they could all see that he wasn't reaching for a weapon.

Rich and Mike moved like lightening, handcuffing Ray's wrists to the wheelchair while Gary bent next to Ray's ear and, in a low voice, said, "We're here for a different reason, Ray."

"What the fuck?!" Twisted Ray exclaimed, jerking his wrists to see if he could protect himself from whatever it was these nefarious agents had in mind. "You can't do this! I know my rights!" he screamed indignantly.

"Sorry, Ray," Gary said a little louder this time. "In this matter, you have no rights. I have a couple of easy-to-answer questions—strictly off the record. First, have you seen Joey V. or heard from him since the bust?"

"I don't know any Joey V. and if I did, why would I want to tell you anything?"

The three agents looked at each other, Rich saying as an aside, "It's never easy with these 'tough guys'."

Rich and Mike's arms shot out and flipped Ray's wheel chair back while Gary walked over to the bed, picked up one of Ray's pillows and fluffed it. Realizing their intent, Twisted Ray, struggled in horror to get his arms out of the cuffs, but couldn't. Gary calmly placed the pillow over Ray's face. This time, Ray kicked his legs and tried desperately to yell for help, but his screams barely made it through the pillow.

After a few minutes, Gary added his weight to the pillow while Mike and Rich pinned Ray's legs to the wheelchair. A few moments more and Gary removed the pillow.

Ray, his face ashen and lips blue, gasped for air.

Gary placed the pillow on Twisted Ray's lap and said calmly, "Let's try that question again, shall we, Ray? Joey V.—your pal with the missing ear—have you seen or heard from him at all since the bust? Just so you know, Ray, I find this kind of interrogation loathsome, so consider this your last opportunity to answer."

Ray hesitated. Gary picked up the pillow, fluffed it again and grasped it firmly in his hands. It took only a fraction of a moment for Ray to conclude that his own life was infinitely more precious than Joey V.'s. "Oh! That Joey V.! Yeah! I remember: He was here earlier!"

"You see, Ray," Gary said, tossing the pillow over onto the bed, "That wasn't so hard after all. Help the man up, guys." The two agents released Twisted Ray's legs and flipped the wheelchair and occupant upright again.

"Take the cuffs off, too," Gary said placidly. As Mike and Rich started to oblige, Gary interposed. "Oh, one final question, Ray. Where is he now?"

"I swear I don't know," Ray pleaded.

Gary tsk-tsked and grabbed Ray's bandaged right index finger—the one Ray had broken earlier swinging at Sal and Dom in Joey V.'s car. Ray tried to yell as Gary twisted, but Rich had recovered the pillow from the bed and placed it once again over Ray's face while Mike grasped Ray's chest from behind. They waited while Twisted Ray thrashed and began to turn blue again.

Rich lifted off the pillow.

Ray again pleaded, "I really don't know!" Gary nodded and began twisting Ray's index finger further. Just then, there was a knock at the door.

"A guy says he's here to take you down to the lobby," one of the guards offered politely. "You want we should let him in, boss?"

Ray instantly regained his composure. "Yeah, let him in!" he gasped loudly, angrily shaking off Gary's grip. The handcuffs disappeared and the pillow resumed its normal position on the bed.

A second later the door swung open and a well-muscled orderly walked in.

"Ready to go home, Ray?" he asked, looking questioningly from one to another of Ray's visitors.

Gary put his hands in his pockets; the other two agents smiled and followed suit. "Well, here's wishing you the best, Ray. Let's go, guys," said Gary. "I think visiting hours are over and Ray's got a lot of things on his mind to attend to, don't you, Ray?"

The orderly, taking Gary's comment as a "yes," proceeded to wheel Ray towards the door, the three agents following the wheelchair in single file. As they exited, one of Sweaters' door guards stepped in front of Rich. "If you didn't carry that badge, I'd remind you what manners are, you motherfucker."

Rich head-butted the guy on the nose. The goon yelped in pain and grabbed for his nose and blood began flowing through the man's fingers. Rich looked the man directly in his tearing eyes. "Yeah, well, I do have a badge. See? Now go get your nose fixed, before you get blood all over that expensive Guinea go-to-jail suit you're wearing." Everyone's attention, momentarily fixed on the altercation, returned to transporting the patient as quickly out of the hospital as possible before any more trouble ensued.

In the ground floor foyer, the three agents watched the hospital attendant push Ray out the front door. "When we find Joey V., we'll find the money," Rich stated.

"Let's hope so," Gary mumbled, and the three resumed their journey towards the front doors.

"Wait! It just hit me!" Rich said to the two men walking on either side of him. "That girl who escaped—the one I went to take care of at her apartment? The guy that was with her was the same one who wheeled off Joey V.'s body to the morgue! I'll bet you my share, he's not on the mortuary payroll."

"So now we have not one, but three leads to where the money is." Gary smiled. "But let's start with Joey V. Since we now know he's alive, we need to talk to him. Then we talk to the girl, who I'm certain we can coerce into identifying her mortuary-attendant-boyfriend before we get rid of her. My guess is that Joey V. or the boyfriend will lead us to the money."

The three agents climbed into their car. "Okay, so while you guys check on Joey V.'s whereabouts, I'll locate the girl and pay her another visit," Rich said from the back seat, wrinkling his nose.

"Good thinking," Gary advanced.

"Guys, check your shoes. Someone's stepped in shit or something." Rich added.

"I don't smell anything," Gary said, sniffing the air about the driver's area.

Mike, sitting in the passenger's seat, followed suit. "Me, either."

Nonetheless, each checked his shoes.

Rich, holding his nose, croaked, "Whatever. Just let's get going! The smell back here is making me nauseous. Maybe you two guys have been together so long you can't tell when the other has shit his pants, but I can tell you this for sure: There's something rotten going on here."

CHAPTER 26

Nick entered his apartment after a brisk walk to the nearest Chinese restaurant, returning with a large brown bag half-filled with cartons of aromatic Cantonese food tucked under one arm. He greatly enjoyed the feel of the warm, afternoon sun streaming down from a crisp, cloudless New York sky. He had been careful during his walk to make certain that he, and thereby Shelby, were not being watched.

Holding the food awkwardly to his chest, he fished into his jacket pocket, located the apartment keys, and sequentially unlocked the four deadbolts while balancing the cartons from escaping from his embrace. Inside, he froze to stare at Shelby and the living room. Stepping back into the hallway, he made a display of rechecking the apartment number.

Shelby, puzzled, had no idea what Nick was doing. "What?" she asked quizzically.

"The apartment!" Nick said with amazement. "It's clean! And there's a beautiful woman in it! I thought maybe I'd entered the wrong one!"

Shelby smiled. "Yeah, I cleaned up the apartment while you were away, and now I need to do the same for myself."

"You look great just as you are," Nick said. "You must be feeling better." He glanced about for somewhere to put down the food. "The place looks so good, I'm afraid to touch anything!"

Shelby let out a grateful sigh, "Well, don't. And, yes, I feel a hundred times better. I can't believe how out of it I've been the last few days."

"I guess whatever they slipped in your drink had to work its way through your system," he commented, looking to Shelby like a sweet, lost puppy dog.

"Please. I don't want to think about it. I can't believe there are creeps like that loose in this world," she said, taking the package from his arms, placing it on the cabinet next to her, and then cuddling into Nick's embrace. Placing her head on his

147

chest, she added, "Honestly, I'm glad the first bunch are all dead. I just hope the other three bastards are, too."

Nick hugged her briefly, guilty for having brought up the topic. "Alright," he said, running his fingers across her forehead and slowly down through her silken hair, "let's not talk about it, then," and he kissed her gently on the forehead. "Hey, I took off from work, so what do you say we get out of the house awhile. I didn't notice anyone hanging around the apartment or following me. I think things have finally quieted down. Anywhere in particular you'd like to go?"

Shelby slid a hand around Nick's slim, manly waist and with the other, entwined her fingers in his. "I should go to my place, pick up a few things and see about having the locks changed."

Nick frowned. When he finally let go of her hand, he reached over for the bag of Chinese food, grinned and said, "Let's eat first. I still haven't showered yet, so I can jump in after you…" His voice trailed off in expectation.

Shelby laughed. "Careful with the innuendo, big boy. I'm well-rested and fully capable of kicking your nice, firm ass now," she said, giving one of his ass-cheeks a playful squeeze.

"Promises, promises," Nick muttered, taking the Chinese food in one hand and Shelby in the other, and directing them to the living room. Sitting side-by-side on the sofa, the two began opening the myriad cartons. Shelby ate a little moo goo gai pan, her favorite, then said, "That's it for me, buster. Why don't you finish this off while I start my shower?"

She got up, yawned, stretched, and walked down the hallway into the bathroom, where Nick heard her turn on the water. Nick finished up and scraped the leftovers into three containers. Looking towards the refrigerator, he noticed a cloud of steam issuing from the bathroom, confirming that Shelby had, enticingly, left the door open. Mesmerized, Nick watched Shelby's reflection in the mirrored wall, as she soaped and slowly shaved her legs with his razor. Then she wrapped her hair into a white towel turban and her body with a white, bath-length towel.

Nick laughed to himself. It was like watching a TV commercial, the alluring woman, just naked enough to excite without exposing any private parts. Nick felt a strong rush of attraction course through his body at the sight of her like this, only to hesitate, afraid the open bathroom door might be accidental.

Shelby suddenly dropped both towels and slipped into the inner mist, pulling the shower curtain closed, then started to wash her hair. Nick, heart pounding, walked into the kitchen, pissed at himself. *You punked out,* he said to himself. *She probably left the door open for you, and you punked out.*

A few minutes later, Shelby padded out of the bathroom, dressed once again in the white turban and dress combination. "I would have showered before you came back, if I thought there was time," she said over her shoulder as she disappeared into the bedroom.

Nick, suddenly glad he hadn't reacted to the open bathroom door, guessed she hadn't been inviting him to join her in the shower, after all. The thought made him feel better for not having done anything foolish, but worse for the lost fantasy. Nick answered jokingly, "You didn't stink it up in there, did you?"

Shelby hissed and laughed, "No, stupid."

So now it was his turn. Nick went into the bathroom and turned on the shower, leaving the door open like Shelby had, thinking to himself, *fair's fair*. Doffing his clothes, he stepped into the still steamy shower, then started: The mist was saturated with her scent! He suddenly felt himself standing where moments ago she had been standing naked. He lathered his face and started to shave, feeling a tug. Great, he thought, touching hand to face and noticing blood on his hand.

He stuck his face into the hot, pelting water and felt another tug, this time on his shoulder. "Wha…?"

"Sorry," Shelby said, directing her eyes over every inch of his body, "but you jumped in before I washed the conditioner out of my hair. I needed to keep it on for a few minutes before washing it out—according to the bottle." Nick turned to face her and Shelby gasped, "Your body's all bruised and you're bleeding!"

Nick sucked in a deep breath of hot, humid air steeped with her scent and explained, "The bruises? Well, let's just say last Sunday was a bad day and leave it at that. The bleeding? Obviously some woman shaved her legs with my razor."

Shelby pouted. "You mean you're harboring another woman here?"

Nick stammered unintelligibly.

"So, you sneak, why didn't you stop me from shaving when you were watching?" Shelby asked, wrapping her slick, soft, wet arms around him. Then she stretched up onto her toes, closed her eyes, and placed her lips on his.

An hour later, the two lovers, still giddy, left Nick's apartment hand-in-hand to walk downstairs into the parking garage. Nick displayed a pumped-up bicep. "I don't know about you, but I'm loving this day!"

Shelby mmmmm'd incoherently, squeezed his strong bicep and rubbed the side of her head against his shoulder.

Nick stopped in front of a cherry red, 1973 Z28 Camaro. Shelby uncoiled herself from Nick to look it over, obviously impressed. "This your ride?"

"Yes, it is," Nick said, rolling her in front of him and pressing her against the front fender.

Shelby, skirt riding provocatively up, braced against the fender, and squirmed in anticipation, purring, "So what are you, some kind of motor-head?"

"What, you don't like me and my car? Sorry, sweetheart, but it's both of us or nothing. So which is it? Or are we already done, before we've started?" Nick taunted playfully.

Shelby tugged her up-riding skirt back down and retorted teasingly, "Oh, shut up, stupid," adding in a husky but sultry voice, "I like your car plenty; it's you I'm not sure of."

Nick pouted, then they both laughed and tumbled into the car.

Inside, Nick began a quick check while Shelby pulled down the visor to readjust her hair and refresh her lipstick, "Oh, don't pout!" she said, admiring him in the corner of the mirror and stretching over the stick shift to kiss him.

Nick returned her tease in the rough, sonorant voice of a trucker: "I'd let you drive, lady, but it's a stick."

"Oh, is that what you call this big, hard thing sticking up between my legs?" Shelby responded in dulcet tones, adding, "You're such a...*man*."

They both laughed heartily as Nick awoke the Camaro and, engine growling and tires screeching, all three animals screamed out of the darkness and into the flagging afternoon sun. Nick drove directly to Shelby's apartment, keeping an unspoken but wary eye out for anything unusual.

As the car growled up to the curb in front of the entrance to her apartment, Shelby said, "So are you going to tell me how you got all those bruises?"

Turning off the rumbling car, Nick turned to her and replied, "I would have told you before, but I was more interested in *your* body. I got my ass kicked a week ago by an overzealous cop."

Shelby's ears perked and she sat up straighter in the warmly aromatic leather seat. "Who? Your father?"

"My father?" Nick said, continuing to sweep the area with his eyes for watchers. "No. Why would you think that?"

"I don't know, Nick. You tell me. I mean if he's really a good cop, then why all the secrecy?"

Nick quit scanning and turned his undivided attention to Shelby. "My father is a good cop. Soon, you'll know what's going on, I promise, but right now it's like... I mean...do you really have a boyfriend?"

"Oh, I see," Shelby said, suddenly quiet and distant. "It's a 'need to know' thing."

Nick looked at her expectantly, hoping she would answer his question. "Exactly."

Shelby managed a weak smile, then began scanning the area herself, knowing that avoiding Nick's "boyfriend" question was driving him crazy. Noticing nothing out of the ordinary outside, Shelby placed a hand on the door handle. "Guess I should go find the super."

Nick awkwardly appended, "I'm coming up with you…if you don't mind, that is."

"Sure. Okay," she responded and climbed out, Nick joining her at the second door of the apartment building. Together they peered in, faces framed with cupped hands pressed against the smoked, beveled glass. They could just make out the outline of a tall man standing in the hallway, alone. Shelby seemed to recognize him and he, her, opening the door for them from the inside.

"Hi, Steve," Shelby said, walking in and casually slipping her arm in his. "Can you help me, please? I lost my keys and I need to get into my apartment."

Steve removed his arm from hers, took a step back and smirked. "What happened, Shelby? Your boyfriend lose his keys, too?"

Number One Bestseller

CHAPTER 27

Nick's face went instantly pale. "I'll be in the car," he said, turning away, angry and dejected.

Shelby grabbed him. "No! Wait," she pleaded, holding onto his arm tightly.

Turning back to the building superintendant, Shelby exclaimed, "I don't have a boyfriend, Steve, and you know it!" Then glaring back at Nick, she asked, "There, are you happy?"

Nick stood surprised and confused.

Steve interrupted, "Hey, how am I supposed to know? The guy *said* he was your boyfriend, and I saw him lock the door the other day when he left your apartment. He was well-dressed, but not a gentleman from his menacing look."

Nick's face dropped, his confusion replaced with concern. "But he's gone now, right? How about you come with us upstairs and open the door?"

"Yeah, alright. He hasn't come back, at least as far as I can tell, though he could have. Let me get the keys. Wait here," he ordered, throwing an inquisitive eye at Shelby as he passed her.

Shelby repositioned herself in front of Nick, clasping his hands tightly in hers, and said, in a low voice, "I hope whoever found my license and keys didn't..."

Nick said nothing, not wanting to scare her further.

"Well, there's one good thing that's come out of all of this," Shelby offered nervously.

"Yeah, what's that?"

"Now you know I don't have a boyfriend!" She said, giving him a stern look. "But the truth is I *do* have a boyfriend. He's not that guy. Or Steve," she added playfully.

Nick, initially relieved, frowned again, and tried to disentangle himself from Shelby's grip, but she wouldn't let go. "Hey, Nick! Don't you get it? So what are you if you're not my boyfriend? My chauffeur?" Shelby asked.

Nick's face relit.

Steve, the building super, returned with the keys, and together, the three walked silently up the stairway to Shelby's apartment. As Steve slid the key in the upper door lock, he turned to apologize. "Look, Shelby, I didn't know the guy wasn't your boyfriend and not supposed to have your keys. I didn't like him, but he didn't look like the robber-type. I mean I can't keep track of everyone in the building, you know. Besides, he flipped me a badge, though I didn't really look at it carefully, it not being any of my business, really," Steve seemed awkward in proportion to his eagerness to offer the information.

Nick cocked his head to one side. "A badge, you say? What kind of badge? Think!"

Steve paused in the process of unlocking the third and final lock. "Like I said, it happened so quick, and I really didn't want to know, if you get my drift." Finishing with the third deadbolt, Steve pushed open the door.

The apartment though dark was clearly a wreck. "Damn! Whoever he was, he sure trashed your place good," Steve said, stepping inside.

From inside to Steve's left, a long, narrow, steel blade flashed, plunging its tip into the notch at the base of Steve's throat. Steve gasped in agony and tried to look back at the two behind him, a look of pain, horror and shock on his already paling face. "Wh...?" he gurgled through a froth of blood as his eyes rolled up and his body went slack.

Nick pulled Shelby back as the knife blade jerked out of Steve's chest and arched above as if to strike again, this time at them, while Steve's body crumpled forward into the darkness. Grabbing the door knob, Nick yanked the apartment door shut on the arm as it slashed through the air to where Shelby, a moment before, had been standing. There was a loud crunch and a scream of pain from behind the door, followed by, "ahh...Fuck!"

Nick braced his foot against the door jamb and yanked the door shut with all his strength, crushing the entrapped arm, the eight-inch, blood-streaked blade clanging noisily from the gloved hand onto the wood hallway floor. Nick yelled over the resulting scream at a horrified Shelby, "I'll hold the door closed as long as I can! Take the car keys out of my pocket, and get out of here!"

Nick's shout brought Shelby back to her senses. "I'm not leaving without you!"

This time, Nick ordered her: "Do as I said...now!"

Shelby slipped a hand into Nick's trouser pocket, grabbed the car keys and yelled back on her way down the stairs, "I'll wait for you in the car!"

"Don't wait for me! Just get the hell out of here!" Nick yelled. "And watch out! This one's probably not alone!"

"I'll be waiting for you in the street with the motor running!" Shelby insisted as she flew down the stairs.

Nick sighed and focused on preventing the person behind the door from forcing it open, trying to figure out what to do next.

On the other side of the door, the man, cringing with pain, reached his free hand awkwardly into the opposite pants pocket, pulled out a gun and began firing through the door.

The first bullet burst out from the middle of the door, narrowly missing Nick's abdomen. Abruptly changing tactics, Nick stopped pulling and, instead, shoved the door open with all his weight, knocking the person inside the apartment down. Several bullets discharged loudly into the ceiling. Not waiting to see the result or who the person was, Nick slammed the door and ran down the stairs.

Rich Pagano lay decked out on the littered and bloodied wood floor, the body of the dead superintendent beside him, momentarily stunned. His gun had flown across the living room from the sudden impact with the door. Rich got painfully up, retrieved the gun in his uninjured hand and ran dizzily out the door for the stairs. The incredible pain from his crushed right forearm and pounding head made it difficult to focus his eyes and navigate the stairs.

When he finally got down to the lobby, it was to see Nick approaching the side of an idling, Z28 Camaro. The woman he was after was in the driver's seat.

Shelby popped open the passenger door and screamed, "Get in!"

The moment Nick's body began to enter, she popped the clutch, smoking and screaming the tires down the street, the passenger door slamming shut from inertia.

Rich, tears obscuring his vision, tried desperately to brace the gun with his good and compromised hands and aimed to shoot, but the pain from the crushed arm made his hands shake so badly he couldn't get off the shot. Noticing pedestrians beginning to look his way, he quickly secreted the gun, ran across the street and jumped into his own car, setting off in pursuit.

To Nick's surprise, Shelby shifted the gears like a pro, screeching right at the next intersection, controlling the swaying car expertly all the way through the screaming turn. She brought the car quickly up to top speed and began weaving in and out of traffic, the man who had killed her friend and super following a lengthening block behind. Shelby, tears streaming from her eyes, cried, "Why kill Steve? Why?"

Nick looked out the rear window. "Maybe he thought Steve, if he lived, could identify him. Or maybe he thought Steve was me...or, more likely, you. I don't know, but let's not be next," he said, adding in the next breath, "Whoa! Truck crossing the road! Stop!"

Shelby slammed on the brakes, and as they screeched to a stop, she slammed the car into reverse.

Rich had only a split second before realizing that the back of the red Camaro he was following a moment ago was now speeding directly at him. Reflexively, he stomped on the brakes and aimed to the side of the onrushing Camaro, hoping to avoid death by direct impact.

Just before impact, Shelby stomped on the brakes again and threw the straining car back into first, screeching off in a black cloud of acrid, burnt rubber.

Rich missed colliding with the Camaro by inches, in the process veering off the road and into the side of a parked van. Momentarily stunned, he looked up and down the road to see the red car roaring away in the distance. Rich swore as he teased his crumpled government car backwards to separate himself from the van he had rammed, then floored the accelerator, directing the car back down the street after his two targets, his right wrist shrieking with pain.

Nick looked at Shelby as she once again shifted deftly through the gears. "Where the hell did you learn how to drive like that?" he asked.

"In Pennsylvania," she answered calmly. "There wasn't much to do there, so my father taught me to race." She looked momentarily over at Nick with a grin. "He was a big motor-head. That's how I got my name. You know, the Ford Shelby Cobra Mustang?"

"A *Ford*? Never heard of it," Nick lied.

"My father would flip if he knew I was falling for a Chevy guy," she said, directing her attention back to her driving. "But I got to admit," she said, patting the dashboard fondly, "It's a great ride."

"Me or the car?" Nick tossed back.

Shelby looked briefly in the rear view mirror. "Both! Hold on," she said and executed another sharp, right turn.

Nick looked out the rear window to see the pursuing white government car reappear around the corner.

"Persistent bastard," he said as they whipped flat-out past a police cruiser.

The cops, momentarily stunned, turned on lights and siren, and screamed out into the street in hot pursuit, just as Rich came barreling through.

Slamming on his brakes to avoid hitting the police car, Rich knew he had run out of room. In defense, he cut the wheel left and screeched up a side street, then fishtailed to a complete stop.

Throwing open the door of his car, he cursed the crowd of people already gathering around him on the side street. "All of you," he screamed flashing his FBI badge, "get the hell out of the way!" Rich stormed to the street corner and watched the cops disappear into the distance. "Fucking cops didn't even see me!" he bellowed.

Shelby, noticing the police car, lights blazing, but no sign of the man who, moments before, seemed so anxious to kill them, eased up on the accelerator. "What should we do?" she asked Nick.

"Did you see what happened to the guy who was chasing us?" Nick asked.

"He made a sudden left when the cops showed up," Shelby said, grinning.

"Go about ten blocks further, then pull over," Nick said calmly.

Shelby pushed the car hard, leaving the police unable to narrow the distance between them, then after nine blocks, began slowing down, finally pulling the car to the curb. The police pulled up twenty feet behind, and tumbled out, guns drawn. One yelled loudly, "Turn off the car and place the keys on the roof."

Shelby did as instructed, tossing the keys onto the roof of the hissing, steaming car.

"Everyone in the car: Put your hands out the windows and keep them where I can see them!" the second officer yelled.

Shelby and Nick complied. The two officers, after calling for backup, cautiously approached the Camaro.

Nick, in the passenger seat, looked at the policeman on his side, and said, "Hey, don't I know you?"

The officer, gun braced and pointed directly at Nick's head, checked the empty back seat, then looked Nick over carefully.

Nick continued talking, careful to make no sudden moves, this time to Shelby. "Honey, remember I told you about the cop that beat me up?"

Shelby sucked in her breath. "Jesus, Nick, is that him?"

"No, this is the guy's partner, Officer Mitchell, right?" Nick said, looking the officer directly in the eyes.

Officer Mitchell peered through Nick's open window at the woman in the driver's seat, and at his partner on the other side of the car holding a gun to the woman's head, then sighed. "Frank, lower your weapon. I know this guy. He's a son of one of our own. We've already fucked up once in his father's eyes, let's not do it again. Lower your weapon."

The rookie officer hesitated, then lowered his gun and called Officer Mitchell to the side. "Mitchell, what the fuck's going on here?"

"That guy's Mack McConville's son, and I'm going to assume this is a life or death emergency, right kid?"

Nick nodded affirmatively.

Officer Mitchell pointed a thumb at Nick. "The kid's name is Nick and he and his father are personal friends of Captain Brown. My former partner recently ran up against Mack, and let me tell you, Mack's not someone we want to mess with."

"Shit. I heard about him at briefing—how Curtis went crazy, and got his ass kicked and thrown off the force."

Officer Mitchell nodded, then smiled and waved at Shelby and Nick, as he shoved his partner back towards their own car.

The two cops limped off without saying a further word to Shelby or Nick.

"Guess that means we can go," Shelby ventured.

Nick grinned. "I guess so. Make a right, get on the parkway and let's put as much distance between us and that killer somewhere behind us as we can."

Shelby hesitated, puzzled. "Why didn't you tell the cops about that lunatic chasing us?"

"Because," Nick said as they drove away, "that lunatic is an FBI agent."

"What?" Shelby interrupted. "Then why does he want to kill me?"

"Let's just say he and his friends went over to the dark side and you're the main witness."

Shelby wasn't satisfied. "I don't get it. Your father's a cop and his friends are all in law enforcement, so why can't they just report these guys?"

"They will, but not until after Sunday."

"Why do I feel like you aren't telling me all of what's going on here, Nick? I think I've been through…"

Nick interrupted, "Alright, I'll tell you," and he proceeded to explain about the money and his father's plan to bet the money so that they could buy Marisol's.

Shelby, listening as she drove, nodded her head every so often to let Nick know she was following the explanation. "So what you're telling me is your father, the good cop, is doing all this bad stuff, not only to catch some really bad federal agents who are posing as good guys, but also to feather your father's own nest in the process?"

"Well," Nick said after a thoughtful pause, "I admit it sounds weird, and that he's having a particularly bad week in terms of breaking the law, but my father's still a good cop. Look at it this way: He saved your life, didn't he? Those three FBI agents certainly have no intention of leaving you alive."

Shelby's face softened. "I know, I know. Well, since you have this new-found wealth, and I can't go home to get any clothes, you're going to have to take me on a shopping spree."

"I'll make you a deal," Nick offered. "I'll pay for whatever you want to buy, but I have to drop you off at the mall and pick you up when you're finished. There's something I need to do while you shop."

"Deal," Shelby chimed. "Just make sure we're not being followed. I don't want to run into that man or any of his friends while while I'm alone and shopping."

"How much time will you need before I come back for you?" Nick asked. "An hour?"

Shelby looked sternly at Nick. "You're not getting off that easy, big boy. I have a black belt in shopping."

Nick's cell phone rang. It was Mack. Nick explained briefly what had happened as Shelby drove on. Mack sounded concerned and made Nick agree to meet him at Nick's apartment while Shelby shopped. The moment Nick hung up, the phone chimed again. This time it was his mother, Annie. She asked Nick if he could pick her up so she could use the washing machine at his apartment—hers was on the fritz. "Sure, Ma, I'll pick you up in about twenty minutes," he said happily, his face a widening grin.

Shelby stared at Nick. "What's so funny?"

"I'm about to host both my parents at my apartment at the same time."

"So?" Shelby asked, her interest piqued, but not understanding.

"Remember I said they hadn't talked in years?"

"You're one devious, deluded kid, Nick, if you think getting them in a room together after so many years is going to solve anything," she said emphatically.

Nick frowned. "What, like they don't deserve another chance? For years, I've been put in the middle. I swear, deep down, they still love each other."

"And now, you're going to *willingly* place yourself in the middle?" Shelby asked.

Nick smirked. "I won't be gone for long. I've got an appointment to meet you at the mall, remember? We're both going to need clothes for our vacation."

Shelby's face suddenly lit up. "Vacation? Where are we going?"

"My father wants us out of here for a couple of days to let things cool off, so it's Vegas, baby! That way we'll be safe and we can bet the game out there, too."

Shelby laughed girlishly, "I haven't been on vacation in so long...and I've never been to Vegas!"

Shelby slowed the car down and cautiously entered the mall parking lot.

Number One Bestseller

CHAPTER 28

Shelby trundled happily off into the mall, while Nick proceeded to pick up his mother and bring her to his apartment.

His mother, Annie O'Boyle McConville—she had resolutely kept her married name—appearing in the best of moods, walked across the threshold of Nick's apartment and stopped, arched her eyebrows, and looked suspiciously around. Though she didn't say a word, she sniffed the air and quietly started doing her wash while Nick packed a carry-on for Las Vegas.

The doorbell rang.

Nick called for his mother to get it.

Mack, impatient, rang the doorbell again only to hear a feminine voice behind the door call out, "Alright, alright! Hold your horses. I'm coming!"

Mack first assumed the familiar voice was Shelby's. Then it hit him. It wasn't Shelby's, it was Annie's! Turning to exit quickly down the staircase, he froze when Annie opened the door. Both blushing red, the stunned couple stared at each other until Anne finally said, "Hello, Mack. Nick's in the back, packing. I came over to do my wash…the washing machine broke again…"

Turning brusquely, she walked towards the kitchen, when Mack, his voice cracking as it returned, blurted out, "So…how are you?"

Annie turned and stared at Mack as if not comprehending what she'd just heard. "How am I? How am I? Are you alright, Mack? That's the most you've said to me in four years!"

Nick poked his head out of the bedroom. "Hey, Dad, shut the apartment door, will you?"

Mack, relieved not to have to acknowledge Annie's comment, stepped in and shut the door.

Mack and Annie, barely three feet from each other, stood wordless and awkward, each waiting for Nick.

161

Nick walked out with a carry-on in each hand. "Guess I'll see you at the bar on Sunday for the game, Dad. Bye, Mom!" He kissed Annie on the cheek.

Annie, totally confused, asked, "Where are you going?"

"Vegas!" he replied happily.

Annie seemed even more confused. "Vegas? How am I going to get all this wash home?"

"Dad can take you. I have to go and get Shelby. Bye!" he said as he passed between them. "There's beer in the 'fridge, Dad," he added, as he opened the apartment door and rushed into the hallway.

Annie looked plaintively at Mack. "Don't look so worried, Mack. I can catch a cab."

"No, it's alright. I'll drive you home," Mack said, and sighed.

They stood, silent again, looking each other over until Annie finally ventured, "Well, this is awkward."

"Yeah. I'm sure your son's laughing his ass off!"

"He definitely takes after you," Annie said, baiting Mack.

"Me?" Mack asked, innocence covering his weathered face.

"Yes, you would find it funny, if it wasn't you he'd just set up."

Mack nodded, "True," adding, "You...want a beer?"

Annie, feeling surprisingly adventurous, said, "Why not," and followed Mack into the kitchen. They sat at either end of the kitchen table, Mack reaching into the refrigerator from where he was sitting and handing Annie a bottle of cold beer. She struggled to open it, then looked plaintively over at Mack who palmed the bottle and examined it. "Your son has expensive taste. This kind needs an opener."

Mack got up and rummaged through a drawer until he found a bottle opener. Standing next to Annie, he took the bottle from her and popped it open

"Thank you, Mack. You always were the gentleman," she said, half hopefully, half sarcastically.

Mack raised his eyebrows. "I know. I suck." Mack, his own beer in hand, got up and backed into the kitchen corner while Annie looked him over carefully.

"You look like hell, Mack. When was the last time you slept?"

"Thanks for the compliment. It's been a particularly tough week."

"From what? Drinking?" Annie replied, a resentful edge to her voice.

Mack shrugged his shoulders. "No. Well, a little. There's a lot going on. The drinking was so I could sleep."

Annie switched to a more conversational tone. "So, who's this Shelby girl Nick keeps talking about? He raved about her constantly on the ride over."

"He met her just recently. I don't know much about her, but she seems nice enough," adding, "I don't think it's anything serious, though."

"I'm his mother, and it sounded serious to me. He's never talked this way about any of his other girlfriends."

Mack tried but couldn't hold back his next comment: "You women make everything into a romance novel."

"You'll see," Annie responded, ignoring the innuendo. "How about you? Any romance in your life, Mack?"

Mack froze, surprised that Annie would dare ask such a personal question. Then it occurred to him that what he and Annie were doing was testing the fences they'd put up. He wasn't really sure if they should. Given the chance, however, Mack hastily decided to stomp right over the fence: "Me, I've sworn off romance," he said, hoping she'd get the message that he was not seeing anyone else and had never forsaken her. Mack dropped his eyes from Annie's inquiring face to the open beer bottle in his hand, then guzzled a drink.

"You mean there's no one you're...interested in?" Annie asked as offhandedly as she could.

Mack felt himself instantly on guard, and, uncomfortable with where the conversation was leading, replied, "Nope." To Annie's thinking, he looked lost and miserable.

Annie, suddenly torn between hope and desperation, changed the topic. "It's nice to talk to you face-to-face instead of through Nick or the lawyer."

"Yeah," Mack grunted, then took a plunge: "How about you? Anyone special?"

Annie didn't want to say anything that would shut him down. "I've made some attempts, but they were mistakes, so in truth there's been no one since you."

Mack squirmed and watched Annie's eyes fill slowly with tears.

"I'm sorry, Mack," she quickly said. "I don't mean to make you uncomfortable..."

Mack turned away from her and looked out the window, his face suddenly flushed with anger. "Yeah, I know about one of the mistakes: that guy you were with while you were still married to me." There, he'd said it. He'd torn the fences completely down and if she denied it, he could put them back up and walk away, this time finally unburdened with guilt. It made him feel good to release the poison he had been steeping in all the years.

Annie stared at her beer and then began sobbing quietly. "I had a feeling you knew, but I could never muster up the courage to talk to you about it. You were so consumed with taking down Jerry Sweaters and...we grew so distant. I thought if I told you, you would hate me, forever. Then when you left, I guessed that you knew. That's why I never asked you why you left. I wish to God the loneliness hadn't driven me into someone else's arms. After I did it, I realized what living without self-worth felt like. I've wanted—needed—to apologize for blaming you, Mack. The big question is, can you forgive me?" Before Mack could answer, Annie stood up and slid over towards him, adding "Please tell me first that Nick doesn't know."

Mack, his chest tightening, tried to breathe, to turn, to take her in his arms, to forgive her, but instead stiffened and whispered, "I would never tell him."

Annie, grasping tightly onto Mack's strong arms, continued. "Hurting you has been something I've never been able to forgive myself for or get past. I know you took a lot of heat from Nick when you walked away seemingly for no reason. I know I didn't do anything to change that. I know now how special what we had was, Mack, before all that…and I wish…I wish…"

Mack thought about telling her about the tape, but quickly realized there was no point. It would only bring more pain. If she honestly knew all he'd gone through, with the tape constantly hanging over his head, she would more than likely *never* forgive herself. Instead, Mack turned and confessed, "I know back then I wasn't there for you when you needed me. My father raised me to not show emotions. In my family, it was a sign of weakness—the John Wayne complex Andre calls it." He looked at Annie, pent up tears from all that had transpired since that fateful day welling in his eyes. "I…I'm so sorry, Annie."

Annie had never in her life seen Mack cry and immediately burst into tears, pleading, "Can you forgive me, Mack?"

Mack, as heartfelt and honest as he could, replied, "I…I don't know. I've never known. But I'll try. And I do know this: My life has been dead without you, Annie. The pain has to stop."

Annie wrapped herself in Mack's willing embrace.

After a few minutes, Mack untangled himself and, sniffling, held her by the shoulders and looked deeply into her eyes. "I think it's time for us to wipe our faces and…try again."

Annie laughed and said lovingly, "Idiot, you mean wipe *my* face," accepting the paper towel Mack was offering her, gently blotting her and then his face.

"There's going to be some big changes this week, Annie."

Annie nodded. "What kind of changes do you mean?"

"After this weekend I could be 'well off' in a financial way." Annie sat beside him and sipped at her beer. "What, you're going to rob a bank?"

"Well, not a legitimate bank," Mack joked.

"Mack, please don't do something that's going to get you killed, not after all we've been through. Please, Mack."

"The dangerous part is over, Annie. I'm just waiting to see how things fall out now. How about I take you to the bar Sunday for the Jets game and I'll explain it all then?"

Annie smiled, opened the refrigerator and reached for another beer, then gave a puzzled gasp at a tiny, bright red dot of light that suddenly appeared in the middle of Mack's chest. Mack looked at her blank face, then followed her gaze to the red light centered directly over his heart. Annie jerked the refrigerator door open further to block the light. The combined sound of glass shattering and a series of rapid thuds on the refrigerator door filled the room as Mack dove on Annie, tackling her to the floor. The two slumped in the corner, backs against the wall, Mack's body covering Annie's. Beer, glass and the contents of a shattered ketchup bottle from inside the refrigerator door splattered across the room and all over the front of Mack's shirt.

Shaking off the shock, Mack crawled to the window, gun in hand, and peeked out the corner of the bullet-shattered window. In the distance, he could make out Rich Pagano, rifle in hand, jumping into a nondescript government car and streaking off.

Mack turned to Annie who was shaking frantically with fear. "Annie, are you alright?"

"Obviously the dangerous part isn't entirely over yet," Annie managed, picking herself up from the floor.

Mack looked angrily at the bullet holes in the refrigerator door. "I don't know how you're going to explain this to Nick."

Annie cleared her throat and took a deep breath. "It's like old times again, Mack. I'm back around you, and within minutes I'm almost killed."

Mack stood up and began awkwardly brushing Annie off. "I'll tell you everything, but right now I have to call Andre and Botch to tell them what just happened…and find out what else is going on."

Number One Bestseller

CHAPTER 29

Mack settled a trembling Annie onto the couch in the living room and called Botch.

"They're putting the pieces together," Botch replied. "You're lucky Annie was there, that guy, Rich, fancies himself a marksman and I'm thinking he thinks he made the kill since he took off like that. He's not one to give up easily."

"He's certainly got balls to try it in broad daylight," Mack replied. "I'm figuring he must have run Nick's license plate. Trouble is, who was he gunning for? If Nick, then they're trying to flush out Shelby. If me, that would mean they know we've got the money, and are trying to scare you two into doing something rash."

"Well, if they know you're involved, and he thinks he got you, they'll likely be watching Andre or me. I'll see if he shows up at tomorrow's meeting. By the way, per you're suggestion, I'll go with Joey V. to pay Amazing a visit tomorrow, just before the game," Botch said.

"Alright, but watch yourself. Talk with you later, Botch. Bye."

Mack keyed off and immediately called Andre to fill him in about Rich's seeming attempt to kill him. Andre listened intently. "That sounds really heavy. Joyce and I are on our way over to visit the in-laws. I'll drop her off and then drive over and give you a hand carrying it, Mack."

Mack could overhear Joyce complaining in the background, "You're not dropping me anywhere! You promised me a quiet evening, Andre: You and me and my parents!"

Mack sighed. "Andre, put Joyce on." Then Mack handed his phone to Annie.

Joyce, hearing Annie's voice on the other end, chimed in, "Annie? What kind of trouble are the men in this time? I can see it in Andre's face..." then Joyce switched in mid-sentence. "Hey! Wait! Are you and Mack there *together*?"

"Yes," Annie replied calmly.

167

"Girl, we spoke just last night and you didn't mention anything about meeting up with Mack."

"I had no idea it would happen. I'll tell you everything at the bar Sunday while the guys watch the Jets game, but for now, please just do as they say."

Joyce looked over at Andre. "Why didn't you tell me Mack and Annie were talking again? Would it have hurt to let me know? I mean, we stood for them at their wedding," adding in the same breath, "and don't tell me you forgot."

Andre tried desperately to get a word in: "That was Annie on the phone?" realizing as he said it that Mack had given him the out he needed. Andre closed his mouth and listened to Joyce as she continued talking on about Annie and Mack.

Eventually Joyce got to the question she'd asked Andre for years: "You mean Mack *still* hasn't told you why he broke up with Annie?"

"I've told you, over and over, he never told me or Botch anything about it, ever."

"I don't believe you," Joyce pouted. "I know you guys have this 'code of silence,' thing, but I'm going to find out this Sunday," she said emphatically, watching to see her husband's reaction.

Andre didn't want to tell Joyce about the money, or worse, that he'd bet it all, at least until the whole affair was over. No sense hearing her call him an idiot twice, though that was exactly how he felt just now: like a big idiot. "Say, why are you going to the bar on Sunday?" Andre advanced, trying to deflect Joyce's attention elsewhere. "You don't like football."

Joyce eyed him suspiciously, "What, you don't want me there? You meeting a girlfriend or something?"

Andre sighed. "Oh yeah, that's just what I need: another woman breaking my balls. Honey, my balls are only for you to break."

"That's right, Mr. 'Avoid-the-Issue-Any-Way-You-Can.' You can be damn sure I'd cut 'em off if I ever heard otherwise."

Andre pulled up to Joyce's parents' house and checked his car mirrors to make sure he wasn't being followed. "I guess I'll have to take the credit card and my mother out shopping," she said defiantly.

"I'm sorry about all this, babe, but I have to meet with Mack. Police business," Andre answered vaguely.

Joyce got out and as Andre started to pull away, she signaled for him to stop and roll down his window. Andre reluctantly complied.

"Andre, what exactly did Mack say to you on the phone that's got you so spooked?" Joyce asked.

Andre squealed the tires and yelled as he drove off, "Between three and four o'clock," leaving a confused and apprehensive Joyce watching her husband disappear in the distance.

Andre grinned, thinking about how many times he'd gotten away with acting like he heard the question wrong. Then he turned his attention back to the fact that Rick Pagano might, at this moment, be hunting him down, and the grin disappeared.

A half hour later, Mack and Andre were talking together at Farrell's over a beer. "I think Botch is right, Andre. That psycho, after unsuccessfully chasing Nick and Shelby, must have run Nick's plates afterwards at the bureau, and I happened to be at that address instead of Nick. You're off for the weekend, right?"

Andre responded, "Yeah, like Botch, I took the week off."

"Me, too, so they wouldn't have tracked either of us from work."

"Do you think they're onto Botch, yet?" Andre asked.

"They will be after Saturday, if the plan works."

"Right. I guess it won't matter if we're seen with Botch after that," Andre admitted.

Just then Joey V. called Mack. "It's all swimming," he said and hung up.

Mack looked at Andre, a broad smile developing on his face. "The money's bet," he said.

Andre looked up and raised his clasped palms towards the ceiling. "Lord, please make this work," he pleaded.

Number One Bestseller

CHAPTER 30

Rich Pagano phoned his comrades, Gary Ross and Mike Smith: "Listen, I'm not showing at the inquiry today. They might bring up my smashing up the company car the other day near the girl's apartment. And a bit of news: I was aiming to take out the girl's boyfriend the other day, but ended up taking out Botch's friend instead. You know, the grey-haired donkey-cop."

After a stunned minute's silence, Gary ventured, "What the hell are you doing taking out a cop? You were supposed to get rid of the girl! I mean, shit, Rich! And why wait to tell us? We're still under investigation, and you go throwing fuel on the fire!"

"Hey! I'm taking care of my part," Rich replied angrily. "With Botch's friend gone, he and that black friend of his must feel threatened. That means they'll run for the money, right? So have you taken care of your part? Have you located Joey V. and where they're hiding the money?"

Silence.

"No," said Gary. "We haven't located Joey V. yet, but Mike just got a lead. We were going to check it out when you called."

This time, the other end went quiet.

"So?" Gary Ross asked, irritated.

"So, I'm wondering what Botch is up to. What if this is a set up to weed out corruption in the bureau?" asked Rich Pagano.

"You're getting paranoid! Our fearless leader hasn't shown his face at work since we met with him and Steiner," replied Gary acerbically. "I don't think he gives a shit about what's going on at the office, if you ask me, but if you've taken out his partner and best friend, then at best, we'll see what his next move is. At worst, you've just incited the wrath of the whole police department on us."

"Fuck," Rich replied. "I mean, I didn't think…"

"Yeah," emphasized Gary, "you *didn't think*!"

"Okay, okay! I'll pick up the girl and her boyfriend's trail soon enough and this time I'll get rid of them both. They can't be far. Call me later." Rich abruptly disconnected.

"What the fuck?" Gary said, staring helplessly at the cell phone in his fist. "God damn loose cannon…"

CHAPTER 31

Gary Ross and Mike Smith left FBI headquarters to check out an auto body shop Smith had located supposedly owned by Joey V.'s younger brother. If they could just locate Joey V., Gary was certain the man would lead them to the millions of dollars that were rightfully theirs.

A minute after Gary and Mike left, Botch pulled into the FBI parking lot and, after scanning unsuccessfully for any sign of any of the three agents, entered the building and traipsed into Walter's office. Botch thought it time to inform his boss of his 'suspicions' regarding the three subordinates currently under investigation.

"Have you looked over the report and pictures of that crime scene from the drug raid, Walter?" Botch began. "I've been going over them and there are just too many discrepancies."

"What's wrong, Botch, jealous?" Walter droned sarcastically without looking up from his desk. "I read that *you* were there and abruptly left. Without informing me, I might add."

"The fact that they didn't notify me of the operation, and the way they acted when I showed up, made me suspect they were up to no good. I just needed some time to confirm my suspicions."

"Botch, Botch," Walter said, even more sarcastically, "I'm hearing a lot of speculation here. How about something concrete?"

"I'm tracking down a witness, but apparently she's not too trusting of the FBI after your golden boys killed everyone who could have talked," retorted Botch vehemently.

"Alright, you've got five days, but if you can't find your witness and get her to talk by then, this case is closed. And, by the way, I sincerely hope you know what you're doing. Your name's now on the official bureau shit-list, and if you screw up anymore, you'll be out on your ass, *sans* retirement. You can't give the bureau a black eye and not expect to pay."

"Yeah, well..." Botch began to reply.

Walter looked at Botch with a fond sadness. "Hell, Botch, I'll even give you a couple of agents to help. That's if there's anyone left in the bureau you can trust and who trusts you. Remember, the boys in Washington are looking to canonize these three guys, so you better make your suspicions good and you'd better do it quick."

Botch thought for a moment, weighing Walter's motives. "New agents are like new school girls: They talk too much. I'm more comfortable alone," Botch said flatly.

Walter nodded knowingly.

Across the city, Mike was directing Gary to an auto shop at Hunt's Point: "Take this side road down to the end and make a right. It's one or two lots in. Ah, that must be it!" he said pointing to a dilapidated sign that said "Chris's Auto Shop" in faded, black letters. "The brother's name is Chris."

The two agents climbed out of the car and peered through the closed, chain-link fence and gate. "That car was Joey V.'s pride and joy, and given the situation, this is the about the only place he could take it for repairs without revealing himself."

Gary grunted and started walking to the right. "I'll check out the yard next door." Pointing back at the gate, he ordered Mike to check out the body shop.

The gate turned out to not be locked, so Mike opened it cautiously, looking around warily for guards or dogs. Not noticing any, a chill crept down his spine. Lack of security at a body shop was not a good sign.

Inside, to the right of the open, oil-soaked yard and behind a couple of large trees, he could make out one of two, long, metal buildings. Inside the closer building, he spotted Joey V.'s car. The exterior appeared fully restored. Two workmen were putting final touches to the interior.

Mike walked up and asked the nearer man, "Hey, there! You Chris?"

The man and his partner stopped what they were doing and looked up suspiciously. "Who wants to know?"

"You thinking of selling that?" Mike asked, pointing towards the car the two men were leaning over. "What year is it?"

"It's a '67 Chevy SS Impala and it's not for sale," the first of the two men, Chris, replied, warier than before.

"I'm a collector," Mike lied, "and I'd like to talk to the owner. I wonder if he'd be interested in selling it?"

"Well, I know the owner and he wouldn't," Chris replied, wiping his hands on a faded towel while approaching the "collector." Mike mirrored Chris' movements, wiping his sweating hands on the sides of his pants and moving closer to the car as if to inspect it.

Chris, the faster, stepped between Mike and the car and blocked Mike's further advance.

"I have something out back that you might like," Chris offered, extending a gnarled hand towards a narrow alleyway passing between the two buildings and on to the back of the lot. Mike hesitated, then extended his own hand, inviting Chris to go first, following the repairman at a safe distance while trying his best to not act suspicious. As he followed, Mike offered that if someone contacted the owner of the restored Impala, he would pay him a generous commission should the owner sell.

Chris ignored him and kept walking.

At it's end, the dark alleyway opened into a fenced-in auto junk yard. Chris led his guest into the yard, directing Mike's attention to a nearly fully-restored 1958 DeSoto two body workers were waxing. Chris hailed the workers and gave them a hand-sign.

The nearer walked over to Mike, smiled, and reached out a hand, but the moment their hands touched, the worker spun the agent around, and arm-locked Mike from behind, while the other worker smiled toothily and kicked their struggling victim solidly in the crotch. Mike groaned and hit the dirt. The two men moved away, the one who kicked Mike slapping a wrench he had taken out of his back pocket menacingly in his palm. The other watched, cracking his massive workman's knuckles.

"So what's your real interest in the Impala?" Chris demanded.

"FBI," came a voice from out of nowhere. "Hands up, where I can see them!"

The three workers turned to see the dark silhouette of a man pointing a gun at them. The three raised their hands.

Gary signaled with the tip of his gun towards Mike on the ground. "Help him up!" the shadow demanded.

The two yard workers reluctantly slipped their arms under Mike's armpits and lifted him halfway up, the mollified agent remaining hunched over, cradling his aching groin. The two men backed off when Mike pulled his gun. With difficulty, Mike waddled up to the guy who had kicked him.

"So you like kicking people in the balls, do you?" he asked, shooting the guy's foot. Then he turned to the man who had held him in the arm-lock. "And you?"

The fellow bolted, clawing a bloody way over the barbed-wire-topped fence.

Mike let him go. Gary, gun braced, approached Chris and whispered in his ear, "You tell your brother, Joey V., he better contact me or I'm going to kill you, him, his wife and his daughter. Tell him his friends who were going to give him asylum said so." Gary shoved a paper with the same message printed on it into Chris' shirt pocket, then struck him sharply on the side of the head with the butt of his gun, knocking Chris unconscious onto the ground.

As the two agents left, Mike waddled past Chris and kicked him in the face.

Outside the front gate, the two agents climbed back into their car. Gary cocked his head towards his partner, and asked with a wicked grin, "Do you think the bug we had put in Joey V.'s car is still working?"

"I would think so," Mike replied hoarsely. "They did a lot of work on his car, but it didn't look to me like they touched the dashboard." Inside the company car, Mike wrinkled his nose. "You fart or something?" he asked.

"What? No," Agent Gary responded as he slipped the key into the ignition.

"Let's get out of here," Mike said with disgust. "The stink around here is sickening."

CHAPTER 32

Chris woke up, legs outstretched in the oily dirt, propped painfully up against the chain link fence. Two of his workers were shaking him by the shoulder. Next to the two, a man was groaning, holding a blood-soaked boot up for Chris to see. Chris pushed it away, inspecting instead his own head and face carefully with his hands. Satisfied that the damage was superficial, he pulled a cell phone from his pants' pocket and called an ambulance for his injured friend.

Chris helped the man who had been shot in the foot limp along the dank alleyway back to where Chris had first encountered the two agents—if, indeed, they were FBI agents. He called Joey V. and passed on the leader's threat.

When Joey V. responded, he spoke slowly and deliberately. "First, are you all okay?"

"The prick knocked out one of my teeth and blew half of Gordo's foot off. That's him moaning in the background, waiting for an ambulance," Chris said.

Joey V. continued in a colder voice. "After I pick up my car there, you should lay low for awhile—until I straighten things out."

"I'm not worried about those two guys," Chris replied haughtily, in the next breath asking, "Are they really FBI?" Gordo moaned again in the background.

"They're FBI alright, but they're bad ones. So lay low like I said, okay? And thanks for fixing my car. Now, shouldn't you be helping Gordo?"

Chris looked at what was left of Gordo's still bleeding foot as the ambulance pulled up. "He'll be all right! He moans like that about everything..."

Joey V. cut Chris short. "So when can I pick up the car?"

"Give me a couple hours and it'll be ready."

"Did you leave the bugs in like I asked?" Joey V. inquired.

"Both of them," Chris said conspiratorially.

"I've got to go visit a hospital, but I'll see you afterwards to pick up my car."

"Some things never change, like me getting my face kicked for some fuck up of yours," Chris laughed, then winced with pain.

"I'll make it up to you, little brother."

"Hey, man. Like, who said I wanted anything?" Chris replied, adding, "And why are you going to the hospital?"

"To put some things right," Joey V. replied in his coldest, cruelest voice before flipping the cell phone abruptly closed.

CHAPTER 33

Joey V. flagged a taxi and directed the driver to Einstein Hospital where Twisted Ray was recuperating from an unexpected relapse. Joey was surprised to find no guards at the door, and Ray's hospital room empty.

Walking back to the central nursing area, he asked the floor nurse where Ray had gone. She was happy to say that the patient was recovering so well that he would be spending his last few days in the solarium.

Joey V. found Twisted Ray dressed casually in shirt and slacks sitting in a wheelchair, back against a corner, flanked by his usual, two bodyguards. Ray was glancing through a sheaf of papers on his lap, but looked up warily the moment someone approached him. Recognizing Joey V., Ray signaled for him to approach, and for his body guards to relax.

"Did you get the tape?" Ray asked, as Joey V. squatted beside him.

"Found it and destroyed it," Joey V. assured.

"If that tape of my daughter ever turns up…" Ray began menacingly.

Joey V. interrupted. "It's done, Ray. I told you, I know how you feel. I have a daughter, too, alright?"

"Alright," Twisted Ray growled, backing off. "Sorry. I owe you."

Joey V. accepted the apology without acknowledgement and began updating Ray about the money being bet and how, if they beat the spread, it would cost Sweaters everything.

"Good! Let the fucker go down."

"Have you heard from Sweaters lately?" Joey V. asked, trying to make the question sound offhand.

"The prick is in the can with no bail. He's trying desperately to find out what happened to the million that he gave you to bring to the Dominican apartment."

"What will you do when he gets out?" Joey V. asked.

"I'm setting some things in motion. I would have had a couple of sit downs

179

already if those FBI friends of yours hadn't come by and messed me up just when I was ready to leave. Shit, I was out the front door, and a couple of hospital orderlies brought me right back in. Guess people didn't like the way I looked. The doctors say my numbers are elevated again, and I'll have to stay here a little while longer. The guys identified themselves as FBI, and they know you're alive. How do you know them?"

"Do you really believe they're FBI?" Joey V. tossed back at Ray.

"I don't know what to believe," Twisted Ray said cautiously, "but what do they want with you?"

"My guess is, they want me because of what I saw in the apartment."

Ray's anger suddenly flared. "I'll never forget that short weasel who grabbed my broken hand. He was testing me, but I was careful to not let on that I knew him. So what *did* happen to Sweaters' and the Dominican's money?"

Joey V. looked Ray in the eyes and lied. "I don't know, Ray. I was with you coming out of the restaurant. They beat you up, kidnapped me, and forced me at gunpoint to take them to the Dominicans' apartment. They needed me to get inside. Then they shot me." Joey V. pointed at his still-bandaged, damaged second ear. "The next thing I knew, I was in the hospital. So what should we do now?"

Twisted Ray stared at the sheaf of papers in his lap for another moment, then dropped them and replied, "Put some people on those three 'agents.' Take these two idiots who follow me everywhere like puppies with you, if you want. Meantime, I'll make a couple calls and see what I can find out. I've already got men out searching for Sal and Dom. Have you heard from them yet?"

Joey V. shook his head in the negative. "No. You still think they might have pulled this off?"

Twisted Ray hesitated as if in thought, then, frowning, replied distantly, "It's still possible, but..."

CHAPTER 34

Botch exited FBI Headquarters, abruptly slipping into a shadow when he noticed Gary Ross and Mike Smith pull into the parking lot fifty feet ahead. They were engaged in an animated discussion and made no effort to exit the parked car, so Botch carefully slipped from the shadows, walked nonchalantly to his own company car, started it, and pulled up behind the squabbling agents. To his chagrin, neither Gary nor Mike noticed.

Botch rolled down his window. "Hey, where were you guys? You missed the meeting!" he asked concernedly.

The two instantly stopped conversing, got out of their car and stared at him. Gary looked surprised. "You mean it's over, already?"

"Where you headed?" Mike added suspiciously.

Botch carefully removed his gun and placed it on his lap, replying, "I came in for the meeting. Otherwise, I'm still on vacation."

"Must be nice to *have so much money* you can take time off whenever you want," Gary probed.

"Oh, yeah, I'm loaded, for sure," Botch returned, draping his left arm casually out of the car window while fingering the safety off the weapon in his lap.

"Need us for something?" Mike asked, in an effort to stall and try to learn more.

"No. Just wanted to check in with you guys. Walter will be expecting you tomorrow, bright and early," he said, adding, "you know: the awards and such," then casually drove off.

Gary and Mike jumped back into their car and followed. Botch, suspecting such, accelerated and began weaving his way in and out of traffic, looking intermittently in the rearview mirror to see if they were, in fact, behind him. He couldn't see them, but just to be sure, he circled back.

One block behind, Mike asked his partner what he thought Botch was doing.

"Cagey bastard! He's checking to see if we're following him. I have an idea: Let's wait for him at the entrance to the FDR. That's where it looks like he's headed. Hopefully, we'll pick him up when he's done with all the diversionary antics."

Botch circled the block a second time, and, not seeing the agents' car and feeling satisfied he wasn't being followed, drove to the entrance to the FDR, past where the two agents were hiding in wait. The agents pulled out slowly, following Botch from as far away as possible.

Botch stopped at Debbie's apartment building in the South Bronx and parked on the street opposite. He walked slowly across the street, checking repeatedly up and down the quiet street just to make sure. As he reached the top of the stairs to her building, he spotted Gary and Mike pulling into a parking spot a block away. *Unbelievable,* he muttered to himself. He hadn't wanted to involve Debbie any further, and now he had brought danger right to her doorstep.

Surveying his options, Botch made his decision and rang the bell, cursing, while flattening himself against the door, hopefully out of the agents' view. Debbie's voice crackled over the intercom, "Who is it?"

Botch replied, "It's me," adding, as he slipped, placing himself once again in the agents' line-of-site, "Shit!"

Debbie, recognizing Botch's voice, asked playfully, "Is that really you, Shit?"

"Let me in...quickly," Botch hissed, once again pressing himself against the door.

Debbie pressed the buzzer and Botch slipped in, trying to be as inconspicuous as possible. He was immediately hit with the smell of musty, old building and rotting garbage. Walking down the narrow hall, he crowded into a small two-person elevator with a fat, older woman, only to be assaulted by the stench of human feces.

Looking down in the corner, there it was: a pile of steaming brown excrement.

The woman next to him, her perspiring bulk occupying the majority of the elevator car, looked where Botch was staring, but seemed impervious to it's presence. As the elevator jerked its way to the next floor, she ventured, "It's dat Bush guy's fault. He don' care 'bout noffin' and no boddy but his own damn sef."

Botch held his breath, countering, "You're kidding? The President came all the way over here just to shit in your elevator? Wow, first no weapons of mass destruction and now this. What's with the guy, huh?"

The woman smiled while outwardly ignoring Botch. The elevator shook violently, screeched, and ground to a stop. The door opened creakily and the woman waddled off. Feeling both nauseous from the smell and light-headed from holding his breath, Botch pulled the collar of his undershirt over his nose and began panting.

The elevator finally jerked to a stop at Debbie's floor. Botch got out and happily pulled the undershirt off his nose only to take in the rank air of the hallway that led to Debbie's apartment. He recognized her apartment door immediately. She had stuffed a towel into the large gap between the bottom of the door and the floor, defying any insects or rodents that might want in.

Botch knocked on the door. Debbie immediately let him in, apologizing profusely like she always did for 'the mess' as she called it. Botch leaned in to kiss her on the lips, but Debbie abruptly turned and presented, instead, her cheek. Botch ignored the slight, pecked her cheek, and told himself it didn't matter, at least for the moment.

Looking around inside at an immaculately clean living room, he spotted Debbie's daughter, Evie, shuffling languidly out of her room. She'd grown since he'd last seen her, and was in the process of changing from a gawky teen into a beautiful woman like her mother. "My sweet little Evie," Botch said, arms outstretched, overjoyed to see her again. Evie ran up and gave Botch a girlish hug. Holding her warmly, Botch smiled, surprised by the feeling of warmth that swept through him for the girl. Never having had children, it hit him: *This is what a father feels for his daughter.* Holding his emotions in check, he let go. "I can't believe how much you've grown!" he said, adding quickly, "I can't believe I just said that. I used to hate it when I was your age and people said that to me."

Debbie interjected, coolly, "You've sure got a good memory, Botch, at least for some things."

"Easy there," Botch returned. "Let's put the knives away for the moment, okay?"

Debbie was thinking over his offer when the phone rang.

"That's for me!" Evie piped up with a typical teen squeal, and ran to her bedroom to take it.

Botch followed Debbie into the kitchen, where he grabbed her by the arms and tugged her towards him. "What's the matter?" he asked.

"Stop it, Botch. You're hurting me," she said, pushing him away.

Botch flushed beet-red and sat at the kitchen table, wanting somehow to get past the awkwardness. "The place looks great," he ventured.

Debbie, frowning, opened the refrigerator and began rearranging things. "Who are you kidding? This place is a dump, but it's all I can afford."

Botch, placed his hands behind his head, stretched and smiled, "Well, that's why I'm here, honey. There's a big change coming."

Debbie stopped rearranging and stiffened, a look of hope on her young but careworn face. The refrigerator door remained open in her hand. "For you or us?"

she asked hesitantly.

"I'm referring to you, me and Evie," Botch replied, standing up and pulling aside one of the kitchen curtains to check the street. He could see Gary and Mike waiting patiently in their car at the end of the street below. "I can't tell you everything right now," he said, adding, "for your and Evie's safety," releasing the curtain and looking into Debbie's eyes. "But if things work as planned, we'll be set for life."

Debbie was visibly shaken. "I want you to know, Botch, that, so far, I've always been there with you because I loved you. I've never expected you to save me or Evie," she said, pacing, shoulders back and head high next to Botch, peeking cautiously out the same window to see what he had been looking at.

Botch grabbed her, held her tightly in his arms, and searched her eyes. "I want it to be 'us' again," he said softly, "and I'm hoping you feel the same, but if you don't...well, I'd understand." Then he smiled. "Of course, I'd be devastated, and would probably do something rash like jump out that window. Truthfully, Debbie, I need 'us' to share our lives together again."

Debbie slipped her willing arms around his strongly-muscled chest and drew him closer. "I love you, Botch, but I don't know if I can go through all the pain it seems to bring. What if you change your mind, again? What if this 'thing' you want to happen, doesn't happen? Does that mean 'us' doesn't happen?"

Botch averted his eyes, letting loose of Debbie, and slipped his hands into his pockets. "No. The thing I want to happen is just an added bonus. It's the 'us' that's really important, and, hell, I'll gladly go through all the pain again if it means 'us' together...forever." Botch pulled both hands out of his pockets and showed her the diamond engagement ring he'd just bought.

Debbie, eyes wide, reached eagerly for the ring. Botch watched her try it on, and then asked, "Will you marry me?"

Debbie seemed stunned at first, then began sobbing, and, leaving the ring on her heart finger, ran out of the kitchen, down the short hallway and into Evie's bedroom without saying another word.

Botch felt confused and dismayed, wondering if he'd offended her. *Does that mean yes or no? It has to be yes*, he told himself. *After all, she took the ring.* Then another part of his bedraggled brain whispered, *Maybe she's just had enough of you and is keeping the ring as payment for services rendered. Or maybe she can't decide.*

A tidal wave of insecurities, disappointments and heartaches from the past flooded his mind, when, suddenly, Evie ran out of the bedroom, face lit up with a big smile, and cried, "Yes! We'll marry you!" almost knocking Botch over as she buried her face in his chest, hugging him as hard as she could. Botch maintained the hug, until Evie, sniffling like her mother, pulled away. "You have to leave for awhile, so Mom can finish crying. She said to please call her later."

Botch hugged Evie again and left, completely ignoring the danger waiting for him on the street.

Number One Bestseller

CHAPTER 35

"The plan has to happen *now*," Botch said a little too cheerfully over the cell phone for Mack's liking.

Mack frowned. "So, don't meet you at your office?"

"No, two of the three agents, Gary Ross and Mike Smith, followed me to Debbie's and they're apparently staying on me at least for the time being. Listen, Mack, this is the chance we've been waiting for. Tell Joey V. to meet me in twenty minutes at his brother's auto body shop."

"Are you sure you don't want us to make a surprise appearance, wherever you are, and help you?" Mack asked concernedly.

"You need to track down the other agent. I have a bad feeling about him. Ever since you told me about him almost taking you out, I keep imagining him lying in wait to pick Shelby, Nick and the rest of us off, one at a time."

"Okay," Mack replied curtly. "Joey V. should already be there. Call him to make sure, and if he's there, give him an advanced warning that you're bringing the two agents with you."

"As long as the car's ready and the bug transmits," replied Botch, "the plan should work fine. Don't worry, Mack, I'll call you if he's not there. Meet you at my office tomorrow."

"Be safe," Mack replied, not entirely sure why he had said it.

"You, too," Botch responded, stepping out of the elevator in Debbie's apartment building, yielding the space to another tenant. Botch pointed to the warm brown pile still lying in corner of the elevator and said, "George Bush." The woman, who had just climbed in, looked where he was pointing and said offhandedly, "You got that right, buddy!" then burst out laughing.

Botch exited the building, stopping just long enough to make certain Gary and Mike saw him. Satisfied, he walked across the street, got into his car and drove slowly away, watching to make sure they were following. In the distance, he could see their car pulling out and breathed a sigh of relief that Debbie and Evie were, at least for the time being, off the agents' radar.

A short time later, Botch slowed his car, its tires crunching on the gravel in front of Chris' Body Shop. Noting the gate wide open, Botch continued in, parking in front of the building housing Joey V.'s car. Joey V., just back from Einstein Hospital, walked over and shook Botch's hand and smiled conspiratorially.

Mike stopped the agency car a distance away so he and Gary could observe the area without being seen. After staring through the government-issue field glasses a while, Gary offered them to Mike. "I guess that answers our question about them being in on it," Gary said.

Mike observed for a while, then asked Gary if he thought they might be gathering at the body shop to divide up the money.

Mike's eyes suddenly narrowed. "Wait! Joey V. and Botch are pulling out in Joey V.'s Impala." Mike reflexively started the agency car.

"Turn on the bug receiver and see if you can pick up on what they're saying," Gary said, jerking his head toward the special receiver mounted beneath the dash.

Mike turned it on and they listened impatiently as Botch and Joey V. talked about the weather. Gary looked at Mike and gave him a thumbs up. "At least it's still working!"

Moments later, Joey V.'s car tore past them in a storm of dust and gravel, the two agents continuing to listen as they followed the Impala from well-behind.

The agents overheard Joey V. say that their partner was on his way to meet them at Hofstra University with the money. "Once we get there, we can split it up and go our separate ways."

Botch: "How far away is Hofstra?"

Joey: "We go to Exit 49—I don't remember the street name—make a left at the Changing Times Pub, go two lights down and make another left by Rudy's Bar, then travel a straight mile to Tara's Tavern on the right. It's a few miles after that on the left. Can't miss it."

Botch: "Where did a nice Italian boy like you learn to give Irish directions?"

Joey: "What do you mean?"

Botch: "You know, go to this pub, then make a left at that bar..."

Mike looked over at his partner. "Bingo!" he said with a smile, then, "Who do you think they're meeting?"

"It's got to be the black guy—the one in the photo in Botch's office—the police captain," Gary explained. "Rich already killed the Irish cop," adding as an aside, "and he should have finished off the girl and her boyfriend by now."

"Thank God the bug still transmits," Mike said. "I guess we're headed to the Island, then?"

CHAPTER 36

Botch scratched on a piece of paper: *Are they following us?*

Joey V. searched the side and rearview mirrors and shook his head worriedly in the negative. Then Joey V. tapped Botch's knee and pointed backwards with a thumb to where a nondescript white car suddenly appeared bobbing in and out of the traffic about a hundred yards back. Botch, assuming Gary and Mike were still listening, began boasting about their success lifting the money out of Gary, Mike and Rich's hands, and how, when the money was split up, Joey V., Botch and their partner would have enough to retire on. Joey V. ended by mentioning how easy it had turned out tricking the three FBI idiots into doing all the dangerous work and then taking the blame for it.

Gary and Mike glared at the car a distance in front of them with outright hatred. Mike struck the steering wheel with a fist and barked, "God damn those mutts; they played us right from the beginning!"

"Don't worry," Gary intervened. "We'll get our money back soon enough. "

Joey V. grinned at Botch, imagining what the men in the car behind them must be thinking. Then, on a whim, he said loudly, "Hey, didn't you say that guy, Mike, had the hots for his partner, Gary?" Botch frowned at Joey V. with a look that said, *don't push it.*

Mike, red-faced and embarrassed, muttered, "That's a bunch of bullshit! I'm not..." but Gary shushed him, choosing to ignore the barb and his partner's revealing over-reaction. At least for the present.

Joey V. turned to Botch and gave a sly smile as they exited for Hofstra University.

Number One Bestseller

CHAPTER 37

As Botch and Joey V. exited the expressway, agents Mike Smith and Gary Ross carefully closed the distance between the two cars. Joey V. knew that after practice Amazing Jones usually stopped at Buttle's, the local sports bar, to make an appearance. Today he would stop there for certain for a live E.S.P.N. television interview. Joey V. and Botch were to intercept Amazing on his way there, and begin implementing "the plan." Joey V. pulled into the parking lot of the Jets training facility located on the university campus. He was the first to spot the jet-black Corvette sporting an "IMAmazing" license plate resting in reserved parking space number one.

Mike pulled the government car into the other end of the lot, far enough away to keep an eye on Joey V. and Botch without being noticeable. Gary, glancing at the many flashy cars parked in the front of the lot, asked Mike offhandedly, "Hey, don't the Jets practice here?"

"Hell, I don't know, I'm not a football fan, or don't you remember, *partner*?" Mike replied acerbically, still smoldering over Gary's reaction to the implication that he might be gay.

"Oh, yeah," said Gary sarcastically. "That's right: You think *real* men play baseball. Hell, the only time I watch baseball is during the playoffs, otherwise it's just too damn boring."

Mike, angered further by the drift of his partner's comment, argued, "I just think there's more strategy in baseball."

"More strategy in baseball? You're out of your friggin' mind, Mary!"

Mike's reply was immediate: "Hey, don't start that shit! I don't watch basketball or hockey for the same reason."

"Well, at least we agree there," Gary sighed. "Bouncing a ball up and down a court seems pretty mundane to me, and hockey's not much different, except for the occasional fights."

At the front of the parking lot, Botch elbowed Joey V. "Here he comes," he said, nodding towards a well-dressed, well-muscled Amazing, slicking his hair back after showering and walking confidently towards his car.

"He's bigger than he looks on TV," Joey V. said, watching the man fold his muscular frame into the Corvette. "I'm glad you're here, given that my brother is injured and couldn't help me after all."

"Thank your friend. It was his idea." Botch replied.

"Remind me to buy Mack a drink when we get back," Joey V. responded before he could stop himself.

Amazing Jones closed the door, fired up his car, and pulled out abruptly, screeching across the lot. Joey V. and Botch followed at a distance, Joey V. watching out his rearview mirror to confirm that Gary and Mike were following them.

A few minutes on the freeway, Mike ventured conciliatorily, "Looks like you were right. The black guy—what's his name?—Andre?—is already spending our money. That's the kind of 'Vette I planned on buying." Gary didn't answer, so Mike continued talking as they followed Joey V. and Botch. "Three against two doesn't sound like the best odds. They're older, true, but they're still dangerous."

Gary hissed back, "It sounds to me like it's going to be four to two. Apparently Rich didn't get the Irishman after all. Didn't you hear Joey V. just say he was going to buy him a drink?"

"Maybe Joey V. doesn't know what happened to him yet."

"Perhaps, madam, you're right, but keep your eyes open, just in case the Irishman suddenly shows. Any idea as to our next move?"

"Well," Mike replied, "I figure the black guy in the black 'Vette—Andre—is taking them to the money where they will divide it. If Botch and Joey V.'s car, say, suddenly spun out of control and off the road, the odds would suddenly be two to one, our favor."

Gary rolled his eyes upward. "Yeah, but if Andre in the 'Vette sees that happen, he'll take off, and we could lose him *and* the money."

"Then we'll have to wait for a perfect window of opportunity," Mike replied, letting off the accelerator pedal.

Ahead, Botch watched anxiously as the black Corvette in front of them began pulling away. Touching Joey V.'s sleeve, he silently mouthed the words, *you're losing him.* Joey V. acknowledged Botch's message uninterestedly, leaving Botch confused.

Reaching under the dashboard and pulling the hot wire out of the FBI bug, Joey V. explained, "I know we're losing Amazing, but right now, it's *them* I'm worried about," he said, gesturing with his thumb back towards the car behind them as he rapidly narrowed the distance between them that a moment ago had been increasing.

Botch, pointing forward towards the distancing Corvette, yelled, "Fuck them, Joey, just don't lose Amazing!"

Joey V. extended his hand, palm down, and began patting the dashboard of the Impala. "Calm down! Under this hood is a 427 big block with nitrous. There's no way Amazing can lose us. Besides, we know where he's going."

Botch folded his arms in front of his chest and grumbled, "So why's he driving so fast? He's got plenty of time before the interview?"

"Just chill out," Joey V. said with finality as he pushed lightly on the accelerator pedal, instantly reclaiming the distance they'd lost. "What did I tell you?" Joey V. asked confidently. "We're right on target, though we've momentarily lost those two FBI agents. Wait! Amazing's slowing! Ha! There's a State Trooper over on the right!"

Mike meantime was weaving in and out of the traffic trying desperately to catch up with the Impala that suddenly left them in the dust, suggesting to Gary that Botch and Joey V. might be on to them, since the microphone suddenly went dead. Gary ignored Mike and pointed forward. "Look! There they are! And... Fuck! Slow down! There's a state trooper with a radar gun just up ahead!" To Mike's surprise, Gary added, "I think we should make our move *now*."

Mike shrugged his shoulders and obliging moved into the right lane to get around a truck that was obstructing them.

Joey V. looked nervously into his side and rearview mirrors. "Shit, Botch, we've lost them, again!"

This time it was Botch's turn to bark, "Forget them! Just don't hit that truck in front of us! Damn! Now I can't see Amazing. Go around the truck!"

"You've got to calm down, Hymie," Joey V. growled, irritated. "I got it all under control," he said as he jumped the Impala deftly into the right lane, at the same moment, Mike abruptly turned left into what a second ago had been an opening just behind the truck. There was a loud crunch as their government car rammed into the side of the Impala they had, a moment ago, been looking for. The impact sent a thunderous shudder through the bureau car.

Mike stomped on the brake with both feet, as the Impala on his left began spinning in a tight circle.

The truck driver, seeing a car spinning out of control in his side mirror, applied his brakes, too. The spinning car suddenly flew alongside and then in front of the truck and towards the center divider.

Joey V., taken totally by surprise, fought the steering wheel in vain, while Botch threw his hands and arms around his head and face. Their car smashed hard into the divider, then bounced back across all three lanes to skid into a ditch on the far right side of the highway in a cloud of dirt and smoke. As the cloud dissipated, a plume of white mist began hissing out from under the wrenched hood of the Impala.

Joey V. groaned. "You alright?" he asked Botch.

"I think so," Botch replied, examining a gash on the top of his head with his hands. "How bad is it?" he asked Joey V., referring to the car while pointing to the cut.

"You'll live, but we're in big trouble," Joey V. stated, watching the column of white smoke roiling from beneath the hood abruptly turn black and begin to fill the interior.

Coughing, the two stumbled out of the car and scrambled up an adjacent knoll to assay the damage from a distance. In the late afternoon light, they could make out the crumpled front, back and sides of Joey's recently restored car. One errant tire rolled to a clanking stop along the roadside ahead. As the black smoke stopped billowing from under the hood, Joey V. shook his head in disbelief. "What do we do now?"

"I don't know. The best I can tell from where we're sitting, we're fucked," replied Botch, shaking and bleeding.

Gary watched the aftermath of the accident out the rear window while Mike, assiduously continued following the jet-black Corvette ahead, its driver oblivious of the accident behind him.

"Where the hell did you learn how to drive like that?" Gary asked in amazement.

"I don't watch football, but I do love NASCAR."

"NASCAR? Really? I'm going to have to start watching it!"

"Now that's a real sport of strategy," Mike offered, gripping the steering wheel to keep Gary from seeing his shaking hands.

"Strategy, is it? I thought it was just cars going in a circle," Gary reminded.

"Look! He's getting off the highway!" Mike interrupted, following Amazing onto an exit ramp.

Fifteen minutes later, they were following Amazing into the parking lot of Buttle's Bar. Amazing parked facing the fence at the end of the lot, taking up two parking spaces so no one would damage his car. Mike pulled up behind, blocking him in. "Now let's locate our money, and recover it before the Irish detective can interfere," he said with finality.

Amazing Jones got out and stared angrily at the two men in the car that had followed him so closely the last part of his journey and were now blocking him in.

Mike looked over at his partner. "Hey! That doesn't look like Botch's friend, the police captain!"

Gary stared. "He definitely isn't the black police captain in the picture in Botch's office. This one's too young. Shit, I wonder what this guy's role is in all this?" The two agents climbed out of their car, guns drawn, ready find out.

Number One Bestseller

CHAPTER 38

In the glowing dusk, Amazing paused, like the football god he knew he was, beside the open door of his 'Vette, adjusting his hand-sewn, silk shirt with one hand while holding his Dolce and Gabbana driving glasses in the other. He was staring at two nondescript businessmen blocking him with a nondescript white car. Absorbed in trying to place what to Amazing could only be two particularly ardent football fans who, he assumed, desperately wanted his autograph, he didn't notice the guns. "So, what's the problem here? Hmm?" he asked nonchalantly.

Gary resisted the urge to laugh, and instead snorted, "*You're* the problem. You're taking up two parking spots."

Amazing walked to the back of his car, and looked to his right and left. "So who the fuck are you, the parking lot police?"

"No, asshole, FBI," Gary Ross quipped. Amazing turned to face two armed men flashing IDs. Gary signaled towards their car. "Get in," he ordered gruffly.

Amazing's eyes widened as he noticed the guns; he shook his head in disbelief. "It's FBI now? Every time I turn around someone's up my ass looking for money. Now it's you fuckers, too? Look, I haven't done shit. I want my lawyer. You nine-to-five crackers are all...Hey, wait! I get it! Give me your IDs and I'll sign them for you so you can sell them and retire!"

Mike, mystified, looked at his partner. Gary answered for the two of them: "The only place you'll be signing autographs is in prison unless you cooperate. Now!" Gary ordered, waving the muzzle of his pistol from Amazing towards the open passenger door of his company car.

Amazing seemed taken aback and genuinely hurt. Then his eyes narrowed and he pointed at the two agents with the end of his folded designer sun glasses. "You'll be working in bum-fuck Idaho when my lawyer gets through with you." Amazing, hands on his hips, continued, "You know what your problem is?"

Gary lunged forward and landed a fist squarely on Amazing's jaw. "Shut the fuck up!" he demanded, looking around nervously to make sure no one had seen him strike an unarmed celebrity.

Amazing stood upright, rubbed his jaw, and, astonished, asked, "Don't you know who I am? Hey, look at me! I'm Amazing Jones!"

While Amazing searched the faces of his two antagonists for any kind of recognition, Mike, incensed with Amazing's self-absorption, punched Amazing in the gut. Gary, following Mike's lead, spun the doubled-over athlete around and clicked on a pair of cuffs. Amazing's thousand-dollar sunglasses clattered across the blacktop and skidded to a stop underneath the 'Vette. Gary and Mike together shoved the struggling superstar into the back of their car.

Slamming the door shut, Gary stopped to look at Mike. "What was that about?"

"The bastard cost me five grand in the Jets-Miami game! He threw an easily-intercepted short pass—he fucking panicked! The most annoying part, however, was when this prick laughed about it afterwards on the big screen."

Gary stared disbelievingly at his partner, then laughed when Mike belatedly confessed, "Alright, alright! So I *do* watch football!"

Amazing, listening from the backseat, piped in, "Hey, just to set the record straight, I was laughing because the lineman who intercepted it and carried it into the end zone ran funny—like a fat guy chasing an ice cream truck!"

Gary climbed into the back seat next to Amazing. "Really? And how funny do you find this?" Gary asked, pointing the barrel of his gun down at Amazing's left knee. "Where's the money?" he growled, as Mike closed the passenger door and climbed into the driver's seat.

Beads of sweat popped out from Amazing's expertly made-up forehead as he looked bewilderingly from agent to agent, true panic in his eyes. "What money?" he asked, adding quickly, "And damn! Which one of you shit his pants?"

Gary drew back to pistol-whip the cowering athlete, when a bewildering array of criss-crossing light beams blazed into the car from every direction.

"Police! Don't move! Put your guns down!"

Gary froze, responding reflexively, "FBI! Don't shoot!" The two agents held their hands, weapon in one, badge in the other, high.

An unseen policeman yelled from somewhere behind the bright lights, "Get out! Slowly!" The driver and passenger doors flew open as if by spectral hands, and Gary and Mike climbed cautiously out into the blinding lights, while Amazing watched in complete bewilderment.

Gary squinted against the lights, and reiterated to the dark forms lurking behind them that he and his partner were FBI.

The lights went off, one-by-one, until Gary could see Botch and Joey V.

standing and grinning just outside a ring of armed police. Gary grimaced as his arms were jerked behind him and cuffs were snapped on. Botch and Joey V. together confirmed, "Those are the guys you want, officers!"

On the other side of the car, Mike, similarly cuffed, sighed helplessly.

Amazing Jones wrinkled his face. "Will someone please get me out of this car! I can't take the smell!" Two officers, one on either side of the car, bent into the back seat to extract the occupant, only to draw back, fingers pinching their nostrils. "Damn!" both said in unison, the one on the driver's side pulling Amazing out of the car but making no move to remove the quarterback's cuffs.

All heads turned towards Botch, who signaled towards the trunk. The nearest police officer reached into the driver's side, removed the keys from the ignition and, walking around to the back of the car, popped open the trunk. Everyone within twenty feet gave a moan and grabbed his nose. The officer in charge directed the two agents roughly over to the back of their car and demanded, "Who are they?" pointing at the bloated and rotting bodies of Sal and Dom.

Mike looked, then closed his eyes and averted his face. Gary, after looking, snarled lowly at Botch and Joey V., "You'll never get away with this," directing his next words to the mass of policemen staring in horror. "Who's in charge here? Listen. I can explain everything! We're FBI agents."

After a moment of pregnant silence, Botch calmly offered, "I'm not so sure about that. We have two witnesses who say that you two killed them."

Gary motioned with his head to Joey V., "Who? This weasel?"

Botch answered smugly, "A girl, too, remember?"

While the two were talking, two more cars pulled up and a bevy of news reporters piled out, flashing identification cards and snapping photos. Amazing Jones stamped his feet in protest, unable to cover his face with his arms bound behind him, cursing loudly when one of the photographers recognized him and began taking pictures of him in handcuffs from different angles.

Ignoring the press, the officers asked Botch what the FBI thought the police should do with Amazing. Botch paused a moment, then smiled. "Take him to a hospital and have them check him over, but keep him in custody. He's a part of this somehow." Eyebrows furrowed, he said quietly to Amazing, "I'll visit you tomorrow in the hospital for questioning." The Plan, as Botch, Joey, Mack, Andre and Nick had taken to calling it, battered by events and tattered with patchwork revisions, was, in fact, working famously.

Number One Bestseller

CHAPTER 39

Mack and Andre sauntered audaciously through the circular rotunda of FBI headquarters and, because of the higher security concerns stemming from the events of the last three days, past *three* over-awed guards, who whispered to each other, "They were the ones that nailed those two rogue agents!"

Andre beamed, enjoying the notoriety, while Mack approached the main guard matter-of-factly. "We're here to see Mr. Bartolato," he said in an all-business tone.

"I'll bet you are," the guard responded. "One moment, please."

The guard called on his walkie-talkie to announce their presence. Waiting for an answer, Mack looked around the lavishly-appointed atrium. Despite yesterday's events, it was still a typical Sunday: There was no one there except the guards and them. The high ceiling suddenly echoed an officious, "Send them up!" that had crackled from the device in the main guard's hand.

The guard pointed toward the bank of elevators at the back. "Mr. Bartolato's office is on the fifth floor. When you get off, take the first right. His is the last office on the left. His secretary's not in today, so just go directly in."

Andre nodded and thanked him, and the two friends walked together towards the elevators. In the elevator, Mack remarked, "Nice set up compared to N.Y.P.D, hey?"

"I knew there was a reason Botch never wanted us to meet him at his office," Andre responded, referring to the building's upscale ambience. "He wants it all to himself."

Botch greeted the two in front of his office. "Gentlemen! This way, please," he said, sweeping his arm in a gesture of royal welcome. Andre and Mack stiffened formally, then walked in, Botch shutting the inner door behind them.

Mack was the first to break the silence: "So *this* is where all my tax dollars go. The places I work, you have to wipe the shit off when you leave, instead of when you enter."

Andre remarked on the large number of cars in the parking lot. "Looks from out there like it should be pretty busy. Where is everyone?"

"Actually, everyone is in one or another emergency meeting. 'Tiger Teams' we call them. Their purpose is to quickly get untoward events, like last night's, out of the public eye in order to maintain the bureau's image. This is what happens here when all the national newspapers carry headline photos of a couple of agents being arrested standing next to a couple of dead bodies in the trunk of their company car. Add Amazing's notoriety, and everyone here's rushing to cover the bureau and their own asses."

Mack and Andre took seats next to Botch's desk. Mack snatched up a folder marked "Confidential – FBI"

"Ooo! Confidential FBI material!" Mack and Andre together chimed, reading the large, red block-printed warning on the cover of the file Botch held in his hands.

"Remember I told you about Walter saying the Dominicans had terrorist ties? Walter had me look further into it, and while I personally think it's all bullshit, I did come across this file on Ross's desk." Botch tossed the folder across his desk towards Mack and Andre. "Now maybe this file was just put together to bolster his story but you never know. The pictures on the left are of one Natasha Sitova, a former, high-ranking KGB operative, and below her a close friend of hers, a former General by the name of Yuri Grachev. Supposedly the two of them have acquired a couple of errant atomic bombs from a former U.S.S.R. vassal state. The pictures on the right are some of the folks supposedly vying to purchase the weapons from them."

Mack studied the folder while Andre hunched over Mack's elbow to see better. "It's a grainy picture but she's a stunning looker, this Natasha with her long, blonde hair."

"She certainly is." Mack agreed. "But what's with the quality of these pictures, Botch? Yuri's is even grainier than Natasha's. The guy was a known General in the KGB, for Christ sakes, and these are the best pictures the FBI can get?"

"Now you know why I think it's something Ross concocted. They don't even have a picture of the guy who allegedly wants to buy the weapons, though the report states that he's a male, and somehow involved with 'North Koreans'." Botch made quote marks with his fingers in the air.

Andre shook his head in disgust. "So you think Ross made this up to throw off the investigation looking into their role in the Dominican Affair?"

"Whether true or not, it's working. The idiots in charge of the investigation still have me assigned, top priority, to look into it, despite what happened to Ross and Smith last night."

"This is so unbelievable, I should use it in my second book," Mack joked.

Botch grabbed the file back from him, and began flipping through the photos of potential buyers. "Now, this picture of a girl who supposedly wants to buy them came out good. Man, if I wasn't getting married, I'd like to meet her. Look at those inviting lips! I bet she could suck a golf ball through a garden hose."

"No word on Rich Pagano, yet?" Mack said, changing the subject.

"No, but the bureau is embarrassed enough to make the manhunt a priority. If Pagano kills again, heads will roll. The super in Nick's girl's apartment survived just long enough to identify a photo of Pagano." Botch dropped his voice, adding as an aside, "There's a certain pleasure in watching my bosses shit their pants, you know. Walter brown-nosed his way to the top, and now that he's been put in charge of a real investigation, he doesn't have a clue as to what to do."

"I thought you liked him?" Andre ventured.

"I do, but I've covered his whiskey-stick-ass too many times."

"So, what's the deal with Amazing?" Mack interrupted.

"Our celebrity quarterback is being held in custody at a private hospital on the Island. Publically, the Jets are assuring the public that Amazing will appear for the game. His and the team's lawyers are working hard to spring him. Even so, the kid is shitting bricks. He's worried that we might be thinking of putting him away for life. I'm going to the hospital later today to 'interview' him about his involvement, which translates to meeting with him about the time the game starts, and making sure he doesn't play in it."

Andre smiled. "So you're telling me all their expensive lawyers and all the political pressure the owners of the Jets will bring to bear isn't going to spring him for the game?"

Botch held up the front pages of several major newspapers. "Have you seen these? Look! Here's a photo of Amazing in cuffs trying to turn away from the cameras, with the open trunk containing the two dead bodies in it behind him. Look at this one! Here's some pictures of Sal and Dom when they were altar boys. The press is making them out to be angels. Amazing's lawyers are advising him to let things cool off awhile, and the Jets owners, in light of all the negative publicity, don't want to get involved in 'obstructing an official FBI investigation'."

"You're sure of this?" Mack asked hopefully.

"Oh, yeah, when the lawyers for Amazing and the club called me, I told them point blank what it could look like they were doing. Their tone changed immediately and they backed off. On top of that, we have the Long Island D.A. and the Feds fighting over jurisdiction, so if that plays out there's another twenty-four hours before he can be brought for arraignment.

Mack was impressed. "And my guess is that no one wants it out that Amazing

Jones won't be playing the game."

Andre added excitedly, "Let's pray the game ends the way we've set it up."

Botch laughed, "Hey, I thought, according to Joey V., it was 'a lock'!"

"Now you're both being dicks," Andre said. "Everything's in motion. All we have to do is not fuck it up."

CHAPTER 40

Agent Rich Pagano entered the Federal building, quick-flashed his ID card to the newest of the new lobby security men recently hired to beef up FBI security, and who at the moment, was too busy arguing with another new security man about overtime pay, to look carefully at the ID card or face. The second floor check-in desk guard, had stuffed the "alert" notice regarding rogue agent Rich Pagano, along with a thick sheaf of other 'priority' notices, into a drawer without looking at any of them. Instead, the guard's attention was fully focused on the bestseller he had brought with him to lessen the boredom of, in his mind, yet another overtime shift on the least-interesting position in the whole building.

Rich approached the guard casually. "Good book," he said flicking a finger towards the cover. "Say, you got a copy of the sign-in sheet for visitors? Someone's parked in my spot and I need to see who it is. This is the second time this week, and I'm getting tired of it."

The young guard put down the novel and shuffled things on his desk until he located the clipboard. He handed it to Rich with an appeasing smile. Rich, eyes following a fingertip sliding down the list, flushed when he noticed Mack's name and realized he hadn't killed Mack after all. Returning the clipboard, he knocked it intentionally onto the floor. As the guard bent over to pick up the list, Rich calmly whipped out a silenced gun, placed the tip near the back of the guard's head and pulled the trigger.

The pop was louder than Rich had anticipated, echoing down the long, deserted hallways to either side of the desk. While slipping the gun back under his jacket, Rich noticed a movement in the mirror behind where the guard had been sitting. Someone had stepped momentarily out from an office and was staring in horror at him. Botch's Debbie, not realizing the killer could see her, covered her silent but open mouth with pale, shaking hands.

Rich turned and looked directly at the woman, and for a moment each regarded the other, wondering what they would do next. Debbie suddenly let out a piercing scream and started running away down the hallway; Rich immediately took off after her.

Debbie opened a stairwell door in hopes of running upstairs to the fifth floor where Botch would be, but then remembered she'd left her security pass on her cleaning cart and would be unable to open the fifth-floor door without it. Looking up and down the stairwell, she thought for a moment of hiding somewhere, but the quick survey revealed nowhere to hide.

The odds being what they were, Debbie decided her only option was to fight, as best she could. Ripping a fire extinguisher off the wall, she pulled the pin and crouched in a corner, watching the second floor stairwell door in anticipation. Rich burst through the door a moment later and gave a startled look as Debbie squeezed the trigger. A thick cloud of dense, whitish foam hissed from the nozzle, hitting Rich squarely in the face, temporarily blinding him. He stumbled forward towards her, frantically wiping away the burning, expanding froth. As he drew closer, Debbie swung the fire extinguisher in a wide arc.

Rich, noticing the movement out of the corner of his red and rapidly swelling eyes, ducked. The cylinder hit the concrete wall with a loud clang and chunks of concrete flew in every direction.

Too blind to shoot, and preoccupied with protecting his face from the flying concrete, Rich lurched forward and blindly tackled the woman, pinning her down with his body on the cold concrete. Debbie started punching wildly, and Rich, having to use both of his hands now to fend off the unremitting volley, decided on an alternate approach.

Replacing the gun in his holster, he pressed his full weight on the screaming woman, then pulled himself up to straddle her waist, one hand behind her neck and the other over her nose and mouth.

Debbie stopped yelling and punching, and grabbed for his hands. Rich, resettling his weight directly onto her hips, shook his head back and forth to flick off the remaining foam from his face, and tightened his grip. "Another word, lady, and I snap your neck!" he hissed menacingly. Debbie forced her shrieking muscles to relax and began withdrawing into the recesses of her panicked mind, preparing herself for the unavoidable wrench and certain death.

Rich, however, had other plans for her. The moment his victim stopped fighting, he slipped his hands beneath her waist, lifted her up with him, and threw her hard at the closed, metal, stairwell door. As she thudded against the door, he pulled out his gun. Signaling with the gun, he directed his now contrite prisoner up the stairs.

Debbie, hoping beyond hope that the crazed agent wasn't, at least for the moment, going to kill her after all, decided to comply, and walked numbly up the stairs. Suddenly, she looked over her shoulder to see if he was going to follow or shoot. He was following, just far enough away from her to defeat any re-attempt at defending herself.

Arriving at the fifth floor, Rich grabbed her by the shoulder and shoved her against the wall nearest the entrance. Opening the door with his security pass, he directed her with the point of his gun down the dark and silent hallway.

Debbie tried desperately to gather her wits. Twice she stumbled. Each time, Rich prodded her with the barrel of his silenced gun, pulling her back onto her feet sharply from behind.

Halfway to the reception desk, Rich pushed her into an office door recess, put a hand forcefully over her mouth and directed the gun ominously at her temple. Glancing back and forth between Debbie and the security person who was seated behind the reception desk at the distant end of the hallway with his back towards them busily filed papers, Rich waited.

At last the guard checked his wristwatch, got up and began his rounds. After a moment, he disappeared down the second hallway ninety degrees perpendicular to where Rich was holding Debbie. "This way," Rich grunted, dragging her further down the hall to Botch's office and pushing her roughly through the outer door.

Debbie, noticing a dark silhouette behind the smoked glass on the inner office door, opened her mouth to yell, but Rich's grip suddenly tightened, as if instinctively reading her thoughts. Debbie, determined to warn her lover, jerked her head to the side and bit down hard on the steely fingers, until Rich, gasping, let go. Pulling his bleeding hand back, he yelped quietly, "You little bitch!"

Botch, hearing the commotion, signaled for Mack and Andre to slip into the shadows and, gun drawn and at the ready, got up and opened the inner office door. The first thing he saw was the barrel end of Rich's silenced gun pointed at Debbie's temple.

"Back the fuck up!" Rich ordered menacingly.

"Let her go, Pagano…" Botch started, but Rich interrupted, finishing his threat with, "or I'll blow her head off!" Rich looked quickly about the room to see if Mack was there, but Botch, watching the man intently, kept blocking his view.

Botch, gun pointed at Rich but denied a clean shot with Debble between them, switched his gaze from Rich to Debbie and hesitated.

That was all Rich needed. Realizing in that second that Botch valued his hostage's life, Rich shoved the gun harder against Debbie's temple. "That's right," he snarled, knowing he now had the upper hand. "Drop the gun and step back!" Rich ordered and kicked the door shut behind him.

Botch continued to hesitate, hoping Rich wouldn't see Mack and Andre in the shadows on either side of the room behind him.

"I said, 'Drop the gun and step back.' Do it now!" Rich yelled, digging the gun sight into Debbie's skin and drawing blood. Debbie winced and despite her best efforts not to, let out a yelp of pain. Botch blinked his eyes as a signal to Mack and Andre, as he slowly backed away, laid his gun on the desk behind him and then moved to the side, raising his hands in the air to keep Rich's attention.

Rich, sensing something amiss, rasped ominously, "Whoever's behind me: Don't even think about trying anything!"

Mack and Andre, seeing the instant pain on Botch's face, also backed off. "So. Where's my money?" Rich demanded flatly to no one in particular.

"What money?" Botch asked, the waiver in his voice confirming to Rich Botch's deep, personal concern for the hostage.

"I'll ask you one more time, then she's dead," Rich threatened "What? You don't believe me?" he asked, pressing the gun sight once again into her skin and drawing more blood. "We figured you guys out," Rich explained, flicking the muzzle of his gun momentarily at the picture of Mack, Andre and Botch together hanging on the wall.

Despite his training, Botch found himself pleading. "Come on, Rich, it's me you got the hard on for. I know where the money is. Leave the girl and take me with you. I'll take you to the money. She's not any part of this."

"Nice try, but right now, her ass is more valuable than yours, boss," Rich said, knowing he had Botch by the balls. "Twenty minutes from now I'll call you on your desk phone. You tell me then exactly where the money is, and the moment I have it, I'll let her go." Laughing evilly, Rich reached behind, opened the office door, and began backing slowly out of the office. Suddenly the agent's face exploded in a shower of blood.

What was left of Rich's body flew forward, past Debbie and directly toward Botch. Staggering, the body fell onto its knees, jerked, and slapped lifeless onto the blood-and-flesh-spattered floor.

Debbie screamed and collapsed. Botch, Mack and Andre ran between her and the door, guns out. On the other side of the doorway stood Walter Steiner, gun in hand, clearly horrified at having just killed one of his own subordinates. The four stared at each other in shocked surprise.

Walter, dazed, suddenly began shaking and mumbling about being grilled by his bosses, who were enraged that Walter had placed the bureau in a position where the bureau was scheduled to publically award what were now clearly three rogue FBI agents. Walter explained how, as he listened, he sensed them setting him up to take the fall for the whole fiasco. Completely overwhelmed, he had walked out of the meeting to the storage closet next to Botch's office to drown his fears in one of several bottles of whisky he always had hidden there. That was when he overheard Agent Pagano threatening Botch and a female hostage. Seizing the opportunity, he dashed back out into the hallway, walked quietly into Botch's office reception area, braced his weapon, and pointed it at the shadows behind the closed door in front of him. When the door suddenly opened and Rich Pagano began backing out of the office, Walter decided and fired.

Walter remained in the doorway, gun now dangling at his side. Blankly watching the white wisp of smoke dissolving in the air before him, the sharp smell of gunpowder permeating his nose and mouth, he dropped the gun dully to the floor.

Mack and Andre helped him sit while Botch crouched beside Debbie and rocked her in his arms, tears streaming. When Debbie's eyes finally opened, Botch's red eyes looked joyfully up at his friends, finally settling on Walter. Nodding approvingly at his friend and boss for showing some balls when it really counted, Botch slowly helped Debbie up. Ordering her to go with Mack and Andre, Botch turned to Walter. "You all right?"

Walter was still trembling. "I...I'll be all right," he stuttered, adding more decisively, "Where are your cop-friends going?"

"I need them out of here. The less people involved in this, the better. I see it this way, Walter," he began, watching Walter's face to gauge his reaction. "Pagano came to kill me and you saved my life."

Walter looked at him with astonishment, tears welling in his rummy eyes.

"How many of your bosses are here in the building right now?" Botch asked.

"Five," Walter answered. "They were meeting in the conference room several doors down to work out the details of my 'sacrifice'."

"And in all this time, not one of them has come to see what the gunshot was about," Botch pointed out angrily.

Botch left Walter and walked down the hall into the meeting room Walter mentioned. All five, as well as their assistants and secretaries, were crouching under the large, mahogany conference table that dominated the room.

Botch scowled. "Thanks for your much-needed backup, gents. Let me guess: You all detest violence and didn't want to get your hands bloodied adding to it." Seeing no reaction, he continued, "I have to go interview a suspect on Long Island. Now that it's over, I don't imagine any of you needs me here anymore, right?"

One by one the bosses and their assistants got up from under the desk and brushed off their suits, trying hard not to make eye contact with Botch. Botch looked them over disgustedly a final time and stated matter-of-factly, "Well, then, I guess I should be going. Damn good thing Walter Steiner was there to take out the last of the three rogue agents. Steiner's a real hero. Saved my life! Thanks for sending him. By the way, I think he could use some help cleaning up my office."

Satisfied he had repaid Walter, at least in part, for saving Debbie's life, Botch turned on his heel and strode out.

CHAPTER 41

Botch drove to the Long Island Peconic Bay Hospital to interview Amazing Jones. It was all part of "The Plan" which, once again, in spite of everything, was proceeding successfully.

The drive was long and harried, the traffic and drivers' tempers being worse than usual. At the hospital, Botch had to fight his way through a veritable campground of reporters. They looked to him like rows of vultures waiting for the hyenas—meaning him—to be done with the carcass—meaning Amazing Jones. Pushing his way past them, he proceeded directly to the reception desk where he asked for Amazing's room number. The stressed-out clerk made a show of looking at the security guards standing to either side, then said to Botch, "How many times do I have to tell you guys? No press allowed inside the building!"

Botch noticed the guards tense as he reached into his pocket. Slowly taking out his badge and showing it, he asked curtly once again for Amazing's room number. The clerk craned his neck forward and stared at the badge, then cleared his throat. "Well...Sir. He's in Room One," he said, pointing towards a small hallway off the main corridor where an elevator with a single floor button marked "Private" took him directly to the uppermost floor.

It wasn't hard to find Amazing Jones. Outside his room the hallway was an out and out freeway, crowded with various law enforcement agency officers, coming and going. Botch waited for a break in the traffic to join the flow and made his way to the FBI officer in charge standing in front of Amazing's door. The officer acknowledged Botch immediately and opened the door for him. Inside, the room was a forest of potted plants and colorful florist bouquets all with bright ribbons around them; through a small clearing in the center, he saw Amazing, sitting up in bed, slipping into a custom-made, silk Jets shirt. Noticing Botch, Amazing pulled the bedcovers over his chest, fell back in the bed and acted like he was asleep.

Weaving through the greenery and flowers to Amazing's bedside, Botch noticed that Amazing was wearing shoes under the covers. Amazing blanched and groaned as if ill.

"Going somewhere?" Botch asked.

Amazing continued pretending he was asleep, then, realizing the ruse wasn't working, sat up and said with attitude, "I got a game to play."

Botch stared at Amazing with unhidden contempt, "You think the FBI, meaning me, would be afraid to walk up to you in the middle of a huddle and formally arrest you while the world watches?"

"At least, that way you'd get it from the fans. The only reason I'm staying in this God-forsaken hospital was so that I wouldn't have to spend the night in jail surrounded by perverts, junkies…and people like you with badges. You don't have shit on me, man. I'm innocent and you know it. I feel fine, so why not just let me go do what I do best, and I'll tell my lawyers to burn all the shit I've had them dig up on you."

"Are you threatening a Federal officer?" Botch asked, eyes narrowing.

"Hell, no! I'm just trying to save your pension fund and shield you from what will, I guarantee, be a very outraged public."

"Thank you, Amazing," Botch replied with a smile. "I appreciate your concern for my well-being, but I'm the one who will decide whether to release you from the hospital, and then, only after you answer my questions."

"I ain't answering shit without my lawyer present," Amazing said, folding his arms together and pouting.

Botch pulled up a chair. "Then don't waste your time worrying about making it to the game. You're not going anywhere until we sort this out. What do you say we leave the lawyers out of this and, until you're ready to talk, we sit back and watch the game together?"

Amazing frowned, then tried unsuccessfully to stare down and intimidate the agent sitting adamantly beside his bed. Botch, in the meantime, turned on the 60-inch, wall-mounted plasma-screen TV.

"You know this is bullshit," a frustrated Amazing Jones said at last. "I didn't even know those guys. They showed me badges, slapped me around and cuffed me. I never did nothing, and I don't know dick about the bodies in the trunk. I don't need to be chilling out with some FBI cracker—no offense—I just need to play!" A helicopter view of a densely-packed football stadium appeared on the television.

"I believe you, Amazing," Botch replied, "but in high-profile-murder cases like this one, I've got to take it one step at a time. For now, I suggest you enjoy the game." Botch sat back in his chair and they both looked up at the TV screen.

The first of two announcers, sitting in what looked like the press box with the playing field artificially-projected behind, was talking about Amazing Jones and his involvement in the double-homicide. Canned crowd noises rose and fell in the background. The other announcer cut in to talk about Amazing growing up in the 'bad' section of Baltimore, and how difficult it would be for anyone to change, coming from such an environment. Amazing sat up, enraged. "They're fucking trying to send me to the chair because of the neighborhood I grew up in! The whole country probably believes this 'Bad Black Guy from a Bad Neighborhood' shit! Listening to them, even *I* feel like I must be guilty!" Amazing looked over at Botch. "They're lynching a nigger, for God's sake!"

The first announcer cut back in and reported with grave authority that the Jets would face more than just an uphill battle today unless Amazing showed up at the last minute as promised. "Backup quarterback Mike Maher has an awful passer rating due to an old injury and a consistent problem reading defenses."

Amazing, disgusted, pointed a finger at the screen. "Man, that Maher ain't no good at all. The game is already fuckin' over," and plopped loudly back down into the bed.

Botch smiled. "You don't think Maher has a chance?"

Amazing gave Botch a puzzled look. "You serious? The team sucks the big one without me. Hell, I *am* the team!"

The second announcer interjected, "The Jets have won the coin toss and have elected to receive."

Botch got up and, in spite of himself, began pacing the room. The pressure was killing him. *What was I thinking betting all that money? I could have retired happily with over a million dollars in my pocket, but, no, it's never enough. We were idiots to listen to Joey V. What had he said, exactly?* Botch suddenly remembered and muttered out loud, "It's a lock. I guarantee it."

Amazing looked from the TV over at Botch. "What's that? You alright, man?"

Botch was surprised by the question. "Fine. Why?"

"I don't know," Amazing said, staring at Botch. "I mean, I thought maybe Joe Willie Namath fell out your ass or something."

"What?" Botch asked, now totally lost.

"You pacing around the room saying, 'I guarantee it.'"

Botch took in a deep breath and let it out slowly. "Don't worry about me. Just watch the game," he said, feeling helpless and alone.

Amazing considered Botch a moment, then pleaded, "Why can't you let me play? We can clear everything up afterwards, I promise."

"Life is more than a damn football game," Botch answered reflexively.

"Hell, you're just persecuting me because I'm black. I've been out of trouble since I was sixteen!"

Botch looked at the frustrated celebrity athlete, thought about what Amazing

213

was doing to Andre's daughter, Tina, and felt a sudden surge of anger. "Don't give me that bullshit. You've got more than just old skeletons in your closet."

Amazing, feeling decidedly uncomfortable with where the conversation was heading, offered glumly, "Oh, here comes the cracker words of wisdom."

"How big are you?" Botch blurted out.

"Six-foot-five. Why?"

"I don't know. Just interested. You're so fucking rich and arrogant, and you act like you're mad at the world. I would say you probably keep a girlfriend half your size somewhere just to slap around. The thing is, you probably think that's alright, yet you don't hesitate to cry foul whenever the world takes a swing at you, like it does at everyone sometime or other."

"Just watch the game," Amazing growled, his reddening face breaking out in a fine sweat.

Botch laughed. "I see I'm right on. What? You suddenly have nothing to say?" he said, cocking an eyebrow at the increasingly uncomfortable athlete.

The big screen suddenly erupted in cheers and the announcer yelled, "The Bills have kicked the ball out of the end zone for a touchback. The Jets have the ball at the twenty yard line. Jets backup quarterback Mike Maher takes the ball from under center. Maher drops back to pass to…Jets wide-receiver, Willie Smith. Smith splits the safeties. Maher launches a bullet pass. Smith's wide open! It's…it's intercepted! Hulse has the ball with no one but Maher standing in his path. Hulse runs past Maher! Touchdown, Bills!" the announcer's voice dissolved into an ocean of heady Bills fans' screaming wildly. "That makes it seven to nothing, Buffalo, after a good extra point," the announcer finally got in.

Botch jumped up and punched the air, yelling, "Yes!" only to realize Amazing was lying in his bed cheering with him. Botch stared at Amazing, confused again.

"What?" Amazing ventured innocently.

"I don't get it. Don't you want your team," he asked bewildered, "you know—the *Jets*—to win?"

"Well, one thing I gotta' tell you," Amazing answered unabashedly. "When it comes to money, I keep it real. They win without me, my value tumbles and in this sport, it's all about payday. No one lasts long in football. You at least agree with me on that?"

"Payday. Gotta' admit, I'm with you there," Botch replied, as he watched the replay, thinking about what Amazing had just said. He didn't give the expected, "It's all about winning" line. Instead, the self-absorbed football star had admitted his own bias, and Botch caught himself momentarily admiring Amazing. The fact that they both wanted the same result would make the afternoon a little less stressful. *God*, Botch thought to himself, *I might just turn out liking this guy!*

CHAPTER 42

The Jets fans could be heard cursing up a storm even from outside Farrell's Bar. Andre and Joyce hesitated before entering just long enough to end up meeting Nick and Shelby just outside of the front door. Andre put a fatherly arm around Nick, "So how was Vegas?" he asked, looking from Shelby to Nick.

Nick was beaming, but offered only a brief, "Fantastic," without further explanation. Shelby giggled and snuggled into Nick's shoulder.

Nick, acknowledging social pleasantries, formally introduced Shelby to Joyce. After returning Joyce's welcome, Shelby offered Andre a friendly, "we've-already-met" smile. .

"Feeling better this time, I hope," Andre returned.

At Andre's insistence, Nick and Shelby stepped into the bar. Joyce, however, stopped just inside the door and asked Andre warily, "What was that all about?"

"Long story," Andre said, giving everyone a shove forward.

Once inside, the four stopped to let their eyes adjust to the darkness, then each looked about the room.

Joyce waved to Mack, who was ordering drinks at the bar, and went straight for the owners' booth where Annie was sitting. Joyce and Anne hugged and kissed. "Okay, what's going on here, girl? What's the big secret? I've been drilling Andre the whole ride over, but he refused to say a word till I saw it for myself."

"Watch the game and I'll fill you in," Annie replied, happy to have another woman to talk with.

Joyce looked at the nearest TV screen and grimaced. "Ugh, football. It's so violent! I only watch it because Tina's ex-boyfriend is the quarterback for the Jets. You know—that creep, Amazing Jones."

Annie looked surprised. "Tina broke up with him?"

"Yep," Joyce volunteered. "I don't know why, and she won't talk about it. I'm just glad they've separated. He's a conceited moron, and look at all the trouble he's in. I couldn't believe it when I heard it on the news. I knew the moment Tina told me about him that that boy was going to be trouble, but two dead bodies in the trunk?"

Joyce shifted her gaze to the far end of the bar where Shelby was clinging to Nick's arm as he waited to help his father carry the drinks over to the ladies. "Hey, are Nick and Shelby, you know, boyfriend-girlfriend?"

Annie turned and looked. "Guess so. I haven't met her. Nick's going to be surprised when he sees me here with Mack."

Joyce held back her burning desire to ask how Annie and Mack were doing, instead continuing, "They do make a cute couple. Wait," she said as if awakening, "You mean, Nick doesn't know about you and Mack?"

"It's only been a couple days, and I still can't believe that we're kind of...you know, back together again. There's still a lot to work through."

"Wow," Joyce said dreamily, staring at Nick and Shelby, "Look at how he's holding her."

"Nick's in love!" Annie replied, so loudly that everyone around them, including Mack, tray of drinks in his hand, turned briefly to face her.

Mack did his best to fake a look of shock as he placed the round of drinks on the ladies' table. Then he returned to the bar and gave Andre a high five and his son a warm, manly hug. Not knowing what to say to Shelby, he cleared his throat awkwardly...and shook her hand.

Andre nodded up towards the TV. "I'd be happy if the score would just stay this way until the end."

"That would be fine by me, too," Mack agreed. Turning to Nick, he added, "So how much did you two lose in Vegas?"

"Actually, we took some of Vegas home with us. We had a nice run, didn't we, babe?" he said, looking happily at Shelby.

"It was a great couple of nights, despite the long flight," Shelby said, adding suddenly, "Nick? Who's that woman waving at us? Is that your mother?"

"Ah, yes, it is," said Nick and Mack together, Nick surprised to see his father and mother in the same building, and Mack anxious to see his son's reaction.

"Why don't you go over and say 'hello' to your mother," Mack said kindly, "and introduce her to Shelby."

Nick looked at Shelby, took her hand in his and squeezed it gently. "I guess it's time."

CHAPTER 43

"Nick, how can I meet your mother looking like this?" Shelby complained.

"Relax, you look great. She's very down to earth. She'll love you," Nick promised, nudging Shelby along.

Nick gave his mother a kiss. "Hey, Mom, didn't expect to see you here, but I won't ask questions, not till tomorrow, anyway."

"Good!" Annie said, surveying the happy couple and thinking of how she and Mack must have looked when they first met. "Let's just say, I didn't expect to be here, either. So how was Las Vegas?"

Nick's smile spread ear to ear. "Great. Mom," adding, "Mom, this is Shelby. Shelby, Mom."

Annie smiled. "Hi, Shelby. I was wondering when I was going to meet you. Nick, go get a drink for Shelby. Shelby, sit, and, please, call me Annie. You've met Joyce already," Annie said, re-introducing the woman at her elbow who was trying hard to take everything in while seeming disinterested.

"We met coming in," Shelby replied, her nervousness beginning to show.

Annie patted Shelby on the arm. "So are you Nick's girlfriend? Or are you just...friends?"

Shelby, thoroughly embarrassed, blushed hotly and said, "I think you should ask your son that question."

"Alright, I get it. I'll stop asking questions. God knows, after all these years, I still don't know where I stand with my own man."

Just then, Debbie walked into the bar. Mack hailed her, and greeted her with a hug and kiss, while Andre stood back and watched with concern. Mack asked her if she was still shook up from what had happened earlier at Botch's FBI office.

"I'll be much better after four or five Rum and Cokes," she said, her cold hands shaking in Mack's.

Mack whispered, "Please don't mention to the girls what happened, at least not until after the game...okay?"

"Not a word, I promise," she replied, visibly stiffening her resolve.

Debbie gave Andre a peck, and Andre pointed towards the owners' table where Annie, Joyce and Shelby were sitting and chatting. "The girls are collecting over there. I'll bring your first Rum and Coke over."

Debbie wound her way through the increasingly crowded bar and over to the ladies' table. After greeting Annie and Joyce, she was introduced to Shelby. Joyce looked over the three women, and dropped her voice so all had to secretively huddle to hear her. "What the hell is going on? When was the last time we were together like this? I mean with the men, and all?"

Annie grinned, "Years. But it feels great, doesn't it? God, I've missed those days."

Nick returned with Shelby's drink and a large appetizer plate from the kitchen. Placing the plate in the center of the table, he gave Shelby a kiss, and re-joined Mack and Andre around the largest TV monitor. Debbie smiled at Shelby and raised her eyebrows as Nick left. Shelby sighed, feeling like one of the ladies at last.

Andre signaled to Mack as Nick sauntered over. "That boy's in love, Mack."

Mack grinned in agreement, "He's certainly acting the lap dog."

Nick, overhearing him, frowned, "Who are you calling a lap dog?"

"No one, Fido," Andre joked.

Nick ignored the comment. Looking up at the TV monitor, he watched the Jets go three yards in three downs, then set up to punt.

"Where the hell is Joey V.?" Andre asked.

"I called him," Mack said. "He's on his way. Why?"

"I won't feel good till I see him."

"Relax. He'll be here," Mack replied, as the bar door opened and in walked Joey V.

Joey V. searched the room and seeing three of his four co-conspirators, pushed his way over to them. "What did I miss?" he asked frantically. "How are they doing?"

Mack responded calmly, "They've punted."

Joey V. gave a long exhale, adding his relief to that of the others. "Excellent. My car's back in the shop again, so I had to take a cab here. I asked the cabdriver to dial up the game on his radio, but he just glared angrily at me. That's when I knew..."

"Buffalo has it at their own thirty," Andre said dryly, trying to redirect everyone's attention to the game on the TV. In the end, however, it proved a worse torture to follow the game together, blow by blow, especially when Buffalo took to simply controlling the ball and calling two or three yard running plays.

"Fuck!" Andre finally volunteered for the whole nervous group. "The way Buffalo is acting, you'd think there was only two minutes left and they had a twenty-one point lead."

"Only seven points and they're happy sitting on the lead. It's...it's stupid!" Joey V. said with ire.

"No, it's *guaranteed*, remember?" Mack stared ominously at Joey V., who looked nervously around the group and then back at the TV.

The Bills set up for a field goal. The kicked ball flew up in the air and Mack, Andre, Nick and Joey V. tilted left collectively willing the ball by their action through the uprights. It landed just inside the right post. The announcer yelled, "It's good! Buffalo's up, ten to nothing!"

Ninety percent of the bar groaned while Mack, Andre, Nick and Joey V. gave each other silent high fives.

At the owners' table, Joyce, Debbie, Shelby and Annie continued talking about what Anne thought had brought about Mack's sudden change of heart. Then Joyce looked over at Andre and yelled, "I might not know much about football, but I know that Jets fans are not supposed to look happy when their team is losing. From here, you all look happy that they're losing! What's going on?" A sudden hush descended over the room, and the four anti-Jets fans cringed in the center of a sea of angry looks.

A moment later, Andre broke from the group and casually walked over to the four women. "Please try to keep your comments to yourself, Joyce, at least until the end of the game, alright? It's a long story, but if you'll all just watch the game, you'll discover what's going on soon enough."

Joyce raised her eyebrows, stunned at the rebuke her husband had given her, and drilled her anger into the back of her husband's head as he walked away. Then she turned to the other women. "He just tried to blow me off! What the hell is this 'watch the game and you'll find out soon enough' stuff? Who the hell does he think he is? Who does he think he's talking to!" Joyce stood as she was talking, intending to go over and confront Andre in front of the whole bar.

Annie grabbed Joyce's arm. "Sit and I'll tell you what I know."

Joyce sat back in her seat with a plop, eager to hear what Annie had just volunteered to reveal.

"Mack told me last night about their latest scheme. He and Andre are just as crazy now as they've been for the last forty years. They're still Jets fans but..." Annie told them everything she knew while Joyce continued to stare heatedly at the back of Andre's head.

Andre, worried more about Joyce than the game, whispered to Mack through the side of his mouth, "Did she sit down?"

"Annie's talking to her, and she's seated, listening," Mack replied. "You've dodged the bullet."

"I know I came on strong, but I couldn't back down and let everyone here think I was some kind of punk."

Mack laughed, "So having her stick her size nine up your ass in front of everyone was a better plan?"

"Humpf," Andre returned dourly.

As the second quarter started, all the girls except Annie watched obediently. Annie, however, was thinking of the many games she had been to with Mack, just to be by his side. Her flashback was interrupted by Joyce standing up and yelling at the TV, "Run, you fat bastard, run!" to an angry hail of, "Sit down and shut up, lady!" from angry Jets fans throughout the room.

The player did exactly as Joyce ordered, a moment later scoring another touchdown, making it Buffalo, sixteen to zero.

Andre watched, abashed, as Joyce jumped up and down screaming, "My man! My man! My man!"

After the extra point, and an impossible to hold inside, "Woo-hoo!" Joyce walked alone, head erect, through the mass of jeering Jets fans over to Andre, put her hands on her hips and growled just loud enough for Mack, Nick, Joey V. and Andre to hear: "So you and your buddies get involved in something *this* big without discussing it with us! You better pray, Mr. Big-Shots, that what you're all doing works."

Joyce sauntered back over to Annie, high-fived her and sat down.

Andre looked at Mack. "Her wrath will be worse than losing the money. I don't know if my heart can take this much longer."

"At least Annie saved you the additional pressure of explaining it all," Mack replied, chuckling.

Andre shook his head, "I don't think I'm going to get off that easy. I know Joyce, and she's watching the game now. When it's over, I'm going to have to explain every play she saw, and why, if I was so worried, I got involved in this in the first place. You don't know my Joyce, Mack. When she focuses on something, she won't let go. If we lose, promise to shoot me, quick."

"Come on. Joyce? She's the warmest, kindest, most understanding woman I've ever met," Mack replied, tongue-in-cheek. "Yeah, she can be strong and direct, but you like that about her, really, don't you?"

Andre refused to rise to the bait, and instead refocused his attention on the TV monitor.

The Jets took the ball following the kick off, the Jets kick-returner almost breaking free along the side line. Joyce and Debbie in the background together screamed, "Stop him! Stop him!"

The second announcer cut in: "The Bills have only their kicker on the field to stop the Jets kick-returner and...Yes! It's a great open field tackle!"

Joey V. couldn't help yelling, "I love that guy! I love him!" The conspirators looked at each other and breathed sighs of relief.

The Jets lined up at their own forty-five. Maher threw a wobbly pass to his running back who took the ball to the Bills' forty. "All right!" the announcer yelled. "This is the first positive pass-play for the Jets, and the first time in this game they've been positioned to score!"

Mack let go and yelled out, "Hold them to a field goal!" to a mob of hisses.

Two plays later, Maher found himself dropping further and further back as Buffalo executed one after another perfect safety blitz. Maher tried to throw the ball out of bounds, but the pass fell short and the Bills intercepted it. Mack and his crowd cheered wildly as the Bills linebacker ran down the length of the sideline to the Jets' twenty yard line where it looked like he was going to be pushed out of bounds. Then, at the last second, the linebacker tossed the ball back to a Buffalo teammate who ran it the rest of the way for a touchdown. Die-hard Jets fans shook their heads in disgust as the score increased to twenty-four to zero, Buffalo, after the extra point.

The Jets fans, watching their team being totally blown out, were becoming increasingly rankled by the boisterous rooting for the Buffalo Bills in what had traditionally always been a dedicated all-Jets bar.

Joey V. rubbed his hands vigorously. "It's a blowout, guys. Didn't I tell ya? Huh?"

Mack silently pleaded with Joey V. not to jinx their luck.

The room grew quiet as the game went back and forth without further scores, until the Jets kicked a field goal, ending the first half, twenty-four to three, with Buffalo still leading. Joey V. grinned, stating for them all, "Twenty-four to three, I'll take that." The men walked over to the girls' table, blatantly proud, confident at last in their overall scheme.

Number One Bestseller

CHAPTER 44

At the hospital, Botch walked out of Amazing Jones's room to call Mack at half-time. "What was that field goal right before half-time? I got a bad feeling, Mack. The Jets are starting to show some life and they scored pretty easily…"

Mack, piqued, cut in. "Come on, Botch, a 'lock' is not a shutout; they're totally different. The Jets would have to score thirty-six points and completely shutout the Bills in the second half in order for us to lose. Relax! We're sitting pretty."

"Alright, alright," he answered, "but I can't help it. Watching the game with Amazing makes me feel crazy. And I still have a bad feeling about this game…"

"Botch? Botch? Are you there?" Mack said, pretending he couldn't hear Botch, and then hung up.

Andre asked, "Nervous Nelly?"

"Who else? He's an insufferable, Doubting Thomas. Always was, always will be. I should have told him to sit on a bedpan during the second half of the game, because with his attitude, he's going to end up shitting his pants more than once before it's over."

Andre's phone suddenly rang. "Hello? Botch?" he said into it, rolling his eyes at Mack.

"Yeah, it's me, Andre. Hey, Mack and I got cut off. Is Debbie there? Is she okay?"

Andre looked towards the girls' table. Joyce, above the general din, was explaining to Debbie and Annie what a four-three defense was. "Oh yeah. She's fine," he answered, wondering where Joyce had suddenly acquired her knowledge of the finer points of football strategy.

"Great," said Botch, relieved, as halftime came to an end and the game resumed. "Tell her not to leave after the game." There was a pause. "Andre! Do you believe that field goal at the end of the first half? I can't believe…"

Andre cut in. "Hello? Botch? Hello? Hello?" and then hung up. Turning to

223

Mack, he frowned. "Now I'm more worried about Botch than I am Joyce. How scary is that?" Mack shook his head in disgust, both returning their attention to the TV.

After a few moments, Andre, intending to tell Debbie what Botch had said, wound his way to where the ladies were huddled together and whispering. Overhearing Joyce's explanation of a safety blitz, Andre changed his mind and instead asked, "Girl, where did you learn all this football jargon?"

"Actually, hon', it's quite easy to figure out," she offered. Andre stared in disbelief as Joyce explained: "Alright! Alright! So I love football, too. When you go out to watch a game with the boys, I watch it at home and listen to what you say afterwards when you return."

"You watch the game by yourself, but you don't want to watch it with your husband?" Andre asked, dumbfounded.

"Don't frown at me like that! You could have at least waited till the end of this game to let me know about all the money—our retirement money—you and your friends are betting on it. I'm likely to drop dead from worry before this damn game ends!"

Andre looked at her, even more bewildered than before. He was about to say, "I *didn't* tell you," but decided, given the situation, to say instead, "I'm sorry, babe," and walked away even more befuddled.

Joyce smiled at Annie. "He thinks he's so slick. I asked him earlier what the 'big secret' was and he pulled away, saying, 'three-thirty,' as if I asked him what time it was. He's been pulling that shit for years, and thinks I don't know his little game. Whoa there! Who the hell gave you that rock?" Joyce switched in mid-speech. Debbie had just reached for her drink, and a diamond flashed on her heart-finger. "Does Botch know you're engaged?" Joyce continued in jest.

Debbie smiled. "I hope so. He gave it to me."

Joyce, Annie and Shelby let loose a collective sigh. "It's beautiful!" Shelby offered as Debbie held her hand high in the air, moving her wrist back and forth. The diamond caught the light of the TV and sparkled like a lighthouse.

Noticing from the men's table, Mack yelled his congratulations, followed by Joey V. and Andre, who immediately returned their attention to the game.

Joyce picked up where she'd left off. "See what I mean? They think they're so slick, but they run and hide the moment they see a ring. I can't believe you finally lassoed Botch!" Joyce continued without stopping, "I thought he'd never get married again!" Joyce noticed Nick, sitting quietly at the other end of their table, and asked, "How come you don't run?"

Nick looked shyly at Shelby and shrugged.

Annie exclaimed, "You guys didn't!"

Shelby gave the nod, pulled out a wedding band and slid it on her finger.

Annie beamed. "I should have known by your faces. A mother always knows."

Joyce shifted forward to the edge of her seat. "Knows what? Come on, what are you holding back?"

"While they were in Vegas," Annie responded calmly, "Nick and Shelby got married."

"You got married?" Joyce blurted out, turning to the couple. "But you've only known each other a couple of days!" Joyce quickly covered her mouth with her hands, wishing she could take back what she'd just said.

Annie looked at Shelby as she pointed to Joyce, "She said it, I didn't."

Nick frowned. "Crazy or not it just felt right."

All eyes turned to Shelby, who took a deep breath, and proceeded to explain. "We talked for hours about it, and in the end we just did it."

"I guess this means you're my daughter-in-law. Please don't think of me as strange, but this is the first time in my life that I've met someone, only to find out they were part of my family all along. I guess any hopes for a big wedding are dashed."

"Not necessarily," Shelby interrupted. "We want to have a real wedding in the future—after the dust settles. And believe me, I understand your reservations. Truly, I do understand," she added, acknowledging each of the people around her.

"Have you told your father that you got married?" Annie asked Nick softly, looking with pleasure at her beaming son.

"Are you kidding?" Nick asked. "Look at him over there, dumbfounded, unable to handle even Botch's engagement! No, I haven't told him yet. I mean, I thought it might, well…"

Debbie lifted her glass. "Well, here's my congratulations!" and the three ladies toasted Nick and Shelby. Shelby smiled happily, while Nick sat and blushed.

"And to Debbie and Botch," Nick said, tipping his glass towards Debbie. All tapped glasses together and drank while Debbie grinned contentedly.

When the toasts moved on to Annie and Mack, Annie seemed suddenly pensive. "Nick," she said, awkwardly breaking the festivities, "How about I tell your father about you and Shelby first?"

All eyes turned reflexively to Nick.

"After the game," Nick responded, and everyone's attention shifted back to the big TV screen blaring above the men's table.

A hush descended throughout the room as players took the field for the second half. Joey V. and Mack looked at each other, and said simultaneously, "This is it," as the Jets kicked off to the Buffalo Bills.

The Bills kick-returner caught the ball at the Bills' twenty-yard line and started running confidently down the field toward the goal, when a Jet player appeared out of nowhere, tackling him and stripping him of the ball. The Jets recovered the fumble. As Jets fans yelled and screamed with joy,

Stunned, Joey V. shouted, "Un-fucking believable!"

Andre, dismayed, added, "The guy barely touched him!"

Joyce, in the background, yelled, "His knee was down!"

The first announcer blared, "There's a flag on the field. The ruling is…"

The TV screen switched to replay, and even the staunchest of Jets fans could see the man's knee was down before he fumbled. Jets fans everywhere groaned, while Mack, Andre and Joey V. shouted, "Yes!"

Midway through the third quarter, the Jets quarterback, Maher, handed the ball to a running back who picked up barely three yards before being aggressively tackled. Mack looked at his companions. "I'm happy with how it's going, but I can't understand why the Jets, down twenty-one points, are playing so conservatively. It's hard to imagine they were so heavily favored."

Andre grunted, "Though I hate to admit it, that asshole, Amazing Jones, must actually be that good."

Mack grinned, "Yeah, well, he's paying for his sins today, watching the game with Botch. Does Joyce know what he did to Tina?"

"Hell, no!" Andre responded, looking around afterwards to make sure no one overheard him. "Tina begged me not to tell her. Joyce would likely plunge a knife in that piece of shit's chest on national TV if she ever got wind of it."

The room hushed as the Jets continued trying unsuccessfully to run the ball, their team members instead succumbing to one injury after another in light of an abruptly more aggressive Bill's defense. "If the Jets keep collecting injuries like this, they're going to run out of offensive players," the second announcer interjected.

Thoroughly bored, the first announcer was about to make a handover comment, when he suddenly yelled, "Wait! Maher's attempting a one deep! Ravitch is wide open! The pass is caught for a forty-yard gain on a third and six."

Joyce yelled, "Shit!" as Maher on the next play threw a bullet to an open Jets receiver in the far corner of the end zone. The Jet's crowd began to cheer, even as the ball continued on, slipping through his fingers to tumble onto the ground. On the screen, the receiver stood staring blankly at his empty hands. The crowds' reaction was deadly: Jets boos and jeers erupted from throughout the stadium and bar.

Joey V. looked at Mack and Andre. Mimicking a heart attack, he said, "We definitely don't want *this* kind of 'momentum' to change."

Next, the Jets tried a running play, but the Bills stopped them dead. Third and seven, Maher handed off to the running back who ran all the way to the line of scrimmage, only to slam into a solid wall of Buffalo Bills defensive players. Andre yelled, "Going nowhere!" as the running back bounced backwards.

Out of frustration, the man flicked the ball back to Maher who, in a moment of untoward glory, somehow hit the tight end for a touchdown. Pandemonium ruled for the next few minutes as the score settled at twenty-four to ten, Buffalo, after a perfectly executed extra point.

Jets fans on TV and in the bar began dancing wildly about. One man, half-drunk, bumped into Mack, almost knocking him over. "That's how *we* do it!" the man screamed at the top of his lungs. "Watch out, Bills, here we come!"

Mack roughly pushed the man aside. "I can take the ball-breaking, but if we end up losing, I'm going to knock the shit out of this fucking bastard!" he said to Andre in a voice that all could hear.

Joey V. paled. "This is not good, guys. Let's not fall apart this early in the game. There's still a lot of second half left, and I don't like seeing things shifting like this."

Mack stared darkly at Joey V., distracted from commenting by the ring of his phone. Mack glared at the number on his cell phone screen. It was Botch. Mack showed the number to Andre and slid the phone back in his pocket.

A moment later, Andre's phone rang. Andre looked at the screen. "Guess who," he said to Mack, and shoved his phone back into his pocket.

Joey V. got up and walked closer to the TV screen. "Actually, we may have just gotten a break. Maher got hit pretty hard on that last play. He looks injured. He might have a dislocated shoulder and have to sit out the rest of the game. If so, that means they'll have to go with the rookie quarterback who has never actually played a pro game," he said, the color in his face returning.

Number One Bestseller

CHAPTER 45

Botch shook his cell phone, unable to comprehend why he couldn't get through to either Mack or Andre. Then he heard Amazing Jones shout, "Shit!"

Botch looked from the phone to Amazing.

"They're putting in Heaney. That stupid ass, Maher, finally got what was coming to him. They're carrying him off the field."

"Heaney, that's the rookie, right?"

"He may look and act like a rookie, but this kid's amaz…" Amazing caught himself. "What I meant to say is, he's almost as good as Maher." Botch panicked and tried to call Mack again. Just then, Amazing's principal lawyer walked in.

Amazing scowled. "Where the hell have you been?"

The lawyer stopped and stared at Botch, then turned his attention to Amazing, explaining cautiously, "I'm really sorry, Amazing, but some idiot swerved in front of me just a block before the hospital and slammed on his brakes. I barely tapped his bumper, but the guy jumped out, moaning, holding his neck and yelling 'Whiplash! Whiplash!' I had to wait for the ambulance to show, and then for the police to interview everyone in the vicinity as if it was a hit and run. After an hour, the victim suddenly recovered and asked the police to drive him home as if they were old buddies. Strange, don't you think, agent Bartolotta?" The lawyer eyed Botch. Botch turned away and looked out the window.

"Alright, alright, so get me out of here!" Amazing said, swinging his completely dressed body out of the bed.

"I spoke to the D.A. and he's not going to press charges. There wasn't enough evidence. The policemen outside have been told to leave. So, we're ready to answer any last questions you might have, Mr. Bartolatta, to put this matter to rest, so my client can resume his life and get ready for next week's game."

Botch clasped his hands behind his back, but didn't move.

"I don't understand," the lawyer continued, "how you could think my client

229

could be involved with those agents when *they* had *him* in handcuffs?"

Botch glanced at the TV to see how much game-time was still left. The trainers were huddled on the sidelines around Maher. Botch calculated how long it would take for Amazing to drive his black Corvette at top speed from Long Island to the New Jersey Meadowlands, and decided that, irrespective of traffic, Amazing couldn't make it back to the game currently in progress in time—in fact, the way Botch calculated it, *he* would barely make it to Farrell's Bar before the game was over.

Satisfied, Botch said in a serious voice, "The handcuffs are the reason I'm going to let him go."

"Then that's it?" the lawyer asked, looking dumbly from Botch's back to his eager-to-go client.

"That's it. All we have to do now is just wait for the paperwork."

The lawyer's eyes narrowed. "What paperwork?"

Amazing, however, was already running for the door with Botch close behind.

The two vied for the doorway, then the first available elevator, and when Botch clearly signaled his uncompromising intention to take the elevator for himself, Amazing ran for the emergency stairs.

Exiting the stairwell, Amazing gave an orderly a hundred dollars for his white hospital coat, and with collar up and head down, Amazing pushed an empty gurney past the milling reporters in the parking lot staring at the entrance to the hospital. Amazing and reporters together watched as Botch ran across the lot and jumped into his car, threw the emergency light on top and tore out of the parking lot, lights flashing, siren screaming. Amazing smiled and sprinted to his Corvette, jumped in and screeched off in the opposite direction to a hail of clicks and flashes from reporters' cameras.

Back at the bar, Mack, Andre, Nick and Joey V. watched intently as Maher rose from the stretcher just enough to give a thumbs up before disappearing down a corridor and out of the stadium. Joey V. shook his head, "They took almost a half hour getting him off the field. I'm going to be bald by the time this is over."

The Bills, after three plays, punted; the ball bounced past the punt-returner and was downed at the Jets' five yard line. "Good, baby, put 'em in a hole!" Joyce cried out.

Annie pointed. "Look, there's a flag!" she shouted as the first announcer declared it against the Bills for holding.

"They'll have to re-kick this one," the second announcer piped in.

This time the Jets called for a fair catch at their own forty-three yard line. A moment later Heaney, the Jets rookie third-string quarterback, walked confidently onto the field and positioned himself behind the center. Heaney called out the signals and the center snapped the ball. Everyone watched in horror as the ball fell from Heany's hands onto the field. Before either of the astounded announcers could comment, a huge pile of players appeared where the ball and Heany had been a moment ago. Joey V. screamed, "Buffalo's ball! Shit Heaney got it back!"

Mack looked at Andre and smiled. "At least Heaney is living up to expectations."

The rookie quarterback glanced nervously at the Jets coach on the sidelines who, red-faced, appeared to be shouting an unintelligible string of expletives at him.

The next play, Heaney dropped back as the Bills' defensive line rushed him. Flushed out of the pocket, he dodged defenders, and, to everyone's surprise, ran the ball to the Bills' thirty-five yard line for a gain of twenty-two yards. Sitting sullenly amidst the whoops and hollers, Mack whispered with concern to Andre, "He looked like Michael Vick on that play. The fucking newbie runs like a deer."

Andre muttered, "Let's hope he doesn't end up throwing like Tom Brady."

On the screen, Heaney took the snap at the Bills' thirty-five and hit his wide receiver with a near-perfect pass, the receiver running out of bounds at the Bills' fifteen yard line. Joey V. looked crushed. "You *had* to mention Tom Brady," he whined at Andre.

The next play, Heaney dropped back and hit his running back with a short pass from the backfield, and the first announcer yelled, "Touchdown, Jets!"

Joyce, the same moment, yelled, "Holding on the tight end!" and everyone in the bar hushed to see if she was right. Seconds later, the camera zoomed in on a flag on the field, the referee calling it exactly as Joyce had. Disbelieving eyes turned towards the women's table, as Joyce explained. "Number eighty-eight mugged the linebacker." The referee paced the ball back to the Bills' twenty-five yard line.

Heaney took the snap. This time, the Bills attacked in an all-out safety blitz and everyone could see the Jets' offensive line didn't picked up on it. The safety dived at Heaney, who, at the last possible second, ducked to avoid being sacked. Then Heaney tucked the ball under his arm and ran forward, dodging defenders, throwing himself head first into the end zone.

Both announcers yelled, "Touchdown!"

By the time the spectators calmed down, the score was twenty-four to sixteen, Bills. The Jets gathered for the extra point, and as the ball sailed between the goalposts, a horn sounded the end of the third quarter. The same obnoxious Jet fan who, a short time ago had knocked into Mack, screamed at Mack from an adjacent table, "Up yours!"

Mack surged toward the guy, but Andre and Joey V. blocked him, admonishing Mack to show restraint. Joey V. was just glad to see Mack expressing his frustration at the Jet fan and not him.

"What's the matter with you?" Nick asked, grabbing Mack's arm and pushing him into a seat.

Mack shook off Nick's hands and pointed to the drunken Jet fan. "That slob over there is getting under my skin." Andre sat next to Mack while Joey V. brushed himself off and headed for a quick toilet break. "That big-mouth mother..." Mack began, the remainder of his comment dissolving into a clamor of renewed Jets fervor as the game resumed.

Buffalo started a drive after receiving the Jets kick-off. The Bills moved the ball slowly, taking up almost five minutes before eventually punting, the Jets returning the punt to their own fifteen. The Jets tried three quick plays with a "no huddle offense," but making no gain, ended up punting the ball back to the Bills.

As the punted ball plunged from its high arc, the Buffalo punt-returner scooped it up and ran hell-bent for the Jets end zone, with only the Jets kicker to stop him. Four male voices shrieked, "Go! Go! Go!" while the rest of the bar moaned as if stabbed mortally in the chest.

As the Bills punt returner approached the end zone, he slowed to check the field just long enough for the Jets kicker to reach from behind and poke the ball out of the stunned man's hands. The Jets punter instantly picked up the loose ball, running it back to the Bills' forty-three yard line.

This time, seven forlorn voices wailed out from amidst whoops and screams of joy by Jets fans.

Everyone hushed when Heaney took the field.

Heaney took the snap, dropped back and threw a pin-point bomb for a Jets touchdown.

Mack, Andre, Nick and Joey V. watched in silence as the Jets made a good point kick, making the score twenty-four to twenty-four. Mack's nemesis looked over at him and started singing, "Slip Slidin' Away," which Jets fans all over the bar took up *en masse*. Mack and Andre looked at each other, trying to decide how badly they wanted to beat up the fellow who started it, when, out of nowhere, Joyce appeared and punched the guy in the chest, knocking him off his barstool saying, "Enough is enough, asshole!"

The fellow, drunk, dazed, and wheezing, struggled to stand, while Mack and Andre dragged him out of the bar. When they returned without the man, and several of the man's friends complained, Mack and Andre showed their badges. "Anyone eager to join him?" Mack asked menacingly, and the bar quieted down to grumbles, attention returning to the game.

Outside Farrell's, Botch approached the front door of the bar, just in time for the man Mack and Andre had just thrown out to bounce off him. "Fuckin' bitch hits me an' they throw *me* out," the man, short of breath, managed to get out in a drunken slur.

Botch stared momentarily at the man, snorted derisively, shook his head sadly and entered the bar. Spotting Mack and Andre, he joined them. "What's the score?" he asked politely. Mack, Andre and Nick stared at him, wondering why he wasn't at the hospital sitting on Amazing. "I stalled Amazing as long as I could," Botch offered in explanation, adding, "My piece-of-shit car radio stopped working on the way here. How's it going?"

"It's tied up," Mack said, pale-faced.

Botch looked confused, then laughed. "Stop breaking my balls! What's the score, really?"

Andre grunted, "It's like Mack said: Tied. Look at the fucking TV!"

Botch looked just in time to see the tie-score slide across the bottom of the screen. "But…but how?" Botch stammered.

Mack and Nick ignored him, returning their attention to the TV, more worried about what would happen next, while Andre visited his wife to warn her sternly to keep in her chair or he'd send her home in a cab. "I'm still the senior police officer here," he stated lamely.

Joyce was rubbing her sore knuckles and staring dagger-eyed at her husband. "Fine," she eventually said.

"Fine," he eventually answered, turning back towards the men's table, but after a couple of steps, stopped, looked back at his equal and said quietly, "Great punch. Couldn't have done better myself."

Botch slipped over to the owners' table, passing Andre wordlessly, to kiss Debbie. Annie and Joyce congratulated him on the engagement; Botch blushed and returned, "Yeah, thanks." Noting Joey V. returning from the men's room, Botch ignored the women and mimicked Joey's voice loud enough for all to hear: "It's a lock! I *guarantee* it!"

Joey V. stopped in his tracks. About to lose his temper, he instead said calmly, "Hey, Botch, shut the fuck up and watch the game. The Jets would have to suddenly score fourteen unanswered points for us to lose!"

No one said anything. Joey V. stared at the ring of stone-cold eyes focused on him. "Someone get Botch a drink…or a muzzle," he said, casually reclaiming his spot in front of the T.V., wondering what could have possibly transpired during the short time he had been away to make everyone so edgy.

Number One Bestseller

CHAPTER 46

All eyes in the bar were glued on the nearest TV screen. Everyone held their breath as the first announcer continued: "Both teams are three and out in a good defensive fourth quarter. The Jets have the ball on their own forty-five. Heaney scrambles out of the pocket...the Bills are tightening the noose around him...and he throws a perfect spiral over the head of the safety! The Jets' wide receiver catches it with one hand...he's running...running...into the end zone for another Jet touchdown!"

The bar erupted into mayhem. Mack, Andre, Botch and Joey V. watched with disbelief as the Jets kicked a successful extra point. The Jets now led by seven. Botch downed his whole glass of Jack Daniels in one gulp. "I think I'm going to be sick."

"We just need the Bills to score another touchdown, and we'll be okay. Then the game will go into overtime." All eyes shifted angrily from the TV to the source of the voice: Joey V. "Well, I'm just being positive. Maybe you should try," he said, shrugging his shoulders while at the same time shrinking behind Nick.

The second announcer abruptly cut in and everyone's attention shifted back to the TV. "...Amazing Jones is back! All charges against him have been dropped! This is turning into what can only be called *the* game of the season!"

"You said it, and I have to agree," the first announcer added, picking up seamlessly on cue. "Amazing Jones is back! And the Jets appear ecstatic. Amazing is being dressed by his assistants as he waves to the crowd. The roar of the Jets crowd is deafening!"

Andre looked blankly at Botch. "I thought you were going to make certain he would be out the whole game?"

Botch, perplexed, muttered, "There's no way he could have driven from the hospital to the stadium that quick!"

Mack pointed to a blue helicopter rising from outside the stadium on TV. "You never heard of a private helicopter, I take it," he announced with finality.

Botch hung his head. "Alright, I fucked up! I tried to call you over and over..."

Andre cut in. "Jesus, Botch, you could at least have slapped him around a bit. At least it might have hurt his ego."

Botch jerked as if slapped himself. "The guy was in the hospital; he was crying, for God's sake!"

Joey V. rolled his eyes and shook his head. "It's on you now if this guy scores another touchdown," he announced with obvious relief.

Botch gave Joey a menacing look. At that moment, Joyce yelled over the crowd, "Too late, Amazing Jones!" as the two-minute warning sounded.

Joey V. gloated and asked self-assuredly, "Who's coming with me tomorrow to pick up the winnings?" The three looked at Joey V. like he had just signed their death warrants.

"God damn it, Joey! The game's still not over! Don't jinx it any worse!"

Joey V. looked from one frightened face to another. "I don't believe in that jinx shit anymore," he said flatly, squaring his shoulders as the Bills continued to work their way yard by yard towards the end zone.

Mack looked from Joey V. to the TV, then back, fixing Joey in a deadly stare, "Well, we do, so shut the fuck up!"

Suddenly the crowd on the TV went wild. The Bills' running back fumbled the ball and the Jets recovered it. From the back, Joyce pointed towards the screen shouting, "Flag!"

The crowd, bar, and first announcer were nearing hysteria, but what all the conspirators desperately wanted to hear, and heard, was "...holding by the Jets' defensive back!"

The Bills had the ball back on the Jets' twenty-five yard line. The tension was thickening the air. The Bills' quarterback set up a shotgun formation and took the snap, the Jets attacking him with an all-out blitz. The quarterback fell backwards trying repeatedly to find an opportunity to throw the ball, only to have it tipped out of his hand and recovered by the Jets' safety. The Bills' quarterback dived at the safety but missed, leaving the safety free to run, unopposed, down the sideline.

The first announcer screamed, "Touchdown!" Botch threw his chair into a corner in rage. It shattered loudly into pieces, completely unnoticed by the shrieking Jets fans.

Joey V. paled and tensed. "I feel like I just got kicked in the balls."

In the back, Shelby turned to Joyce. "What does all this mean? Is it over?"

Joyce explained, "If the Jets make the extra point, which is almost certain, there will be only twenty seconds left. Even under the best of circumstances, the

Bills won't be able to cover the field and score in that little time. The final score will be thirty-eight to twenty-four: a fourteen point spread, which will make the game, in the betting world, a 'push.' What it means is that we lose everything." Everyone watched transfixed as two more injured players were helped off the field.

As the Jets lined up to kick the extra point, Botch saw Amazing Jones trundle onto the field to take the snap and hold the ball for the kicker. "I can't believe it! That self-absorbed bastard's going to get himself into the game one way or another!"

Joyce yelled from behind, "Shank it!" while Annie put her palms together, fingers pointed upwards, and silently prayed.

Amazing Jones took the snap and then, to everyone's surprise, stood up, tucked the ball under his arm and scrambled to his right. The kicker, equally surprised, awkwardly attempted to block for him.

Joey V. yelled, "The showboating bastard is going for extra points!"

Amazing scanned the field, and calmly threw the ball cross-body towards the far left corner of the end zone, where the Jets' tight end was waiting, wide open. Adrenaline sparked, lightening-like, through the stale bar air in counterpoint to Mack and his group's groans, when out of nowhere the Bills' cornerback cut between the tight end's fingers and the descending ball to intercept it. The Jets receiver stared at his empty hands while the Bills cornerback ran unopposed down the side line. Bills fans throughout the stadium yelled and screamed, jumping up and down in a frenzied ecstasy.

The moment the touchdown was announced, Botch and Joey V. clutched their chests at the same time. Andre smiled broadly as the Bills took the extra point, making it a remarkable thirty-eight to thirty-one, Buffalo Bills, when the clock read all zeros.

Fans flowed from the bleachers onto the field. In the distance, Amazing Jones was being chewed out by the Jets' head coach for not running the very play he had called. The camera suddenly zoomed in tightly on Amazing Jones' lips as he ripped his helmet off, "Fuck you! This is *my* team, not yours!" The coach, livid, ripped off his headset and threw a hard right at Amazing, knocking him onto the ground.

Half of the Jets team grabbed Amazing's arms and legs and dragged him off the field, while the other half cheered and clapped for the coach. Andre looked at Botch. "Now why couldn't *you* have done that to the son-of-a-bitch?"

Botch laughed. "Are you kidding? Right now I could kiss that kid," he said and walked over and kissed Joey V. on the cheek. "Never doubted you. Not once," he added, smiling childishly.

The girls abandoned their table and descended on the men, Annie hugging Mack and Mack giving her a long, dramatic kiss to his comrades' lengthy hoots.

Debbie looked askance at Botch. "You kissed *him!*" she said to Botch while pointing at Joey V. "What about *me*?" she asked, grabbing Botch in her arms, arching over him and implanting a passionate, French kiss.

Mack pretended not to notice, shouting instead, "Drinks for everyone!"

At that announcement, the glum Jets crowd suddenly brightened.

Nick turned to Shelby and began, "*Now* I can tell you everything…"

"Men! Of all the…" Shelby interrupted, shaking her head. "I figured it all out an hour ago, but thanks for trying to spare me the anguish of the game. So does this mean we're rich?"

"Let's just say the future is on me."

Mack lassoed a tray of drinks and called the gang around him. Looking carefully to make sure no one outside their circle could hear, he whispered, "Listen: No one spends any of the money until *all* the smoke has cleared, got it? And let's not go crazy tonight. We've a lot of serious collecting to do tomorrow."

"Let's hope we don't run into any problems with that," Botch added to hisses and boos all around.

Joey V. couldn't help but issue a missing-ear-to-missing-ear grin: "As long as Sweaters is in jail, I'm the one who'll be telling the bookies to pay off. My good friend, Twisted Ray, made sure of that by putting me in charge."

"I'll drink to that!" Mack, Botch and Andre called out together, raising their glasses, downing the libations in one gulp.

Joyce followed suit, then, seeing her husband suddenly turn pale, gasped, "What is it, baby? What's wrong?"

All a dazed Andre could say was, "We're rich…we're rich…"

Mack lifted his empty glass. "A toast to Amazing Jones!" Everyone, except Andre, responded happily, dry-toasting the man who, at the last moment, had made it all happen.

Andre, thinking again about how Amazing had treated his Tina, put his glass down in protest. Mack smiled and continued the toast: "To Amazing Jones, the most selfish asshole to ever wear a Jets uniform. May he never live it down!"

Andre hesitated.

Mack, lifting an eyebrow, toasted again: "To a man who deserves to be K.O.'d in front of the whole, damn, disgusted world!"

This time Andre lifted his glass with the others and laughed, as everyone touched glasses. "Here, here!" he said, and everyone began hugging each other gaily.

It was Joey V. who finally broke the wild celebration. "Wait," he chimed as he ran to the bar to order another round of drinks.

Mack shook his head in the negative. "I said we should take it easy tonight," he said as Joey V. returned with the tray and passed out a fresh round of drinks.

Joey V. stared at Mack with a look of hurt and surprise. "So you're the only one here that can give a toast?" Then turning to Botch and Debbie, he took one of the glasses from the tray and said, "To Botch and Debbie on their engagement."

Mack looked guiltily at Andre, embarrassed they hadn't thought to congratulate Botch and Debbie. In the excitement of the game, neither had thought about all that was transpiring outside of it. Everyone had new lives to look forward to, and in the process, they had also become a unified group again. Lifting his glass, Mack said a simple, "Congratulations," nodding to each couple...then Annie, adding at the last moment, "I guess marriage isn't that bad, really."

Joey V. raised his glass and piped out, "To the marriage of Nick and Shelby!"

Mack repeated the toast, brought his glass to his lips and then sprayed it out in shock, to everyone's laughter. Shelby turned red. Nick took her hand and looked towards his mother. Mack looked at Annie to see if it was a joke, then, his voice returning, Mack wiped his chin and asked gruffly, "Is it true?"

"Yes, it is," Annie replied matter-of-factly. "It happened in Vegas."

Mack downed the rest of his shot smartly.

"Whatever you might be thinking," Shelby explained, "I want you to know that we thought it out and talked it over before deciding."

Nick quickly cut in. "Hey, Dad, you just told Botch marriage isn't so bad a thing. I figured you'd be happy that I'm finding that out for myself."

Mack nodded curtly at Nick, then looked knowingly at Annie, smiled and raised his eyebrows. "It's been a wild day," he said, smiling from one friend to another, and lastly at Joey V.

Joey V. shrugged his shoulders. "Nothing compared to tomorrow, I'll bet."

Number One Bestseller

CHAPTER 47

Early next morning, Mack, heavily hung over, was regretting his idea of having the family meet at the bar for a celebratory breakfast for Nick and Shelby. "How should we work this?" Mack asked Joey V. on his cell phone, Mack's other hand on his aching head as he smiled at Annie. "Call Joe Nator, Joey. Let him know I'll be picking him up about eleven."

"I'll bring Sweaters' payoff money. I don't know yet if Twisted Ray is going to send someone with me, though," replied Joey V. There was a pause. "Actually," Joey V. continued, "it's nothing for you to worry about. Joe knows what he's doing. Like I said, all the bookies love him!"

Mack grunted affirmatively, placing his palm over the cell phone to ask Nick, "What about the bets in Vegas?"

Nick smiled and asked his new wife, "Do you think you could handle an early anniversary trip to collect the bets we made in Vegas?"

"Sure! When?" Shelby replied eagerly.

"In about an hour," Mack offered, looking at his watch. "Take a limo to your apartment and then to the airport. Fly first class." The two lovebirds smiled at each other and left.

Joey V. continued. "Mack, what time does Sweaters go in front of the judge today?"

"Now it's my turn to say, 'don't worry.' The court officers will 'accidently' lose his file. Sweaters won't be out until late afternoon."

"I hope Twisted Ray doesn't suddenly have a change of heart and start giving a shit about Sweaters' money or question where it's going," Joey V. said, his voice revealing an edge of concern.

"If he gives you any problems, let me know right away. And Joey, we should plan on having most of the money back here tonight. After a quick accounting, we can begin moving it." Mack paused. "Maybe I should give Tommy Chang a 'heads up' call?" he added as a postscript.

"Is that the guy you always talked about when we worked for Sweaters?" Joey V. asked cautiously.

"Yeah, the guy that was going to hook me up overseas."

"Right, I remember you always talking about moving to Singapore," Joey V. mentioned cautiously.

"Seoul," Mack corrected. "He was going to put me in charge of one of his businesses there." Mack's voice trailed off: "Things…evolved since then."

Joey V., sensing Mack's resistance to give out any further information about Tommy Chang, ended the conversation with a well-wish, which Mack returned.

"I'm happy things are finally working out for you, Mack," Annie said as Mack signed off.

"Yep, I guess you can say my…*our* ship has finally come in."

Annie tensed and asked, "So what's the rest of your plan? You always have one."

"Retire. Go into partnership with Botch, Andre and Tommy Chang. Oh, yeah, and I almost forgot, your son."

Annie ignored the *your* son. "Partnership? In what?"

"You remember our favorite resort in the Canaries?" Mack asked.

"Of course. I loved it. I miss our trips there and…" Annie suddenly became misty-eyed. "Life's funny."

"How so?" Mack asked, not catching her drift.

"Well, I finally have you talking to me again, and already you're planning to move away."

Mack grinned. "So why don't you come with me?" he asked, reaching for her hands with his.

"I…I really don't think that's a good idea," Annie replied softly.

"Why?" asked Mack thoughtfully. "I don't know what will ultimately happen for us, but is there any reason why we can't try, you know, take it slow and see how it goes?"

Annie thought a moment. "You drank a lot and we were up really late last night. Let's go back to my place and sleep on it awhile. Let's see how you feel about it in, an hour, say."

"Hey, I'm fine," Mack blustered. "But if you insist…"

Annie grinned. "Oh, I do. And when you roll over in bed and look me in the eyes, and ask me again, I'm pretty sure I'll say, 'Yes'," she whispered.

Mack smiled lovingly, like old times. "Even better," he said, feeling his heart begin to fill once again with love for Annie.

CHAPTER 48

The collecting later that morning and early afternoon went without a hitch. Joe Nator tipped the bookies well; they were happy to accept Sweaters' money and then turn around and pay Joe. After the last collection, Joe relaxed a little to reveal, a little too matter-of-factly for Mack's comfort: "I'm done with gambling."

Mack looked carefully at the man in the passenger seat next to him. Joe's face showed the wear and tear of years of stressful living. His sallow face, snow-white temples and the myriad creases in the corners of his eyes and mouth made him look almost mummified. "You should be, Joe. When you think about it, in the long run, the house always wins."

"Yeah, I know that, but I've enjoyed living large. I made a lot of money, Mack, more than you can imagine." He gave Mack a sly grin. "And I spent most of it on wine, women and song. It's the rest that, thinking back, I spent foolishly. Seriously, I'm taking whatever money you give me and heading for Arizona to make a fresh start. I've a daughter there, can you believe it, and grand-kids, too."

Mack's face softened. "Just get out of town before Sweaters comes looking for you. Once he finds out you won all of the money that Joey had you deliver, he's going to try to get it back and make sure you have an unfortunate accident in the process."

On the other side of town, Twisted Ray was too consumed with trying to figure out what to do about Sweaters to worry about what his new lieutenant, Joey V., was doing with Sweaters' booking money. This left Joey V. able to cover the payouts on all the bets without raising any red flags. Sweaters' empire was crumbling, but Sweaters wouldn't be aware of it until it was too late. And Twisted Ray was already plotting to kill Sweaters outright, but that required permission from Sweaters' bosses, Sweaters being a made man. It was enough for the moment to know that Sweaters' losses wouldn't sit well with his makers. No, Twisted Ray thought to himself, he would bide his time before he made his big move, but when the time was right...

Late that afternoon, Sweaters, striding back and forth like a caged animal in his holding cell at the Bronx Criminal Court, resolutely demanded of his lawyer, "What the fuck is going on? Why am I not out? I haven't heard word one from Ray since I've been in here!"

Sweaters' principal lawyer anxiously watched Sweaters pace. "We should have you out of here by late today. Phil's waiting for you outside. The District Attorney is aware that the state doesn't have a strong enough case against us to prosecute effectively," the lawyer responded nervously.

"Against *us*?! Oh, that's a good one! *I'm* the one in the cell, asshole, and as far as getting me out 'later today,' you better, or you and your high-priced flunkies will be out a job!" Sweaters snapped. "They haven't got shit on me! I don't need you to tell me that! These are trumped-up charges! I want you to sue for defamation and damages as soon as I'm out!"

Sweaters' lawyer stiffened. "Yeah, and I'm sure with your colorful background..."

Sweaters slammed a fist on the bare table in front of him. "I'm not paying you to be a wise ass! I'm paying you to get me out of jail! Look around, asshole. Where am I? Don't try and get cute with me!"

The lawyer went pale. "Hey, I have it all worked out. Don't worry. I'll have you out today, guaranteed. They're just having trouble locating your file."

"That figures. Don't give me excuses, make things happen!" Sweaters demanded.

Sweaters' lawyer nodded gravely and signaled for the guard. Exiting the cell, he thought about speaking yet again with the assistant district attorney, one of Sweaters' bought men.

An hour later, a court officer brought Sweaters in front of the judge, where the court clerk blandly read a long list of charges. Sweaters' attorney interrupted, pointing out what were the first of many discrepancies in the complaint, expressing outrage over what he claimed amounted to a personal *vendetta* against his client. The judge looked sourly at the assistant district attorney, who shrugged his shoulders, to indicate that Sweaters' attorney was right.

The judge wrinkled his nose and, calling the two lawyers close, whispered, "There's a case here, but it appears weak, at best." Flipping casually through the list of charges, he turned to the two lawyers and continued. "I see there's a violation charge in this list."

Realizing this was the out they needed, the assistant district attorney turned to Sweaters' lawyer and said quietly before the judge, "If he pleads to the violation, the state will drop the other charges."

After a brief consultation, an angry Sweaters yelled at his lawyer, "So I have to admit to this trumped-up charge and pay a fine to get out?" Looking about the courtroom for sympathy and seeing none, he scowled but reluctantly agreed.

Sweaters and his lawyer were joined, on their way out of the courthouse, by 'Fortunate' Phil Iaccono, one of Sweaters' lesser but currently rising lieutenants. Sweaters, fuming, stopped halfway down the courthouse steps to confront Phil directly. "What the fuck is going on?" Sweaters demanded.

Fortunate Phil, puzzled, frightened, and feeling not so fortunate to have Sweaters confronting him directly in public, asked, "With what, boss?"

Sweaters grabbed the front of Phil's shirt and ranted, "With what? I can't get hold of Twisted Ray or Joey V. or anyone else but you with your dumb questions, that's what!"

Phil felt dismayed at being treated like a nobody in front of the growing mob of reporters hanging on every word they could catch. "There was a lot going on while you were—away—and Ray's had me jumping through hoops."

Sweaters stared at Fortunate Phil with total contempt. "Give me your phone," he commanded menacingly, ripping it from Phil's hands the moment it appeared.

Sweaters released Phil and turned his back on him. "Ray? Where the hell are you?"

"At the club," Twisted Ray answered, holding back the anger welling inside of him at the sleaze who had somehow entangled his daughter into appearing in the nude and taped her having sex in front of a camera.

"Stay there," Sweaters ordered, adding, "and just so you know, I'm out!" Sweaters deliberately ended the call before Ray could respond.

Ray looked at the phone and squeezed it as if it were Sweaters' throat. "Have a heart attack, you fat fuck!"

The last couple of days Ray had been making discrete inquiries, having heard rumors the big bosses were tiring of Sweaters' hijinks, and that they might warm to taking out Sweaters. Twisted Ray paused, a contorted smile on his face, imagining himself in Sweater's place, a made man.

Sweaters bee-lined it to his club, The House of Mirth, entering through the back entrance leading directly into his private office. Opening the door, he bumped into Twisted Ray. Ray jumped and turned, hand inside his jacket on his weapon, to face his old boss once again. "Ah…welcome back, boss," he croaked loosening his grip on the weapon but not offering his hand.

"Welcome back?" screamed Sweaters. "I'm in jail all this time and don't hear a word from you! Now it's, '*Welcome back, boss*'?"

Ray showed Sweaters the brace on his hand and pointed to the still-resolving bruises on his face. "I've been in the hospital."

"And what have you been doing since you got out?" asked Sweaters dismissively.

"I was busy tracking down the guys that ambushed us at the Dominican place. How come you didn't call, boss?"

"I tried," Sweaters said in a calmer voice, symbolically brushing himself off, "but I was only allowed one call a day and the phone there didn't work well."

Fortunate Phil appeared from behind Sweaters. "They were holding you for child porn, boss. Did you think the guards would do anything to help you? You're lucky they let you connect on the phone with your lawyer."

Realizing Phil was right, Sweaters, placated somewhat by being back in his club and having his men around him again, muttered, "Whatever," then addressed Ray. "So what happened to my million?"

"The money's gone, Sweaters. And they killed Joe Buddha. I woke up on top of him the next day in a dumpster."

"Why didn't they kill you?" Sweaters asked coldly, eyeing Twisted Ray with suspicion.

Ray looked from Sweaters to Phil. Moments ago, he had been thinking of how to knock off Sweaters and take his place. Now he wondered anxiously if it showed. "Dumb luck, I guess," he answered, shrugging.

"Well, your 'dumb luck' better get my money back," Sweaters advised.

"They killed Sal and Dom," Twisted Ray said in a whisper, anticipating further rage.

"And what about Joey V.?" Sweaters asked, showing absolutely no concern at all for his nephews.

"I've got him trying to find out who was behind all this."

"And you trust Joey V.?" Sweaters looked astonished and began backing away.

Ray explained quickly. "The guys who attacked us were genuine FBI; we think they were dirty agents, though, acting on their own. I figure Joey V. and I were lucky to get out alive. Two of the agents were caught out on the island with Sal and Dom's rotting bodies stuffed in the trunk of their car. No offense, boss, but we figure Sal and Dom were dealing with them, and once the agents got the money, they didn't need the twins anymore so they took them out. The whole thing was in the papers."

Sweaters shook his head in disbelief. "So let me get this straight: I tell you to watch my money and you lose it. Then I tell you if there's any problem, to kill Joey V., but he's still alive and out doing what you should be doing. For years, I tell you leave Joey V. alone because he's a good earner, and you beg me, 'Let me kill the little prick; I'll gut him like a deer'—those were your exact words! Now when I have suspicions about him and give you the okay to take him out, you give him a God-damned pass? What the hell's going on inside that damaged Sicilian skull of yours?"

Ray felt his blood boil and growled, "Joey V.'s alright, boss. I know it, that's all."

Sweaters looked at Phil, and then behind Twisted Ray at several of Sweaters' men approaching from inside the club, and laughed. "Suddenly Joey V.'s 'alright!' Was I in jail for ten years or something? Or has the world suddenly gone mad?" Sweaters faced off squarely with Twisted Ray. "Okay, fine. You say Joey V. deserves a pass. Alright, you bring him here to answer a few simple questions I have for him, and I'll be the judge. And if I don't like his answers, someone will pay. You 'comfortable' with that, Ray?"

"Ah…no problem, Sweaters," the question on Ray's mind at the moment, however, being whose side the men surrounding him would be on?

Ray cursed under his breath, and watched impotently as Sweaters made some more calls on another minion's commandeered cell phone. All the while Ray searched the eyes of the men standing around. *Who will these men ultimately back when I make my move on Sweaters?* he wondered. None, he knew, were big fans of his—at least, not yet. He had just begun winning them over in Sweaters' absence, but he knew they were tired of Sweaters and his increasingly frequent, ill moods.

As Sweaters signed off, Ray informed him respectfully of Sal and Dom's wake that night at Sisto's Funeral Parlor.

Sweaters glared daggers. "I can't be there! You just told me they helped steal my money! I'm supposed to spend the night with a couple of stiffs who tried to ruin me?"

Twisted Ray seized the opportunity to continue turning Sweaters men. Looking each of the men standing around him in the eyes, and hoping they would get the message about what they could expect from Sweaters if and when their time came, he said boldly, "Those two were family, Sweaters. They were your own flesh and blood, for Christ's sake."

"My going to the wake won't bring back those two morons. And as for being family, they were just two slobs on my payroll as far as I'm concerned. If they'd been more careful, they would still be here."

Phil and the other men looked hard at their boss, disappointment shadowing their faces. *It's working*, thought Twisted Ray.

When Sweaters realized what effect he'd just said was having on his men, he ordered them out to the bar. When the last man left, Sweaters shut the outside door, looked at Ray and snorted, "And where did you get your balls from all of a sudden?"

"Hey, Sweaters," Twisted Ray replied, concerned that Sweaters might call him out prematurely. "Boss," he added judiciously, eyes watching Sweaters' hands to anticipate any attempt, "I'm just saying it wouldn't look good for you to not go to the wake, that's all."

"Well, thanks for your fucking 'help,' I'm now obligated to go. While I'm there, I'll put on the show, but I don't want to have to deal with their families, you understand? You keep them away from me!"

Ray wiped off the mist of sweat that had formed on his brow. "Don't worry, boss. I'll make sure the families won't be a problem." Then Ray added, "But Sal's wife, Astrid, will be there. She was looking to dump Sal, you know."

Sweaters looked confused. "So?"

"She'll need consoling, and, besides, you can't sit there and act like you don't know she's always had a thing for you." *Play to his ego. You've got to play to his ego*, Ray thought to himself.

Sweaters suddenly perked up. "Really? Get out of here."

"No, I'm serious, boss," Twisted Ray said collusively. "She has great legs and the inviting sort of ass you like. She's had the hots for you for years, and now she's a widow. Someone's got to console her."

"What time does this wake start?" asked Sweaters, rubbing his palms.

"People will arrive between five and nine this evening."

"I guess it wouldn't hurt to stop by to pay my respects." Sweaters' silky voice suddenly turned ice-cold: "In the mean time find Joey V."

Ray joined Fortunate Phil and the other men at the bar, mumbling just loud enough for them to hear. "I can't believe that Sweaters."

"What?" asked Phil and several men in unison, curious how the confrontation between the two had proceeded.

Ray shook his head sadly. "I tell the man about Dom and Sal's deaths, and all he wants to do is go to the wake so he can make a play on Sal's wife, Astrid."

Phil looked astounded. "You gotta' be kidding!"

Ray, sensing the effort was working, decided it was time to throw gasoline onto the fire: "Poor Sal, not even in the ground, yet. This kind of shit is just wrong!"

Ray walked past them and sat at a table close by, idly twirling an ash tray while listening carefully to Phil. "So that's what the fucker thinks of us. He wasn't even going to go to the wake, until he realized he might have a shot at a new piece of ass. Something's happened to Sweaters. He isn't the same since he went into jail, you know? And look how bent-out-of-shape he got when Ray tried to explain to him what we'd been doing. Wait till he finds out how much he lost on the Jets game—that, on top of the million he lost in the Dominican raid! The man's gonna explode!" The men standing around Phil nodded their worried assent.

Sweaters suddenly yelled from inside his office, "How much?!" then, "Where's Ray! Get that man's sorry ass in here! Now!"

All eyes turned to Ray, but to everyone's surprise, Twisted Ray just shook his head sadly, got up and walked the other way, out the front door of the club.

"Guess Sweaters just found out," Phil said worriedly. "This might be a good time for us to disappear, too, and give Sweaters a chance to cool off."

As the men made their way towards the door, they heard Sweaters yell from his open office doorway, "Where the fuck are all of you going?!"

Stopping in their tracks, the men looked anxiously back at a livid Sweaters, hands on his hips, a crazed look in his eyes. "Where's Ray!?" Sweaters roared.

Phil looked at the other men. "I think he left to get Joey V. like you ordered, boss."

Sweaters pointed a menacing finger at Phil. "You! Come with me!"

Phil followed Sweaters into the office. Sweaters slammed the door shut. "Phil, who was minding the store while I was in jail?"

Phil, surprised at Sweaters' sudden civility, gladly shared. "Well...I was. At least, at first. I mean, we didn't know what happened to you...or Ray for that matter. Then Ray called me and told me Joey V. would be running things until Ray got out of the hospital. Why?"

"I just got off the phone, and I'm hearing that Joe Nator went for more than just a few mil on the Jets game, and actually put up the money to back it. Now, if I know anything, it's that Joe Nator hasn't won shit in years! The man barely has a pot to piss in! So where did he suddenly come into big money like that?"

Phil cleared his throat. "The...ah...word going round is that he recently inherited a load of cash." Phil was, despite his unease, enjoying Sweaters' anguish.

Sweaters seemed baffled. "So why is Joey V. paying him off with my money on a win like that? Joe Nator should have disappeared in a wood chipper somewhere instead of getting paid!"

Phil took the defensive. "It wasn't by me, Sweaters. Ray was out of the hospital when Joey V. paid up, so Ray must have approved it."

His anger building again, Sweaters yelled, "I'm in the joint less than a week, and when I return, Joe Nator comes into a big inheritance and I'm wiped out? Don't you think that's a little odd? As of this moment, you're my new right hand, Phil. Bring me Joe Nator. I want to find out who fronted him the guarantee money. I'm not going down that easy. Heads are going to roll, and the faster I get my money back, the fewer will have to die."

Number One Bestseller

CHAPTER 49

"Thanks for everything, Joe," Mack said as he surveyed his congenial passenger. "Everything from this last stop is yours. Try not to blow it all in one place."

Joe Nator shook Mack's hand vigorously. "Thanks, Mack. I've learned my lesson. I'm outta' here." Joe started to open the car door to get out, but Mack abruptly stopped him.

"Wait, Joe. Who's that over there?" Mack asked, slipping his gun out.

"My neighbor, Tom," Joe said, patting Mack's arm in effort to reassure him.

Walking briskly towards the car, Tom signaled for Joe to roll down the window. "Hey, Joe," he said. "A couple of guys just broke into your apartment! I looked around and couldn't see that they'd taken anything, but I called the cops." The man stood as if waiting for a response.

Joe Nator's face went pale. "Thanks, Tom. I'll talk to you later."

Joe asked Mack to drop him off around the corner. "They're probably watching for me." Around the corner, Joe looked nervously about before exiting the car.

"Guess Sweaters found out faster than we thought," Mack offered.

"Not fast enough to stop the pay offs," Joe Nator asserted with pride.

Mack nodded his assent. "Well, you can still go to Arizona and not look back. I'll drive you to the airport if you like."

"Just leave, Mack and take care of you and yours. I'm going to walk around and make sure no one's sitting on the place. I've memories there, Mack—pictures of my deceased wife, my daughter and grandchildren—I want to take them with me."

A look of pain welled in Mack's eyes. "That's crazy to my mind, Joe. Listen, if they do happen to catch you, tell Sweaters it was me who took his money."

Joe Nator laughed. "Now who's crazy? I'd rather sandpaper a bear's ass than

251

rub that one in Sweaters' nose."

Earlier across town, Andre was waiting in his car for Joey V. to stop at the last couple of places and act like he was paying out to Joe Nator, so Sweaters wouldn't get suspicious. Finished at last, Joey V. and Andre returned to Farrell's to help Mack sort and count it.

"There's a horse running called 'It's a Lock' and..."

Andre looked at Joey V. with disbelief. "I didn't hear that, Joey. After Sunday's football game, I'm never betting again," Andre confessed as they joined their waiting comrades.

Joey V.'s cell phone chirped. Looking at the caller display, he replied to no one in particular, "Shit! It's Twisted Ray!"

Everyone stopped what they were doing to listen.

"Where are you?" Ray's voice crackled suspiciously.

Joey V., moving his hand as if jerking off, replied, "I'm checking on my car. Why?"

"Sweaters wants me to bring you in."

Joey V. looked from face to face, for some suggestion as to what to say. "Sorry, Ray, you're breaking up. I can barely hear you. Ray? Ray?"

"Bring your fucking ass in! Now!" Ray yelled. Joey V. pulled the phone away from his face. "Okay, okay. Will aspirin do? Hello, Ray?" Joey broke the connection. Looking plaintively at Andre, Joey explained. "I overheard your wife mention you pulling that shit on her. Maybe it'll buy me a little time, but basically, I'm fucked."

Mack lifted the additional duffel bags full of money laying on the floor at his side. "Whatever happens, we've got enough money to get you, Joey—and your family—out of town. Or to the Canaries, with us, if you want." Everyone nodded in agreement. "What we need to know is whether Twisted Ray has the balls to take Sweaters out," Mack ended.

"Maybe its time *we* took Sweaters out," Andre stated.

Joey V. looked from Mack to Andre with appreciation. "Good idea, but it wouldn't work. Remember, he's a made man. Every wannabe gangster would start looking to kill us to make a name for himself. There's no way Ray will get up the balls to try and knock out Sweaters without permission and me prodding him. Either way, I need to get to Ray fast."

"How about telling Ray that Sweaters is planning to take him out?" Mack advanced.

"Hmm. That might just work," Joey V. responded. "I could say Sweaters wants me dead, too, which wouldn't be much of a stretch. Then he and I could bond against a common enemy." Joey V. lowered his voice: "Hey, Mack, that's the first time you mentioned me, my family and the Canary Islands in the same sentence. I must admit, it sounds appealing. Wherever we end up, I don't want to be looking over my shoulder the rest of my life." Joey V. shifted uncomfortably. "Right now, it's time for me to talk to my new best friend, Ray, and then meet with Sweaters."

Mack sighed. "Well, if things get too hot, tell him I'm the one behind it. I'm the one who took his money."

"For God's sake, Mack!" Andre cut in. "Why do that? Won't it just irritate him more?"

"Well, I'm pretty sure he's figured things out by now, so it wouldn't matter and it might make Sweaters think Joey's on his side if you ratted me out."

"What makes you think he's figured it all out so fast?" Andre asked Mack.

"Some thugs broke into Joe Nator's apartment and, in spite of my offer to take him directly to the airport, Joe insisted on going back to collect his family mementos. Just in case they caught up with him, I told him to tell Sweaters it was me. Either way, I figure Sweaters would need to get permission to kill a cop," Mack replied.

Joey V. raised his eyebrows. "The guy's nearly finished, Mack. If Sweaters gets more pissed, I don't think he'll wait to ask permission to take you with him."

Mack shrugged. "It might not have been the smartest move, but I figured, what the fuck: If they're watching Joe Nator's apartment, they probably saw us together anyway.'"

Andre frowned. "Who are you bullshiting, Mack? We all know that you want Sweaters to know it's you, no matter what the consequences, just for the sake of revenge. Jesus, Mack, have you thought about how this is going affect the rest of us?"

"You're right, and I'm sorry," Mack acknowledged. "Maybe it's time for *me* to get out of Dodge," he said. The group fell into awkward silence.

Joey V. stared awhile at the floor. If Mack left, that would leave Joey to deal with Sweaters on his own. Mack, noticing the worry lines on Joey V.'s face, said, "Don't worry, Joey. I'm not going anywhere. If you can't get Ray to move on Sweaters, then I will, no matter who comes after me before or after it's done. When Sweaters figures out it's me behind it all, it's likely he'll stop looking for you or anyone else."

"I just hope that if they catch Joe Nator, he doesn't force our hand by mentioning you," Andre said to Joey V., his tone suggesting it would undoubtedly happen if Joe Nator were caught and threatened.

"Don't worry. Joe Nator's my cousin," Joey V. said flatly, still staring at the floor.

"Jesus Christ! How come you never told anyone Joe Nator is your cousin?"

asked everyone together.

"It's a long story, but the gist is that *no one* knows he is, and he won't say shit. The bookies we dealt with won't say shit, either. I've known them all my life. They hate Sweaters. Even so, Sweaters is no fool; he'll eventually figure it out and exact his revenge."

"And knowing this, you're still willing to meet with Sweaters?" Andre asked incredulously.

Joey V. frowned, "If I duck him, I'm dead. I'm just going to have to get into Ray's head first and push Ray to make his move."

"It's suicide," Andre proffered. "There's got to be a better way. Think, everyone!"

"Maybe it'll be suicide, maybe not," Joey V. said with finality. "But no matter who Sweaters blames, I'm already in the thick of it." Joey V. looked from conspirator to conspirator with a cheerless smile. "Do any of you honestly have a better plan?"

CHAPTER 50

The front door of Farrell's Bar flew open, and Botch strode confidently into the room, asking happily as he stared at the large duffel bags scattered over the floor, "So have we got all of it?"

Andre was the first to answer. "Yeah, we've got it all. We were just waiting for you to come over here and help us count it!"

"I'm more than happy to help, especially now that there's enough to retire to the Canaries." He looked, puzzled, from one morose face to another. "So who just died?" Botch noticed a particularly despondent Joey V. "What's with you?"

"Sweaters wants to meet him and most likely knows by now that Joey and I are behind everything," Mack stated flatly.

"How could he know for sure about either of you?"

"Let's just say I didn't try to keep it from him," Mack countered evasively. Botch growled. "Mack, you thick-headed donkey! We've taken all these precautions to preserve our anonymity, and you walk up and spit in Sweaters' face? That's what you did, didn't you? I *knew* you were going to find a way to let him know it was you, but for God's sake, couldn't you have at least waited until our families were safe?"

Mack nodded contritely. "You're right. *All* of you are right. I fucked up. I should have waited, but I couldn't..."

"Damn right you fucked up! I would have never signed on knowing..." Everyone sighed, thoroughly fed up with Botch's volatile negativity. "Now we're going to have to kill the prick. We're going to commit out-and-out murder! This ain't 'Nam, Mack! What about those two girls who got killed on the roof? What about..."

Andre interrupted. "We all feel bad, but none of us knew it was going to play out like that."

"They were innocent girls!" Botch interjected, shaking with pent-up frustration. Mack placed a hand on Botch's quivering shoulders while Botch continued. "Hey, I want to see Sweaters get his as much as the next guy," Botch said, trying to shake off Mack's hand, "but I didn't want any of us having to pull the trigger."

Mack's shoulders and voice dropped. "I feel bad about those girls, but then, like now, we have to play the cards we're dealt. I still sweat them…as well as the people I killed in 'Nam. I have nightmares about them, but I'm sorry, I don't sweat over getting revenge on Sweaters. I'll gladly pull the trigger if that's what it takes. It's something I've dreamed of for years. I have the opportunity now to bring it all to an end. You're right that I should have waited until we were *all* safely set up in the Canaries, but…"

Mack's cell phone rang. He opened the lid and showed the call identification screen to everyone. It was Nick.

"Nick? Did anyone give you a hard time collecting?"

"Not at all. We're being treated like royalty."

"Your mother and Joyce went to Atlantic City to collect on some bets Babe made for us through there, and they're getting the same treatment. Stay in Vegas a couple more days and enjoy yourselves," Mack offered.

"I've wired the money to the island account number you gave us. See you in a few days!"

Nick disconnected.

"How are the newlyweds doing?" Botch asked, not wanting to return to their earlier discussion.

"You know, I was going to ask him, but I suddenly couldn't remember her name," an irritated Mack shot back.

Andre, Botch and Joey V. shouted together: "Shelby!"

"Right," Mack acknowledged. "I guess I still can't believe they are actually married."

Andre laughed. "Hey, maybe you'll be a grandfather in nine months."

Mack's face changed. It looked harsher around the edges yet somehow softer, almost dreamy. "Real…fucking…funny."

Joey V. rolled his eyes. "Tell me more about this place in the Canaries."

CHAPTER 51

Andre's face lit up as he revisited the resort in his head: "The place is on La Palma Island. It's called Marisol's, which I think means 'sea and sun' in Spanish.

Botch grinned, "*Maravilloso*! So, you *do* know Spanish?!"

Andre scowled, waving Botch's comment aside. "The place isn't like the Plaza or anywhere else you can imagine. It's an unspoiled, white-sands beach resort with pool and restaurant, and it's located just outside of town: total comfort, but untouched by commercial developers. It still has its ethnic charm."

Botch added, "What I like best about it is that you can relax on the beach during the day, then party at the Tiki bar during the night."

"How big is the resort?" Joey V. asked, his nearly earless face acquiring a misty, faraway look.

"The pictures!" Mack said, and walked into the bar's kitchen to retrieve them.

Andre, in the meantime, continued, "Select rich folk go there from all over the world to relax. The island is up and coming. We want Marisol's to be *the* place to be."

Mack returned with a manila envelope and poured a number of pictures onto the table. "Check these out," he said, offering Joey V. one. "That's the front. It's the first and last thing visitors see."

Joey's face lit up. "Wow, this *is* nice. I was imagining straw huts or something. This is a tropical island paradise!" Mack handed him another picture. "This is the check-in lobby."

Joey V. looked longingly at the island decor. "Guys! This isn't any 'no tell' motel. It's incredible!"

Mack pointed at the rest of the pictures. "Go through them and see for yourself. There's the pool. There's the beach, and there are some pictures of the nearest village."

Joey V. said excitedly, "The pool. Does it have one of those swim-up bars?"

Mack and Andre looked at each other and smiled. "If it didn't, we wouldn't have gone there in the first place." Mack rifled through the photos and located one showing one of several swim-up bars with Botch, Mack, Annie, Andre and Joyce toasting at it. Botch pulled the picture from Joey V.'s hand. "This one's my favorite bar!"

"The place is actually huge! Do they ever fill up at the resort?" Joey V. asked.

"Weekdays are quiet and slow, but weekends, it jumps."

"How many times have you been there?" Joey V. asked, looking from one smiling face to another.

"Awhile back," Mack said, with Annie in his eyes, "we went almost every year, usually for a month at a time. Once you're there, you'll hate to leave."

Joey V. pointed to another picture. "Who's that guy? I've seen him in a couple of these pictures. He always seems to be lurking in the background."

Mack laughed, "That's my friend, Tommy Chang. He hates cameras. He's the one that turned us on to the place. He's the one who's putting up the other half to buy it."

A cloud passed over Joey V.'s countenance. "How did you hook up with him, again, Mack?"

"One day in 'Nam, we got us a couple of weeks R & R in Australia. We ran out of weed at the airstrip waiting for the plane, so I went to pick up some more. I got back just in time to watch the plane and all my friends here taking off down the runway. There wasn't anything I could do, so I asked the duty guard where the two other planes warming up on the tarmac were going. I was told one was headed for Hawaii, the other for Seoul. I'd been to Hawaii a number of times, so I figured I should see what's going on in Korea and hopped on the plane.

"Anyway, there I was, all by myself in Seoul, Korea, and let me tell you, it was great. You could still go there today and see hordes of seventeen-year-old girls, listening to the same rock and roll music we listened to in the sixties and seventies. Well, anyway, I met this beautiful Korean girl, moved in with her, and eventually ended up AWOL—you know, absent without leave. Her brother was Tommy Chang.

"Tommy was a few years older than me and an up and coming big-shot international businessman. His sister said that they had been separated from their family, as well as each other, very young, and that after Tommy made his fortune, he came back for her. She doted on him and, well, he liked me, and so she and I did whatever we wanted.

"Tommy was never afraid to spend money. He took us all over the place, and the three of us became...close. He promised me a job after the war, but he wanted me to finish my service time in 'Nam. 'No skeletons in the closet, Mack,' he used to say. So eventually I went back.

"I expected to have the book thrown at me, but all my paperwork was mysteriously lost, and I slipped back in through the cracks without the Army even knowing I had been gone."

"What happened to the girl? You never told us about her before," Botch said.

Mack's face darkened. "Well, Tommy Chang had planned on setting her up while I finished my time with the Army, but, oddly, just before I left, she began begging me not to leave her. She kept saying, 'Don't go back there. You'll get killed.' Even so, at Tommy's urging, I left.

"In her first few letters, she sounded frantic, but that all changed when she discovered she was pregnant. She was happy again, and couldn't wait for me to return. A few months later, Tommy Chang wrote saying she wasn't doing well. Female cancer, he said. She was still early in her pregnancy, so I went AWOL again and stayed with her to the bitter end."

All three men looked blankly at the floor.

"I married her just before she—and the baby—died. She wanted to be married. That was the last time I saw Su Lee."

"And you've stayed in touch with her brother all these years?" Joey V. said, breaking the long, awkward silence that followed.

"Yeah," said Mack distantly. "Tommy Chang and I remained close. He's a great guy. I mean, he could buy Marisol's on his own. He doesn't really need us."

Joey V. frowned. "Then why doesn't he buy it himself? Why have to deal with partners?"

"His reasoning is something like this: What's the point in having money, if you haven't anyone to enjoy it with? He's older now and wants to get out of the rat race, but the only time he really enjoys himself, he says, is when he's on vacation with us."

Andre suddenly laughed. "Yeah, and boy, do we have a good time!"

"The partner thing was so we wouldn't feel like we were living off him," Mack ended.

"Now we can all be equals," Botch added. "Over the years, we talked about how to make it happen, you know, ways to finance the deal. We also talked about the changes we would make to the place if it was ours. He liked all our ideas."

"This deal was between him and you guys, so do you think your friend will have a problem with another partner?" Joey V. asked Mack.

Mack paused decisively, acting like he had to think hard about it. "Actually," he smiled, "I already talked with the group and with Tommy about you and Rose. We all agreed your cut, should you two decide to join us, would give us just the cash cushion we need to implement our ideas for the place. So, Joey, you and Rose want in?"

"I have one requirement, Mack."

Botch frowned; the other two sobered and backed off slightly. "What's that?" they asked in unison.

Joey V. grabbed a picture and pointed. "See that barstool in the corner? I want that to be my spot. I want to take book there until I'm a hundred and twenty."

The four stared at each other, as if sizing each other up, then Mack laughed, "I think we can make that happen, but you might be in your eighties before the resort develops enough to see any big action."

Joey V. asked, "Does it have satellite TV for the ponies?"

"If it doesn't, you can surely afford to buy it," Mack offered, the others nodding in agreement. Mack walked over to the bar, reached behind it and dug around, pulling out a bottle of 80-year-old, single-malt whiskey. Brushing the dust from it, he opened it lovingly and poured out a shot for each of them. "Drinking the same reserve as Sweaters these days?" Joey V. asked as he swirled the amber liquid in his glass and clinked it against the other's.

"This *is* Sweaters'," Mack said, savoring the warming libation as it slipped down his eager throat. "I figured Sweaters wouldn't have anything to celebrate anymore," and then laughed heartily.

"What's your buddy's name again?" Joey V. asked, shot glass to his lips.

"Tommy Chang," answered Mack.

"Did he say anything about me joining?" Joey V. asked, drawing a deep breath of the rare liquor.

Botch answered for the group. "Don't worry. We lied about you."

Joey V. searched Botch's eyes for a moment, then snorted and smiled. "Good idea," he chuckled, downing his drink and adding his empty glass to the three on the table.

Satisfied with their new arrangement, the four proceeded to counting and stacking the money while talking about the resort and changes they could imagine to the resort to make it even more desirable. Suddenly Mack paused, pumped up his chest and said, "Aw, fuck it! There's way more than enough here for our half. I'm calling Tommy now to let him know to draw up a contract. We're so close to the dream, I can taste it."

Mack checked his watch, calculated the time in California, and flipped open his cell phone, switching it onto speaker phone when Tommy answered.

Tommy Chang, in a thick, Korean accent, said, "Yaw bo seh yo. Hey, that you, Mack?"

"Yeah, Tommy, it's me. Listen. I don't want to take up your time, but I wanted you to know that we're all a 'go' here." Mack paused for Tommy's reply.

"Great, Mack. Time to quit that dangerous work of yours. I surprised bullet not found you yet, considering number of times bullets find you as soldier."

"God knows, many have tried, but none stuck. Now I'm ready to retire while I'm still in one piece. I'll be putting in my papers as soon as..."

"Great news, Mack," Tommy cut in. "but prease, my friend, be careful. Many people, as they prepare for retirement, end up dying last minute on job. Better do quick as possible."

"Okay," Mack piped in cheerfully. "I'll begin the process as soon as I hang up. Marisol's is still for sale, isn't it?"

"Spoke with owner just today. We still only ones in line."

"Is that good, or bad?" Mack half-joked.

"*Vely,* vely good, Mack. This way, I negotiate from position of power," said a suddenly serious Tommy Chang, all business-like.

Mack added hastily, "What I meant was, I wondered if nobody wants it for some reason we don't know about."

"Mack, Mack, Mack," Tommy Chang's voice chimed, "After all these years, you still do not know how many deals I make for much more money than this?"

"I know you know what you're doing, Tommy," replied Mack, "It's just that this is my lifelong dream—and not just mine, but that of my friends and our families, too."

"Andre and Botch in agleement?"

"Yes, plus Nick, my son, and my old friend I told you about, Joey V."

"It will be nice to have some 'young blood,' as they say. What about other guy, Joey V.?"

Mack, holding the phone in one hand, stretched out the other, palm down, rocking his outstretched fingers. "Tommy, Tommy, Tommy. After all these years..."

Tommy Chang laughed heartily. "Will have papers drawn up today!"

"Great. Will you be swinging by New York anytime soon?"

"Already, plan to swing by this week. In L.A. right now. Have new construction here, but Amelican contractors sit on asses all day do nothing. I schedule meeting with them and unions for later this week. Hey, know what? I fly in this Fliday or Saturday, soon as talks over! We can sign papers, cerebrate, and, how you say, 'shoot the broads'?"

"'Breeze,' Tommy," Mack said, laughing. "It's 'breeze' not 'broads'." Mack suddenly stared ahead in the distance. "Speaking of bullets finding me...I've got some business to finish with Jerry Sweaters before you arrive."

The voice on the other end stopped abruptly, then returned after a long pause. "Jelly...'Sweaters'?"

"It's nothing, Tommy, I was just thinking out loud," Mack replied.

"Okay. I call you when finished with contractors and unions."

"Sounds good," Mack replied. "Talk to you then. Bye!"

Mack hung up and looked at the other three. "You heard it with your own ears. We sign papers Friday or Saturday."

Andre smiled, "Assuming we successfully conclude that old business you spoke of."

Joey V.'s phone chimed. It was Twisted Ray—again. "Well, I hope I live long enough for me and Rose to meet Tommy Chang and sign the papers," Joey V. said as he walked behind the bar, alone, to take the call.

CHAPTER 52

"Where the hell are you?" Twisted Ray yelled into his cell phone.

On the other end, standing behind the bar at Farrell's, Joey V. responded cautiously. "I'm stuck in traffic on the Hutch—must be an accident or something."

"Listen, Joey: Sweaters is pissed at *both* of us," Ray offered, accepting Joey's explanation."I spoke up for you, and I think he's going to give you a pass this time. It's important you and I talk first, though. Meet me at Cecil's Bar."

"Alright," said Joey V. "I'll be there quick as I can."

Joey V. hung up and walked toward the front door, saying wistfully over his shoulder to his compatriots, "Wish me luck! I'm off to meet my good buddy, Ray."

The other three men stopped counting the stacks of money. "Do you want one of us to follow you?" Mack asked.

"Nah, my new best-buddy just wants 'to talk' before we meet Sweaters. I'm guessing he may actually be getting up the balls to make his move and he's wanting to make sure he has my support as well as that of Sweaters' men. That's what I'm hoping, anyway."

Botch walked up to Joey V. and placed his hands on Joey's shoulders. "Even so, it's suicide unless he gets Sweaters' bosses' permission. You said so, yourself."

Joey V. shrugged. "Yeah, well, since he didn't kill Sweaters right away, I figure that's what Ray's waiting for. It would most likely have to come from Sweaters' uncle."

Andre frowned. "Who's his uncle?"

"Gus," Joey V. answered.

"Just 'Gus?' Not 'Gus-with-The-Mole-on-His-Balls' or 'Gus-Slickstick' or some other nickname? Jeeze, this guy must really be top-level."

Joey V. frowned at Andre. "His name's just Gus, and he thinks of himself as a beneficent 'godfather,' you prejudiced prick. From what I hear, Sweaters' uncle is so embarrassed by his nephew's mess, I think it likely he'll let Ray whack him."

"Let's hope so," Andre muttered, returning reluctantly to his counting.

Botch signaled for Joey V. to walk outside with him.

Alone together in the parking lot, Joey V. ventured, "What's up?"

"Put this on," Botch said, pulling a roll of white bandage and a small button microphone out of his pocket. "I meant to somehow attach this onto Amazing, after we beat him up. Since he and Andre's daughter aren't a couple anymore, I'm guessing we won't have to beat him up and bandage him afterwards."

Botch wound the bandage around Joey V.'s head and tucked the microphone inside. "Now you're not alone. I'll be following you. If you need anything, just hint one way or another and I'll do everything I can to help." Botch stepped back to admire his work and pulled out a portable receiver to make certain the microphone worked.

"Damn," said Joey V., smiling at his new friend, Botch. "I was just getting myself used to crying alone."

CHAPTER 53

Thirty minutes later Joey V. pulled into the lot at Cecil's Bar, a scaled-down caricature of Sweaters' swank House of Mirth, to meet with Twisted Ray. Joey V. sat alone in his car, going once more over the approach he planned to take with Twisted Ray.

Cecil's looked dead—an ominous sign. After assuring himself that no one was watching, Joey V. walked up to the unlocked, flaking, black door and into the dark room beyond. The bar was empty save for a tall bartender.

Joey V. sat down, face to the door and waited.

A moment later, Twisted Ray appeared behind him from out of nowhere. "Hello, Joey," he said with calm impertinence.

Joey V. steeled himself. "So, Ray, what's up?"

Twisted Ray lifted a hand and two fingers to the bartender, who immediately placed a drink in front of each. Sitting on the next stool, Ray ventured, "Let's just say you better not wipe your ass without first making sure one of Sweaters' goons isn't watching. As for me, I'm on the outs for not killing you. I stuck my neck out for you, Joey, to buy us both some time." It was the "us" that gave Joey V. his first hint that the approach he had planned might work.

"Word on the street is that your time is running out, Ray."

"Me?" Twisted Ray exclaimed, setting his drink on the bar top. "He wouldn't, that son-of-a..."

Joey V. decided to push a little harder: "I heard if Sweaters doesn't get *all* his money back by the end of the week, we're dead meat, you and me both."

Twisted Ray frowned. "No shit? Well, hopefully that'll be just enough time to talk his uncle into letting me take him out."

Joey V. forced an agreeable smile. "Takes some balls calling the uncle and asking permission to kill his nephew."

"Well, I haven't been able to arrange a private sit down with Gus, so I've got a couple of people with juice trying to feel him out before they ask his permission on my behalf. Of course, then I'll owe them…fucking politics! I'm hoping to get the okay late tonight—you know, right after Sal and Dom's wake."

Joey V. raised his eyebrows. "Is Sweaters actually going to show there?"

"Yeah, I told him Sal's wife had the hots for him. Everyone knows that's the only reason he's coming. I'm trying to use that to work his men to my side."

Joey V.'s confidence was quickly growing. "Don't worry, Ray. They'll listen to me when you make your move."

"That's why you're second in charge," Ray said, eyeing Joey V. obliquely, trying to gauge Joey V.'s reaction.

Joey V., all business, replied, "We still need to get Sweaters out of the way. Wait! I have an idea: At the wake, I'll need you to somehow let on to Sweaters that Astrid is a little hard of hearing. Can you do that, Ray?"

"Why?" Twisted Ray asked, surprised, suddenly all ears.

"So he'll get his face really close to her. It'll look like he's making a move on her. We can use it to play up to everyone what a real weasel he is."

Twisted Ray paused in thought. "I like the way you think. Okay, I'll do it. Let's go to the wake."

The parking lot of Sisto's Funeral Parlor was packed by the time Joey V. and Twisted Ray arrived. At the door, they were greeted by an evil-grinning, black-suited, Fortunate Phil. "So you found him?" Phil asked, his voice dripping venom as if he couldn't wait to see Joey V. get his.

"I was never missing," Joey V. said, staring Phil in the eyes and challenging him to act.

"Where's Sweaters, Phil?" Twisted Ray interjected. "He wanted to see Joey V."

Phil leered malevolently. "He just got here. He's in the head, preparing himself to give you two a nice, warm reception."

Joey V. situated himself chest-to-chest with Phil and asked indifferently, "So what are you so happy about, Phil? Word is that Sweaters isn't very happy with your screwing things up while he was in the can." Seeing Phil's face morph from smugness to fear, Joey V. continued to press. "I don't know what Sweaters has been telling you, but the man's been polling everyone about whether you might have been working with Sal, Dom and the three crazy agents."

Phil paled. "Me?! I never met those agents."

Catching Joey's drift, Ray shrugged his shoulders. "Joey V. here's just telling it like it is, Phil. You know how once something gets in Sweaters' head there's no changing it."

Phil's shoulders slumped and his chest caved. "Yeah, well…"

"You got to admit," Joey V. added, "you, Sal and Dom were close."

"That's bullshit!"

Joey V. retreated, patting Phil on the back. "Hey, I'm just suggesting you watch your ass. When Ray was in the hospital and you were in charge, that's when the shit hit the fan. I mean, it just doesn't look good."

Phil looked at Ray. "*You* told me to step aside."

Ray shrugged his shoulders again. "Yeah, well, that isn't how Sweaters sees it. I told him different, but like I said, you know Sweaters. Who else is here?"

Phil looked around stealthily. "Everyone, Ray. You name 'em."

"I mean of our men?" asked Ray, stressing the "our."

"Pretty much everyone except Mark and Vinny who are keeping an eye on things at the club."

There was a commotion in front of the men's room, to the side of the coat room. "Here comes Mr. Wonderful now," Joey V. offered sarcastically.

Sweaters, noticing Phil with Ray and Joey V., pushed everyone aside and strode directly up to the three. "Well, if it isn't Joey V., back from the dead. Where the fuck have you been hiding?"

"Hiding?" Joey asked, looking quizzically from Sweaters to Ray. "Ray here told me you wanted to see me, and here I am."

Sweaters eyes narrowed. "Where's my money, you little rat?" he asked, pushing Joey V. into the coat room.

Joey V. maintained a look of surprise as he regained his footing and smoothed his rumpled shirt. "That's what I was checking out when Ray called and said you wanted to see me."

"Okay, Joey. So tell me: What *did* you find out?" Sweaters asked venomously.

Ray interrupted: "Come on, Sweaters, this isn't the place to talk business," and nodded towards the crowd in the wake room shifting its attention from the two caskets towards the coat room.

Sweaters looked at the crowd darkly, then at Joey V. "Alright, Ray, but don't let this scumbag go anywhere."

"I'm not going anywhere," Joey V. piped out as if irritated by the whole discussion. Joey V. walked confidently past Sweaters into the wake room, and sat down respectfully.

Ray immediately snapped, "Phil! Follow Joey V. and don't let him out of your sight. I need to talk to Sweaters a minute."

As soon as Phil had joined Joey V., Ray turned to Sweaters. "I just wanted you to know, boss, that Astrid has a hearing problem, so you'll have to get close if you want to talk to her. Otherwise, you'll have to shout and everyone will end up hearing what you're saying."

Sweaters grinned, pleased with Ray's concern. "With those sweet melons, I can't help but get very close," he said.

Ray winked and followed Joey V. and Phil to pay his respects to the deceased twins, Sweaters following at his side. Sweaters grasped Ray's arm in the process and whispered, "I don't know who that is next to Astrid, but I need him out of that chair when I'm done paying my respects, got me?"

"No problem," said Ray smoothly. "I'll have Phil handle it immediately."

Twisted Ray split off, as Sweaters walked up to Dom's casket, made the sign of the cross, knelt, and acted as if he was praying. Ray, in the meantime, walked over to Phil and whispered, "Sweaters wants the guy sitting next to Astrid out of that chair," adding with disgust, "I tried to stop him, but the prick plans to make his move on the widow, right here, right now, right in front of everyone—can you believe it?"

"You can't be fucking serious," Phil whispered back to Ray.

Ray continued, "The guy's utterly heartless. He gets off on this sort of thing."

Phil looked over at the man sitting next to Astrid. "Jesus, Ray, that's Astrid's brother." Phil turned towards the first of the ring of Sweaters' men standing stiffly around the perimeter of the room, and signaled for him to get rid of Astrid's brother. Each of Sweaters' men inclined his eyes towards Sweaters, kneeling and sham-praying before Dom's casket, and shook his head in resolute disgust.

When the man he'd signaled didn't move, Phil realized that in order to avoid a scene, he was going to have to do it himself. He walked casually over to Astrid's brother just as Sweaters was getting up to pray over Sal's casket. "Excuse me," Phil said politely to the grieving man at Astrid's side. "Could I talk to you for a moment in the next room?"

Astrid's brother looked Phil up and down indignantly and waved the man off, whispering, "We can talk later. I need to be here for my sister," as he continued stroking his sister's back with the other hand, while she continued quietly sobbing.

Phil leaned closer, and showed him the butt of the gun inside his jacket. "I'm not fucking asking, I'm telling."

Astrid's brother stared at the gun with shock, but refused to budge.

CHAPTER 54

After looking discretely to make sure no one was noticing or overhearing him, Phil pointed to the door and hissed, "Get up! Now! And calmly follow me out that door or, I swear, you'll end up a cripple the rest of your life."

Astrid's brother blanched. He turned to his sister, excused himself politely, and quietly followed Phil into a small, private mourning room off to the side of the main room. Sweaters, noticing, got up from Sal's coffin, walked over to the empty chair next to Astrid, hugged her closely, and put his lips to her ear. "Whoever did this is going to pay," he promised.

Joey V. turned abruptly towards several of Sweaters' men, who were watching their boss with equal mixtures of awe and disgust. "Did you see that? He stuck his tongue in her ear!"

First one then another of Sweaters' men awkwardly shifted his gaze away from the lewd scene unfolding before their eyes, grumbling about how Sweaters had reached an all-time low.

Joey V. smiled, scanned the audience and noticed Sweaters' uncle, Gus, sitting in a back row, surrounded by bodyguards. Walking towards the lobby as if to have a cigarette, Joey V. caught the old man's eye, hoping the distinguished-looking don would remember him. Gus did.

A moment later in the lobby, Gus greeted him. "Hey, Joey," he said somberly, flicking a finger at Joey's turban as if in token acknowledgement of both their recent losses.

"Gus, how are you?" Joey V. said, shamming surprise.

"Tough times, these," the man offered, nodding sadly towards the two coffins at the front of the room. Smiling emotionlessly, he continued, "But at my age doing bad is still doing something. How about yourself, Joey? You recovering okay?"

"Oh, this?" Joey V. said, pointing a finger at his head bandage. "Guess I should be glad to be alive. I mean, what can I do about it, cry?"

"You still like driving the old cars?" the man asked, while giving the guard standing next to him permission to leave.

"Yeah, I'll always love the old classics. The fifties and sixties were good times," Joey V. returned.

Gus put a hand on Joey V.'s shoulder, "You know, you're just the guy I've been wanting to talk to. I'm looking for a Caddy. White. Convertible. Sixty-five to sixty-eight. You know, to cruise and be seen in when I'm down in Florida. What do you think?"

"They're a classic ride no matter which year you choose. Say, you know who could hook you up? Ray. He's got connections. I'd ask him now, but he's pretty upset. He was very close to Sal and Dom and their deaths hit him hard, but I'll tell him what you're looking for at the first opportunity." Pausing, Joey V. tried to look pensive, then added quickly, "You know, maybe it would be better if you called him yourself. I know he has a line on a white sixty-six—the classic of classics."

Gus shrugged his shoulders affably, "Hmmm. I'm not going back for a week or so..."

"In that case," Joey V. offered, "You could have it checked out before it's shipped."

Gus nodded in the affirmative. "Alright. You tell him and I'll call him later. Sorry, but I got to head out. Party to attend," Gus said winking. "By the way, have you seen my nephew recently?"

"He's over there next to Astrid," Joey V. said, making certain that Gus followed his outstretched finger.

Gus could see Sweaters and Astrid shoulder-to-shoulder, Sweaters' face buried in her hair next to her neck. Gus frowned in disgust, collected his bodyguards and walked out, rethinking for the hundredth time the organizational structure with his nephew, Sweaters, out.

Seeing his plan working, Joey V. signaled discretely across the room at Ray, who immediately got up and walked over to greet Gus as the don and his contingency entered the foyer to put on their coats and hats.

Gus stopped and extended a hand. "Ray. Sorry about the loss. I want you to know how much I appreciate your concern for the family," he asserted, placing his other palm sympathetically over their interlocked hands. "Listen, I'll call you soon about taking care of something for me."

Twisted Ray stopped shaking hands. "Whatever you need, Gus. You can always count on me," he said, heart pounding.

"I know," Gus said warmly as he released Ray's hand and turned to leave.

After watching the benevolent-looking aristocrat leave, Ray immediately sought out Joey V.

"I saw my life pass before me," Twisted Ray said to Joey V. "I thought Gus was going to say I'm a dead man for even hinting at asking his permission to kill his nephew. Instead, he said he wanted me to take care of something for him. I think that was the green light, Joey, and, thanks to you, the guys are really pissed at Sweaters and ready for a new boss."

Phil walked over to the two conspirators and asked permission to interrupt. When Twisted Ray acknowledged, Fortunate Phil chose his words with care. "Ray. Listen. Me and the boys can't take this anymore. Sweaters is practically sucking on Astrid's neck in front of her dead husband," he said. "Sweaters just ordered me to go find Joe Nator."

Phil left with two of Sweaters' tougher-looking henchmen. After rechecking the Berretta hidden in the small of his back, Joey V., tried his desperate best to think of a way to get away from Ray long enough to make certain Botch had overheard Phil's comment about going after Joe Nator.

Looking over Ray's shoulder at where Sweaters was sitting, Joey V. pretended to notice Sweaters signaling. Looking puzzled and pointing a finger at Ray, he mouthed, "Who? Ray?" directly in front of Ray. As Twisted Ray looked over his shoulder towards Sweaters, Joey V. told him that Sweaters had signaled he wanted to talk to Ray. Ray snorted derisively, then began swaggering towards Sweaters, mumbling to himself, "What in hell does the prick want now?"

Pressed for time, Joey V. rushed outside the Funeral Home and started talking into the air like a homeless person. "Botch! You listening? Botch? Warn Joe Nator to hide. Jesus, I hope you're getting this!" He repeated himself, then turned to go back into the funeral home, and froze. Twisted Ray was standing just behind him with a suspicious look on his face.

"Who you talking to?" he asked, looking from side-to-side and seeing no one.

"I…I don't like praying in front of others, so I said a prayer for Sal and Dom out here," Joey V. said, thinking fast.

"Well, thanks for telling me Sweaters wanted me," Ray said, clearly pissed.

"Why? Did he change his mind again in mid-stream? The guy's becoming a nut case," Joey V. said nervously.

"No, but he tried ripping me a new ass for interrupting him with Astrid. You know, you're right, Joey. The guy's getting looser and looser in the head. Damn! If we don't do something about him soon there's no telling what he'll do next!"

Number One Bestseller

CHAPTER 55

The look on Twisted Ray's face told Joey V. that his plan was still working. Then Joey V.'s cell phone chirruped. "Aren't you going to answer it?" Twisted Ray asked after the fifth ring.

Joey V. reached in his pocket and pulled out the phone with trepidation. The caller number confirmed his worst fears: It was Botch.

Joey V. flipped open the phone and stared at Twisted Ray, hoping for some distance, but Ray showed no inclination of affording him any privacy. On the other end, Botch was saying, "I heard you. We're trying to track him down. Any idea where he'd likely be?"

On his end, Joey V. replied loudly, "Phil? Is that you? You're breaking up!" After a short pause Joey V. flipped the phone shut.

"What's up?" asked an overly-anxious Twisted Ray.

"Couldn't understand him," Joey said curtly, trying to think of how to divert Ray's attention elsewhere.

Ray looked back towards the wake. "I told Sweaters we'd meet him at the club later. Let's get out of here and grab another drink together."

"Sounds good to me," Joey V. said, relieved that the subject had changed, but not liking the new direction in which things were going. "But not Sweaters' club, alright?"

"Right," Ray replied. "We need to be careful not to draw any suspicion until it's over and I'm in charge. Let's go somewhere we can talk freely, and then head on over to the club at the last minute."

Botch, Mack and Andre watched from a distance as Joey V. handed over responsibility to another of Sweaters' lieutenants, and then he and Ray drove off together. "Shouldn't we follow them?" Botch asked, holding the suddenly silenced phone in his hand.

"Joey didn't look anxious. I say we drop in at Sweaters' place in about an hour.

Right now, we need to make certain Joe Nator is out of harm's way. What do you think?" Mack asked.

Andre stared as Joey V.'s car disappeared into the distance. "I don't know, Mack. Aside from Joe's apartment, which was empty, do you know where else Joe might hang out while waiting to 'relocate'?"

"I know a couple places, and knowing Joe, his new-found wealth will direct him to one that's running ponies." Mack started the car. "Let's try a couple of his favorite betting haunts and see if they know if he's left town yet, then we can meet up with Joey V. at Sweaters' club."

"Do you think Joey's safe alone with Ray?"

Andre, surprised at Botch's change in attitude, offered, "Like he said, Ray's his new 'best friend'."

Botch winced and fell silent.

Phil, in the meantime, was finding that locating Joe Nator was likely going to prove an all-night endeavor. He and his men were having no luck whatsoever. Their last remaining lead was a bar called Rudy's IN, where Joe was said to sometimes hang out and lick his wounds or, more rarely, tout a gambling victory.

To Phil's surprise, Joe Nator and another man were sitting in a corner of Rudy's bar, faces directed towards a small TV monitor mounted above the bar. On the screen, a group of horses were racing, neck-to-neck. Phil signaled for his men to sit at a table just inside the door and keep low.

Joe turned to the bartender and ordered another round of drinks for everyone, meaning himself and the man next to him. The bartender refilled the two men's glasses and waved away the repeat offer for himself, instead pouring drinks and sliding them down the bar towards the three men who'd just walked in. Joe suddenly yelled drunkenly, "Come on, Mister B! Come on!" and when his horse finished sixth, "Ah, shit!"

Joe Nator turned to the man sitting on the barstool next to him and asked in a slurred voice, "Who've we got in th' eighth?"

The man started to answer, but Phil, who had been silently gliding across the floor, interrupted. "Hey, Joe. You need to come with me. Sweaters wants a word with you."

Joe Nator's thoroughly inebriated friend turned and, wobbling noticeably, faced Phil. "Excuse *me!* I wasn't done talking to this gentleman here…"

Phil, in one motion, had the guy by the hair with one hand, while shoving the barrel of a gun into the man's mouth with the other. "Aw, gee. Where are my manners? I'm sorry, I thought your conversation was over. By all means, go ahead and finish whatever you were saying, please."

The man gagged.

"Oh, so you're finished?" Phil snarled, ramming the barrel further into the wide-eyed man's mouth. Joe's 'friend' nodded his head, "Yes," and Phil slipped the gun out of the man's mouth and back into his coat. Shaken, the man on the barstool next to Joe Nator turned towards his on-the-house drink, downed it in a single gulp, and began to get up and leave, barely able to set the glass down for all his shaking.

The bartender backed off and pleaded from a distance, "Gentlemen! Please take it outside. "

Phil grabbed Joe Nator's shirt at the throat and shook him violently. "You heard the nice bartender, so gather your shit and let's go."

Joe clumsily grabbed his keys and money-roll off the bar, letting himself be dragged away. Halfway between the corner and where Phil's men were waiting at the table, Phil said, "I hear you came into some luck lately. The boss wants to celebrate your new-found wealth with you."

Joe Nator, waking momentarily from his drunken stupor, balked and called out to the bartender, "I finally win a couple of shekels and everyone wants to break my balls. Ain't that some shit?" The bartender didn't respond. Instead, he silently returned his attention to cleaning shot glasses with his towel.

Joe Nator, realizing the gravity of his situation, tried talking as best he could for his life. "Hey, bartender, do you believe this? When the game's not going his way, Sweaters wants to take his ball and go home."

Phil threw a menacing look at the bartender. Deciding the man posed no real threat, Phil returned his attention to Joe. "Alright, you've had your fun, Joe, so let's go." Phil tightened his grip on Joe's shirt and started dragging him again towards the door. Phil's henchmen stood and joined them as they passed.

Joe, in a last ditch effort, grasped the bar with both hands and yelled, "No, I'm *not* finished yet. You can tell Sweaters to suck my ass!" Momentarily shaking free of Phil's grip, he gathered himself to run, but tripped and fell backwards after Phil slapped him solidly across the face.

"Oh, I will, Joe. I will," Phil answered, locking onto one of Joe's arms, once again pushing the struggling man towards the door.

Joe Nator dug in his heels and brought his free hand up to his reddening face. Then he slid out of Phil's grip, straightened himself up and walked calmly out. Looking back over his shoulder, Joe shouted to the receding bartender, "If I'm not back in five, tell everyone you know not to bet with Sweaters. He's a welcher, a thief…and a murderer!"

Phil and his men drove a considerably more sober and concerned Joe Nator directly to The House of Mirth, Sweaters' private nightclub. Pushing him through the front door, they weaved their way through a riotously dancing crowd. A cloud of cigarette smoke hovering from the ceiling to barely three feet off the floor parted in their wake like the Red Sea before Moses. At the bar, Phil stopped a moment to gawk at two slender women, who took places on either side of him. Both wore black fishnet stockings with black lace garters and black patent-leather high heels. Phil pretended to ignore the two mostly naked women, turning instead to Joe Nator and asking him condescendingly, "You want a last drink?"

"No," Joe Nator said shakily, his fear overtaking him at last. Phil snickered and told the bartender, "Jack and Coke for me, and give these two whatever they want," referring to his two new female companions.

Phil let loose of Joe's elbow. "You should have a drink, Joe. You might not get another chance in this lifetime. Right now, alcohol's probably your best friend."

"Scotch and soda—make that a double," Joe Nator said loudly, turning his back to the bar to watch the two semi-naked girls dance for Phil.

One began gyrating seductively directly in front of Phil.

Returning his attention to Joe Nator, Phil said silkily, "Those sweet legs just seem to go on forever, don't they, Joe? And that little forest of hers—she moves it like a genuine belly dancer. A nice view to take with you to the next world, don't you think?"

The girl continued grinding in front of Phil, finally spreading her legs brazenly in front of him. Phil laughed and slowly placed a hand into the folds of the dancer's Mohawk-shaved crotch. As if on cue, the door to Sweaters' office suddenly flung open and Sweaters yelled from within, "Phil! Why are you standing there with your dick in your hand? How fucking long do I have to wait for you to bring me Joe Nator?"

Sweaters looked around the club haughtily; the party crowd filling the room didn't even notice his outburst. "Bring him in here! Now!" Sweaters yelled above the din. Four grim-looking men appeared from behind Sweaters and obediently pushed a path through the revelers. They were halfway across the dance floor before Phil could get his hand free to comply.

Annoyed at being embarrassed in front of everyone, Phil yelled back, "Alright, alright!" and turned back to the girl. "You! Don't move! I'll be back soon for the rest," he ordered, waving his wetted finger cruelly in front of Joe Nator's nose.

Sweaters stalked back inside the office, slammed the door, and paced behind a massive wooden desk. He let out a long sigh, then plopped into the soft, Italian-leather desk chair. Hearing a barely audible knock, Sweaters looked towards a couch on the other side of the office where two completely unclad dancers were snorting cocaine off the glass coffee table. Frustrated when neither got up to answer the door, he muttered, "Surrounded by fucking morons," then shouted loudly, "Come in!"

Phil nudged Joe Nator into Sweaters' office. The door thudded heavily behind them, and the pounding beat of the live dance music changed instantly to graveyard silence in the soundproofed room. Sweaters' four henchmen, trying to maneuver into the room and out of Sweaters' line of sight, sat and blended with the girls on the couch.

Sweaters stood, then walked silently around Joe Nator and Phil as if inspecting them while the girls snuffled another line of cocaine. Sweaters stopped pacing and with a chivalrous gesture offered Joe a chair directly in front of the desk. Sweaters' eyes suddenly widened. "Fuckin' shit! Everyone! Take off the shoes!"

Joe Nator slumped into the seat Sweaters offered and began to slowly remove his shoes, and everyone else in the room hastily followed. "You know, Phil, if you had done a better job minding the store, I wouldn't right now be in the process of having to liquidate just about everything I own."

"Don't blame me for this mess, boss," Phil retorted, instantly on guard. "Ray put Joey V. in charge during your absence, so maybe you should take it up with him. And what's with taking off the shoes?"

Sweaters took a step back, visibly offended, and pointed down at the rug. "This rug is from the movie, 'The Godfather Two.' Cost me over two hundred grand!"

Phil shook his head in disbelief, "Two hundred grand? Why the hell put it on the floor of your office, then?"

Sweaters face flashed red. He stepped closer to Phil and hissed through gritted teeth, "Because I wanted to be able to say that it was here in *my* office. Did you hear me, Phil? I said, 'wanted.' Past tense. Like in 'gone.' Get it?"

Sweaters walked menacingly over and sat on the edge of his massive desk, in the process giving Joe Nator a soft slap on his cheek. "Well, now, if it isn't my favorite customer, Joe Nator."

Joe folded his arms across his chest and replied with all the nerve he could muster, "Funny, how you never invited me over here when I was losing money."

"Oh, you got me all wrong, Joe. I'm just curious as to what you did to change your luck, because over the last week, mine has changed in the opposite direction. All for the bad! I thought maybe you could give me some tips on how I might fix things, you know, back to the way they were."

Joe shrugged. "I wouldn't know, Sweaters. Luck is luck. Things just sort of fell in for me."

Sweaters raised his eyebrows and pushed himself off the desk. Walking behind Joe, he replied, "I left word on the street before this mess not to take any action from you, unless you showed the collateral to back it up. So tell me, Joe, where did you get the millions to back up all these 'lucky' bets you made?"

"You should know, Sweaters. I recently inherited a big chunk of money from a rich aunt who died."

Sweaters threw a wicked punch to the side of Joe Nator's face from behind. "Wrong answer," he said dryly. Joe Nator flew forward out of his seat and hit the floor with a thud. Sweaters immediately yelled, "Get him off my rug!"

As soon as Sweaters' men picked up the bloodied Joe Nator and set him back in the chair, Sweaters continued. "Joe. I checked out that line of bullshit you've been spreading. The only family you have left is that lovely daughter of yours and her children in Arizona."

Joe Nator winced. "Okay, I have some people that trust my judgment, and they were willing to back me, as long as I guaranteed their anonymity."

Sweaters looked savagely at Phil then back at Joe. "So you're trying to tell me you know some big-money people willing to back you on a whole series of multi-million-dollar bets. Joe, you haven't won a meaningful bet in thirty years. I know your resume. You've gambled everything away. You lost two houses and everything that wasn't nailed down. You even lost two wives in the process. How is it that these mystery people suddenly see something wonderful in you that I've never seen, and suddenly want to back you so generously? Tell me who they are, Joe. I'd like to meet them, and maybe do some business of my own with them— you lying sack of shit."

"I can't, Sweaters. Really. I'm telling you the truth. I promised I'd never name them. It was part of the deal," Joe said, frantically looking from Phil to Sweaters and back to Phil.

Sweaters looked at Phil and nodded towards a nearby cabinet. Phil, shaking his head, got up and pulled a length of well-used rope out of the cabinet after which he emotionlessly tied Joe Nator's arms to the chair. When Joe squirmed to resist, Sweaters' other men came silently forward and held him in place.

Joe Nator started kicking frantically and yelling at the top of his lungs, "Come on, Sweaters! It's no one you'd know!" On a signal from Sweaters, Phil positioned the light on the desk so it would shine directly into Joe Nator's eyes while Sweaters retrieved a jar from a desk drawer.

"Well, look what I found, Joe: A jar of battery acid. Hell-of-a place for someone to leave something like that, don't you think? I should dispose of it..." Sweaters' disembodied voice rankled at Joe from somewhere he couldn't make out behind the brilliant light.

Sweaters stepped to the side so that Joe could watch him remove the lid from a glass jar filled with a thick, clear liquid. Then he placed a small paint brush in the jar and moved the smoking brush and jar slowly towards Joe. "Phil says he found you at a bar drinking. How about a little of..."

Joe Nator struggled as Sweaters swung the wet brush towards Joe's lips. Joe screamed, "Alright, alright! I'll tell you! Just don't..."

Sweaters burst out laughing, "Jesus, Joe, I didn't even get to explain in detail how this stuff slowly burns the skin off your face."

Joe, staring in horror at the fuming brush, mumbled, "The Irishman. It was him, Sweaters. I swear! It was him!"

Sweaters placed the jar back onto the desk after handing the smoking brush to one of his men. Then Sweaters leaned closer. "You'll have to be a little more specific, Joe. I know more than a few donkeys. Which one?"

"Mack!" Joe blurted out. "It was Mack...him and his friends."

Sweaters, his face turning ashen grey, stared at the hopelessly struggling man.

Phil interjected. "I can't believe what I'm seeing! Earlier today, Joe, you were such a tough guy! I distinctly remember you saying that you were going to tell Sweaters to do something of a rather personal nature."

Joe Nator, heart racing, spit at Phil and said, "Fuck you, you bastard!"

Phil explained to Sweaters: "Back at the bar where I collected him, Joe here said he wanted you to suck his ass, Sweaters," and laughed.

Sweaters, seething, picked up the jar of acid and slushed it threateningly in front of Phil. "And you find that funny, do you?"

The moment Phil stopped laughing, Sweaters switched his rage back to Joe Nator. "So you want me to suck your ass, do you? How about *you* sucking *my* ass? But, hey, let me fix those burbling lips first," he yelled, holding the open jar menacingly directly above Joe's mouth.

Sweaters turned back to Phil. "That donkey-mutt is going to suffer before I kill him. I'll make him watch that ex-wife of his turn into a crack whore. I'll..."He suddenly paused, as if a light went off in his head and pointed at two of his men. "You two! Go pick her up and bring her here!"

Sweaters suddenly went silent, appearing as if trying to remember the train of his conversation, as all four henchmen ran for the door. "Oh yeah, then after that, I'll put down whatever 'friends' helped him..."

Phil interrupted Sweaters' errant rambling. The man seemed to be cracking. "How about we take care of this tough guy first, huh, boss?"

"Yeah, right, where was I? Oh yeah: Phil, hold his head."

Phil iron-gripped Joe Nator's head as Sweaters brought the hissing jar to Joe Nator's lips. Joe let out a blood-curdling scream as Sweaters directed a glob of the viscous liquid onto Joe's trembling lips. Joe Nator's screams changed to desperate gasps and finally to strangling gurgles as his lips turned ghostly white and began

Number One Bestseller

foaming.

CHAPTER 56

Ray sat at the bar, hunched over, staring into his glass of bourbon as if it was a crystal ball. Ray took out his heavy iron and weighed a small Beretta automatic in the palm of his hand. He hoped to God he wouldn't have to use it during the meeting. If he did, it would mean the situation had spiraled out of control, and he would be fighting for his life with little more than a pop-gun to defend himself. Slipping it into a spinal holster and the holster into the small of his back, he returned to his drink. After several thoughtful minutes, he downed the drink and turned sullenly to Joey V. "It's time to go."

Joey V. tossed his head back and enjoyed the clink of the ice in the glass as it bounced off his upper lip and teeth, sucking in and savoring every last drop of the warm, invigorating whiskey. Placing the glass next to Ray's, he asked calmly, "So what are you going to tell Sweaters?"

"I still haven't heard from Gus yet. Now that the horse is out of the barn about me wanting Sweaters dead, it would require an unquestionable accident—not so easy a task—without the big boss's permission. I figure we just bide our time and wait," Ray replied morosely.

Joey V. looked into the mirror behind the bar and adjusted his tie. "Well, Gus called me briefly and said to tell you if you got a call from him and he mentioned something about a Caddy or Cadillac, that meant you had his blessing to go ahead and rub out Sweaters. The code word was 'Caddy' or 'Cadillac'."

"Got it. But why tell you and not me?"

"Because he doesn't want any possible connection with what you're going to do for him, not until it's successfully finished," Joey V. said matter-of-factly and changed the subject. "If Sweaters orders his men to search us, we'll have to run for our lives."

Ray, in the middle of adjusting his own tie in the mirror, scooped up his automatic and paused. "Why?"

"Think about it: Have you ever been searched by Sweaters? If he has you searched, that means that word's leaked out and you're a dead man."

"I see what you're saying, Joey, but I've known Sweaters longer than anyone, and believe me, if he really wants one or both of us dead, he'll set some kind of a trap and enjoy watching us walk into it. All I can say is, wear your tap-dancing shoes, because he's going to ask some tricky questions either way. Whatever happens, we need to stall Sweaters until I get the okay from Gus."

Joey V. pulled out a roll of cash, removed the rubber band, peeled off a ten dollar bill, and tossed a twenty along with it as a tip. "I got a bad feeling about this, Ray."

Ray looked at the thirty dollars on the bar, pulled out a roll of his own, placed a ten, a twenty and an extra twenty next to Joey V.'s. "That's for luck. Just don't pussy out on me now, Joey," he said, getting up.

Twenty minutes later, Ray placed his large automatic in the glove box of the car and the two sped off to the parking lot of The House of Mirth. There, an anxious Joey V. searched the area as inconspicuously as possible, hoping to locate any sign that Botch and Mack were somewhere there waiting. Despite his best efforts, Joey V. saw nothing that indicated anything of the sort.

Hoping for the best, Joey V. got out of the car, and walked with Twisted Ray towards the front door steps of the club. Joey V. entered first, only to smack into a wall of acrid blue-grey smoke, blazing lights and deafening music.

Inside the packed house, everyone was partying like the world was about to end. Several patrons sitting at a perimeter table noticed Joey V. One of the table occupants stood, cupped his hands about his mouth and yelled ineffectively for Joey V., then signaled with his hands for Joey to come over and join them.

Gauging it safe, Twisted Ray slipped in and stood beside Joey V. The man who had, a moment ago, invited Joey V. to join them at his table, abruptly turned away. A suddenly silent, staring crowd parted as Joey V. and Twisted Ray worked their way across the dance floor towards the door to Sweaters' office.

The bartender nervously signaled and the two girls who had danced for Fortunate Phil a short while ago walked out, totally nude, into the center of the dance floor. The DJ, seeing the crowd's attention shift to the two naked women, put on a screamingly loud, body-thumping techno song, even louder than before. In seconds, the fickle crowd was copying the girls' energetic, uninhibited pelvic thrusts and provocative arm-waving on what quickly became a re-packed floor.

Ray followed Joey V. the rest of the way to Sweaters' office. Ray stood for a moment, then made an executive decision, and pulled open the door without knocking.

Across the room, Phil recognized the two intruders and, pointing a finger, yelled loudly, "Frisk 'em!"

One of the two henchmen left got grudgingly up off the couch, the two cocaine-laced girls purring and pawing at him from either side, re-adjusted his clothes and hobbled slowly over towards an uncompromising Twisted Ray, and an uncomfortable-looking Joey V. The man frisked Joey V. but stopped dead when he moved to Ray and noticed Ray's darkening scowl.

Seizing the moment, Ray demanded, "What the fuck do you think you're doing?" The man looked lamely back at Phil, as Sweaters walked out of the side bathroom, drying his hands on a couple of towels.

Momentarily taken aback, Sweaters proceeded the rest of the way across the office to his desk, deliberately ignoring Ray and Joey V., asking his man with a look of suspicion, "Any weapons?"

"Joey V. seems clean," he offered, punting the responsibility back to Sweaters.

Sweaters studied Ray's face as if looking for any crack in the man's armor. "You guys come together?" Sweaters finally asked, rearranging the items on his desk.

"Yeah, why?" Ray replied with what he hoped sounded like justified annoyance.

"I don't know," Sweaters said, tossing the towels at a bodyguard. "You guys seem quite chummy all of a sudden."

Ray frowned, knowing that Sweaters was baiting him. "I don't know what you're getting at, but, whatever you say, Sweaters."

All eyes turned to Sweaters, who decided to change his approach. "Take your shoes off. Both of you."

Joey V. looked around the room as he slipped off his shoes, trying to unobtrusively plan an escape should the situation degenerate any further. Looking at the couch where two girls were chatting and laughing together, his attention was drawn to a groan from behind two of Sweaters' burliest henchmen standing close together on that side of the room. Joey V. walked quietly towards and around the nearest man to see his cousin, Joe Nator, tied in a chair, the man's lips and nose blistering gruesomely before Joey V.'s eyes. Having witnessed Sweaters' acid trick before, and, disregarding his own safety, Joey V. marched calmly into Sweaters' bathroom, grabbed a towel and placed it under cold running water. Then he strode out of the bathroom with the wet towel back to where Joe Nator was.

As Joey approached, the nearer of Sweaters' two men moved to block his path. Joey V., without hesitating, threw the huge man a thundering punch to the face, audibly cracking the man's jaw, and knocking the unfortunate guard backwards onto the rug. Wide-eyed, the other guard backed away. Joey V. compassionately placed the wet towel over his cousin's swollen, cracking, bleeding face.

Joe moaned, and looked to the side. Recognizing Joey V., he squinted one eye to signal Joey V. that he hadn't revealed Joey's part in the Sweaters swindle.

Sweaters dispassionately watched the drama unfolding before him. "You should be worried more about yourself, Joey," he said blandly, and then, changing before everyone's eyes from a mannered Dr. Jekyll into a malevolent Mr. Hyde, Sweaters screamed, "Where...is...my...fucking...money?!" Then, returning just as quickly back into the outwardly courteous Dr. Jekyll, he added icily, "And if you say you don't know, I'll redo your lips next!"

Joey V. repositioned the towel, careful not to acknowledge Sweaters. Instead, he looked sadly at his cousin's contorted, disfigured face, and decided that, regardless of Ray, the time had come for action. "Can't stand to see a real man caring for another, can you, you fucking animal!"

The room went instantly silent. The girls on the couch stopped chatting and looked up to see Sweaters' reaction. The man Joey V. had punched stood awkwardly up, holding his jaw, and looked to Sweaters for a signal as to what to do.

Sweaters glared at Joey V. with amazement, then broke out in laughter. "A fucking animal, am I? What's happened to *you*, Joey? I go to jail for a couple of days, and suddenly you think you're the boss? What have you been doing in my absence, fertilizing your balls to make them grow bigger?" Sweaters looked begrudgingly from Joey V. to Joe Nator and then to the man Joey V. had punched, and to everyone's surprise signaled his man to cut Joe Nator loose. Moments later, Joe Nator was in the bathroom, alternately plunging his face into a sink full of cold water and sloshing the water around inside his mouth, letting out one agonizing groan after another.

Sweaters watched with malignant pleasure, then turned back to Joey V. "Now, I'm asking you again, Joey, all civilized-like: Where's...my...fucking...money?!"

Joey V. shrugged, extending his arms and hands. "Hey. You watched it all on the news. Those FBI agents set us up." Pointing to the dressing around his head, Joey V. added, "I almost got my fucking head blown off, you know!" Sweaters seemed to relax a little at the explanation, so Joey V. continued: "Ray and I figure Sal and Dom were working with them." Joey looked at Ray. It all depended now on whether Ray actually bought the con he, Mack, Andre, and Botch had so meticulously constructed.

Still no word from Gus, Ray looked feebly at Sweaters, then raised his eyebrows and cocked his head to the side, acting as if he didn't know what Joey V. was talking about.

"Sal and Dom? Those two morons?" Sweaters hissed, his attention now riveted on Joey V. "They had to sniff to find the bathroom, so don't give me that bullshit. Listen, I know about your pal, Mack, backing your quick-to-talk cousin here. What? You think I haven't known all along that Joe was your cousin?"

"You're right about Joe being my cousin," Joey said matter-of-factly, "but I got nothing to do with that Irish prick. Once he began wearing a badge, he and I no longer…"

Sweaters pointed to the seat next to his desk, previously sat in by Joe Nator. "Sit. We have some sorting out to do."

The back door to Sweaters' office suddenly banged open loudly, and Phil jumped out of the way as Annie, Mack's ex-wife, was dragged in by two more of Sweaters' goons. Annie, struggling, broke loose and dived at Sweaters in an attempt to gouge out the man's eyes with her fingernails. At the last moment, however, Ray stepped in and grabbed her by the talons. Annie, on gut reaction, spun around and raised a knee as high and hard as she could into Ray's groin.

Ray let out a horrific scream, grabbed his aching privates and fell to his knees. Then, in a last-ditch effort to save face, he tackled Annie to the floor and rolled on top of her, in his rage swinging as hard as he could at her.

Annie screamed, barely avoiding the merciless punch. Phil drew a gun and began to move towards the struggling couple, only to be knocked aside by Joey V., who dove on Ray. "You're going to kill her!" His scream accompanied hers, until Phil intervened. "Stay out of this, Joey," Phil ordered.

Sweaters, principally out of concern for the rug he was soon going to have to part with, added, "Enough! Take her into the bedroom."

The two gorillas who had dragged her into the office pushed Annie towards the door to an interconnecting bedroom Sweaters had had built onto his office in order to enjoy, at his leisure, the best of his porn movie stars—those he allowed to work at his club.

Bruised, determined and angry, Joey V. pushed the men away. "You scumbags get the fuck away from her. I'll take her," he said, sliding a supporting arm around Annie's waist as she went limp, laying her on the bed.

"Yeah, Joey," Sweaters mumbled with a wicked scowl. "You'd best 'take' her and right now. On the bed. Because when I finish with her…"

Number One Bestseller

CHAPTER 57

Mack leaned forward and rested his elbows on the back of Andre and Botch's seat backs. All anxiously watched the front entrance of The House of Mirth. Having given up finding Joe Nator, they had arrived in time to see Joey V. enter, followed by Twisted Ray, and were becoming increasingly alarmed by what they were hearing transmitted from the microphone hidden inside the bandages wrapped around Joey V.'s head.

Mack wrinkled his brows. "I don't know what that was about, but it didn't sound good. What do you think is going on in there?"

Andre continued to stare at the receiver speaker. "I'm not sure, but from the sound of it, someone caught a beating, though not Joey V., since the microphone is still transmitting. It sounded to me like two people, a man and a woman, have been hurt. I think we should go in."

Botch leaned back in the driver's seat, butting Mack in the nose with the back of his head and, stretching out, began digging in his pockets. Pulling out his cell phone, he banged in some numbers. "Let me try something, first," he added, rubbing the back of his head while Mack rubbed his nose.

Inside Sweaters' office, Ray was sitting, one hand cradling his throbbing groin, the other reaching for his cell phone. He answered between shallow breaths. "Yeah?"

Andre asked Botch in a whisper, "Who you calling?"

Botch covered the phone, placed a vertical finger to his lips, then started talking, dropping his voice a full octave. "Ray, that you? That thing with Sweaters I said I'd call you about. Yeah, well you've got the green light." Botch, heart racing as if he were speaking to the devil himself, quickly hung up. "That should shake things up a bit," he said with a grin.

Mack nudged Botch from behind. "So what exactly did you just do?"

"Joey gave me Twisted Ray's cell phone number as a precaution. Ray's been stalling for time, waiting for this particular call to happen. I thought it might be worth a shot to nudge things along. That way, we won't have to go in and worry about getting our own asses blown off."

The three hunched together around the hand-held receiver and listened to see what Botch had unleashed. A loud, rustling sound was followed by a whisper from Joey V. "Mack? If you can hear me, they got Annie."

Then they heard a louder, second voice. "Who the fuck are you talking to?"

The blood drained from Mack's face. "Did Joey just say that Annie's inside?" Mack threw himself out of the car, weapon drawn "Guys, we've got to get in there! Now!"

Andre and Botch slid out of the front of the car to find two of Sweaters' men, guns drawn, materialize from the shadows. "Hands on top of the car!" one yelled, shifting the point of his pistol continuously from one to another of the three. Mack, Andre and Botch reluctantly complied.

Andre, noticing Mack tensing to strike, hissed quietly through clenched teeth, "Not now, Mack. Not now."

The man closest to Andre snapped to attention. "Did I say you could talk, Shine?" he asked, slashing the butt of his gun viciously at Andre's forehead. The second man frisked the threesome while his partner kept his gun pointed at the center of Andre's profusely bleeding head. After making certain that they had confiscated all the weapons, the second man said, "Keep your hands where I can see them, and head towards that door over there."

With two guns pointed at them, Mack, Andre and Botch did as they were told, in the process blundering into another of Sweaters' men in a rush to get to Sweaters' office. The gunman who had punched Andre yelled, "Steve? Where the hell have you been?"

"Running my ass off to get to the end of Long Island and pick up this fucking videotape for Sweaters. Wouldn't you know: The guy's got two live asses in his office, and he orders me to drive here with a God-damn tape! One of the few left after his stash was inexplicably burned. By the way, take your shoes off and make these guys do the same before you go in. Sweaters is planning to sell his 'Godfather Two' rug, that, in his crazed mind, is going to get him back a chunk of the money he recently lost." Mack smiled with satisfaction, then ventured a look at the tape under the man's arm, wondering if it could be another copy of Annie's infidelity that Mack thought destroyed. Then it occurred to him that he didn't care anymore. All he wanted was to take Sweaters out before Annie was harmed.

The group could hear voices on the other side of the back door to The House of Mirth raised in anger. Fortunate Phil was asking Joey V., "Who's on the fucking other end of this?" to which Joey V. answered, "Believe me, no one you want to mess with."

Phil's voice suddenly dropped to a whisper. "I swear to you, Joey, that if anything goes wrong tonight, I'll personally kill Joe, the woman, you and everyone else involved. And since you don't want to tell me who you're talking to, you can tell Sweaters." Joey V.'s voice receded behind the door as he answered, "A lot of things are going to go down tonight, Phil, and I'll say it again: You don't want to be on the wrong side when the dust settles."

Everyone outside the door had stopped to listen to the dialog inside. There was a sudden scuffling, and then Phil told Joey V., "No more of your double-talking bullshit! I'm not letting you suck me or Sweaters in like you nearly did Ray. Now get going!"

Phil shoved Joey V. in front of Sweaters. "Look what our friend here has hidden in his bandages," he said, showing Sweaters the tiny microphone. Phil enjoyed watching Joey V. squirm.

Sweaters looked darkly from Joey V. to Twisted Ray, when Ray's cell phone rang a second time. Everyone's stare turned from Joey V. to Twisted Ray, who looked completely baffled.

No one moved.

The phone continued to ring.

Sweaters, turning the microphone over and over in his hand, said, "Well, Ray, why don't you answer it? In fact, put it on speaker phone so we can all enjoy what very well may be the last words you and your pal, Joey V., ever hear."

To everyone's shock, the call was from Gus. Gus, hearing Ray pick up the call, didn't wait for him to speak but launched right in. "Ray. How are you? Sorry I couldn't talk to you further at the wake. Listen, I want you to know that I appreciate you handling the Caddy deal for me; I want you to do the delivery personally. We'll talk more afterwards." Ray replied for all to hear: "Understood, Gus. Consider it done."

"Do what you gotta do," replied Gus on the speaker phone. "I just want it before I leave."

"You want me to call you then when it's done?"

Gus growled, "No need, just do it."

Staring at the phone as he hung up, Gus chuckled, then looked at the crime bosses assembled around the table. "All that for a white 1966 Cadillac? I almost feel guilty that he's going to get me the car, and then I'm going to have him whacked when he drops it off for wanting to take out my nephew." Gus accepted a proffered drink and continued. "Now, back to business. As I said, I know Sweaters is a problem, so, who do we have to fill his shoes when I ask him to step down?"

The room fell silent. Finally Big Frank Da Da, nicknamed for his stuttering problem as a kid, a fellow don and one of Gus's closest allies, relit his cigar. "I think we're beyond Sweaters stepping down, Gus, and I know I'm speaking for the rest at this table. He's brought too much attention to our work. He just got arrested for child porn, for God's sake. He's not just a problem. He knows too much, Gus, and we simply can't afford to let him continue to hang around."

Gus's mouth flopped open. "Child porn?"

Sensing the opening, Frank threw all his cards on the table at once. "Gus, dear friend. My lifelong colleague. I know he's your nephew, but right now he's so busy trying to bang the wife of one of our own recently departed, that he didn't even approach you at the wake and apologize for the mess. Stupidity is one thing, Gus, but disrespect like that cannot be tolerated in the family."

A round of guttural assents swept the table.

Gus nodded sadly in agreement. "To tell you the truth, I'm getting the same from the West Coast dons."

"Who called you from out West?" Big Frank Da Da asked, taking another puff off the glowing Cuban torpedo sticking from his mouth.

"Rhino," Gus said emphatically, watching Big Frank Da Da's face intently to see what the man's reaction would be.

"Rhino? I'd heard he was remaking a name for himself out in California after being shut away for thirty years. He's one dangerous son-of-a-bitch and not one to cross!"

"So gentlemen, who do we have to do the job and take Sweaters' place?"

"There's Fortunate Phil," Big Frank Da Da offered, knocking his cigar ashes into a silver ashtray at his elbow. "He's a perfect fit. He knows his shit and he's a good earner."

Gus shook his head in disagreement. "I hear he's a loose cannon. What about Joey V.?"

"A low level bookie," replied Big Frank. "He'll *never* be a leader; he doesn't have the stomach for it. Listen, I have Phil's number here. He's our best choice. Really, Gus." Big Frank wrote Fortunate Phil's cell phone number on a piece of paper and slid it to the don sitting to his left. Heads bobbed in agreement as the paper traveled around the table from don to don towards Gus.

Gus accepted the paper and said, "Look. This is a big change, and frankly, I don't know the man personally." Stretching an arm towards Big Frank Da Da, Gus offered the paper back to him. "Since you know him, you call him. Feel him out. Make sure he's our man."

"I've known him for years," Big Frank replied with conviction. "He's like my own family; Hell, he calls me Uncle Frank. You met him at the wake, Gus—the tall guy by the door. You hit him accidentally with the door when you were leaving."

Gus laughed. "Oh, yeah, I remember the guy. His father was a good earner. I don't know what it is about Phil that he doesn't stand out in my mind, but I've heard the rest of his crew respects him."

Back in Sweaters' office, Ray snapped his cell phone shut, considering why Gus would call him twice in a row to order him to do the same deed. *He was probably just making certain I understood the message*, Ray told himself. *Maybe because Gus hadn't mentioned 'Caddy' in the first call. Or were the Dons just getting so old that their minds were slipping? Either way, it didn't matter. He was now absolutely clear about what needed to happen next.*

CHAPTER 58

"So, Ray? Now you're getting chummy with my uncle? What is this all about..." Ray started to reply, but before he could speak, Sweaters held up the microphone and yelled, "Shut the fuck up! I'm talking about *this!*" Ray slowly raised his eyes from the cell phone in his hand, and looked blankly up at Sweaters. *"What?!"*

Sweaters threw his hands in the air. "What the fuck is the matter with you? Didn't you just hear? Phil found this wire on your friend, Joey! For God's sake, Ray, Joey's been playing you for a fool! Are you such a total moron that you can't see what's going on?"

Suddenly the back door to Sweaters' office again swung open and in marched Mack, Andre and Botch lead by three more of Sweaters' men. Sweaters, sensing the tide now turning solidly in his direction, announced, "Well, well, well! The whole gang's here, and, hey, everyone's got his shoes off. Nice work, guys. At least *somebody* still fucking listens! And I see you brought the video tape. Good! You stay, Steve. You other men, outside. It's getting crowded in here!" Sweaters looked triumphant.

"Mack," Sweaters continued, searching Mack's eyes. "You God-damned, back-stabbing son-of-a-...mic! All these years you've been not-so-secretly trying to ruin me. I guess you forgot that I was the one who put you to work when you returned from Viet Nam and couldn't find a frigging job anywhere. After all I did for you, you steal my money and try to ruin me!"

Mack looked around the room for Annie, frowning when he didn't see her. Mack looked directly at Sweaters and snarled, "You expect people to stand by while you fuck with their lives and the lives of their children?" Pointing at the videotape under Steve's arm, Mack continued: "You're just lucky you've had such a long run."

Sweaters laughed. "You, of everyone, ought to know what happens to people who get in my way. In the end, Mack, they disappear. Poof! And that's that! So tell me how you think this evening is going to play out."

Mack replied defiantly, "You really think you're the one in control here? What about Twisted Ray over there? He's just waiting for the right moment to take your place. What about all the men you just sent away? You think they don't know your days are numbered? What about all the people you now *owe* in trying to pay off your losses? You think anyone's going to welcome you back after the mess you've made? The only thing you're going to be greeted with is a hail of bullets, all with *your name* on them. You're done, Sweaters! Washed up! *Finito!*"

Sweaters looked nervously around the room. A single drop of perspiration dripped silently from his glistening temple onto his cherished rug.

CHAPTER 59

Sweaters' men began returning one-by-one to the room to witness the drama. "...besides which, by now, this place is surrounded by cops and feds," Mack added.

Sweaters' eyes narrowed. "Like you'd risk exposing yourselves as the thieves you and your buddies are. You're bluffing, Mack. But look, I'll make it easy: Tell me where my money is and I promise I'll kill each of you quickly. Or, if you prefer, I can take my time and rip the information out of you slowly, like I did with Joe Nator here."

Mack hesitated. "Now *you're* bluffing, Sweaters. . ."

"Either way, you're going to end up telling me what I want to know before I kill you," Sweaters continued confidently.

Mack hissed. "You don't get it, do you, Sweaters? I don't have your money— the feds do. The stolen money was a setup to flush you out. If anything happens to us in here, the feds outside will hit this place like a stampede of wild boars and break you and your gang like a paper *piñata*."

Sweaters, visibly shaken by this latest news but refusing to be fazed, broke in. "Always the tough guy, aren't you, Mack? But I'm not going to be taken in by you and your lies."

"Maybe you're right. But how about your men here? I don't sense any love for you, and killing a defenseless woman, a federal agent and two of New York's finest wouldn't be a great career move." Several men awkwardly shifted their position.

Sweaters, sensing the change in his men's resolve, snarled back, "You always had a good line of bullshit, but it won't work on me or my men here. Steve, give me the tape. And since everyone's all back together, Phil, bring out his old lady."

Fortunate Phil looked morosely from Joey V. to Sweaters to Mack, knowing whatever he did would likely make him "Unfortunate" Phil from here on.

Shuffling slowly into the other room where Annie was starting to awaken, Phil extended a hand and politely asked her to come with him. Phil escorted her into Sweaters' office where everyone stood waiting to see what would happen next.

Sweaters gnashed his teeth and shoved the videotape into his VCR. The big screen across the room came alive in a swath of snow and lines. "Oh, you are going to love this one!" Sweaters said, looking first at Mack and then at Annie with dark malice in his cold eyes.

Annie, noticing Sweaters index finger hovering over the "play" button of the loaded VCR deck, paled, not knowing what to expect.

Seeing the blood suddenly drain from Annie's face, Mack prepared to lunge for Sweaters, and Andre and Botch, sensing Mack's intention, steeled themselves to follow. Just behind Sweaters, however, a bound and surprisingly relaxed and smiling Joey V. made vigorous head signals towards the VCR. At last catching Mack, Andre and Botch's attention. Joey repeatedly mouthed, "Relax."

At the last second, Mack, deciding against what would likely have meant certain death for him and all around, instead, relaxed as his pal, Joey V., advised. Joey breathed a sigh of relief.

Sweaters touched his finger to the play button, only to be distracted this time by a ring from another unseen cell phone. "Whose God-damn, fucking, phone is that?" he screamed, looking around the room, his finger suspended on the play button.

Phil looked at Sweaters and shrugged. "It's mine, boss" he said, and leaving Annie to stand shakily on her own, he walked back into the adjoining bedroom and closed the door. Everyone waited until Phil walked back into the room and rejoined them.

"What?" said Sweaters angrily, "Am I talking to the walls here? Everybody— that includes you, Phil—for the last time—shut up and watch tonight's feature." Sweaters hit the play button hard, smiling and saying as he did, "You're going to love the cast."

The screen changed from static to the vague outline of a naked woman behind a glass door taking a shower. The person doing the recording walked up and slid the glass door open, exposing the back of a young girl rinsing herself after shaving her private parts. All eyes turned momentarily to Sweaters, who had a puzzled look on his face, but the eyes immediately returned to the big screen when the girl turned the shower off and turned towards the camera. "Hey, isn't that Ray's daughter?" one of the men shouted, pointing at the girl who gave a yelp while trying unsuccessfully to cover her wet breasts and hairless crotch with two hands. Then she slowly removed her hands and posed, displaying herself to the camera.

"You mother-fucker!" Twisted Ray yelled, whipping out the small automatic from his spinal holster and aiming it at Sweaters' chest.

Sweaters, barely quicker, grabbed the jar of acid on his desk and threw it point-blank at Ray. Ray shot several rounds into the ceiling before dropping the weapon and grabbing at his face. Blind, screaming in agony, he ran frantically towards the bathroom, instead hitting the wall just to the right of the doorway, and falling to the floor. Writhing and moaning on the floor, he tried inanely to claw his way on hands and knees into the bathroom. Sweaters watched with interest, and followed Ray into the bathroom.

Continuing to talk as he went, Sweaters intoned, "Just for the record, Ray, I was set up. It was supposed to be a different tape, but being as it was this one, I thought you should know that your daughter's got a very, very tight..." and with that, Sweaters picked up the Baretta Ray had dropped on the floor and pulled the trigger several times. Ray's hissing, steaming face exploded in a flash of red, his body thudding heavily onto the bathroom floor.

Sweaters tossed the smoking gun onto Ray's twitching body, turned, and walked across his office to the door separating his office from the club. Opening it a crack to assure himself that the partying outside hadn't stopped, he then walked to an outside window. Peeking through the blinds, he returned his gaze to Mack. "That's several gunshots. Where's this army of cops and FBI agents, Mack?"

Turning to his men, Sweaters explained coolly, "I told you he had a good line of shit. He never fooled me; though, I must admit switching tapes to the one with Ray's daughter on it was brilliant, just brilliant."

Sweaters looked with anger at the puddle of acid, hissing, smoking, rapidly carving an expanding hole in the middle of his carpet where moments ago Ray had been standing holding a gun on him. "Fuck!" he yelled, stamping his feet. Turning to Mack, Andre and Botch, he pointed at the hole in the rug and screamed, spittle flying in every direction, "Every fucking one of you is going to pay for that!"

Sweaters walked menacingly over to Mack. Placing two shaking fists in front of Mack's face, he asked in a dead monotone, "One more time, Mack. Where's my money?"

"Eat me, clown," Mack replied boldly.

Returning his shaking fists to his sides, Sweaters spat in Mack's face and yelled, wild-eyed, "Okay, Mack, then watch your wife and friends die."

Facing his six prisoners, Sweaters addressed them coldly. "I could shoot each of you like I did Twisted Ray, that traitor, who was, like *you* said, just waiting for an opportunity to do the same to me, but, like *I* said, I want my men to see that I'm not the 'bad guy' here when you finally spill your guts."

"You," Sweaters said to Steve, "start with Mack. Put him in Joey V.'s chair and tape his hands onto the chair arms."

You," he pointed to another of his men, "tape his mouth shut. And you," he pointed to a third man, "You get five more chairs and some clothes pins!"

Steve retrieved two rolls of silvery duct tape from the cabinet against the wall that housed the rope used to bind Joe Nator, and began taping Mack, Joey V., Andre, Botch, Joe Nator and Annie's hands onto the armrests of the six chairs. The second man followed directly behind Steve, running more duct tape around the six's jaws, effectively sealing their mouths.

Sweaters narrated as they worked on the victims. "I could use the black-plastic-bag-over-the-head trick, Mack, but I want you to see your friends and finally your wife suffocate, one-by-one in front of you, begging you with their eyes to tell me where the money is! I want you to see them curse you for valuing the money above their lives as they each die!"

Sweaters walked down the line, checked the tape around each of the captive's hands and mouths, then took the clothes pins from the third man, and carefully clipped them on Andre, Botch, Joe and Joey V.'s noses, pausing between each, just long enough so that each would have time to die before the next.

Joey V. looked at Botch, shrugged his shoulders…then paradoxically winked. Botch watched Joey V. with dark finality, amazed that Joey would joke at a time like this. Joey V., however, slid as far forward on his chair as possible. Then started rocking.

His back to Joey V., Sweaters was too wrapped up in describing to a wide-eyed Mack, in detail, how suffocation was the most agonizing of deaths, and how after watching each of the four in turn die, he'd get to watch Annie die as the *finale*. Meanwhile, Joey V. tipped his chair over, and rubbed the clothespin against the rug until it popped off his nose.

Botch and Andre attempted to follow Joey's lead, while Sweaters, taken by surprise, hesitated just long enough for AnnIe to tilt her chair into Andre's, for Andre's to bounce into Botch's, for Botch's to tilt onto Joe's, and for Joey V. to hook a foot around one leg of Joe's chair. Jerking the foot of Joe's chair firmly, the whole group toppled over in domino effect onto the carpet.

The impact knocked the clothes pins off Botch's nose, leaving AnnIe, Andre and Joe desperately rubbing their noses against the rug like Joey V. had done until their clothes pins, too, popped off.

Sweaters yelled and signaled frantically with his arms, until his men reluctantly righted the five, this time separating them so they couldn't topple each other again.

"This time, I want each of you men to hold onto a chair!" Sweaters snarled.

Sweaters' men, horrified by what they were being asked to do, reluctantly complied, turning their faces away from their equally horrified victims.

"Okay, now that you've had a chance to see the preview, let's try it again, this time with my men here making sure each of your friends remains upright to the bitter end!"

Phil's cell phone rang. This time Phil took the call, ignoring Sweaters' indignant screams. "Hello? Yeah, but not for long. Okay, you didn't tell me that before."

Sweaters managed to get out, "Hang that up or I'll..." before Phil reached into a pocket, pulled out a stiletto, flicked the blade out, and plunged it into Sweaters' side, immediately thereafter deftly directing the point upwards into Sweaters' beating heart.

Sweaters stared in disbelief as Phil pulled the knife out. Everyone watched in disbelief as Sweaters, still standing, helplessly tried to hold back the rush of blood that rapidly filled the hole in the rug made by the acid.

Sweaters looked uncomprehendingly from the expanding pool of blood beneath him to his killer and then his own bloodied hands. Phil coldly kicked the foundering man, now glassy-eyed, onto the carpet. "That felt better than I thought," Fortunate Phil said, wiping Sweaters' blood off the knife blade onto a clean area of the rug.

Sweaters gasped and moaned.

"Inconsiderate bastard. Can't just die, can you? Instead you have to continue to bleed all over *my* carpet. Well," Phil said, signaling to the circle of men standing about the room to drag Sweaters into the bathroom and dump his body alongside Twisted Ray's, "the value of the carpet will just continue to grow."

"In other words, time for some house-cleaning," Phil said matter-of-factly, as, knife in hand, he approached a shocked Mack, who had been rocking himself between his companions and Phil.

Mack looked from the twitching body being dragged away to Phil looming before him, and braced for the worst. Phil, quick and cat-like, slipped behind Mack and cut Mack's wrists free.

The moment Phil removed the tape from Mack's mouth, Mack said cautiously, "I...ah...couldn't have done it better myself, Phil."

Phil shrugged indifferently, and continued down the row of chairs, cutting the tape around the victims' hands and carefully removing the tape from their mouths. "In case you were wondering, Mack, those first two phone calls were from one of Gus's dons." Turning to the suddenly disinherited gangsters watching him with mouths agape, Phil said, "You all answer to *me* now."

"So where does this leave us?" Mack asked, placing his arm around an exhausted Annie. Andre, Botch, Joe and Joey V. looked on, successive waves of revulsion, satisfaction and concern playing across their faces, as they listened to

299

Mack and Phil's continuing repartee.

Phil seemed pleased to explain: "Well, first of all, you're lucky I didn't turn my cell phone off like that miserable fuck ordered me to."

Mack, surprised, asked, "His uncle really ordered him out of the way?"

Phil frowned, "Not entirely. More important, it seems you have an influential friend."

Anne, Andre, Botch, Joe and Joey V. looked at Mack, confused. "Don't look at me like that," Mack quickly interjected. "I don't know who or what he's talking about!"

Phil smiled and said, "Let's just say the last few minutes here were brought to you by Tommy Chang."

Mack looked totally baffled. "Tommy Chang? But..."

Phil continued, "I can imagine how you must feel. We almost ran out of time, you know. In the first call, Big Frank Da Da, one of Gus's most trusted dons and a longtime friend of mine, asked me if I thought I could conveniently waste Sweaters and take over his operation, which I told him I would be pleased to do. Unfortunately he made no mention of me getting between you and Sweaters, so I thought he wanted you and yours wasted, too. I was to wait for the final confirmation from Sweaters' uncle, Gus. My plan at that time was to just stand by and let Sweaters do you and make my work easier before I did him. The second call, also from Big Frank, said to make sure none of you were harmed. Too bad for Joe Nator the call didn't come earlier. I could have saved him a lot of grief and plastic surgeries. But you've got to remember, I was just following orders. "

Everyone stared at poor, disfigured Joe.

"The third call was from Gus, and, well, you know the rest."

Everyone stared at Fortunate Phil until Mack asked the question that was playing on all their minds. "So, what about us? Are we good to go?"

Phil shrugged his shoulders again in his uniquely uncaring way. "Hey, I never had any beef with you from the beginning. I'll walk you out, however, so you don't walk into a problem with any of Sweaters' stray men in the lot. Oh, and, of course, we wouldn't want all those feds and cops waiting out there to get the wrong impression, now, would we," he said, winking.

In the parking lot next to Botch and Joey V.'s cars, Phil suddenly extended a hand to Joey V. "Hey, no hard feelings."

Joey V., not wanting to piss off his, for the moment, new boss, replied, "Yeah, forget it," smiled and shook the proffered hand. Phil then turned to Mack, as Mack slipped behind the wheel of Botch's car. "A quick word of advice: Just so you know, the word is, don't *ever* fuck with Tommy Chang." Mack nodded and drove off as soon as Annie was seated safely beside him, and Andre and Botch were settled in the back.

They drove to the first traffic light in silence. Then Mack stopped the car and turned back to face Andre and Botch. "How about we go to the bar and celebrate. I told Babe to wait up for us."

Andre looked at Botch, and Botch at Andre. "Sounds good," Botch answered, "but I don't like drinking in pants I just pissed in."

Joey V. and his cousin, Joe Nator, pulled up beside them. "I need to take my cousin here to a hospital, Mack. Meet you at the bar afterwards, okay?" Joe Nator, still in considerable pain, added with difficulty, "I'll...be...fine..."

As Joey drove off, Mack turned and said, "Well, thank God tonight turned out just as we planned," to which everyone, including Annie, chimed in together, "Asshole!"

CHAPTER 60—Epilogue

On Saturday, Mack and Annie, Andre and Joyce, Botch and Debbie, Nick and Shelby, Joey and Rose, all dressed formally, climbed into a black stretch limousine waiting to take them to an exclusive private club in downtown Manhattan for a celebratory dinner with their host, Tommy Chang.

At the club, they were greeted by an impeccably liveried man who escorted them into a private room, where they were seated in high-back oak chairs around a large, formally appointed, 18th-century oak table beneath a massive crystal chandelier.

Andre surveyed the oak-paneled room with its rows of heavy, purple-velvet, French drapes. "Our host isn't here," he half-asked, half-observed.

"He's probably waiting for us to settle in before making his grand entrance," Mack answered, fingering the small, white placard just above the dinner setting with his name written on it in flowing, gold, Edwardian script.

Joey V.'s wife, Rose, taking in the grandiosity of it all, gushed, "I've always dreamed of someday dining in a place like this. It *looks* expensive, and there's no menus. I'm told that, if you have to ask about the price in a place like this, it's not right for you."

Mack pulled a waiting magnum out from one of eight ice buckets standing nearby. "Champagne, anyone?"

Annie sidled up to him lovingly. "Absolutely."

Mack poured champagne for everyone, finishing just in time to look up and see Tommy Chang, in formal black-tie, enter. "And here he is, the man of the hour!" Mack exclaimed.

Tommy Chang bowed and said with a distinctly Korean accent, "Herro, dear flends!" and walked around the table hugging Mack, Andre and Botch and kissing Annie and Joyce. Mack then introduced Debbie, Nick, Shelby, Joey and Rose. After greetings, Tommy Chang signaled, and eleven male waiters dressed like butlers appeared from nowhere. One attended to each guest, while a sommelier presented the champagne to Tommy Chang, and with his approval, popped open another three magnums of chilled champagne. For the next half hour, the group drank, laughed, toasted and re-toasted the successful conclusion of their adventure with their host and benefactor.

Loosening up, Botch raised an instantly-refreshed glass. "Here's to Andre, Mack, and myself, who all put in their retirement papers the same day, and are now beginning a new chapter in their lives!" All, including Tommy Chang, laughed aloud and downed the contents of their glasses. Then Botch yelled over the din, "The best part is that both the FBI and the police force had just given us commendations and promotions, so we're retiring at even higher pay!"

Going around the table, it was Joey V.'s turn to toast. "Well, I can't say that I've got a pension, but at least I now have a shot at living to a ripe, old age—and in style." The group drank to his health, then Tommy Chang swept an arm before the table, which was quickly laden with a bewildering array of hors d'oeuvres. Within the hour, they were feasting on one course after another of the best food they had ever eaten, Tommy and Mack together making certain there was never a shortage of champagne.

Towards the end of the dinner, Joey V. hugged Rose, and began talking excitedly with her about the new life awaiting them at Marisol's. "Not to offend, Mack, but he rearry necessary?" Tommy Chang whispered as an aside to Mack.

"He's an old and dear friend, Tommy. I know he's a little rough around the edges, but, trust me, if you ever needed someone at your side, he'd be the man," Mack said, adding, "He was instrumental in the whole affair."

"If your trusted fliend, Mack, then also mine. Hope you right about him, though. Not good for business, I think."

"Trust me. He'll grow on you," Mack assured Tommy, motioning for Rose to come and join them. Rose took a seat on the other side of Tommy Chang. It only took a few minutes for 'the Rose' to quickly win over Tommy Chang, and soon the two were laughing together like old friends. A few minutes later, Tommy called Mack back over and whispered in his ear, "Don' worry what said about Mister V. Rose make up prentey for him."

Mack let out a sigh of relief, glad that his last big concern had been laid to rest. Seizing the moment, he stood up and tapped a fork to his glass. "Quiet! Quiet! Let's not forget to honor the most important person in all this—the one without whose initial suggestion—and final intervention—we would not be here celebrating tonight. I mean, of course, the man standing next to me, my dear friend and our new business partner, Mr. Tommy Chang. Tommy, we all want to thank you for the request you made at the crucial moment last week on our behalf."

Tommy Chang's glass dipped slightly and he frowned. "Request?"

Mack returned the frown with a fake one of his own. "Okay, I get it. We won't talk about it," but he and all around the table raised their glasses to Tommy nonetheless.

Tommy Chang smiled, re-raised his glass, took a long draught, then, still looking puzzled, asked quietly, "Seriousry, Mack. What request?"

Mack grinned. "Let's just say I didn't know you had juice like that in the underworld."

All eyes turned to Mack and Tommy Chang. The instant silence was deafening.

Tommy Chang looked cautiously from guest to guest, then shrugged his shoulders and laughed politely.

"You know," Mack whispered. "Jerry Cannistraci. Sweaters."

Tommy Chang nodded, "Oh, him! Yes! All work out, then?"

Joey V., who had joined Rose behind Tommy Chang, slapped Tommy on the back, and put an arm around him. "Work out? Shit! We wouldn't be here if it wasn't for you! You're the only man I know who's ever made Gus jump!"

Tommy Chang shrugged off Joey's arm and backed away, giving Joey V. a long hard stare.

It was Botch who finally broke the awkward silence by saying aloud, "Come on, Joey, give our benefactor a break. He saved our asses, and now you want to grill him?"

Joey V., despite all the champagne, suddenly realized he'd overstepped an unspoken line, and quickly apologized. "Hey, Tommy. I mean, Mr. Chang. Whatever I've just done, I didn't mean to put you in a difficult place. I'm most sorry. I just wanted to personally thank you for saving Rose and me—and all our friends here."

Tommy Chang switched quickly from frown to grin and, appearing satisfied with Joey's approbations, looked briefly at Rose and then back at Joey V. "Is awright. But see need to exprain something."

They all grew silent. "Have hotel deveropment in Ros Angeres. Middle of constluction, find work not get done. Investors very concerned. Not sure you aware, but organized clime wide-splead in construction industry in USA. Had to negotiate with despicable peoples. Sit down, make new agreement with man called, 'Rhino'—get name from *big* nose, I think—now, no more probrems."

Joey V. and Mack's mouths dropped open. "Can't be!" each said to the other.

"What can't be?" asked Rose nervously.

Joey V. ignored her and asked Tommy Chang, "Did you happen to catch the full name of this 'Rhino' guy?"

"Exchange business cards," Tommy Chang replied, extracting a card from his wallet which he handed to Joey V.

Joey V. looked at the card, sucked in a deep breath and turned as white as the tablecloth as he showed Mack the card.

"Holy shit!" Mack exclaimed, also aghast.

"What *is* it?!" Rose asked a second time.

Joey slowly read the name on the card out loud. "Jay Bisignano," he said mechanically, adding under his breath, "So my brother is still alive?"

Everyone caught their breath.

"It was always assumed," Joey V. slowly continued, "that my maniacal brother had…died. As his brother, I'm glad to know he's alive, but I'm even happier he's no longer any part of me or the Bisignano family's life."

"Tommy, you have something more to add?" Mack ventured, seeing the look of concern on Tommy Chang's face.

Tommy Chang looked carefully at Joey V. "Thought you rook verry famiriar! Same nose, but different ears. I mention Jerry Sweaters to—your brother—and need probrem fixed for my fliend, Mack. Rhino say he knows Sweaters and wirr take care of it personarry. Everything work out, yes?"

Mack alone, within the horrified audience, belly-laughed. "Everything may have gotten changed a bit in translation, but, in the end, thanks to you, Tommy, my problem is gone, yes!"

Tommy Chang's look changed to serious. "Am deepry invested in construction, Mack. Grad to hear 'Sweaters' not bother you anymore." Tommy Chang continued, "Grad, in small way, to help all my new flends."

The men around the table each looked at Tommy Chang anew, trying to decide, each for himself, if he thought Tommy Chang was as innocent as he was portraying himself to be, or if he was playing them exceptionally well. Over the rest of the evening, each came to the conclusion that, in the end, it didn't really matter. What had happened, happened, and they were individually and collectively glad for a new life before them.

The ambience became more relaxed, and after another hour of revelry, Tommy Chang called for everyone's attention. Extending a gold-ringed index finger pompously into the air, a gorgeous, long-haired, blonde dressed in tight, black patent leather suddenly appeared, carrying a black leather briefcase, which she ceremoniously handed to Tommy Chang.

Everyone tensed, each couple realizing this was *the* pivotal moment in each of their futures. Tommy Chang looked from one to another of his guests, noting their collective tension, as he removed the sheaf of papers he'd brought for everyone to sign in order to complete the Marisol Resort agreement.

Everyone sighed with relief. "Vely edgy bunch," Tommy Chang commented off-handedly to Mack. "Called bank yesterday. Aw money transfered successfurry," Tommy observed, closing the briefcase and tossing the papers and a pen on the table.

One by one, each signed his or her name to the joint-purchase agreement. After the signing was complete, Tommy Chang smiled...and reached his right hand into the inside of his dinner jacket.

Again everyone tensed. This time it was Tommy Chang who sighed, as he removed a stack of pictures he'd recently had taken of the resort, to share with his new partners. As the pictures passed around, each partner had the opportunity to express his or her approving oooh's and ahhh's.

"My fliends," Tommy Chang said at last. "Now must go. Much work to do. Call you in morning, Mack."

Each guest, one by one, bid Tommy Chang their personal goodbyes. While bowing to each, shaking hands with the men and kissing the women, Tommy Chang noticed out of the corner of his eye the woman in black standing near one of the French windows, trying to catch his attention. Tommy Chang barely finished shaking Joey V.'s hand, before walking across the room to talk with her.

Botch unbuttoned his dinner jacket and sat back down at the table next to Mack. "Me, I've got to visit the head."

Mack stood up and rubbed his swollen belly. "Right behind you."

"And you guys talk about us women always going to the bathroom together," Shelby couldn't help piping up.

Mack and Botch stood to the laughs of their wives and friends. On their way across the dining room, Mack and Botch watched Tommy Chang talking intently with the stunningly beautiful blonde in black. Tommy Chang, noticing, escorted the woman through the heavily-draped French windows and onto an outside porch. There, Tommy Chang's signature smile and Korean accent instantly disappeared. "Nicole! You were to wait in the car for me!" he said brusquely.

Ignoring the reprimand, Nicole shook out her silky, blonde hair enticingly, then looked down at the briefcase with a sly smile. "I see you've successfully negotiated your retirement."

Tommy Chang let out an aggravated sigh. "What's up? Why are you here?"

Nicole looked around to make certain they were alone on the outdoor portico. "This news couldn't wait: I just learned the Middle Eastern players are once again trying to negotiate a deal with Yuri and Natasha."

"Damn it, Nicole!" Tommy Chang replied angrily. "I promised to make it all happen, and somehow I will. You take care of your end of it! If they ask for a meeting, set one up and make certain all the players remain on La Palma. And notify me at once! I'll handle the rest. Now leave before you draw any more suspicion."

Inside the men's room, Botch seemed to awaken from his heavily-liquored stupor. Mack picked the urinal next to his friend and the two starting relieving themselves. "What's up, Botch?" Mack finally said.

"I'm suddenly feeling uneasy about all this, Mack. I mean we just handed over a fortune for a promise. For all we know we could have just given our millions away."

Mack searched Botch's face, then replied with disappointment, "Why must you always find something to worry about even when things are going well? Trust me, Tommy Chang knows what he's doing."

"I can't help it, Mack. I'm Italian and Jewish, remember? It's in my DNA." Botch's voice turned serious. "What if something were to happen to Tommy, Mack?"

"What do you mean?" Mack asked as he flushed the toilet, walked to the nearest sink, and began washing his hands.

"Suppose he...falls and breaks his neck...or gets himself killed or something?"

Mack paused while drying his hands. "Wow! I was worrying about exactly the same thing! Like what if Tommy suddenly was killed in a tragic blimp accident."

"Really?" Botch asked with surprise.

"No!" Mack said, shaking his head as he flung the wet towel into the trash receptacle. "I'm trying to point out how ridiculous you sound!"

Botch froze, then splashed some cold water on his face and looked at his reflection in the mirror above the sink. "Yeah, I guess you're right. Okay, I'll stop with the worrying. Hey, did you notice the girl Tommy was talking to?"

"She's a knockout," Mack replied, glad his friend was finally letting go of his fears and moving on to a lighter and more interesting subject. "Tommy knows how to pick them. I was wondering if she was some kind of high priced call-girl—you know, the black leather and all? Who knows what Tommy's into nowadays. To be honest, Botch, she looked vaguely familiar."

Botch looked at Mack's reflection in the mirror beside his. "That's odd. I thought the same thing the moment I saw her. Well, if she is a call girl, I bet she's worth every penny. Did you see those luscious lips? Man, she could suck a golf ball through a..."

It hit Botch and Mack together at the same time: The girl Tommy met was the same one in the file Botch had lifted from agent Ross's desk. The two ran out of the restroom back into the dining room and tried to locate Tommy Chang, but to no avail. The portico door was closed, the heavy drapes redrawn and the portico empty. The two had gone. "Wait a minute, Mack! What would we say if we *did* find them?" Botch asked.

"I just wanted to ask Tommy what was going on and find out if he knew who the girl was. Maybe she's playing him! Like you said, Botch, he's suddenly a richer man."

Botch grabbed Mack's arm. "Mack, what if this lady really is the one in the photo? That could make Tommy Chang the unknown terrorist 'financier' to whom we just gave away all our money. If Ross's report was actually for real, we're talking about atomic bombs and thousands, maybe millions of lives, here."

Mack stopped Botch for a moment to regain his composure, "Maybe, but at this moment, it's just wild—negative—speculation! We don't really know *any* of this for sure."

Botch let go of Mack's arm. "Maybe we shouldn't say anymore until we know about the girl and check out Tommy a little more first. Is that what you're saying, Mack?"

"What I mean, Botch, is that you gotta' be kidding! Tommy's like a brother to me!"

"Yeah, and Joey probably felt like that about his brother, Rhino, at one time."

Mack reluctantly acquiesced. "Alright. Fine. We'll play it from your angle for the moment, but you're going to see how wrong you are about Tommy. We'll have to do this very delicately, or we could lose Tommy's trust. Let's check with the hostess first and see if she knows where the two went."

Mack and Botch walked to the main desk where they were greeted by the hostess. "Good evening, gentlemen. May I be of assistance?"

"We're looking for our host for this evening's dinner, Tommy Chang." Mack replied.

"I'm sorry, but I have strict instructions not to give out..." Before she could finish, Tommy Chang ambled up, pulled out his wallet and flipped her a credit card. "Good evening, Mr. Park," the hostess said, looking from Tommy to Botch and Mack. "I hope everything was to your satisfaction?"

"Everything verry good, thank you." Tommy Chang said, bowing to the hostess while giving Mack and Botch a wink.

"Mr. Park?" Mack ventured.

"Mr. Jun Sun Park, at your service," Tommy Chang replied, continuing in a collusive whisper, "Use different name after meeting with Mr. Rhino. Am cautious businessman, Mack."

Botch raised his eyebrows suspiciously. Mack, however, seemed satisfied, and bowed politely, then bantered in a normal voice, "So who was your stunning, blonde, leather-clad assistant, Mr. Park?"

Tommy Chang's face grew dark. "Business associate, Mr. McConville, from whom seek advice flom time to time."

"Mack has the hots for her," Botch interrupted, not wanting Tommy Chang to become too suspicious. "He couldn't stop staring."

Tommy Chang's darkness changed instantly into a broad grin. "Expranation accepted, Mr. Bartorata," he said, bowing quickly and slightly. Turning back to Mack, Tommy smiled even wider and continued: "How could anyone not have 'hots' for her?" The three laughed stiltedly.

Given this newest exchange, to Mack's mind, Botch was at least partially right: They would need to quietly investigate this new Tommy Chang and make certain the money they had transferred to buy Marisol's was, indeed, where it should be before Tommy left the country. "You know, Mr. Park, I would settle for just knowing her name. Then again, maybe I'll reconsider arresting you for solicitation," Mack said with a grin.

"Arrest nobody, Mr. McConville. Remember, you no ronger cop anymore. 'Retired'." Tommy hesitated a moment, then pulled some papers from inside his dinner jacket. "Awmost forget. Invitation for new business associates to fry first-first crass on private jet to La Palma—whenever wish."

Mack sucked in a deep breath, imagining himself and Annie flying to Marisol's, in a private jet, 'first-first class.' She would like the touch. Botch visibly relaxed. "Wow, a private jet. I suddenly feel like I'm in the big leagues. Thanks Tommy…er…Mr. Park. Will you be coming with us?"

The hostess, following the men's discussion with interested discretion, was distracted by a phone call. Reluctantly abandoning the conversation, she announced the restaurant-hotel name and listened. "Yes, he's still here. One moment, please." The hostess called Mr. Park to the phone: "For you, sir."

Tommy politely excused himself and reached for the phone.

Mack and Botch backed off politely to give him privacy, but listened and watched carefully as he took the call. Mack was unable to help wondering if the strong, feminine voice on the other end of the phone might actually be Natasha Sitova, and if Mr. Jun Sun Park, or Tommy Chang, or whatever he was really called, her notorious financier. "I'll tell you one thing," Botch whispered aside to Mack. "If the pilot on that private jet has a parachute, I'm not getting on it."

Mack gave Botch a puzzled look. "What are you worried about now?"

"Getting all of us together on board a private jet flying over the open Atlantic would be a convenient way to get rid of all of us without firing a shot."

"Good God, Botch, maybe you should start wearing diapers. I mean, you never know what might happen," Mack replied as Park/Chang handed the phone back to the hostess.

"So?" Mack asked off-handedly, "Will you be joining us on the flight to La Palma...Mr. Park?"

Tommy lowered his voice, "Unfortunatery, not possible, Mack," he replied with genuine sincerity, nodding at each man honorifically. "Must take care of some new business first. Then meet you at Marisol's," Tommy Chang ended with a warm but thin smile.

"Is there anything we could help you with?" Mack asked.

Tommy looked deeply into Mack's eyes, then into Botch's, as if sizing them up. Putting a friendly hand on Mack's shoulder, he whispered quietly to the two, "Thank you, Mack. Like when you with my sister. You true fliend. Perhaps so. Maybe other associates' advise and help, too?" Tommy patted Mack's shoulder and walked off.

"What the hell was that all about?" Botch asked, his worry renewed, as he and Mack thanked the hostess and began walking back to the private dining-room to join partners and friends reveling in their newfound wealth.

"I'm thinking the word 'retirement' is going to have a different meaning for us," Mack said with equal amounts of enthusiasm and concern.

About the Author

Born and raised on the streets of the Bronx in New York, **Brian Morley** experienced growing up with the warmth and love of his family on a tree-lined street, while other parts of the borough struggled with gang violence and murder. Living with these two faces of the Bronx plagued many growing up in the city; Brian's life path, however, followed that of his father in law enforcement. Known for his ability to lay back and fit in while listening to people from all different walks of life share stories,he likes to develop and interweave these stories into realistic fiction. Sometimes humorous, sometimes terrifying, but always serious, the result is an accurate reflection of life "on the beat."

Number One Bestseller

If you enjoyed *Number One Bestseller* consider these other fine books from Savant Books and Publications:

A Whale's Tale by Daniel S. Janik
Tropic of California by R. Page Kaufman
Dare to Love in Oz by William Maltese
Today I Am a Man by Larry Rodness
The Bahrain Conspiracy by Bentley Gates
Called Home by Gloria Schumann
Kanaka Blues by Mike Farris
Poor Rich by Jean Blasiar
The Jumper Chronicles by W. C. Peever
William Maltese's Flicker by William Maltese
My Unborn Child by Orest Stocco
Last Song of the Whales by Four Arrows
Perilous Panacea by Ronald Klueh
Still Life with Cat and Mouse by Sheila McGraw
Mythical Voyage by Robin Ymer
Falling but Fulfilled by Zachary M. Oliver
Manifest Intent by Mike Farris
Hello, Norma Jean by Sue Dolleris
Richer by Jean Blasiar
Charlie No Face by David Seaburn

Scheduled for Release in 2011:
Ammon's Horn by Guerrino Amati
*In Dire Strait*s by Jim Currie
Blood Money by Scott Mastro
In the Himalayan Nights by Anoop Chandola
The Treasure of La Escondida by Carolyn Kingson
Wretched Land by Mila Komarnisky
My Two Wives and Three Husbands by S. Stanley Gordon

http://www.savantbooksandpublications.com